THE WOLF VS THE WITCH
THE HIDDEN CITY SUPERNATURAL SLEUTH

LAURETTA HIGNETT

Copyright © 2025 by Lauretta Hignett

All rights reserved.

No part of this publication may be reproduced, distributed, or transmitted in any form or by any means, including photocopying, recording, or other electronic or mechanical methods, without the prior written permission of the publisher, except as permitted by U.S. copyright law. For permission requests, contact Lauretta Hignett info@laurettahignett.com

The story, all names, characters, and incidents portrayed in this production are fictitious. No identification with actual persons (living or deceased), places, buildings, and products is intended or should be inferred.

No generative AI was used at any time in the story and artworks of this book.

Editing by Cissell Ink

Book Cover by Atra Luna Graphic Design

First Edition 2025

CAST OF CHARACTERS

Daphne Ironclaw — Our hero. An optimistic, unhinged wolf girl. Last seen behaving even more unhinged than usual by running out on her date in a panic, holding two containers of tiramisu.

Romeo Zarayan — Warlock, High Priest, Lord of Shadows, and determined stalker of Daphne. Currently missing two containers of tiramisu.

Dwayne — The less said about him, the better.

Bella — Romeo Zarayan's foster sister and best friend. Yep, that's right, Daphne's boyfriend has a Girl Best Friend.

Perrina Montezuma — a dryad, a religious fanatic, and a terrible mother.

The Soul Stealer/Stephen — Pompous scumbag witch pretending to be a pigeon shifter. Delights in making Daphne's life a misery.

Myf — Formerly a mysterious agoraphobic Welsh pantry-dweller, now a seriously depressed dragon shifter and a mean drunk.

Lennox Arran — Lion shifter, world champion boxer, rich playboy, and now (because he muscled Daphne out of her own challenge and stole her kill) the Alpha Shifter of Philadelphia. Lennox wants Daphne to be his Shifter Princess and will not take no for an answer.

Monica — Manager of the Otherworld department of the CPS, the personification of bureaucratic anxiety, and Daphne's boss. Never stops moving, and is ninety-nine percent made up of caffeine.

Judy — Daphne's colleague, nosy witch and office bitch. Still weirdly addicted to yogurt.

James — A lovely hardworking O-CPS colleague of Daphne, and part dryad.

Cindy — A Gothflower pixie and Otherworld Drug and Alcohol counselor.

Countess Ebadorathea Greenwood — A sorceress with a terrible (and deserved) reputation.

Asherah — the Fae Diplomat of Philadelphia, exiled princess of the Winter Court, and Dwayne's current main squeeze. An absolute psychopath.

Christopher Jupiter — the oldest Jupiter brother, former heir to the Jupiter fortune, now married into the Russian High Priest's family. Now that Alexei Minoff is dead, Christopher has taken the title of Worst Person Alive.

Mina and Wesley Jupiter — Christopher's parents, matriarch and patriarch of the Jupiter family. Absolute assholes.

Troy Jupiter — The youngest Jupiter son and Daphne's lying, cheating ex-boyfriend.

Holly LeBeaux — a smoking-hot witch and Troy's reluctant fiancée, trying desperately to get out of her marriage contract.

Levi — a witch, covenmate and devoted acolyte of Romeo Zarayan. Looks like a hot Tolkien elf.

Micah — Former assassin and another covenmate of Romeo Zarayan. Not a witch, but actually a sexy raven-haired vampire.

Cole — Another loyal covenmate, again, not actually a witch, but a stocky, sandy-haired cheerful lynx shifter.

Brandon — The final covenmate, another former assassin and, surprise surprise, not actually a witch, but a dragon shifter.

Veronica Sterlington-Hyde — Enormously wealthy sculpture artist and socialite. A self-absorbed nightmare of a woman.

Azerad — vampire nestmaster of New York. He's not in this one, but is lurking behind the scenes, up to no good.

Alexei Minoff — Polar bear shifter, literally the worst person in the world. Luckily for us he's dead!

Zofia — Former vampire nestmaster of Philadelphia. She's still dead too, but rates a mention.

CHAPTER
ONE

I wasn't sure if the woman I was interviewing was even alive anymore. She sat so still and held herself so stiffly, I was worried she might topple over and shatter into a million pieces any second.

She was alive, though; I could hear her heart beating. I eyed the rest of Mrs. Montezuma's apartment surreptitiously, trying not to be rude, while I waited for her to answer my question. The place was clean, with the kind of floral-patterned armchairs and sofas that old ladies in sitcoms favored—the only thing missing to complete the image were the plastic slip covers. Houseplants and low-light shrubs covered most surfaces. There was no coffee table between us. She hadn't offered me a drink anyway, so at least I didn't have to hold a cup awkwardly with no place to set it.

My patience had worn down to nothing, and we'd only just begun. It was bad enough that I was working on a Saturday morning in the first place, but we all had clients who couldn't take time off during business hours to see us. All my colleagues were doing the same thing as me—squashing in as many out-of-hours appointments as possible before heading into the office for our bi-monthly team meeting. I'd been hoping to wrap this up quickly, but it seemed that every time I asked Mrs. Montezuma a question, it required a full sixty-second period of absolute silence and preternatural stillness while she thought about her answer. It was absolute torture for someone like me—someone who found awkward silences to be roughly on par with waterboarding. Nevertheless, I forced myself to keep my mouth shut and waited.

Stab her.

I pinched my lips together harder and hissed at myself internally. Stop it! Why is stabbing people the solution to all your problems?

I don't want to stab everyone. Brain-Daphne shrugged. *Just the ones who deserve it.*

You don't know that she deserves it.

Yeah, I do. I'm always right. Trust me. I'm your intuition.

No, you're not. You're my lizard brain, that's what you are. You're my survival mode. You have no idea what this woman's deal is. We give everyone the benefit of the doubt. She might be a victim, too, you know. Look at her!

Brain-Daphne eyed the woman in front of me. Her assessment was much harsher than mine had been.

Perrina Montezuma's file said she was twenty-seven, but she looked much, much older. She was a white woman with bushy chestnut hair, a long face, an immense forehead, pointed chin, and a small mouth. She looked fairly sturdy at first glance, but her skin texture was papery and ashy like a woman in her eighties. Her fingers were clasped together into a fist on her lap, her knuckles bone white. She wore a feminine billowy dress with a flowery print that swamped her, disguising the rest of her figure. Her hazel eyes were cold and hard.

After what felt like hours, the tension in her jaw cracked, and she opened her mouth. "No, Ms. Ironclaw." She whispered the words very slowly. Her voice sounded like the rustle of leaves. The soft tone was an odd contrast to the tension of her body. "You must be mistaken. My son does not do Physical Education. So, he could not possibly have been observed rolling up his pants to play soccer."

"Mrs. Montezuma..." I stifled my sigh. "Leif attends a public school. Physical Education is a mandatory class in public school."

Her eyes hardened even further. "I informed the school that my son has a religious exemption from participating in Physical Education. If they made him join the class, then they are impinging on our religious freedom, and I will have to take the necessary legal—"

"Well, from what I understand," I interrupted, my patience already at its limit, "the class had a substitute teacher who was not aware of your request that Leif not participate in P.E."

She stared at me in silence.

A wriggle of discomfort squirmed in my gut. Leif was only eight years old. I hadn't been able to speak to him directly yet—Mrs. Montezuma was keeping him confined to his room down the hall. So far, she had refused to let me see him. But the substitute teacher who'd made the report told me that Leif had joined the soccer game not just willingly, but with the kind of joy and enthusiasm usually reserved for a prisoner finally let out of a dungeon.

Finally, Mrs. Montezuma cracked her mouth open again. "Leif would have informed the substitute teacher that he is forbidden from participating. I will need to speak with my lawyer."

Told you, Brain-Daphne snarled. *She's obviously an evil monster, and we're just wasting time here. Let's get to the stabbing.*

I couldn't jump to conclusions. I just needed her to answer my questions so I could get to the bottom of this situation. While I wondered how to proceed without making things more difficult, a sad honk and a very wet sniff broke the silence.

Brain-Daphne's bloodthirsty focus wavered. *Do you think he's ever going to stop crying?*

I certainly hoped he would, because he was making me look a little unprofessional. Taking a deep breath, I shot a look at him out of the corner of my eye.

Dwayne—my guardian, the Lord of Chaos, Master of Mayhem, The Alpha of Anarchy—was depressed. The poor guy was suffering from the aftereffects of two weeks of solid partying.

He hadn't said much about it—and I wasn't keen to press him on the details since most of his explanations seemed to involve illicit drugs, sex toys, and multiple felonies—but I assumed that most of his sadness was just the inevitable come-down of alcohol depression. I was also aware that his new girlfriend, the terrifying fae princess Asherah, had gone home to Faerie for a scheduled visit. I was happy about that, but Dwayne appeared to be sad that she was gone. He'd been moping for days and hadn't left my side.

Right now, Dwayne nestled on the chair next to me, his head stuck underneath his wing. Every now and then he let out a sad little peep, or a honk that sounded like a tired, depressed truck horn.

It was nice that he wanted to stick close to me, but I wished he would blow his nose every now and then. He let out another very wet-sounding sniff.

Mrs. Montezuma's expression didn't change, but a flare of disgust shone in her eyes. "Please ask your companion to wait outside," she said in her whispery, leaf-rustle voice.

"No." I stared at her.

"I don't need an emotional support animal."

Dwayne was still wearing his service vest. "He's not here for you," I said. "He's here for me."

I knew this callout would be tough. Perrina Montezuma and her son were dryads, and dryads originally came from a culture that, for very good reasons, I was trying really, *really* hard not to think about right now.

I wasn't sure how much Dwayne knew about what was inside me, because I could never tell him. I couldn't tell *anyone*. But I knew he always had my back, and I could rely on him to distract me if the darkness overwhelmed me. "He has to stay," I told the dryad woman. "He's my boss."

She considered that for what seemed like hours.

"Fine." Mrs. Montezuma eyeballed me steadily. "But this is a waste of time. I will be speaking with my lawyers. Leif should not have been forced to participate in his P.E. class."

"Forgive me, Mrs. Montezuma, but that is not the issue I am here to discuss. We have mandatory reporting here in Philadelphia. The teacher observed multiple whip marks and bruises on Leif's body. I'm here to ask you about them." I eyeballed her right back. "Do you know where the marks came from?"

She stared at me. The silence stretched on. I pressed my lips together hard and waited.

Leif had told the school counselor that the marks had always been there. If he'd said his mother had hurt him, we'd be having a very different conversation.

Dwayne let out a sad, pathetic honk, breaking the silence. My emotional support animal needed an emotional support animal of his own.

Finally, she cracked. "He is my son. He is not allowed to participate, so he did not participate. His teacher, again, is lying. Probably to cover the fact that she has violated my religious rights."

Told you. She's evil.

"Please answer the question, Mrs. Montezuma."

She sat stiffly. I waited. My jaw hurt from clenching it so hard. Be patient, I told myself. I had to give her the benefit of the doubt.

"I don't know what you're talking about," she finally whispered.

My hands twitched towards my Orion blades in the

hidden sheathes at my back. I forced my fingers to be still. It would be tough getting the blades out, anyway—it was cold in here, and I still wore my heavy motorcycle jacket.

Mrs. Montezuma didn't believe in Physical Education, and she clearly didn't believe in heating her apartment either. It was a miracle that the big fiddle-leaf fig in the corner survived. She was a dryad, though, and her magic was botanical. She probably forced her babies to put up with the cold and ordered them to thrive anyway. "So, you're not aware of the whip marks on Leif's legs? Or the bruises?"

She stared at me, unmoving. I waited.

She could be a victim, too. Mrs. Montezuma was a widow—her husband had died six years ago, when Leif was just a toddler. She might have a new dryad man. Or woman.

The silence stretched on, and my mind wandered. In ancient Greece, dryads were always women—they were nymphs, goddesses, spirits of the trees. Typically, they liked to do the nasty with whoever tickled their fancy, and most of the time, any offspring they bore were basically humans without magic. But, eventually, due to thousands of years' worth of interbreeding with similar mortal realm-bound spirits of the forest, ones from different cultures—the Lunantishee in Ireland, for example, or the Ghillie Dhu in Scotland—we now had a species of tree-loving, botanically-powered supernatural humanoid creatures who called themselves dryads just to make things simpler. In more rural areas, dryads would sleep in tree trunks and dance naked in the woods. Here, in the city, they were award-winning landscapers and highly paid groundskeepers.

Mrs. Montezuma *could* have a new partner who was beating Leif. She finally cracked her mouth open again. "No."

I'd forgotten what I asked her in the first place, so I continued with my train of thought. Maybe it was a new partner getting rough with the poor kid. Another dryad, maybe. Or something else. In the past, especially before the Suffocation, most supernatural creatures were more relaxed about who they hooked up with.

Not so much anymore. Every single species had taken a massive hit. It was now considered almost traitorous to date outside your race.

A thought occurred to me. Carefully, mindful of my mental state, I examined it. As far as I was aware, dryads didn't have a religion. They didn't worship any gods. They worshiped nature, and nature worshipped them. Thousands of years ago, they used to party with the gods like they were frat buddies, but there wasn't an organized faith surrounding dryads.

I decided to investigate that thought a little further. "Can you tell me more about your religion, Mrs. Montezuma? So, I can understand the situation a bit better?"

She didn't move, but a light flared in her eyes. "We are dryads. We are the spirits of the trees. Our sacred duty is to be tree-like. To become as we were supposed to be."

"You... uh. You want to become..." I frowned, confused. "Like... a tree?"

That would account for her uncanny stillness and the leafy rustle of her voice. "Yes."

"Um." I blinked. "You live in a high-rise, though. And this is South Philly."

Her chin tilted up slightly. "That's because of the Suffocation. We had no choice."

That was fair. The Great Suffocation was an unprecedented event where the sentient magic of the Great Agreement ballooned out of control and started choking supernatural creatures in the street. The only way to survive this magical apocalypse was to hide behind closed doors, where no normie could see you.

Public spaces meant normie eyes were everywhere. Creatures that would normally take shelter in the woods and rivers suddenly found that there was nowhere to hide.

"You didn't want to live in the Hidden City?" I asked her. "At least there's a park there."

Disgust shone in her eyes. "With all the other riffraff? Of course not."

Okay, that was a bit mean. The Hidden City wasn't that bad. It was true that it was the place where the poorest, most vulnerable people had fled to. When I first arrived, it was one step up from being a ghetto. But it was much nicer now that the old apartment board had been fired.

Actually, now that I think about it, they'd been fired twice now. A board made up entirely of Orbiters—nonmagical humans—had been installed.

In the past week, the new Apartment Board had fixed the cellular communications between the pocket dimension of the City and the outside world and started construction on my dream project, the kid's drop-in center. Firing the old board and hiring new Orbiters to sit on it was the best idea Romeo had ever—

We need to tell him.

I choked on my own spit and desperately wrestled my thoughts away from the Warlock. I couldn't think about him now. I couldn't, because whenever I did, I started thinking about the new battle we had on our hands. A new crisis, the one where Christopher Jupiter had seen what was inside of me—

An inky-black tentacle within me smashed against the side of my psyche, jolting me in my seat. I froze, locked down my thoughts, and mentally counted backwards from one hundred.

Mrs. Montezuma's face twitched when I reached forty-eight. She cracked open her mouth and whispered, "Is there something wrong, Ms. Ironclaw?"

"Oh. No. Not at all."

There were so many things wrong, I had no idea where to start. Thankfully, Dwayne poked his head out, emerging from underneath his wing, and glared at me. **Can you not think of someone other than yourself for a change, baby girl? Can't you see I'm dying of heartbreak here?**

The distraction worked. The only thing Dwayne was dying of was drug and alcohol withdrawal symptoms. And possibly one or two faerie STDs.

I cleared my throat. "I was just thinking of your religion, ma'am. Is it, uh, is it new?"

Her expression barely changed, but I registered her

sneer. "Of course not. We are the eternal spirits of the gods and goddesses of the woods. They are eternal, and in our adoration, so shall we be. Eternal and forever, just like the woods."

Okay, that didn't sound so bad. Worshiping trees was nice. Especially nowadays, with so much deforestation going on. But it didn't explain the cuts and bruises Leif's teacher had reported. "It's an old religion?"

Her chin moved slowly upwards. "The oldest. We are dryads."

"Yeah, but..." I wasn't sure how to approach this without insulting her.

First of all, the woman in front of me was nothing like a dryad of Greek mythology. She was wearing too many clothes, for starters.

A connection pinged in my brain. "Do you, um." I swallowed. "Is your religion based on becoming more tree-like? As in, not moving, talking in whispers, that kind of thing?"

"Of course."

"Is that why Leif isn't allowed to do P.E. at school? You don't want him to move around too much?"

"A tree does not run," she whispered. "A tree does not sing, jump, or play."

A chime went off in my head. So that's why Leif was so excited to join the soccer game. The poor kid wasn't allowed to even *move*.

Dwayne, too, was finally pulled out of his despair. He stared at Mrs. Montezuma. **This woman is batshit crazy.**

For a long moment, I was truly speechless. Leif was

eight years old. Dryad kids were like any other kid. They weren't quiet, and they didn't stay still.

So, she beat him.

The darkness churned within me, fueled by a desperate hopelessness. The worst part of my job was the fact that Perrina Montezuma wasn't doing anything illegal. Here, in the great state of Pennsylvania—just like all parts of the United States—it was totally, one-hundred percent legal to physically discipline your kids.

If there were injuries or marks, we could get involved and investigate. But if she argued that she was beating her kid within the framework of the law, as in, she was doing it to prevent misconduct, promote safe behavior, and not hurting him enough to leave permanent, lasting damage, then she was free to keep doing it for as long as she liked.

It was enough to make me want to burn down the whole world.

It didn't matter that the vast, overwhelming weight of science showed that corporal punishment didn't work. It only made kids more violent and resentful. At best, it just conditioned young people to expect violence from the ones who loved them and set them up for a life of domestic abuse with their romantic partners later—as either the victim or the perpetrator.

But voters wanted to be able to be free to hit their children if they so desired, so it was still legal to beat the shit out of your kids. It was just one of those things that truly baffled me.

Even looking at the hardness in Mrs. Montezuma's

eyes, I knew that parenting classes and counseling wouldn't work. What the hell could I do now?

My fingers twitched. *I've got a few ideas.* My brain threw up a visual of me, stabbing her in the belly with my Orion blades, over and over again.

I'm so sad and exhausted. Dwayne rested his head on the sofa arm and let out a miserable sigh.

I loved Dwayne with all my heart, but now was *not* a good time. I shot him a glare out of the corner of my eye.

He gave a little goosey shrug. **I mean, I'm not sure if I've got the energy to deal with this psycho right now. Do you want me to switch places with your stalker boyfriend? He's still outside in the hallway.**

Desperately, I wrenched my thoughts away from Romeo Zarayan and back onto the woman in front of me. I fixed her with a hard look that probably rivaled hers. "Let me make sure I understand you correctly. Your religion dictates that you become as tree-like as possible."

"Of course. It is as the great priest Hama decreed. We are dryad."

I hadn't heard of this Hama before. Maybe he was new in her life. "So, you whip Leif when he is singing, jumping, or playing? Or does your priest do it?"

Her lip—very slowly—curled. It was a moment before she replied. "It is my duty as mother to discipline him when he blasphemes."

I stared at her. "So, you whip him. You whip him when he moves."

Her expression turned flat. She was doing a great job becoming tree-like. "I correct his behavior to bring him closer to his true nature."

Okay, I've had enough of this. Let's just start getting stabby.

I couldn't. For starters, Mrs. Montezuma wasn't breaking the law. I'd have an uphill battle convincing my boss Monica that this kid—who by all accounts only had a few bruises and red welts on his legs—needed to be removed from the custody of his only remaining family and placed with strangers.

It might be easier if Leif was one of the more common supes. If he was a vampire, I'd be having words with the nestmaster. Except there still wasn't a new one, since I'd sawed off the last one's head.

But if Leif was a shifter, I'd—

Yeah, I still wasn't talking to the new Alpha Shifter.

I cringed into myself. Gods, when did my job become so complicated?

Oh, yeah. Day one.

It wasn't much consolation, but if Leif was a witch, Mrs. Montezuma would probably already be dead. There was no way that Romeo Zarayan would let his people beat their kids like this.

But Perrina Montezuma and her son were dryads. There weren't enough of them in Philly to require their own species representative on the Otherworld Council.

I stood up abruptly, dusting off my hands, and felt a jolt of satisfaction when the stiff woman in front of me flinched at my sudden movement. "Okay, I'm done here."

Alright, alright, alright. Dwayne sighed, unfolded himself from beside me and ruffled his feathers. **I suppose we're doing an eye for an eye, then, are we?** He hopped off the sofa, waddled over to the fiddle leaf fig tree in the corner, and snapped off a long, thin branch with his beak.

Mrs. Montezuma rose to her feet so slowly I barely saw her move. "Good." Her lip was still curled into a sneer. "I would appreciate it if you do not bother us again."

I shot Dwayne a look. "Oh, don't worry. I won't be bothering you again. But for what it's worth, your religion is a made-up bunch of horseshit."

She gasped.

Whip-crack. Dwayne whipped her with the little branch, smacking her on her legs. **No blasphemy, sister.**

She froze in place, staring at me, her mouth wide open in outrage. I shrugged. It couldn't have hurt that much; she was covered in fabric from head to toe. "He's doing you a favor. You're supposed to be tree-like, and trees don't gasp or flinch, Mrs. Montezuma. Now"—I crossed my arms over my chest—"I don't follow your religion. Your rules don't apply to me, so I'm going to keep talking. See, I grew up in a cult, so I know a thing or two about wacky made-up religions."

Mrs. Montezuma opened her mouth.

Woosh-snap.

"Uh, uh." I held up my hand. "Trees don't protest. They are silent, so you should be, too. But, for what it's worth, I'll explain myself so you can see where I'm coming from. The original dryads were goddesses. They weren't men. They were nymphs, they were *women*. So why are you listening to a male priest?"

"Because—"

Swish-crack.

She let out a shriek but cut herself off quickly. Her eyes bulged.

"And secondly, the original dryads were the *spirits* of the trees. The spirits." I paused for emphasis. "They moved, they ran, they flew, they sang." I glared at her. "And you're trying to tell me that a dryad is supposed to be still? And it's not an insult to the tree, who can't move?"

"But…" A *whip-crack* cut her off as Dwayne smacked her again. "Ouch!"

"And, on that note, why are you wearing clothes?"

She gaped at me, outraged.

"Dryads don't wear clothes. They never did. Trees don't either. But I'm guessing that this Hama priest of yours says that it's your responsibility to be modest. I suppose he said something like, *cover yourself as the trees sheath their trunks in bark to conceal their shame.* While at the same time, he's gathered a bunch of female acolytes who take turns visiting him at night. I bet he changes his tune on the modesty rule after dark, huh."

Her mouth dropped open even further.

I chuckled mirthlessly. "Bullseye. Well, these holy priests seem to use the same playbook, no matter what religion it is. You know what it boils down to? Control. They say the same contradictory bullshit, and they smooth talk over any glaring inconsistencies in their doctrine. They use physical punishments on you, and they ask you to punish others. The ones who are vulnerable." I arched an eyebrow. "Tell the truth, Perrina. I bet it feels good to hit your kid when he disobeys you, doesn't it?"

Her lip quivered in outrage. "You—"

Whip-crack.

"Ouch!" she screamed.

Woosh-snap.

"Now, now." I wagged a finger. "You'll be offending your... priest? Is that what this Hama guy is?" I made a mental note to do some research when I got back to the office. "You're not supposed to make loud noises, right? Or move. But I suppose you do that when you whip Leif, too, right? You're not supposed to move, so you can be more like a tree... but you can beat your kid if *he* moves?"

Her eyes flashed almost black. Hatred, hot and poisonous, streamed from her.

It didn't bother me in the slightest. My phone buzzed. I had to wrap this up. Moving closer, I got right in her face. "Listen up, Mrs. Montezuma, because I'm only going to say this once," I said softly. "You've been brainwashed. Hoodwinked by some horny asshole with a drop of dryad blood and delusions of grandeur. Try some critical thinking, get some therapy, stop hitting your kid. And we won't have a problem again."

Her whole face trembled. "How... How dare you!"

Okay, we were going to have a problem.

Whip-crack.

She whirled around to face Dwayne, her whole face trembled in outrage.

Looks like we broke her. He swung at her again. *Crack.*

She let out a yelp and shuddered oddly, clearly torn between exploding in rage and keeping as still and as quiet as possible. Maybe we really had broken her.

Though, I had no idea if I'd even managed to make a dent in her religious psychosis.

My phone buzzed again. I shot a look at the screen and cursed inwardly. Myf was calling. Again.

I had too much on my plate right now, too many balls in the air. There was probably no point continuing with this conversation anyway. I wasn't going to get through to Mrs. Montezuma. If she was indoctrinated enough to believe she had to beat her kid whenever he moved...

Reason wasn't going to work. I liked to think of myself as a reasonable person. I always thought the best of people. I believed in redemption, as long as there was remorse and accountability.

The truth was, sometimes, violence *was* the answer.

Dwayne dropped his stick to wipe his nose on his wing, and Mrs. Montezuma took the opportunity to move. She thrust her finger in my face. "I am a child of a goddess,' she snarled. "It is written in our holy book—"

"What's the book made of? Paper?"

She mouthed wordlessly, past the point of outrage.

"It's paper, right?" I smiled without humor. "I suppose Priest Hama has an excuse for that."

She blustered for a moment, desperately trying to lower her voice. "You understand *nothing*," she hissed venomously.

There was no getting through to her. "I see we're going to have to change tack here. How about this? Look at my boss over there. The one trying to pick up that stick with his wing."

She turned very slowly.

Dwayne lowered his head and narrowed his eyes at her. A low hiss erupted out of his beak. The barbs on his tongue glinted like tiny razors in the dim lights.

I kept my voice soft, like hers. "You know what he is? He's a real god. An *actual* one."

She looked at him properly for the first time. Her eyes widened in shock when she stared into the fathomless black depths of his eyes.

I loved staring into Dwayne's eyes. For me, the endlessness of his gaze comforted me. I was just a tiny insignificant speck drifting through infinity.

But Mrs. Montezuma stared into his eyes and saw Chaos.

"Reason won't work with you, I can see that now," I said. "My job—my only job, the only thing I've ever wanted to do in my whole life—is to protect vulnerable kids. Your child Leif is vulnerable. He's only eight years old, and he's relying on you. You're all he's got. You're hurting him by not letting him play, you're hurting him by not letting him speak, and you're hurting him *physically*. Hurting him to the point his teacher called Child Protective Services. You are an awful person, and you're a terrible excuse for a parent."

She froze, caught in the snare of the eyes of a god of chaos.

"Don't worry, I'm not going to take your kid away from you. I probably couldn't do it, anyway, considering the law is on your side. Leif's bruises and welts are fresh, and they will fade. I was a lot like Leif, you know." My tone turned conversational. "My mother brought me up in a religious cult. We were physically disciplined for existing, we were tortured and told our suffering would bring us closer to God. My mother raised me in that environment. And you know what I did?"

I waited until the dryad woman wrenched her gaze back to me. Then, I leaned in closer. "I killed her."

Her eyes widened in horror. *Now* we were getting somewhere.

"So, this is what we're going to do." I stepped away from her and slid my laptop into my backpack. "You will stop hitting Leif, effective immediately. You will take this"—I whipped out a small card with a series of numbers on it—"and you will make an appointment for therapy. You will retract your request to forbid Leif from skipping P.E, and you will get better." I paused and met her gaze. "Or you will die. Do you understand me?"

She panted softly, her nostrils flared.

Whip-crack.

Dwayne had to ruin the moment by honk-crying miserably. **Asherah woulda loved this.**

CHAPTER TWO

My phone buzzed again as I walked out of Mrs. Montezuma's apartment. This time, I answered. "Myf? Are you okay?"

Her voice screeched through the line at me. "Yessssh babe. Yes, I'm great! How are you?"

Oh, no. Myf was drunk again. "I'm fine," I said cautiously. "Just working, you know."

It had only been two weeks since Myf burst out of my bedroom window, turned into a dragon, flew down to the ground and roasted the Alpha Shifter with her fire breath, before flying awkwardly away again. Luckily, she'd been wearing a confusion-illusion charm at the time, so the crowd hadn't seen a dragon.

Nobody was sure what they saw. The most common story was that it was actually Dwayne covered in curry powder and carrying a flamethrower.

"How are you doing?"

"Great!" Myf's overly perky voice hurt my ears. "Listen, babes. Bestest roomie ever," she cooed drunkenly. "Daphne. Babes, I need a favor."

I walked down the hallway towards the elevators. The lights above me flickered; every third one blinked out, blanketing every second doorway in shadow.

Despite the sudden horror-movie aesthetic, the sight of shadows soothed my ragged nerves. Romeo was close. Suddenly, I could breathe a little easier.

"What do you need, Myf?" I said as I marched down the hallway.

I already knew the answer.

Her voice turned wheedling. "Can you pick me up a bottle of wine, babes? Just a little tipple? Some rosé? Maybe a bottle of mother's ruin, perhaps?" Her voice didn't echo. She was back in the pantry again. And drunk. *Again*.

"You know I can't do that, Myf."

Silence. I kept walking.

"Please?"

God, she sounded so young. She *was* young. That was the whole point. "I can't buy you alcohol. You're only seventeen, Myf. I'd be breaking the law."

"Only in America, babes. In three short months it will be legal for me to drink in the U.K."

"You're not in the U.K. You're in my pantry again." We hadn't made much progress on that front. The reason for Myf's agoraphobia hadn't exactly vanished, after all. She was still terrified of what she was.

Aren't we all, my brain added dryly.

"Let's pretend we're in the U.K. then," she said cheerfully.

That wasn't going to work. "You're still seventeen, Myf."

"Then, uh. Let's go with Belgium. I think the drinking age is sixteen there," she slurred. "I think it is, anyway. Go on, bestie. Pick me up a bottle, would you?"

Suddenly, I was exhausted. My feet felt like they were made of lead. I had no idea how Myf was getting her hands on alcohol in the first place. It was likely she was taking a leaf out of Dwayne's book and just stealing it during the brief moments she felt brave enough to leave the apartment.

I paused and glanced behind me, seeing the hallway empty. Dwayne hadn't followed me out of Mrs. Montezuma's apartment. He was probably still whipping her with the branch every time she breathed too heavily.

I couldn't bring myself to worry about that right now. I had a whole other bag of problems to worry about, like my underage, drunk, Welsh pantry-dwelling dragon roommate.

This new relapse was my fault. I had been encouraging Myf to experiment with moving around outside a little more. Now that Alexei Minoff was dead and she wasn't going to get activated and shift by accident, I felt like it was safe enough.

The problem was that she was still a dragon.

Poor Myfanwy just happened to be the rarest and most sought-after shifter species in the world. Two very powerful, very secret societies had been set up thousands of years ago, one devoted to using her kind as currency and weapons, the other devoted to worshiping her kind. They'd both lied to her for her entire life. She'd been indoctrinated, brainwashed, and abused, while being smashed back and forward like a tennis ball in a sadistic game. The People of the Claw and the Welsh Guardians had both messed her up to the point where she didn't feel safe leaving the confines of my pantry.

My shoulders slumped. "Myf..."

"G'wannn, babes," she pleaded. "I just need something to drown out all this shouting in my head. Please?" Something clattered near her; she'd knocked some tin cans around in the pantry.

I exhaled heavily. I still had a full day of work ahead of me—all my client visits, the staff meeting, and a pile of paperwork to get through. But I couldn't leave Myf drunk in the pantry at ten in the morning. She needed professional help, and I wasn't sure I could give it to her. Myf's problems were fairly unique, so it was going to be a nightmare finding someone who could both keep a secret and understand what she was going through.

"Listen," I said. "I'll come home. I'll be there soon."

She let out a happy chuckle. "Good on you, you're a right one, Daph. Love ya!" The phone clattered to the ground.

I sighed again, pocketed my phone, and took the stairs down all twenty flights of steps to the bottom.

Romeo couldn't follow me if I got into the lift. The lights were too bright. And I wanted him to follow me. It was the only thing keeping me sane right now. It was the contradiction of the century—I could barely think of him, but I had to have him close by.

Thoughts were funny things; it took discipline to keep them on track. The events of two weeks ago were still too fresh in my mind. It was a constant effort to keep my mind from veering towards the thing I definitely shouldn't think about.

I can probably help with that, you know.

"Can you?" I was too surprised to keep my thoughts internal—I spoke to Brain-Daphne out loud.

Good grief, girl, when are you going to remember to trust me? Sure, I can help if you want. I'll start with pointing out the fact that it doesn't matter if these bitches inside us get stronger, they ain't getting out no matter what.

The darkness within me stirred. I clutched my head. "You asshole."

Stop being a coward. You know as well as I do that we'll sacrifice ourselves before we let that little bitch Christopher Jupiter open us up.

I counted backwards from fifty.

Keep counting, because the clock is ticking. We need help, so we gotta tell the Warlock. And soon. My brain was relentless. *It's that or death.*

CHAPTER THREE

My natural optimism reasserted itself as soon as I hit the ground level of Mrs. Montezuma's building. It was a bright, sunny winter's day in Philadelphia—my favorite kind. The cold air brushed my skin, causing it to tingle, invigorating me, and the bright sun burned away the sense of impending doom as soon as I moved through the revolving doors of the building. Pausing on the steps, I took a deep breath of the crispy fresh air and exhaled it all out, watching it as it turned to vapor and float away on the breeze. I took another deep lungful of air and held it for a second, before releasing it in a long, *ahhhhh*.

There we go. Oxygen, one of life's great mood improvers.

I bounced down the steps, heading towards my motorcycle, another great mood improver. The Kawasaki was parked just down from the building.

Suddenly, I caught a whiff of street garbage, stale fries, and death. I hesitated.

After a moment, a deep baritone came from just above me. "Baby, baby, I've been thinking of you," the voice crooned.

And just like that, my mood sank again.

"Sweet baby, baby, you know my love is true," he sang again. Despite the cheerful key of the song and the sweet, saccharine words, the tone was off. Forced. Pained. The voice sounded like a baritone version of a Tiny Tim song playing in a horror movie. I ground my jaw.

Where is that little fucker?

I kept walking. A flutter of wings sounded above me. My bike was just up ahead. I paused, took my gloves out of my satchel and pulled them on.

The pigeon landed on a ledge on the second story. Normally I could jump that far, but there was a basement stairwell just below the ledge he'd settled on. The sunken stairwell was dark and deep, making it a two-story jump instead of just one. He was too far out of reach, and he knew it.

The fat little pigeon strutted back and forth for a second, then his beak opened. "Oh baby, baby, don't make me feel blue. Without you in my life, I don't know what I'll *doooo*."

My patience evaporated. I stopped, looked up, and glared at him. "Does he know I hate this?"

The soul stealer gazed back at me through the pigeon's beady black eyes. "I did inform the Alpha that you don't appear to enjoy being serenaded. He replied— and I am quoting directly here..." The soul stealer changed his tone, mimicking Lennox Arran's cheerful, confident voice, "'How can she hate it? It's romantic. Chicks dig romance. Maybe it's the song, Steve. Try a new song. Keep going, she'll come around eventually.'" The soul stealer switched back to his normal oily, haughty voice. "Understand, child, I do not enjoy this either."

I sighed. "But you're doing it anyway."

"I have no choice. Lennox Arran is the new Alpha Shifter." He sneered down at me. "And that's *your* fault. For fifty years I served Alexei Minoff, and the favors I received were worth the humiliation I occasionally had to endure as I served him. Then *you* came along," he spat. "You engineered a coup and had your lover, Lennox Arran, kill the Alpha for you."

I pinched the bridge of my nose and exhaled. "That's not what happened."

He wasn't listening. "Two weeks ago, I would have thought it impossible to find a man with an ego bigger than Alexei Minoff. But now, because of you, I am forced to ingratiate myself with a man who believes that—and again, I am quoting directly here—his 'shit smells like roses.'"

I had no words.

"Lennox Arran believes this to the point where he insists on emptying his bowels every morning with the door wide open," the soul-stealer continued, his voice dripping with disgust. "So, everyone in the compound can bask in the magnificence of his morning defecation."

My shoulders slumped. I could have gone my entire life without knowing that.

"That man makes Narcissus look like a spotty teen

with anxiety and depression," the soul-stealer snarled. "His delusions of grandeur consistently take my breath away. And *you* were the one who engineered his rise to power."

"No, I didn't," I moaned.

"You *did*. It is now common knowledge that you and he are in a long-term relationship, dating back from the time he spent in Castlemaine during the Suffocation. I confess I am rarely wrong about anyone, but you appear to be far more manipulative than I originally thought. It's entirely your fault that he now leads the shapeshifters of Philadelphia." The pigeon strutted back and forth on the ledge, thrusting out his chest. "And now for some reason, you're refusing to join your lover in the shifter compound, and he's sent me to lure you back. This is beneath me."

"He's not my lover," I spat out through clenched teeth.

A subtle fizz of elderberry hit my nose; I recognized it and relaxed a little.

"Of course." The soul-stealer tossed his head pompously. "Not now, anyway. You've dumped him since you've gotten your way. Alexei is dead, which is what you always wanted. I don't understand how you managed to make Lennox Arran think you were destined to be his princess, but then again, I've never been susceptible to the sexual wiles of the females of the species." He paused and glared at me in disgust again. "I suppose it is because of your big bosoms."

The elderberry fizz wafted towards me again. My

focus drifted to the dark stairwell underneath the ledge where the pigeon strutted.

"Whatever the reason, a man with the most unbelievable delusions of grandeur now sits on the shifter throne. He is too intelligent to be called a buffoon, but I am tempted every day. Lennox Arran actually believes if I follow you around and sing love songs dedicated to you, eventually you'll realize how foolish you're being, and you'll run back to him and fall into his arms. Like some god-awful cheesy nineties romcom." Stephen the soul-stealer strutted back and forth angrily on the ledge. "The fury I feel that I am now forced to serenade you on a daily basis is tempered by the knowledge that you hate it."

"I don't know why I even have to say this out loud, but you're not a shifter, Stephen. You're a witch." I pointed at him. "Does Lennox know you're not a shifter?"

"Of course not," the pigeon drawled. "The man might be an unbearable buffoon, but he is still the most palatable Otherworld leader in this fine city. The others are not susceptible to my talents of flattery and manipulation." His expression grew pensive. "Although I may revisit my options when a new vampire nestmaster is elected. Hmm. Perhaps I can convince them that I am a rare breed of vampire pigeon."

"So, Lennox doesn't know you're not a shifter," I confirmed.

"Oh, there is no point in you telling him, child, I've made sure of that. Despite the fact that Lennox Arran has declared that you are to be his princess, he certainly has a low opinion of your intelligence. I merely had to inform him that you held a grudge against me for orders I had to issue while I was under the employ of the former Alpha. A sort of 'shoot the messenger' scenario, if you will," he added, waving a wing airily. "I planted the idea that you might seek to make up outrageous stories to push me out of his favor, and Alpha Arran laughed heartily, nodded, and said, "yeah, chicks do that." Ugh." The pigeon bristled, opened his mouth to say something, hesitated, then shut it again.

We had company.

Two youngish men in sports jackets and chinos were approaching. I pretended to fiddle with my riding gloves, staring at the ground and waiting for them to pass by. We were in public, the Great Agreement was still in effect, and the normie men would freak out if they saw me having a vigorous discussion with a talking pigeon.

We could probably get away with killing a pigeon with our bare hands in public, though.

Could we? Maybe. I still couldn't reach him, though.

The normie men slowed down as they approached me. I wasn't looking, but I could feel their eyes slide over me appreciatively.

Keep walking, fuckers, my brain seethed.

Both of us knew they wouldn't. This was a quiet street, there was nobody else around. Both of them had rigid hairlines and were dressed in expensive sports-luxe clothes. I hated judging people on looks, but they looked like newly graduated frat boys heading to the golf course to talk about the corporate jobs daddy had arranged for them.

And I was wearing bike leathers and pulling on riding gloves. It was an easy conversation starter.

"Hey, girl," one of them called out as he came closer. "You riding somewhere?" Both men stopped in front of me. "Where are you going?"

There was never any right way to deal with unwanted male attention. If you were polite and carefully rebuffed them, they would persist. If you were rude, they might get violent.

And look. That's fine, too. Except we probably don't have time for police statements and court dates right now...

If you lied and said you had a boyfriend, they'd say something like, "Oh, are you not allowed to have friends?" And if you told the truth and said you weren't interested, they considered it a challenge to try and change your mind.

One of the men chuckled, reached forward, and patted my arm. "Oh, don't be shy, sweetie. We're good guys!"

The elderberry fizz smell bloomed again, and the darkness in the stairwell pulsed menacingly.

And *that* was another way to deal with unwanted male attention. To have another man—a huge, muscular, terrifyingly powerful, and overwhelmingly overprotective man—step in. That was the worst way, in my opinion. First of all, it wasn't often that a man like that was around to step in and help you. Secondly, the fact that he had to do it in the first place was an insult to everyone. I shouldn't have to "belong" to another man to get someone to back off.

There was no right way to deal with being hit on when you were just out and about, trying to live your life.

But there was an easy way. I'd learned from the best.

I glanced up at the men who had stopped right in front of me and widened my eyes as far as I could make them. "I'm going to see my dead mother," I said loudly. "But that's okay. It's a closed casket. Her face is gone, but it's okay, all her cats are still alive."

They both stepped back, their expressions horrified.

It was important to keep your voice inflectionless. I took a step forward. "Do you like cats? I have eight British shorthairs and five ragdolls, but that's okay, I have room for more. None of them like each other, but that's okay. Mom's cats are all Persians."

The men exchanged a glance.

Great, it was working. I wished I was as good at this as Chloe, one of my guardians—she was a far better liar than I was. And I wish I enjoyed it as much as Prue, her best friend. Once, when Prue was visiting Castlemaine, a guy hit on her in the local bar. She backed him into a corner and gave him a monologue about the history of scarecrows—straight-faced, without taking a breath or even blinking, for twenty-three straight minutes. He ended up having to duck down and crawl along the floor to get away from her.

The best I could do was wide eyes, repeated phrases, and cats. Loving cats seemed to be a sleazy man's kryptonite.

I stepped forward again, and both men took another step back. "Actually, I'm glad you're here. I could use some help," I said, keeping my tone devoid of all inflection. "How many cats do you think you can carry at once? One? Two? Three four five six seven..."

"Oh!" The men's eyes dropped, looking anywhere except me. "Uh, is that the time? Sorry, honey, we've, uh. We've got meetings." They split up, walked around me, and power-walked to the other side of the street, disappearing around the corner quickly.

A glow of satisfaction warmed my chest. Prue would have been proud.

"Well, that was an interesting display." The soul-stealer's claws tapped on the ledge above me. "More evidence that you are far more manipulative and cannier than anyone gives you credit for. It's an odd thing, isn't it?" He tilted his head. "When you've made up your mind about someone, it really is hard to see them in a new light. I suppose you use that to your advantage. When I first saw you, a silly, pretty young girl chasing her rich boyfriend, I wondered how on earth anyone could be so stupid." His eyes narrowed. "Despite all the subsequent evidence, it is still very difficult to see you as the wily, manipulative maneater you clearly are."

My jaw clenched. "Stephen. Aren't you supposed to be singing?"

"I think I'm done for the day, child." He ruffled up his feathers. "I can go back to my Alpha and tell him I sang the song, and you rebuffed me, and it will not be a lie." The pigeon scowled. "For a mere shifter, Lennox Arran seems to possess an uncanny ability to tell when someone is lying to him, which I suppose comes from his feline beast intuition rather than any magical power."

"You're forgetting something. He's not your Alpha. You're not a shifter."

He chuckled pompously. "We've already been over this. I do what is best for me, child. I have unique abilities, and that enables me to choose who I serve."

The darkness in the stairwell grew very still.

The soul-stealer didn't notice. "Once Lennox Arran loses interest in sending me to sing for you, he will pay me for information in the same way Alexei Minoff did."

"That's not the point I'm trying to make."

"Well?" He tapped his little clawed feet towards the edge of the ledge. "What is your point?"

I jabbed my index finger at him. "You're a witch."

"Yes, I am. What's that got to do with anything?"

I smiled. "You already have a master."

Shadows shot up out of the stairwell, wrapping the pigeon in darkness. The soul-stealer disappeared.

There was a loud crunch. The dead pigeon dropped to the ground.

The shadows settled back down into the stairwell.

I waited for a second, carefully checking my train of thought. I was okay. The sun shone brightly all around me, and it was almost easy to ignore the awful, horrible sense of impending doom.

I begged Brain-Daphne silently. Please help me keep my focus. Don't let me think of the evils. If we give them attention, they'll eventually become too powerful for me to handle. I just know it.

Fine. You're not giving us enough credit, though. I'll keep the thought train on the tracks.

"Romeo?" I licked my lips and cleared my throat. It suddenly felt very dry. "Can you come out?"

Do you think he could give us a lock of his hair? I know he keeps it cropped short, but maybe he could give us a lock of his pubes instead.

Why?

I want to make a voodoo doll. Gonna finger it.

Romeo Zarayan walked out of the shadows. Every time I saw him was like the first time, almost shocking, like being punched in the eyeballs by the most desirable thing in existence. He was probably the most recognizable man on the planet right now—the young bad boy billionaire, the man who'd dumped a European princess.

The media called him a heartthrob worthy of a romance novel. That firm jawline, those high cheekbones, that smooth dark-tan skin, those lips, the hardness in his silver-gray eyes, the stormy fury whirling beneath his brutally handsome facade. A dark fae prince, they called him. The Lord of Shadows. They would never know how right they actually were.

I blinked at him, dazzled by his overwhelmingly masculine beauty in the morning light. "You should spend more time in the sunshine."

"I know." The storm in his eyes settled down. "That's why I'm following you."

I smiled. "I don't mean me."

The last time I spoke to him, he told me I was like the sunshine, chasing the storms away. Being with me made him feel calmer, and he felt at peace for the first time in his entire life, like everything was right in the world.

It was exactly the same for me. We were almost exact

opposites in every way, but we matched each other perfectly. The sun never needed to wonder what the moon was doing; she already knew. "I mean you should spend time in the actual sunshine. It suits you."

He didn't smile—Romeo rarely smiled—but his eyes softened a little more. "It suits you more." A crinkle appeared between his eyes. "Are you okay?"

"Yeah." I took a deep breath. The last time I spoke to him, I was running out of the most expensive restaurant in Philadelphia, holding one plastic container filled with a rib eye and potatoes and two with tiramisu to my chest.

After a couple of hours—and after devouring both servings of tiramisu—I calmed down, and wrote him a letter, which Dwayne delivered for me. I explained that I had something important to tell him regarding Christopher Jupiter, but there was a very good reason why I had to avoid most of the topic. As soon as I worked out how to tell him without putting anyone in danger, I'd do it.

"I'm sorry, again. Not about the tiramisu, though," I added. "I'll never be sorry for that; it was the highlight of my entire existence. I'd never had tiramisu before. If I knew what it was like, I would have ordered it for myself instead of stealing yours."

His eyes grew hot. "I wish I was there to watch you eat it."

Warmth bloomed in my belly.

"Anyway," he shrugged. "The maître d got me some more. I think he felt bad that my date ran out on me. I ended up taking a whole tray of tiramisu home."

I gasped. "A whole *tray?* You monster!"

His lip twitched into a faint smirk. "Guilty as charged."

I gazed at him for a moment, feeling my heart hammer in my chest. Good grief, he was perfection. *This* was perfection. I would savor this feeling as long as I lived.

Too good, my brain muttered. *It feels too good. It's too much. I want to murder him and bury him and dig him up and roll around on his week-old dead corpse like a dog.*

Brain-Daphne still hadn't quite gotten the hang of being in love. I sighed. "I *am* sorry."

"Don't be. You never have to explain anything to me, Daphne." God, I loved the way he said my name. "I'm the one who should be sorry. I told you I'd wait for you to be ready to talk. I didn't feel the need to clarify I'd be waiting six feet away, hiding in the nearest shadow, stalking you."

I smiled. "You know I knew you were there the whole time."

"I know."

It was just so easy with him. He knew. I knew. We barely even had to speak. "There's one thing, though. How are you managing your High Priest duties and all the Jupiter companies when you've been following me around for the last two weeks?"

He shrugged. "I'm not. I've delegated most of the High Priest stuff to Levi. Cole and Brandon are handling the businesses. Micah is on espionage duty. Another close friend is helping me with some research." His expression softened for a second; he was talking about someone he loved deeply, like Aunt Marche. A yearning gripped me—I wanted to know this close friend. I wanted to know everything about him.

Hopefully, we had time. His eyes grew warm. "You appear to have tempered my control-freak nature."

"Liar." I grinned at him again. "I can hear you on the phone from the shadows, you know."

"They still need guidance." He exhaled wearily. "It's probably a good thing for me to try and let them help more, anyway. They're all smart guys; they can handle a crisis."

"But you're still the boss."

"You know what our world is like, Daphne. There has to be someone in charge. I didn't want it to be me..."

"Which makes you perfect for it."

He nodded. "Thanks to you, I understand why Aunt Marche did what she did. If it's not me, it will be someone like Wesley Jupiter. Someone like Zofia. Someone like Alexi Minoff." Suddenly, he scowled, his expression thunderous. "Someone like Lennox Arran. Did you know he's started a YouTube channel?"

"Yeah." The less said about that, the better.

Romeo rubbed his brow. "Someone needs to make the hard choices, and someone has to stand up to the monsters. It might as well be me."

My gut churned at the mention of monsters. I gave myself an internal poke. *How are we doing?*

Fine. Tell him the story, see how that goes.

I took a deep breath. "Romeo..."

He waited. After a second, he took a step towards me and nudged the dead pigeon with his boot. "I wish I could kill that soul-stealing bastard," he muttered. "But he jumps out so quickly every time I get a hold of him." The pigeon's body rolled into the gutter and down a storm drain. "I'm sure the rats will appreciate the snack. Okay." He nodded at me. "Go ahead."

I checked to make sure my thoughts were on track. "Did you know there is a god of sourdough bread?"

Romeo frowned. He clearly wasn't expecting this. "No. I'm not surprised that you know that, though, given your passion for carbs."

"There's a god of everything. Every action, every feeling, every inanimate object. Everything in every single universe has a spirit attached to it. How big or small that spirit is depends on how much attention we give it. Sometimes a god is so big, it has lots of different names. The sun god—Ra, Helios, Shamash, Mithra. The god of the ocean—Neptune, Poseidon, Ceto, Tangaroa..."

He nodded. "I'm following."

"The god of sourdough is called Levaina. She was a small god. Back when we all lived in mud huts, mortals used to say a prayer to her when feeding the starter. She was invoked, and she was pleased, and she helped craft the perfect loaf. But over time, they began to mention her name less often. Maybe it was because new religions sprouted up and it was considered heresy to thank the god of sourdough for the role the starter played in a good loaf of bread. Or maybe it was because Levaina was such a small god, people forgot her name. But over time, they stopped invoking her when they baked. The quality of a loaf dwindled. Levaina languished. Forgotten, she began to fade away. Sourdough bread didn't fade, of course, because bigger gods stepped into the gap. Sif, from Norse mythology, the god of bread. Hestia, the Greek goddess of the hearth, picked up the brunt of baking. But there wasn't any god specific to sourdough. So, over time, with Levaina's worship vanishing, sourdough just wasn't as good for you as it used to be. Not as perfect."

I paused and took a deep breath.

We're good. You're doing great. Go on.

"Then the pandemic hit. Suddenly, people were stuck at home, and a few of them took up baking. Now, I'm not sure exactly what happened or when it happened. Maybe someone spoke lovingly to their starter one day and mispronounced the French word for starter—levain. Maybe they took it a little further, imagined their starter to be a little goddess, and decided to worship her, hoping to produce a perfect loaf. The worship gave Levaina the power she needed to remind the baker of her name. For whatever reason, people started remembering her. So, she grew."

A light went off in Romeo's eyes. "Gods require worship to survive."

I knew he'd get it. "Even speaking of them gives them power."

He was silent for a second. Then, he nodded. "I understand."

"Now, because Levaina is being worshiped again, she's so much stronger. Sourdough loaves are exquisite, and they're incredibly healthy for you."

"This is just straight-up carb propaganda, Daphne, but I think I'm following you. And I know where this is going. Levaina is a *good* god."

"Exactly." Relief surged through me. "I need to be

able to tell you, but I can't. Speaking of the gods gives them power."

He nodded and stepped closer to me. I surrendered and let him pull me into his arms. He tilted my chin up, gazing into my eyes. "We'll find a way, Daphne," he whispered. "Don't worry." He bent down to brush his lips on mine, and my head swam.

My phone buzzed.

I pulled back. "Shit. I forgot about Myf."

Romeo's thumb stroked my cheek. "Can I follow you?" He gazed into my eyes.

The darkness waved back at him.

I squeezed my eyes shut and cursed. "I'm so sorry. This is hard. But yes, please. Even though this is hard, I feel better with you walking next to me."

"It's okay." His beautiful deep voice pulled me out of the darkness. "We'll figure it out."

CHAPTER
FOUR

The countess had gone on vacation.

I had no idea where she was. She hadn't been in contact at all. I'd had no phone calls, no messages, no emails, not even a rolled-up note in a raven's beak. It would have given me deja vu from when Dwayne had gone missing and we found him blind drunk in a shrinking ward with a bunch of sex toys, except Ebadorathea Greenwood had announced her departure eight days ago and bid me farewell, surrounded by her Louis Vuitton suitcases. When I asked her where she was going, she said "abroad," picked up her luggage, and left.

It wasn't until she'd gone that I googled "abroad," wondering where in Europe that was, and found out that "abroad" just meant "to a foreign country."

I couldn't help but feel a little pissy about her leaving. Now was *not* a good time. I desperately needed the countess's help, especially with handling Myf. The countess was the only person I trusted to go into my apartment while I wasn't there. It would have been so much easier to ask her to pop next door and keep an eye on Myf.

Instead, I had to go home and check on Myf myself. I had so much work to do today. I still had to get to the office for the staff meeting at eleven-thirty.

On second thought, considering the countess's penchant for cocktail hour starting mid-morning, it was probably a good thing she was gone.

I got on my bike. Romeo had parked his Ninja around the corner—I could smell that beautiful beast across the whole city. He rode behind me the entire way home, shadowing me closely. We wheeled our motorcycles through the new brick wall entrance in the abandoned building in the parking lot of the Devil's Pocket.

The weather inside the Hidden City always mimicked the outside. It had snowed last night, and the trees were still blanketed in a bright-white cover of icy flakes.

Thick banks of snow lined the pathways. In the clearing around the lake, framed by the willow trees, a dozen or so kids in all shapes and sizes—horns, wings, and extra feet—played happily in the snow, bundled up in bright colored jackets and thick pants.

This place felt like home, and that was a new sensation for me. I'd always felt like a stranger in a strange place, but finally, after falling through dozens of alien realms, after surviving countless harsh worlds, after running from terrifying beasts and magical behemoths, I was back in the world where I was born, and I'd finally found a place where I felt like I belonged.

Another intense emotion gripped me as we moved

through the park—a fierce protectiveness. This was my home, and I wouldn't let anyone take this away from me. I had worked hard to change the Hidden City for the better. I'd made sure the kids here were happier. The whole place was cleaner, brighter. It was better, and it would keep getting better. Nobody was going to change it for the worse.

The darkness inside me bristled.

That's right, fuckers, Brain Daphne hissed. *This world is mine. Stay in there and rot.*

My eyes kept drifting towards Romeo, riding very slowly next to me, constantly checking to make sure he was still there.

I told you it wouldn't be so bad. All we have to do is not think about the inevitable conclusion—

Christopher Jupiter. He knew.

I swallowed my fear as the darkness bristled inside of me again. It was going to be okay. Romeo would help me find a way.

We rode slowly down the path to the West Tower and left our bikes in the storage garage. Romeo's phone kept buzzing. "Go ahead." I nodded at him as we walked into the elevator together. "Answer it."

He let out a gruff sigh. "It's probably best if I don't."

"Why?" I hit the button for the forty-fourth floor. The doors shut. Instantly, the tension in the tiny elevator rocketed. My skin tingled.

Romeo's eyes met mine. "I haven't been making the best decisions lately. My temper has been... much shorter than usual."

I felt my cheeks redden. His short temper was my fault.

Our first date had ended on a disastrous note—with me running out of a very fancy restaurant like a coward, abandoning Romeo right after he told me what Christopher Jupiter was planning to do. I didn't even have the grace to leave a glass slipper on the steps on my way out.

Immediately after that, Romeo had gone straight to the Jupiter mansion, formally evicted Mina and Wesley, and threatened to burn the whole thing down if they didn't leave immediately. I'd heard this directly from Dwayne, who, for some insane reason, decided to sneak back into Wesley's office that night with Asherah so they could bang on his desk again, under the watchful eye of the ghost of Augustus Jupiter himself. Apparently, being watched by ghosts turned Asherah on. I could have gone my whole life not knowing that.

Nevertheless, Dwayne was there when Mina, Wesley, and even Troy and Holly, were forced to carry their own suitcases out of the mansion and leave immediately.

I had also heard that Romeo publicly refused to acknowledge Lennox as the new Alpha Shifter. Not only that, the New York vampire nestmaster, Azerad, had put forward one of his own vampires for the position of Philadelphia nestmaster, claiming that the vamp population in Philly was so decimated that they needed a leader from outside the area. Romeo had refused to acknowledge this new nestmaster, too.

Firing the Hidden City Apartment Board and installing only Orbiters in their places seemed to be the cherry on top for a lot of Philly's supernatural elite. The idea of having non-magical people making decisions for magic folk rubbed everyone the wrong way, even though it turned out to be the best decision for the residents of the City themselves.

Everyone was mad at Romeo, and Romeo was mad at everyone. This whole thing had become a diplomatic nightmare. "I'm sorry."

"You're not responsible for my actions," he said softly. "Besides, I didn't do anything I wouldn't normally do. I was probably just a little more forceful than usual. It's not all bad news." He shrugged idly. "The rest of the country seems to be settling down. The hellmouths in Delaware are finally closed. The Shifter King and the Vampire King will be back in the capital soon, and they'll take a lot of pressure off."

"Oh yeah, I heard." It was great news.

"They all hate me, but—" Romeo stopped. "Wait. How did you hear that?" He frowned down at me. "Delaware has been dark for over a year. Even *I* struggle to get information from the supe royals there, and that's not because they hate me. It's because the whole place is locked down."

"Not the whole place. Just the magic towns." The mortal population was totally and blissfully unaware of the anarchy that had broken out on the periphery of the human city. "The supe royals did a great job of keeping that whole mess quiet." I breathed out a sigh of relief. "And now it's almost over."

"Yeah, but I doubt that information has even got back to anyone in Castlemaine yet. I was only informed as a matter of courtesy, because I'm High Priest. It's classified information," Romeo added pointedly. "How do *you* know?"

"Oh." I blinked. "Shit. Sorry."

He waited.

I squirmed for a minute. How could I have not told him? "Well, uh, you know, this is kind of your fault." I wagged my finger at him. "You seem to understand me so well that I keep forgetting I haven't really told you much about myself. About my family."

"I know you're from Ironclaw in Castlemaine. That pack is infamous, Daphne. I just assumed you didn't want to talk about it, because of how horrific it was." He shrugged. "And I know you got lost in a slipway. You've been off world longer than you've been on it, so your digital footprint is tiny compared to a typical twenty-two-year-old."

"Well, yeah..." I made a face. "I might have forgotten to mention that my uncle Nate is dating Amelia, the Vampire Queen of the South."

There was a long pause. Romeo's mouth dropped open.

I cringed. "And my guardian Chloe is mated to Malik Malleus."

"Malik Malleus." Romeo's face twitched. "He's *literally* a god."

"Well... So is Dwayne," I said in a little voice. "I should probably get this all out. The Shifter King is married to Chloe's best friend, Prue."

His eyes bulged a little. "Prudence *Nakai?* The Daughter of the Beast?"

"That's a little mean, but... uh... yeah. The Vampire

King of the North and his wife, Queen Imogen... Imogen's like my crazy aunt. I love her so much. Whenever Sandy—she's Chloe's other best friend—comes to town, Imogen shows up and tries to force-feed her bananas, which I never really understood when I was a kid, but apparently, it's a whole inside joke."

Romeo seemed to have lost the ability to form words. He stared down at me, silent.

I barreled on. "Anyway, Imogen called me the other day to let me know that they should all be heading back to their respective homes soon." I shrugged. "And that's it. That's how I know."

Romeo closed his eyes and pinched the bridge of his nose. "Do you mean to tell me that the most powerful people in the supernatural world—the people that despise me the most, the people who will most likely come back here to kill me as soon as they're done cleaning up Delaware... They're your *family?*"

"I realize this is a conversation I should have had with you a while ago—regardless of how busy we've been with, y'know, war and death and whatnot. For what it's worth, I never liked telling people about my family because it made me sound like a nepo baby. It's one of the reasons why Lennox Arran wants me so badly, you know."

A low growl escaped his lips.

"If it makes you feel any better, none of them like Lennox. *At all.* The only person that really liked him was my Uncle Nate, but Uncle Nate is a terrible judge of character and prone to idolizing toxic men. Everyone except

Nate always disappeared whenever Lennox showed up in Castlemaine."

"That doesn't make me feel better. They don't like Lennox, which I can understand, given his personality. But they *hate* me, Daphne. They all want me dead. The only reason they haven't killed me already is that they've all been busy in Delaware."

"That's not true!" I looked away and murmured under my breath. "The only reason they haven't killed you yet is because they're all good people, and you killing Aunt Marche in a challenge and becoming High Priest was all legal and above board."

He exhaled gruffly. "They all hate me, and they want me dead."

"They only hate you because they think you killed Aunt Marche."

"I *did*." His voice rumbled through me.

"Yeah, but she tricked you into it. Once you tell them what really happened, they'll understand. They'll forgive you."

"I can't tell them." He stared at me for a long time, his silver eyes growing darker. "I still hate her for what she did."

"I understand." I nodded carefully. "Have you considered therapy?"

He ground his jaw. The elevator dinged.

"In my defense," I said, walking out the open doors, "I honestly assumed you must have known all this already. You're a High Priest. A simple background check would have uncovered my Castlemaine contacts."

"I wanted to do this the right way. The old-fashioned

way. I didn't want to do a background check." He frowned. "Micah should have run a check as soon as you mentioned Carfanon, his old agency."

"It wouldn't have uncovered anything. Chloe's brother worked for Carfanon. He's dead now, though. She, uh, she killed him. Or it might have been Malik. Actually..." I wrinkled my nose. "It might have been me. I can't remember. It seemed like back then, there were lots of people showing up to kill us. Me and Dwayne built a lovely bone sculpture in the rose garden. There were a lot of bones." I was wildly aware that I was rambling, but I couldn't seem to stop.

Luckily, Romeo avoided that little tidbit. "I wanted us to talk, to get to know each other properly. I've told you my whole life story, and I'm just finding out now that you're the adopted child of supernatural royalty. Who all want to kill me," he added savagely.

"Romeo." I turned at my door and threw him a bright smile. "*Everyone* wants to kill you. Everyone, everywhere, all of the time. You've gotta be used to it by now."

Moving on to the next door, I knocked loudly. "Countess? Are you home yet?" I waited. No answer. "Damn it."

He moved behind me. Even now, while he was a little pissed at me, his presence was so reassuring, like a giant storm cloud at my back, threatening to destroy anything that might sneak up on me. "Where has she gone?"

"Abroad."

"What does that mean?"

I whirled around. "I didn't know either! I had to google it." I grinned at him. "She's out of the country. I'm assuming she's still on-world." I walked back to my own door and knocked again. "It's me," I called out. "I've got Romeo with me."

Myf's voice slurred from the pantry. "Good. Maybe once he gets his fat one up ya, you'll be in a better mood."

My cheeks burst into flames. Sometimes, having enhanced hearing was the worst thing ever.

"I don't want to hear you guys bang on the sofa right now," Myf said cheerfully. I heard something clatter next to her. "So come in and give me my booze, and go bang in the countess's place, would you?"

Romeo frowned down at me. "What's she saying?"

"Nothing." I cracked the door open and walked inside. Romeo followed me, a looming thundercloud.

"How are you doing, Myf?" Walking into the kitchen, I opened the cupboard and got out a container filled with peanut butter choc chip cookies. They were a little too salty—Myf had cried into the mixture while she was baking. "Are you okay in there?" Piling the cookies onto a plate, I talked directly to the pantry door. I could just make out the shape of her through the slats.

"Box of birds," she slurred. "*So* happy. Everything's A-okay in my world, babes. It's just me, an empty six-pack, twelve boxes of instant mac and cheese, and this giant bottle of olive oil. Why do we have so much macaroni, anyway?"

"Dwayne likes it."

"Pfff. He would, the silly old duffer. You know, I made an award-winning mac and cheese once? The secret is always using four different types of cheese, but you can't grate it, you gotta melt it really slowly, all together. Now, where's my gin, babes?"

I kept my tone soft and even. "I don't have any gin for you, Myf."

"Some whiskey, then?" Her voice turned wheedling. "Did you bring me some whiskey, Daph, my bestest friend?"

"No, Myf, I haven't brought you anything to drink. I told you, you're underage, and it's illegal."

Her mood flipped almost instantly. She let out a snarl. "Fuck off then, you fat cunt."

"Myf!"

"G'on. Fuck off. You're not helping me, so you might as well piss off. I'm stuck in this fucking pantry, my world is crashing down around me, and it's all your fault."

I shot a look at Romeo. He stared at the pantry door, the lines of his shoulders tense.

"All your fault!" Myf thumped around in the pantry loudly. She might have been trying to stomp her feet against the wall. "You're a meddling fucking do-gooder whore."

The atoms in the apartment began to vibrate in a not-safe way. Romeo didn't like this at all.

I cleared my throat, getting his attention. He turned, and I shook my head at him. "It's fine," I mouthed.

A little of the storm in his eyes died down. He stepped back, moving out of the kitchen. Myf might be drunk, but at least she was predictable. Her path to mental health wellness was less two-steps-forward, one-step-back, and more of a wild roller coaster.

But the roller coaster always stayed on the same track. First, Myf would get the courage to venture out of the pantry, head downstairs, and walk through the Hidden City. Then, something would remind her that her whole life was a lie, and everything she believed about herself was wrong. She'd freak out and scurry back to the only place she felt safe—my pantry—somehow stealing a few bottles of alcohol on the way. Then, once she was safely ensconced among my dry goods, she'd drink to dull the pain, until she was cheerful and happy.

The cheerful, happy stage didn't last very long. Myf was a mean drunk. We were now in the "lashing out" stage, where she'd say the most awful things she could possibly think of.

Lucky for her, we all had thick skin. She called Dwayne a "twinky little bottom bitch with a big loose butthole" the other day, and he laughed so hard he fell off his chair. It wasn't the reaction she was hoping for.

"It's all so easy for you, isn't it, Daphne?" Myf's voice was filled with drunken scorn. "So easy, with your big tits and your dumb face. All you have to do is blink those doe eyes of yours, and all the boys will be rushing to come and solve your problems. You're like a prostitute. A scheming whore, flaunting your goodies to get what you want. Wah, wah, wah," she mocked. "I got lost when I was a widdle girl, but I'm all big now. Look how big I am! Oh no, the Alpha Shifter is being mean to me! Pweease, big High Priest man, come and save me!"

I held Romeo's gaze and rolled my eyes, just to let him know how seriously I took Myf's insults. The tension in the air dialed down a little.

"And now you've got Lennox Arran wanting to marry you. *You!* You don't even like boxing." Her voice rose to a shout. "You don't deserve his attention. You can't even shift! You're just a dumb, stupid, broken werewolf whore!"

"Go on," I sighed. "Get it all out."

"It's all your fault." Myf started to sob. "You messed me up."

Oh, good. We were moving through the "lashing out" phase much quicker than usual. It was time for phase three—crying so hard she got severely dehydrated.

"Everything is so much worse now," Myf cried. "Before, I knew what I was, and I knew I had to stay hidden. But now..." She let out a mournful howl.

I walked over to the cupboard and rummaged around, finding two hydration tablets. I filled a glass of water, dumped the tablets in, and watched the water fizz.

Freedom was a scary concept. For Myf, it was much worse. Her whole life, she'd been told she had a monster —or a terrible god—inside of her.

Now, she knew the truth. She was just a shapeshifter. Her dragon was a part of her. It wasn't something separate she could hate. It wasn't some demon that lived in her body. It was just her.

She was having trouble coming to terms with all this.

I put the glass of water on the floor by the pantry, opened the door, and slid it inside. Myf wailed wordlessly for a minute or two, before she went on. "Nothing has changed, but everything is so much worse. I still can't leave. If anyone finds out what I am, I'm still in danger. The People of the Claw are still out there somewhere. I could still transform at any moment and kill everyone close to me—"

"You won't." We'd been over this a million times. "Alexei is dead, Myf. The activation words died with him."

"The People of the Claw still know them."

"You were programmed using his voice. And, if I can remind you, you managed to resist him and the words. I have never heard of any of the Stolen Ones being able to resist the activation words."

She let out a little mew of misery. "The Guardians taught me how to lock down the beast. Now, I know they were just training me to resist the words."

I ground my jaw. Out of the two ancient institutions that worshiped dragon shifters, I held the least contempt for the Welsh Guardians. At the very least, they rescued Myf from her captors and treated her kindly. But they still lied to her.

I voiced my thoughts out loud. "They lied to you about a lot of things, Myf."

"They *died* for me," she sobbed. "They're all dead. My da, and my brothers and sisters…" She wailed. "And I didn't help. I never helped them! The People firebombed the house. They came in with guns and blades, and they slit their throats, and I never did anything to help!"

I shut my eyes. God, poor Myf.

"I didn't help. I stayed down in my bunker, and I did what I'm doing right now. I cried. I listened to them being slaughtered upstairs, and I cried and cried and cried."

Her guilt felt almost visceral, like an extra person in the room. "Honey..." I licked my lips. "You know it's not your fault. That's what they trained you to do. They literally conditioned you to hide and stay human." That was the Welsh Guardian's whole MO for dragon shifters. Hide, stay human, stay with them, and let them worship you as an earthbound god.

"I'm so weak." Myf's voice dropped to a whisper. "A coward. A stupid weak coward."

"You're the opposite of that, and you know it. You escaped from the People. You found an Orbiter gang to smuggle you here. You resisted Alexei when he came for you. You resisted *torture*, Myf. That's how strong you are."

"I could have saved them."

That's what it all came down to. Now that Myf understood that she'd been lied to, and the dragon wasn't a separate entity just inhabiting her body, she realized she could have transformed into her dragon form and saved the Guardians.

"You saved me," I told her. "The second you understood you were your dragon, you transformed, and you saved me. I never would have survived that fight with Alexei if you hadn't blasted him with your fire breath."

"Too late," she moaned. A thump came from the pantry—she was hitting herself in the head again. "I was too late. And I was too cowardly to stick around and help more. I flew away."

Romeo, still brooding over by the front door, moved, crossing his arms over his chest, instantly capturing my attention. "Brandon was never able to resist his activation words, no matter who said them."

Myf stopped thumping herself in the head. She might have forgotten that Romeo's coven mate was a dragon shifter, too.

"He still has trouble with it. It's one of the reasons he has to drink a potion to inhibit the shift." Romeo took a step closer to the pantry. "The other reason is because we still don't know who bought him—whoever he was programmed to obey is still out there somewhere, so it's a necessary precaution. But even now, after eight years of therapy, he still gets twitchy when anyone says the word 'toaster bath.'"

I raised my eyebrows and mouthed at him. *Really? Toaster bath?*

Romeo wobbled his head slightly in a gesture I interpreted as *I'm not telling Myf his activation words, are you kidding? That's just asking for trouble.*

He turned back to the pantry door. "Brandon was the very first assassin sent to kill me. He almost succeeded. I've still got burn scars from his breath and a claw mark on my arm." His mouth became a hard line. "He has to see the scars he gave me every time we spar. Imagine how bad he feels about that."

I kept my expression blank. Romeo was laying it on thick. It would have been different for Brandon—he'd been activated by whoever bought him and sent him to kill the new High Priest. He had no control over his own actions at that point. That was what the People of the Claw did—they turned dragon shifters into good little Winter Soldiers and sold them to the highest bidder.

Myf sniffed. "Can you make me one of those potions?"

"If you want. It's up to you. Something tells me you don't need it, though."

"The People could still find me," she whispered.

I opened my mouth.

They'd have to get through me first. Dwayne kicked open the door and marched in, a box of tissues under one wing and a whiskey bottle under the other one. He paused to throw Romeo a meaningful glare I didn't quite understand, then stomped miserably over to the pantry. **Move over, you sappy ginger cow. I'm coming in.**

Myf gasped. "I... Daph... I think I heard Dwayne's voice in my head. I heard—"

Dwayne wrenched the door open with his beak and stomped inside, disappearing into the darkness of the pantry. **Move, bitch.**

"Ouch! Okay, okay. Oi, sir, give me a second. Yes, I'll move over, hang on." The sounds of rustling and thumping came from the pantry.

I grinned. Looks like Myf had gotten herself a new Alpha.

Time to eat a bag of cement mix and harden the fuck up.

The smell of whiskey bloomed in the air, and my smile vanished. "Oh, thanks, sir," Myf said. "Don't mind if I do."

"Dwayne!"

CHAPTER
FIVE

I was running late for the staff meeting. It was lucky my bike went fast. I giggled like a hyena as I tore through the backstreets, heading into the city. Romeo shadowed me as close as he could, but I pulled away a little as we hit the busy streets, winding through the traffic, almost brushing the cars and trucks as we sped by. This was what I was best at.

This is why they nicknamed me Yūrei—The Ghost—on the MotoGP circuit. I rode like I was already dead. There was something about the speed that soothed me on a level that I never really understood. Maybe it was because I'd spent years hurtling through time and space at light-speed, with no control over where—or when—I was headed. Finally, I could go fast, and I could control the destination.

I parked outside the main DHS office and pulled off my helmet. Three seconds later, Romeo pulled his matt-black Kawasaki Ninja in beside me, looking like the Angel of Death riding in on his mighty black steed. God, I wished I could handle that thing, but it was far too heavy for me.

He glowered at me as he pulled off his own helmet. "You will be the death of me."

"You didn't have to try and chase me, you know. You knew where I was going."

"As if I was going to let you out of my sight."

I giggled and pulled off my gloves, my heart still racing. "Sorry. It's just... it's better than therapy. It relaxes me so much. Even the smell of motor oil and grease... hmmm." I sighed. "There's just something about dominating a machine like that." My dark silver ZX-14R was perfect for me, but I'd love something with more power.

Involuntarily, my eyes drifted down between Romeo's legs.

"Stop eye-fucking my bike," he growled playfully, flipping the kickstand and getting off.

My cheeks blazed. I wasn't looking at the bike, but I was mesmerized by the masterful way he handled it. I could ride fast—quick turns, split-second gear changes—but Romeo rode with power. His Ninja was one of the most powerful bikes in existence, and he used it like an extension of himself. "I wish I could handle it."

He stared down at me. His eyes darkened. "Are you talking about the bike?"

"No."

The heat in my cheeks migrated downwards. My phone buzzed. I jerked. "Oh, shoot! I forgot about the meeting!" Yanking my phone out of my backpack, I glanced at the screen. Eleven thirty-five. I was already five minutes late. "Are you coming in?"

"Of course. You won't see me if you don't want to. I can stay in the shadows."

I could barely look away from his beautiful silver eyes. God, he was perfect. "I do want to. This"—I waved my hand towards him, gesturing back to myself—"I thought it would make it all worse, but it's easier than I thought it would be."

Yeah, Brain Daphne said cheerfully. *Because your train of thought keeps heading straight into the gutter.*

So that was it. My survival expert lizard brain was redirecting my thoughts from the inevitable terrifying future, bypassing the important conversations I had to have with Romeo, and focusing solely on how much I wanted to rip my fingernails down his back.

Romeo moved closer, bringing me back to the present. "If you're sure."

"I am sure. I want to see you. Although, it means everyone else will see you too, but there are fewer people around since it's Saturday. You're not cleared with security, though. It's pretty tight these days, you're supposed to check in all your weapons." I didn't check in any of mine, but you'd have to pry my Orion blades out of my cold, dead hands. "You'd have to sign in as a visitor. That might mean a little unwanted attention..."

"Nobody else will see me." He hitched his enormous shoulders in a careless shrug. "I have some messages to reply to, and I've got some research to do. While I was watching you racing through traffic like a person with a death wish, I had a few ideas on how to tackle our various problems—" He stopped, instinctively knowing to back off from the topic of what we *couldn't* talk about and rolled his bottom lip through his teeth in a mind melting sexy gesture. "I'll stick to the shadows. But I won't be far away."

I swallowed. "Okay." Nodding, I turned to go.

"Daphne."

I turned back.

He bent down and kissed me. It was hard, passionate. I threw myself at him. We came together like we were fighting, like our tongues were desperate to wrestle, like our lips were frantically trying to mold themselves to fit, our mouths hungry for the taste of each other. Like a match thrown on a gas-soaked bonfire, my core burst into flames. I melted against him.

Bite him.

My hands explored him. Hard muscle. Bulging biceps. Rock-hard chest. I never wanted it to stop...

Just a little bite?

His hand wound around the back of my neck, holding me, then moved up, fisting my hair gently. I arched my body against him. He gasped against my lips.

"I needed that," he murmured.

I did too. I would have said so, but he'd left me breathless. Like Brain-Daphne, who was making *gnaw-gnaw-gnaw* bite noises, I couldn't even form coherent words. Instead, I let out a weird squeak.

Finally, he let me go, and I remembered I was really

late. I pirouetted on my toes and lurched like a zombie up the stairs, into the main building. I didn't have to check to make sure he was following me. The black-cherry fizz of an invisibility spell bloomed behind me, and I knew if I turned around, I wouldn't see him.

But my heart knew exactly where he was.

CHAPTER
SIX

Judy looked up from her pot of yoghurt and glared at me as I raced into the office. "Well, well, well." She narrowed her eyes, glaring at me, her bushy, bleach-blonde hair quivering around her head. "Look who the cat dragged in."

"Sorry I'm late." I directed my words not at her, but at Monica, my boss. "I got stuck with a client."

Monica, looking whip-smart in a new red pantsuit that matched her thick-rimmed red glasses, twirled the whiteboard marker in between her fingers. "The dryad kid, was it, Daphne? How did that one go, was it alright?" Twirling the marker again, she shifted her weight from side-to-side, keeping up her typical machine-gun speech patterns. The woman didn't know how to stay still, possibly due to her caffeine addiction. "I'm very interested in that one, Mrs. Montezuma's lawyer called me six times yesterday and even twice this morning, he's been curiously silent since the time of your visit, though, you'll have to debrief me later, Daphne honey, we've got some things to get through, first, numbers."

I think your boss might be the mortal embodiment of white-collar anxiety, my brain mused. *Chloe might have missed sending one of the archetypes back to the Wilds. Maybe we should stab Monica, see if she explodes in a ball of white light, what do you say?*

I managed not to roll my eyes. Brain-Daphne would do anything to avoid sitting through a staff meeting.

I sat at my desk, nodding at James, my only other colleague, who gave me a quick smile. James never said much, but he was a workhorse and a fabulous dresser. Today he wore a moss-green textured suit that hugged his tall frame, and black glasses sat on his nose.

Speaking of noses...

James had been introduced to me as an Orbiter, but my enhanced olfactory senses picked up a hint of Otherworld around him. Now, with the lingering scent of Mrs. Montezuma fresh in my nostrils, I realized that he had dryad blood. It was hard to be sure, since Judy, for some reason, had an enormous bunch of red roses on her desk, which threw an overpowering floral odor into the air.

James's heritage was none of my business. The roses weren't either. I tried to pay attention as Monica marched back and forth in front of the whiteboard, running through some reports—client numbers, cases, referrals, budget notices...

My attention wavered quickly. The bureaucracy side of things wasn't interesting to me; I was only concerned about my clients. Judy was more animated than I'd seen her in weeks, though, especially when Monica informed us that the office would soon be going completely paperless. "Everything will be online from now on, sweethearts, so get used to it as soon as possible."

Judy trembled in rage. "They're not taking my files! And I need my pens! Are we all going to be slaves to these screens? Turning into mindless electronic-dependent zombies? The world has gone mad!"

"You can keep your pens, Judy," Monica reassured her, stalking back and forth in front of the whiteboard. "It's not only for environmental reasons. We just don't need to be keeping paper files anymore."

"Woke nonsense!" Judy howled.

"And storage reasons, Judy, dear, there's no need for us to be storing six million boxes of old client records in the basement anymore. For efficiency, too, it's so easy to pull up a client's file on a secure server these days."

"What if the server crashes?" Judy screeched. "What if the power grid fails? What if we're hacked? This insane reliance on technology will destroy us all!"

I had no idea why Monica put up with Judy; the woman barely ever did any work. But I suspected she must be very well connected.

Judy was a witch from the Sagwood coven. It wasn't the wealthiest coven in Philadelphia. In fact, when I first started at the O-CPS office, she'd rubbed her connection with the Jupiters in my face, thinking it was impressive. It wasn't anymore, but I'd since learned that the Sagwood coven had a reputation for being very crafty. They'd proven that by staying out of the alliance Mina and Wesley had formed with Alexei Minoff, when he laid siege to the Hidden City.

The Sweetgrass and Gemini covens were still reeling from it. Romeo hadn't even had to hunt down the traitors and punish them—most of the witches who took part were already dead. The ones who tried to run didn't survive the aftermath.

"The sky isn't falling, Judy, honey." Monica's pacing was getting faster and faster. "You'll get the hang of using your laptop eventually, doll, all you need to do is follow the—"

"We're only days away from singularity you know, Monica," Judy screeched. "Days! At any point.... any *second* now, the machines are going to become self-aware, and you know what they're going to do?"

Monica blew out a breath and spun the marker in her hand. "I suspect they'll throw themselves off the nearest cliff to avoid having to deal with us anymore, Judy."

Idly, I wondered if Judy had put some kind of spell on Monica. A "don't fire me" charm. Or an "ignore my shitty behavior and keep paying me" spell, maybe. I'd never caught any hint of magic coming from my boss, but that didn't mean she wasn't under some kind of magical hold. Some spells were undetectable. I concentrated on Monica, trying to catch a whiff, but the smell of the giant bunch of red roses on Judy's desk overpowered my nose.

Distracted, I turned towards her desk. Why the hell did she have a giant heart-shaped bouquet of red roses?

James saw me looking. "They were for you," he murmured softly, not making eye contact with me. His voice was so low, it was almost subsonic. Monica and Judy—still yelling at each other—didn't hear him. "There was a card. It's in her trash can now."

I met his eye and nodded in silent thanks, even though my stomach churned. Romeo hadn't sent me those flowers, I knew that for sure. While we hadn't had much time to share personal details about ourselves, our likes and dislikes, favorite colors and pizza toppings, there was no way in hell he'd ever think that my favorite flowers might be red roses.

Red roses were probably the worst flowers I could think of. When I was about nine years old, I spent months of my life on the run, chased by a bloodthirsty queen in a wild-magic realm. That darn madwoman insisted I should paint all her white roses red. And when I refused, she kept trying to cut off my head.

Consequently, I wasn't fond of red roses.

"Okay, enough." Monica clapped her hands. "Judy, I take your point, but it's not up to me. This is happening at a federal level, so if you're still put out, maybe take it up with your district congresswoman, now we have to move on, we've got a lot to get through, and we've only got five more minutes."

Judy scrunched up her face and opened another pot of yoghurt as Monica ran through some policy changes that affected our department. My attention drifted again. I could hear Cindy in the meeting room on the other side of the office, holding one of her group therapy sessions. Poor Cindy was working on the weekend, too.

Cindy wasn't part of O-CPS—she fell under a tiny Otherworld Social Services program for supes that had drug and alcohol dependency issues. Since we often had to refer parents to her for counselling and education, it made sense to have her as part of the office.

"Finally," Monica said, whirling around and tapping the whiteboard, "I'm pleased to announce that Daphne has completed her hours and is now fully registered as a social worker. Congratulations, Daphne, you're now one of us."

James murmured darkly in his low, rumbling tone. "One of us. One of us."

"She can't have!" Judy looked outraged. "She's supposed to do at least six months of full-time work to get her hours. She's been here just over a month!"

"She's done six months of full-time work already, Judy."

"It's not possible!" Judy launched into a rant about the diminishing standards and giving hand-outs to people who didn't work for them. All of us ignored her.

The meeting room door opened, and Cindy fluttered out on tiny black wings. Gothflowers were a species of pixie—off-world creatures from Faerie. I'd met a flutter of them once while I was trying to get home, but they were rare here. They didn't come to the human world if they could help it, mostly because of their powers.

Pixies of all species excreted magical dust, and a gothflower's pee and poop was a powerful aphrodisiac. My friend Prue used to have a friend who was a gothflower, and she told me the most hilarious stories about her when I was a kid. When I came back, Prue couldn't talk about her friend without crying, so I assume the poor little pixie died during the Suffocation. So many of our people had died.

My brain growled. *Christopher Jupiter. It was all his fault. And now he's running around Greece, trying to—*

I derailed that train of thought, my heart sinking down to the pit of my belly when I realized my brain was right—this whole Christopher situation was getting urgent. He was on the move.

But how the hell was I supposed to do anything about it when I couldn't even think about it? And I couldn't even tell anyone what he was after?

We have to trust ourselves. We can do this.

Okay, stop. I clenched my fists. Focus. We've got other things to worry about. Christopher Jupiter is not urgent.

He is.

I ignored her and wrenched my attention back to Cindy, fluttering out of the meeting room. As usual, Cindy's aesthetic leaned heavy on the goth part of her name. She wore a black micro-mini, ripped fishnet tights, and a black-and-white striped t-shirt held together with safety pins. Her tiny heart-shaped face was painted corpse-white, with black liner ringing her eyes and swooping upwards towards her temples in a spiderweb pattern. Tiny pentagrams dotted her nose like freckles.

"Right." She flew into the office, scowling, and pointed at Judy. "Shut your yoghurt-hole, Judy. Your meeting is over."

"But—"

"I said shut it," Cindy snapped. "I have vulnerable clients who are in earshot of you, and nobody wants to hear your yapping." She flew right into Judy's face, narrowing her little spiderweb-decorated eyes. "How about you try something new. Write down your feelings in an email. Then take that email, shut your laptop, and shove the whole thing up your ass."

Judy looked like she was about to have a heart attack. She mouthed uncontrollably for a moment.

"Oh, and nice flowers, Judy," Cindy added, her tone dripping innocence. "Who sent them to you?"

Judy's face went white. "Uh, they were, uh, from an, uh, from a client—"

"Really? Because the card in your trash can says, *Be mine forever, all love, Lennox*."

I cringed. I should have known.

Cindy was relentless. "Why is Lennox Arran sending you flowers?"

A vein in Judy's forehead throbbed. "I've, uh, I've always been a big fan. I was the first one to subscribe to his channel, you know. Perhaps he sent them as an, uh, acknowledgement to his biggest supporters."

That was interesting. Judy was normally an awful snob when it came to other supes. But then again, everyone loved Lennox. He just had that big, brash, confident personality, that charming ruffian thing white woman seemed to melt over.

Cindy fluttered her wings like a hummingbird and moved, zipping up, then down, before coming back to eye level, holding a little card. "Then why does it say *P.S. I can't wait to pound you into the next dimension. When I'm done with you, your pussy will look like ten pounds of tenderized wagyu beef*."

Judy stammered and went bright red.

Cindy raised her eyebrows in a silent challenge while her clients filed out of the meeting room behind her—

two witches, a young werewolf man, and a lamia in her snake form who morphed effortlessly back onto two legs before she left the office.

An idea occurred to me. "Actually, Cindy, can I have a quick word with you?"

Her head whipped towards me, and the hard look on her face vanished. "Sure." She waved her arm. "The meeting room is free."

"No, it's not." Judy gnashed her teeth. She finally found her voice. "I have it booked. I have two clients—"

"You're not fooling anyone, Wario Parton." Cindy rolled her eyes, fluttered behind me, and started pushing me back towards the empty room. "Everyone knows the reason Daphne's completed her hours already is because she's done all of yours for you." Cindy shoved me inside and slammed the door behind her.

I turned and grinned at her. "Wario Parton? I don't get it."

"Wario is the evil Mario from Mario Bros. Judy tries to look like Dolly Parton—with the hair and boobs and her waist trainer sucking her in—but she's not a saint like Dolly Parton. Judy is the opposite of Dolly, so she's Wario Parton."

"Oh," I chuckled. "Good one."

Cindy pushed me towards a chair. "You don't have to pretend you understand any of those references, Daphne."

"Thanks, I didn't." I'd have to google them all later. "But I want you to know that when I do, I'll laugh really loudly, and I didn't want you to miss out on my reaction."

Cindy rolled her eyes, but there was no meanness in it. "You're a peach." She fluttered down and sat on the table across from me, cross legged. "So, what can I do for you?"

"I need some advice on how to deal with my roommate." Keeping it brief, I told her about Myf and her new fondness for booze, with little hints about her trauma, leaving out any incriminating details about her true nature. When I was done, I held up my hands. "What do you think? What can I do to help her?"

"Hmm." Cindy tapped her little pointed chin. "That's a tough one. Dragons are tricky."

I jolted. "Huhhhh, what?" My mouth dropped open. "How did you guess?"

"I didn't guess." Cindy's tone was deadpan. "You made it kinda obvious. She's got a temper. She's got red hair. She's *Welsh*. Come on, Daphne. You didn't even have to tell me she's a scary shifter with lots of trauma in her past and a ton of survivor guilt. I saw the dragon thing a mile away. Next, you'll be telling me she's a mean drunk. Dragons are *always* mean drunks."

"Oh, she is," I breathed out. "I don't know what to do about her."

Cindy thought for a second. "Well, it doesn't sound like she's an addict. If she was, she'd be leaving your pantry to find more drugs and alcohol. Even if she was actually agoraphobic—and you don't think she is, do you?"

I shrugged. "Not in the strictest sense of the word. Myf's not scared of the outside. She just feels safer when she's hidden."

"Right. So, she's not agoraphobic. If she were an addict, then getting her hands on more alcohol would be the only thing she could think of. No, I think she's self-medicating to numb the pain. Your best bet is just to ride it out. Keep listening to her. I have to warn you though, she'll get worse before she gets better. She'll get meaner."

I let out a weary sigh. "I don't see how that's possible. She's *so* mean."

"Oh, she can. Believe me. Your dragon roomie is desperately trying to make sense of her whole world right now. She hates herself, so she's going to do everything she possibly can to make you hate her, too."

"I could never hate her."

Cindy stared at me darkly. "You say that now. Trust me, I know for a fact that there are limits even the most compassionate person in the world can endure." Suddenly, her expression shifted, and I saw a deep sadness—an endless grief—in her eyes. "I'm only four years sober, you know. The last time I relapsed was at the start of the Suffocation."

"Really?"

"Yeah. I was living in D.C. at the time. People started dying, and nobody knew why. I relapsed because I was so scared. I locked myself in a warded box with twelve bottles of vodka, and watched as my best friends came home, crying, after losing another one of their people. I hated myself so much for relapsing, and for being such a coward, so I kept drinking to numb the pain. Eventually, I wanted my bestie to hate me too, so I started saying the most awful things I could about her—her stupid slutty outfits, her old beefcake husband, her dumb nail art... Nothing was off-limits. At first, she understood me lashing out, because she was scared too. But at least she was doing something about it. I was such a coward."

Tears welled up in Cindy's eyes; she dashed them away with her fingers. "Anyway, we kept losing people, and the stress was making her crazy. It was making *all* of us crazy. We started fighting all the time, and eventually, during one of my drunken rants, I told her she was one step away from turning into her father." Cindy pressed her lips together and looked away. "It wasn't the first time I'd used her bio dad as a weapon against her, but it was the first time it really hit a nerve. She'd been overextending herself trying to help supes get to safety, and she knew she was becoming... bossy." Cindy paused and shrugged. "More bossy than usual, anyway. When I said it to her, I saw the look in her eye, and we both knew I'd gone too far." She shook her head sadly. "But at that moment, I felt *so* much satisfaction. I finally got her to hate me as much as I hated myself."

"Oh my gosh," I breathed out. "I'm so sorry, Cindy."

The little creature met my gaze. "Take this as a cautionary tale. Your fiery little roommate might do the same thing. You might think you're prepared for whatever she throws your way, but believe me, it could be unforgivable."

"Oh, Cindy." My own eyes welled up with tears, too. "That's awful. I'm so sorry. Did you ever make up with your best friend?"

"Not yet." Cindy looked down at the desk. "After that day, I drank myself into a coma. When I woke up, I found out that she'd gone with her husband to try and clean up some of the Suffocation disaster zones. I knew I'd hit rock bottom, and I'd die if I didn't do something, so I left D.C. and went up to New York, got clean, finished my certification in Otherworld drug and alcohol counseling, then came here to try and start again. I haven't seen her since. I've sent letters begging for forgiveness, but I haven't heard anything back yet." Her eyes glistened with tears again. "I have to make amends. But I also have to respect her feelings. She might not want to get in contact with me."

I reached out to hold her hand, then stopped, awkwardly realizing my own hand was bigger than her entire body. After flailing my fingers awkwardly for a second, I extended my index finger and tapped her very gently on the knee. "I hope you manage to make contact with her."

"So do I. The Great Suffocation makes everything hard. We all lost so much." She blinked back tears. "Do you want me to try and talk to your roommate? We do have a few things in common. Both of us were sold as slaves, for one."

"Actually, yeah. That would be awesome." My attention wavered for a second.

A weird intensity was building in the atmosphere. Not here, but out in the office. I could feel it, just outside the meeting room door.

I refocused on Cindy. "Thanks so much for your time," I said, getting to my feet, noticing that the office outside had gone very, very quiet. "I really appreciate it." I opened the door and looked out.

Romeo Zarayan stood at my desk. He glanced over and caught my eye. "Hey. Can we talk?"

Nobody in the office looked at him. Nobody said anything. Judy appeared to be staring at her computer, but her neck muscles were bulging hard with the effort of keeping her head fixed on her screen. A light sheen of sweat glistened on James's brow. He tapped on his keypad carefully, as if he was defusing a bomb instead of filing a report. Inside her glass office, Monica was pacing so fast, she looked like a video game character stuck in an underground level.

Cindy, coming up behind me, let out a shriek, and zoomed backwards, hitting the wall behind her.

"It's okay, Cin—"

"*Eeeeehyeeeeeehhhhhhhhhh!!!*" She barreled off the wall, shot out of the door, and streaked through the office, a sparkly black comet, heading straight out the window.

CHAPTER
SEVEN

The Lord of Shadows took me to lunch.

It seemed we both learned the lessons from our first disastrous date. We didn't speak as we walked out of the building. Romeo didn't tell me where we were going, but he took my hand, and we walked in the direction of a local burger joint, only one block from the DHS office.

This is a good test to see how well he knows us. If he doesn't take us to Benny's Burgers, then we get to eat his kidneys. Deal?

I ignored Brain-Daphne. The strangest feeling fluttered in my stomach, and it had nothing to do with the idea of Benny's Burgers. The sensation was exquisite—a delicious anticipation, a secret excitement, like when you were a kid, and you saw real magic for the very first time. I didn't want to pepper him with questions for fear I'd break the spell.

I got nervous when we drew closer to a very expensive sushi place. I wasn't a fan of sushi, because of all the raw animals I'd forced myself to eat as a lost kid just so I could stay alive. So I breathed a sigh of relief when he walked past without hesitating.

We crossed the street and walked directly into Benny's Burgers, and I exhaled happily. We stood at the podium and waited until the hostess came back. She was seating another couple and seemed in no hurry.

I eyed Romeo carefully. If he looked like himself right now, she'd be sprinting over. The delicious zing of berry-scented magic told me he had cast a glamor right after we left the O-CPS office, but he still looked like himself to me. A huge, sexy, brooding beast of a man wearing black leather motorcycle pants and a dark gray Henley shirt under his jacket.

He must be wearing a double-layer glamor. The same as what Holly wore when she came to warn me about the Jupiters betraying him. I smiled up at him. "What does everyone else see when they look at you?"

He met my gaze, and his eyes softened. "Just a guy. I look like a man from a car insurance commercial. Generic, nondescript..."

"Harmless."

"Exactly."

He didn't feel harmless though. Like always, I could feel his immense power radiating out of his body, a thunderous presence—dark, moody, explosive. It was bewildering to me that nobody else could feel it.

I grinned at him in silence like an idiot until the hostess finally came back and led us disinterestedly to a corner booth. The place was crowded but comfortable, the air thick with the delicious aroma of flame grilled beef and salt on hot fries. I settled back into the comfy plastic seats, listened to the generic, unexciting buzz of conversation around me, tasted the air, and exhaled happily. "I don't think I've been this relaxed in years."

"Good." His gray eyes settled on my face. "That's what I was hoping for."

My belly warmed. He really did understand me. Anybody else would be more relaxed in nature—lying on the beach, listening to the crash of waves or in the woods, watching the stars. But not me. Hell, no. I'd spent too much time in nature on high alert, trying to avoid things that kept popping out to eat me.

My stomach flipped. "Wait. Why did you want me to be relaxed?"

"I've been thinking about our... communication issue. I have some things I need to tell you, but it might get close to the boundary you told me about. I've discussed it with my friend, the expert—"

I smiled. "The one who is helping you with your research?" I couldn't wait to meet this guy Romeo clearly adored. In my head, he was a male version of Aunt Marche.

"Yeah, that's the one. We talked it over, and I want to try something."

I swallowed, suddenly nervous. "Okay."

"We don't need to talk about specifics right now. I just want to try something first, and I think it would help if you were as relaxed as possible. I wanted to bring you somewhere where you would feel safe. Where you would feel powerful."

Gods, he got me. Here, in the city, in civilization,

surrounded by normies, sitting on a plastic seat, and enveloped by the odor of comfort food, I'd never felt safer. Nodding slowly, I thought about what he might be trying to do. "I feel safe with you. But I don't necessarily feel powerful. I get that you have things you need to tell me, so you might as well go ahead."

"Well, I've got another idea. I'm going to cast an illusion. Are you ready?"

I nodded. A fizz of black cherry magic bloomed around me, and suddenly, I wasn't sitting in a booth in a trendy burger joint anymore. It was night. The air was cool, and I was sitting on an upturned milk crate.

My Kawasaki was beside me. Tall buildings with neon signs in hiragana script surrounded me. I smiled. "Yokohama?"

"As best as I can remember it." Romeo sat beside me on a milk crate of his own, wearing motorcycle leathers. His gray eyes twinkled silver in the neon lights. "You broke three world records that day."

"Unofficial world records."

"Well, they can hardly make official records for illegal Japanese street racing."

"Fair point." I closed my eyes and inhaled, tasting flame-grilled burgers and salt. "Yeah, this works. I feel amazing. I've never felt more powerful in my whole life than when I was racing here, in the city." I opened one eye and squinted at him. "Will you let me know when the waitress comes to take my order?"

His eyes twinkled. "Sure. She's on her way." The sound of revving engines soothed me a little more. A blonde woman wearing an apron over her motorcycle leathers sashayed up to us, brandishing a notebook. Romeo had opened the illusion to include our waitress. "What will it be, kids?"

"The triple-stacker-cheesy Benny's Bad Boy burger," I said without hesitation. "Cheesy fries. Large raspberry soda. An extra serving of curly fries."

Romeo's lips twitched. "I'll have the same." The waitress scribbled our order down and wandered away. "You didn't even have to look at the menu."

I waved my hand, the delicious anticipation making me giddy. "I'll never be more relaxed than I am right now, so you better go ahead."

His eyes darkened. "Christopher Jupiter is still in Greece," he said, his voice low. "I have a tail on him, and he's been visiting temples and talking to priests."

The evils stirred within me. I focused on the sound of revving engines and hardened myself. "Okay. Go on."

"He's started to hunt for some sort of ancient artifact."

Fuck.

I flinched.

Romeo hesitated. "Are you okay?"

"I'm fine." As long as we didn't talk about them out loud, I could do what I always did and pretend they didn't exist. I waved my hand and forced my shoulders to relax. "Go on."

"The expert friend of mine, the one who is helping me with the research—she's my foster sister, actually—"

She? This expert is a girl?

Not now, Brain. Breathe in, breathe out.

"—she's an expert on ancient magical artifacts. I've

put her on the case. I've given her all the information I've received from my PI. She'll be able to figure out what the artifact is, and we'll be able to find it first."

Breathe in, breathe out. Breathe in… In the distance, I heard an announcer call the next race over the loudspeaker. I was doing just fine.

"I know what it will be," I said, wondering how to proceed. The artifact he was talking about—I'd seen powerful sorcerers from parallel realms use them before, but I wasn't sure I could bring myself to explain it all right now.

It took me a moment. "If Christopher Jupiter is trying to summon—" I didn't want to say her name. "Someone from mythology, then he'll be looking for an ancient artifact, at least three thousand years old. It will be a very large gemstone with exceptional clarity. And it will be surrounded by copper or gold. A powerful conduit of some sort."

Romeo nodded thoughtfully. "The thing he's looking for is a *Stella Ostium*, isn't it?"

It meant "Star Door" in Latin. "Yeah."

"Will it work?"

I shrugged. "Both of us know that with enough power, anything is possible."

"Okay." Romeo furrowed his brow. "I just would have thought that if it was possible, someone would have done it."

"There's a reason why it's not easy. I—"

The darkness stirred.

Think of a different realm. And maybe eat some fries while you talk about it.

Good idea, thanks, Brain. I shuffled around on my milk crate. "This might be easier while I'm holding my burger."

"A comfort burger. No problem." Romeo sat back. "We can talk about something else while we wait for our food."

I was desperate for him to tell me more about himself. "Enough about me. Tell me about this foster sister of yours."

"Her name's Bella," he said, his face softening. He relaxed back on his milk crate. "She's been my best friend for a long, long time."

"She's a witch?"

He shook his head. "No, she's an Orbiter."

I smiled. Any other witch would have said she's "*just* an Orbiter." Not Romeo, though. I waited to see if he was comfortable sharing anything else. Like me, his childhood and adolescence had been horribly traumatic.

"Bella and I met when I was five, and she was seven. We were both placed together in a group home." His jaw hardened a little. "It wasn't a nice place to be. It wasn't the worst placement I'd had, but it was far from the best. I don't remember why I was moved there, but I probably did something awful, and my former foster family asked for me to be rehomed. There were eight other kids in that home, and all of us were fucked up beyond repair."

My heart ached. Nobody was broken beyond repair.

But I understood what he was saying. In order to be able to empathize with some of my clients, you needed to understand exactly how they felt, and why they sometimes did awful, terrible things. And that was why. Some kids felt like they were fucked up beyond repair. Unsavable. Unlovable. Like Myf, trying to reinforce her own view of herself, and make me hate her as much as she hated herself.

Trauma was a bitch. I nodded. "Go on."

"Bella was the only one who was kind to me. She protected me from some of the older boys as best she could."

"I love her already."

His gaze softened. "She was a firecracker, even at seven years old. Bella was actually the one who gave me the idea to try magic spells in the first place. She was obsessed with everything magical, and even though she was an Orbiter, she always insisted it was real.

"How did she become an Orbiter in the first place?" An Orbiter was a normal human who'd been exposed to the supernatural world and had the veil on their eyes—the thin cover that shielded them from seeing magic all around them—removed.

It might be a tough question for him to answer. There were two ways to become an Orbiter. The soft way was to be born into it—maybe born human and magicless, but brought up around werewolves or wizards, so the veil naturally eroded away as the child grew.

The second way was the hard way—violent, shocking, and illegal. Usually, the transition from normie to Orbiter happened because of something terrible, like if a crazed vampire fed from them and didn't have the grace to hypnotize them afterwards to make them forget. It was rare, but it did happen. "Was it the soft way or the hard way?"

"I don't know," Romeo replied. "Bella doesn't know, either. She's always been able to See. She was an orphan like me." His expression grew sad. "Her mom was a sex worker who was murdered by a client when Bella was just eight months old."

"Oh, no," I whispered. "The poor girl."

"So, she grew up in foster care like me. There was no father listed on her birth certificate, so again, just like me, potential adopters were reluctant to take her on. Nobody wants the bio dad to show up one day and sue for custody. And," he added, the hardness in his jaw easing a little. "Like me, Bella was a hellcat. We were difficult children together. She would read fantasy books out loud to me and explain that magic was real, we just couldn't see it yet, but one day, we would. Our case workers and foster carers kept taking the books from her and sending her back to therapy to drum into her that it wasn't true. A hairy half-giant wasn't going to show up on a magical flying motorcycle and rescue any of us and take us to a magic school. But she insisted magic was all real. And I believed her."

I nodded but stayed quiet.

"Bella wasn't ever delusional," he continued. "Later on, I guessed her mom must have been a witch, because she somehow intuitively knew the basics of spellcasting. Circles, objects of power, incantation, intentions, that kind of thing. She would sneak out of her girl's dorm at night, and we'd sit together on the floor of my bedroom, and she'd try over and over again to gather some magic. But it never worked for her."

My heart throbbed. The poor girl.

Romeo glanced away. "It worked for me, though. I never told her my spells worked. I still don't know if it was the right thing to do or not. I kept it to myself and worked my little spells, making protection charms that kept our foster parents' attention off us and kept the older, meaner kids away. We stayed in that group home together for four years, and she never gave up hope that one of her spells would work, but it never did. I still feel guilty about it."

I could tell; I could see it in his eyes.

After a moment, he continued, "As you know, I started experimenting with blood magic. Just little things—using my blood, trapping spiders, crushing little bugs. They gave my spells more power. I had no idea how bad it was, how much of a slippery slope it all was. Everyone around me was violent and horrible, so it was just normal for me. When Bella would come back from a fight with our older siblings with their blood on her knuckles, she'd use the blood to make a spell. Again, it never worked for her." He lapsed into silence.

"What happened next?" I asked gently.

"Well, eventually, the inevitable happened, and the group home got audited. One of the older kids got brave enough to snitch on our foster carers. The authorities found out some of the girls had been pimped out. The home got shut down, and they separated us all. I was terrified." He shook his head once. "Bella was my big sister, my only protector, so I couldn't bear the idea of her going away. By then, I knew that spells powered with blood were stronger, so I killed a rat, drained its blood, and tried to make a spell to tie her to me so we could never be separated." He trailed off.

"Did it work?"

After a beat, he shook his head. "No. I don't know why. Most of my spells seemed to work out even though I had no idea what I was doing. With magic, intention is everything. They placed us in different homes. Bella was sent out of state, up to Vermont."

"And what happened to you?"

Some of the shadows disappeared from his eyes, and the hard line in his lips softened. "Aunt Marche happened."

"Oh."

"She found me a few days after I was dragged off to another group home. She explained what I was, confirmed that magic was real, and gently admonished me for killing animals to use their blood in spells. To be completely honest, I didn't understand why it was so bad at first. Everyone I know eats the flesh of dead animals. For me, blood was just an ingredient. But Aunt Marche explained that it wasn't the blood that fueled the magic. The blood itself is just a conduit. The power is in the suffering—*that's* why it's considered an evil art. Because the more you make the creature suffer, the more potent the magic is, and the more addictive it is, until you need more blood, more suffering..."

That's why he wants us, my brain whispered. *That's why he wants them so badly. They will make him so powerful.*

I shivered, and interrupted Romeo and my own train of thought, trying to get back onto safer ground. "Then what happened? After Aunt Marche found you?"

"She had me put into the O-CPS system instead. I got placed with a nice witch couple in Pittsburg, who put me on the straight and narrow. Lesbians," he added, with the hint of a smile. "I used to call them the witch wives. I hated them at first, but as it turns out, it was the best place for me. They didn't put up with any of my bullshit. They made me finish school, and they taught me the right ways to use my magic."

"And what about Bella?"

"Oh, we always stayed in touch. She got adopted by a very strict normie family—academics—and changed her name. They put her through some very intensive therapy, and eventually, things worked out for her, too. We got to hang out again when she was sixteen, and I was fourteen. She finally gave up on trying to use magic and became obsessed with magical artifacts instead. Her normie family sent her to university. She studied archeology and ancient history and began traveling around the world with her professors and consulting on excavations. Eventually, she discovered some really valuable antiquities in the remains of an ancient temple in Sri Lanka and made her fortune." He gave me one of his rare smiles. "She's like a female version of Indiana Jones."

I smiled. The countess loved those movies. She'd made me watch *Raiders of the Lost Ark* a few times. "Cool."

"So, Bella was the first person I called when I realized Christopher Jupiter was—"

"Hold that thought." I could smell the burgers approaching, and I needed to jam some fries in my mouth before I felt truly capable of handling this conversation. "The server is heading this way. How are we going to do this?"

Romeo waved his hand, and the table materialized between us. We waited in silence while the leather-and-apron wearing waitress placed our plates on the table and shimmied away.

I ate a few cheesy fries, took a huge bite of my triple-stacker-cheesy Benny's Bad Boy burger and nodded at Romeo. "Okay. I'm good. First, you wanted to know why Stella Ostiums exist, and why nobody has used them in recent history." I took a deep breath. "Do you understand the tidal universe theory?"

He shrugged. "Only a little."

"Well, to give you the short explanation, all realms, as they exist right now, are constantly moving. They drift in and drift out again. Sometimes we're close together, and then, after a few thousand years, we'll drift further away. Our mortal realm has been rubbing up against Faerie for a few thousand years—sometimes it's even closer, like it was in the seventeenth century. Back then, you didn't even need magic to get there; you could just fall into a fairy circle and disappear forever. We used to be much closer to the Norse realms back in the eighth century than we are now." I paused and swallowed. "Some of the creatures in those realms were so powerful that humans here at the time called them gods. You know all the stories about Loki and Odin and Thor?"

His brow furrowed for a minute, then he understood. "Yeah."

"Well, all of them are true. The Norse parallel realms were once aligned so closely with our mortal realm, they overlapped. You didn't really need anything to move from one realm to the other. You could just go over a body of water and let your intention carry you to the next world. In time, as the realms drifted further away, you had to travel the Bifrost or use the branches of the World Tree to travel to the different worlds. When they came to Midgard, the most powerful denizens of Asgard were called gods, and they went where they pleased and did whatever they wanted."

"I understand." Romeo swallowed a big bite of his burger and nodded. "Go on."

"As time went on, and the Norse parallel realms got farther away from the mortal realm, it became harder for the gods to come here. They poured their power into their own magical artifacts to help them travel. First, they used world keys, which we still use to get to other similarly aligned realms now. Then, as thousands of years passed and we drifted farther away, the vibrations of our realms were no longer aligned. So, these gods needed more powerful artifacts. Something that would open a wormhole, and also something to help transform whoever was traveling into the right vibration so they wouldn't arrive at the other end as a steaming hunk of barely-alive flesh."

The darkness within me quivered. I paused, swallowed roughly, and ate a handful of fries before I could go on. "So, they used Stella Ostiums—Star Doors. The gem is always vibrationally aligned to the foreign realm."

Romeo chewed thoughtfully. "The gem came from that realm?"

"Usually, yeah. Or it was created by the gods themselves. I heard a Norse priest boasting about a Star Door he once held in his hand, an old white gem that was apparently made from Odin's sperm."

Romeo pondered that for a second. He raised his eyebrows. "Okay."

"I have no idea if it's true or not," I added, shoving some fries in my mouth. "But one thing is certain; the gem in a Star Door is not from this world. It might look like an emerald or a diamond, but it's not from earth. A geologist would say it's unique in clarity or that it's an exceptionally rare specimen or something like that."

"But Star Doors don't work anymore." Romeo pulled out a pickle from his burger and offered it to me wordlessly.

I ate it, equally wordlessly. I loved pickles. Once I swallowed, I answered his question. "It's not that they don't work. It's that our realms are too far away for them to work as easily as they used to. All the old priests and priestesses would have stopped trying after a while. And remember, once you stop giving something attention, it loses its power. They're not calling the gods anymore, because the gods aren't answering. And the gods aren't answering because we're not calling them."

We ate in silence for a moment. "But it *is* possible."

I nodded grimly. "Like I said, you and I both know that with enough magic, anything is possible." I took a sip of my soda and waited a moment. "I need to tell you everything, Romeo, I know that. We're not going to be able to stop him unless I share everything with you, but I just can't, and I don't know a way around it."

To my surprise, he didn't look too upset. "Bella actually had some ideas about that."

"She did?" My heart thudded. The idea of not having to carry this burden alone made me so giddy, I could have bounced out of my seat.

"Yeah. I've been doing more research into wards." Romeo's jaw hardened as he clenched it. "Because of that asshole Christopher Jupiter using a *micşorându* ward on Dwayne. I need to find a way to break them, in case he ever tries anything so evil as a shrinking ward ever again."

"Agreed." I stuffed the rest of my fries in my mouth.

"So far, I've got nothing. But an idea came to me. You find it easier to talk to me when you're relaxed and confident and in control, right?"

"Right." I peered at him. "So what are you thinking?"

"Well, since I don't really know what the problem is, I'm thinking of a multi-layered approach." He held up his hand and ticked off the ideas on his fingers. "We get Levi to lock us both in a hard ward, and I project a scene like this to get you as relaxed as possible. Then we get Micah to put you under vamp hypnosis."

I chewed my lip thoughtfully. "Huh."

"We put your body to sleep, then access your subconscious, bypassing your conscious state. I ask your subconscious questions, and you answer."

I thought about it. No, it wouldn't work. If he were speaking to my subconscious—my spirit—my soul would still be in my body, and my body would still be right there.

The evils wouldn't be asleep. They would still be able to hear me.

But if he could separate my spirit from my body...

"There would have to be some distance," I said. "I'd need to get pulled out completely."

"Out of your body?" He caught on immediately. "Astral projection?"

"Yeah."

"Have you ever done it?"

"Nope." I shrugged. "But I'm willing to try. And only if you stay out of the hard ward. My body can stay in the hard ward. Alone."

Romeo's eyes narrowed. "Is it really that bad?"

I nodded. I didn't say anything.

"No." He shook his head. "No deal."

I smiled at him. "Then no deal. We're not doing it."

His expression grew savage. "I'm going in there with you, Daphne."

"Only if you promise to kill me if anything goes wrong, Romeo," I sang back.

"Never." He glared at me.

"I don't see why this is a dealbreaker for you," I said. "I won't be in there anyway. If all goes to plan, I'll be floating around the room like a ghost, staring at the top of your head. You'll just be stuck inside the hard ward with my body."

Romeo stared at the table in silence for a while, then let out a gruff sigh, leaned over, and took my hand. "Let me think about it some more. In the meantime, we need to get moving on finding this Star Door before Christopher Jupiter. But you don't have to worry, if anyone can track down an ancient artifact, it will be Bella. I've got her on the case."

Brain Daphne growled softly. *This Bella bitch sounds like trouble.*

I ignored her, but an odd feeling squirmed in my chest. It felt... icky. Dangerous.

That's jealousy, you dumb whore.

No, it couldn't be. I'd never been jealous of anyone in my whole life. I'd been envious, covetous, resentful, and just downright sad... but I'd never been jealous before.

I don't like it. He talks like he likes her too much. Trust me, we have to take her out as soon as possible. Stabby, stabby, stab.

Wordlessly, I shushed her. She was Romeo's *sister*.

Foster sister, she hissed. *Trust me, she's bad news, I just know it.*

I ground my teeth, mentally wrestled Brain-Daphne to the ground, held my hand over her mouth, and forced myself to concentrate on Romeo.

"In fact—" He pulled out his phone and tapped out a message. "I'll just let Bella know what you said about it having to be a rare, high-clarity gemstone with gold or copper surrounding it. She probably already knows, but it won't hurt to share." He sent the message, then met my eyes. "And you don't have to worry. Bella will take care of it; she's getting ready to head straight to Greece now. We'll find that damned artifact before Christopher Jupiter, I promise."

The darkness twitched; I forced it down. "It won't be in Greece."

He paused and frowned. "No?"

"Nope."

Romeo's frown deepened. "I thought you didn't know where it was."

"Oh, I don't. I don't know where it is or what it looks like. But I know it won't be in Greece."

"Why not?"

"It's an ancient artifact, Romeo. More importantly, it's a big, rare gemstone wrapped in valuable metal. It's pretty, rare, *and* expensive. Ever heard of the Elgin Marbles?"

"Oh." The scowl vanished. "Of course."

"Exactly." I shot little finger-guns at him. "Greece has been occupied by foreign invaders dozens of times over the last few thousand years. Usually, it's the English that have sticky fingers when they're colonizing or even "liberating" an occupied country. This is just a calculated guess, but the Star Door is most likely to be in the Tower Museum or wrapped around the neck of some royal or set in a tiara somewhere."

He rolled his bottom lip through his teeth. "I didn't think of that. I don't think Bella did, either. She's in New York, on her way to the airport to head to Greece now. I'll divert her." He thumbed his phone again. "So, London?"

I shrugged. "Maybe. It could be anywhere in the world." Just like the countess, the Stella Ostium was "abroad."

Romeo grunted. "It's probably better to have Bella come to meet us at my place for now, then. We need to figure out a plan of action. There's no point in her jetting off anywhere if we don't know where to go."

I raised my eyebrows. "She's got a jet?"

"Yeah." He tapped out a message on his phone. "Two, actually. No, wait, she sold the Lear and bought a Mirovski last year, I think. So just one jet and one helicopter."

She's super-rich, huh? That sickening, squirming feeling writhed in my belly again. *Wonder how she got all her money? The tomb raiding business pays well, I suppose.*

Bella was none of my business. And she was Romeo's sister.

Foster sister.

I ignored Brain-Daphne. "Well, I just don't want Bella to waste her time," I said, picking up the tiny crispy shards of fries remaining in my basket. "If your sister is a magical artifacts expert, she should know about Star Doors, and she might have an idea of what to look for. Huge, rare gemstones tend to leave a bloody trail throughout history, so no doubt she'll find something. I'll start to worry once Christopher Jupiter leaves Greece because then we'll know he's on the trail." My hand shook a little as I went to pick up another fry.

Romeo met my eyes, reached out, took my hand, and squeezed it. We stared at each other in silence for a long moment. "I need to know what's going on with you." The muscle in his jaw ticked. "It's killing me."

Me too.

CHAPTER
EIGHT

My hour was up; I had to go back to work. I had two clients coming to the office today, and I had to consult with James first, as he'd handled both cases before.

Romeo followed me back to the office, retreating to the shadows. I could hear him every now and then, murmuring into his phone, giving orders for his P.I. to follow Christopher more closely, and try to find a description of the artifact he was chasing.

To my surprise, I found Dwayne in the human CPS, sitting outside our office, still looking absolutely miserable. Two equally sad looking children sandwiched him, cuddling him gently. One of them—a little white girl wearing clothes unsuitable for the cold weather—had her face buried into his feathers.

I paused in front of the sad little group. "Are you comforting them, or are they comforting you?"

He sighed. **A little of column A, a little of column B.**

Dwayne's hangover had gone on for far too long. I was starting to get a little worried. But first... I pointed at him. "Is Myf okay?"

She will be. Eventually. Once she wakes up.

"She's asleep?"

Kind of.

I glared at him. "What does that mean? *Please* don't tell me you let her drink herself unconscious."

Of course not.

I exhaled heavily. "Good."

I knocked her out.

"Dwayne!"

That girl is a mean drunk, little one. I'll admit, I overestimated my capacity for empathy. I thought we'd have a miserable little drink together, but I haven't been roasted so badly since that Baltic witch lured me into her cottage.

"But... sir..." I spluttered. "You knocked her out?"

He rolled his eyes at my expression. **She's a dragon. She'll be fine. Besides, the sleep will do her good. I left her some Advil.**

I stared at him for a moment, finally noticing that one of the kids nestled into his side was looking at me like I was crazy.

Oh, right. I was in the normie CPS office, and I was having a one-sided conversation with a goose. Cool, cool, cool...

Well, it was too late now; I already looked crazy. I stabbed a finger towards him. "We'll talk about this later," I hissed, and stalked off, heading into the O-CPS office.

James was still out—his desk was empty. Our meeting to compare notes was booked at one-thirty. I checked my watch; we had ten minutes to go.

I pulled my laptop out of my backpack and placed it on my desk, took off my jacket, and settled in to write up some notes before our meeting.

Judy, unfortunately, was back from lunch, or maybe she'd never left. Sometimes, she would stay in the office over her lunch break and use it as an excuse to go home early, even though she barely did any work while she was here. Now, she sat at her desk with her phone glued to her ear, whispering into it with a scowl on her face.

Unfortunately for me, with my enhanced hearing, I could hear every word she said. "... must be sleeping with almost everyone in this city. No, I don't think Lennox wants her. He's a tremendously smart guy, and he's too smart to be hoodwinked by big boobs and a pretty face. I think he must just be intrigued because the High Priest has hired her to do something—he keeps showing up to talk to her—so Lennox is pursuing her so he can find out what Zarayan is up to." Judy let out an exasperated sigh. "Honestly, Debbie, at this stage I'm ready to take a feline transformation potion and swap sides. Zarayan has bypassed all the high-ranking witches in the city and put his friend Levi in charge. Nobody knows what he's up to, and nobody is happy. We're looking at the fall of witchcraft as we know it, and I, for one, think Lennox Arran is a far better leader. At least he's not corrupt."

I sat at my desk, closed my eyes, and concentrated on my breath. In for five counts, out for five counts. In... out... in... out...

"Of course he is; she is, too. I'm sure she's sleeping with one of the higher-ups here at the DHS. How else could she get her certification so quickly?"

Darkness crept in around the edges of my vision. Oh, shit, I was getting dizzy.

"I bet that's why she was working from home a week ago. She was probably lying on her back with her legs in the air—"

Brain-Daphne took over my mouth before I could stop her. *"Judy!"*

She whipped around to face me.

I still had to work with this woman. Desperately, I wrestled myself back under control and met Judy's eye calmly. "Did you know I can hear every word you're saying?"

Judy wrinkled her nose and stared back at me, totally unrepentant. "You know what they say about eavesdropping, don't you, Daphne? First, it's rude. Second, you shouldn't do it, because you might not like what you hear." She turned away and put the phone back to her ear. "Anyway, Debbie, I don't think there's anything I can do about it. Yes, I've already made a complaint, but if that complaint is going straight to someone she's already sleeping with, then what's the point?

My fingers twitched towards my back. I clenched my fists. I felt my smile widen.

In my mind, Brain Daphne was collecting wood, piling it around a stake, and whistling a jaunty tune while she gathered up some ropes. *Time to burn this witch.*

I clenched my fists a little harder and concentrated on my breath. We can't kill her. She's just gossiping.

We can gossip, too. You know what? I heard Goody Proctor saw Judy Sagwood talking to the devil. In the vision in my mind, Brain-Daphne dumped another armful of wood on the fire. Then, she opened a bottle of kerosene, and, whistling a happy tune, sloshed it over the wood.

We can't.

Yeah, we can. What's gotten into you, anyway? You used to trust me. You don't trust yourself anymore, babes, and that's a big problem.

Judy sighed. "I should go, Debbie, I've got more clients to see this afternoon. I'm trying to squash as many in as I can since seeing clients on a Saturday makes me look really dedicated in my performance reviews. Ha, of course not, I'm taking Friday off next week. Okay, sweetheart. Bye." She hung up the phone and started tapping on her laptop. Slowly. Using only one index finger.

I needed to be the bigger person here. It wasn't like I didn't already know that Judy was talking shit about me. And it didn't matter what she said. Sticks and stones.

Just sticks, Brain Daphne corrected. *Stones don't burn. Wait... they did use big stones to crush witches back in the dark ages, didn't they? Okay, you're right. Sticks and stones. Let's use both.*

My natural optimism was struggling to reassert itself. Something was bothering me badly, but I couldn't figure out what it was.

That's because there's too many things bothering us, my brain chipped in helpfully. *Christopher Jupiter, Dwayne's troubling extended hangover, the countess's mysterious absence—*

She's fine. She's gone abroad.

You don't even know where abroad is. Then, there's Myf, of course, knocked out in your pantry. And the fact that for some reason, you've decided to become a doormat and let that bitch Judy walk all over us.

My brain was right, that wasn't like me. Sure, I liked to lead with kindness and compassion, but Judy had already more than tested those limits.

If you're asking me, I think it's more to do with the fact that the man we love appears to love someone else much more.

I blew a raspberry; that was ridiculous. "She's his sister," I breathed out, too irritated to keep my response internal.

Foster sister. They're not blood related, and they're bonded by trauma. It's almost as bad as being horny stepsiblings. Have you not watched porn, like, ever?

"I trust him."

Yeah, but do we trust her? I bet she's obsessed with magic because she's trying to find a way to get him to fall in love with her. Like, properly. I'm telling you, babes, she's bad news. I can feel it.

"We don't know her," I ground my teeth and muttered under my breath. "We don't even know what she looks like." Almost violently, I shoved an image of Indiana Jones—the modern, older one—in front of my brain.

But Brain-Daphne reached out, tore it up, and shoved an image of Lara Croft back at me.

I flinched. That awful, sickening, churning feeling squirmed in my chest again.

I'm telling you, babes. I'm your intuition. She's bad news. We should act quickly. Stabby, stab, stab, stab...

"I'm just jealous," I whispered to myself. I had no good reason to be. Romeo was here with me, not running off with his foster sister. The intensity of emotion I felt for him was bound to mess with my emotions.

Where was he, anyway? I reached out with my senses, desperate for the comfort his presence gave me.

It didn't take me long. The meeting room's lights were switched off. He was there, hiding in the shadows. I caught the scent of a handful of spells and activated charms—one for silence, probably so he could talk on the phone without anyone hearing him. Another for lingering darkness, so he could shadow-jump when he wanted to leave. A fuck-off charm to make anyone who wanted to go into the meeting room feel so uncomfortable they decided to hold the meeting in one of the cafes downstairs instead. Reluctantly, I tore my eyes away from the meeting room door and looked around.

Monica, back in her glass cage, had her Bluetooth headset on. She was talking to her direct manager about budgets while performing lunges behind her desk at the same time. I reached out with my senses and found that Cindy wasn't in the office. Last I'd seen her, she was fleeing out the window, trying to get away from Romeo.

James walked in, and I glanced up. Through the gap in the door, I could see Dwayne lying down on one of the bench seats, surrounded by children. All of them patted him and stroked his feathers gently.

Something is up with him, too. It's our intuition, babes. We gotta learn to trust ourselves.

On this one, I agreed with her. But how did I learn to trust myself again?

CHAPTER NINE

Judy left the office a few minutes later, and miraculously, my mood improved. That woman was like a vacuum cleaner that spat out dirt rather than sucked it up.

My consultation with James went smoothly, right until I asked him about Leif Montezuma. When I mentioned that his mother had fallen victim to what seemed like a brand-new dryad religion, he flinched. I prodded gently. "Do you know something about that?"

"Yeah." He paused for a moment. "Let's just say I can relate to what Leif is going through." Good grief, his voice was so deep. He met my eyes. "You can keep this between us, right?"

"Of course." I gave him a gentle smile. "You never need to ask me to keep your secrets, James. Your business is your business."

"Some people can be really judgmental—"

"She's not here, and you can say her name. Judy." I grinned. "Judy can be really judgmental."

He exhaled. "Yeah, she can. I've been here five years, and I learned really quickly that it's best to keep my mouth shut and my head down. I'm here for the kids and for nobody else."

I kept my expression neutral, even though I was burning with fury on the inside. "Someone really needs to do something about that woman," I murmured.

James shot a look towards Monica in her glass cage. "Believe me, I've tried. I don't know how she does it, but any time I've tried to raise an issue, Judy comes out of it lily-white and innocent, and I look like a whining brat."

I gnawed on my lip. "It's gotta be a spell or something. Judy does almost no work at all. I don't understand why Monica hasn't gotten rid of her yet."

"Whatever it is, I haven't managed to figure it out." He exhaled a low, weary sigh. "And to be fair, I don't mind doing her work for her. I'm a workaholic, and she's only going to mess up all our cases anyway. I just wish we didn't have to put up with her badmouthing anyone that's not an upper-middle-class witch." The corner of his eye twitched. "Or the new Alpha Shifter. Her bigotry doesn't seem to touch handsome, charming men like him. Did you know he's put up a statue of himself in front of the shifter compound? A huge bronze statue. It's not even on his private property. He's put it in The Woodlands by the community garden so all the normies can admire him."

I didn't want to talk about Lennox Arran. "Can you tell me more about this crazy new religion that Perrina Montezuma is involved in?"

"It's not a new religion," he said. "It's just a revival. It happens any time there's a vibrational shift in the mortal realm."

I swallowed roughly; a lump had sprung up out of nowhere. "Can you elaborate on that?"

"Judy assumed I was an Orbiter. It's mostly true—my mom was an Orbiter, but my dad was a dryad. I don't have any magic at all. I've got a green thumb, and that's about it. But dryads are more sensitive to vibrational shifts, so we notice them more. Especially if it turns out to be an energy surge that matches our magic."

Ice crawled up my spine. "What do you mean by that?"

James let out a rumbling sigh. "My mom left my dad when I was two—over twenty-seven years ago. He'd suddenly become gripped with this crazy new religious fervor that all his friends were caught up in. He thought we should burn ourselves as a sacrifice. Like, burn our bodies to pay homage to our dryad ancestors."

I blinked. "I'm not following that logic. Not at all."

"It's not logical. It's not supposed to be. To be frank, there's not much about Greek mythology that's logical. Absolutely batshit crazy things happened all the time."

The darkness writhed within me. I clenched my fists. Not now.

James didn't notice. "Mom, of course, took me and ran. But not before I sustained some serious burns. I talked to my paternal grandma about it when I was older, she told me these things seem to go in cycles. I did some research, and it appears that we go a little nuts whenever the mortal realm swings closer to any of the Hellenic realms."

Oh, no. No, no, no.

Christopher Jupiter was hunting a Stella Ostium. I'd been worrying about what he'd do to make it work—what blood sacrifices he'd make. How many innocent people he'd torture to death to get the power.

If what James was telling me was true, then it was about to get much, much easier.

My chest suddenly felt tight; I couldn't breathe deep enough. *Warning, girlfriend, we need to evacuate now.*

The door slammed in. Dwayne had kicked it open. He waddled in, sniffed, and wiped his nose with his wing. **It's okay.** He took a deep, quivering breath. **I'm here for your emotional support.**

I opened my mouth and closed it again. What the hell was wrong with him?

Before I could ask him, the air around me rumbled. The shadows in the meeting room surged, splitting open. Romeo walked out, massive shoulders tensed, his expression thunderous, and his eyes focused only on me.

"We have to go." His voice was ice cold. "Christopher Jupiter is in London *now*."

CHAPTER TEN

After I sent Dwayne back home to tend to Myf, we rode back to Romeo's place—the old church near the river, a massive spooky gothic building.

"The guys will meet us at home," Romeo said, his voice gruff in my earbud.

We zoomed through traffic like it was standing still, the combination of speed and Romeo's voice in my ear soothed my ragged nerves almost instantly. The wonders of mortal realm technology meant that we could race and keep up a conversation at the same time. It still felt like magic to me. The *erlyn* beasts I'd ridden in Svartalfheim didn't have comms systems.

Unfortunately, Romeo's mood hadn't improved at all. He roared behind me like a dark thundercloud. "I didn't want to rush you. But—"

"No, I get it." I dropped a gear, leaned down, and took a corner so fast my knee brushed against the blacktop, stinging for a fraction of a second. "You need to know what's going on, and I need to be able to tell you as soon as possible. None of this is fair on you."

"That's not it." His Ninja roared behind me, catching up. The acceleration in that thing was insane. "You can't tell me what Christopher is after, because it causes you pain. If I had my way, I'd make sure you never had to tell me." His voice dropped an octave, rumbling through me. "I never want to cause you pain, Daphne. I hate that we have to do this before you're ready."

"You're not causing me pain. *He* is." I ground my jaw, seeing the traffic slow to a crawl up ahead. The inbound city lane was practically empty, though. I put on a burst of speed, turned, and slid into the left lane, heading directly into the oncoming traffic. "This is Christopher Jupiter's fault and nobody else's."

Romeo growled in my ear. "Daphne—"

"I can't have you feeling bad about this, Romeo. You just have to accept that this is going to be incredibly painful." A huge semi braked last-minute, throwing off my timing; a premonition hit me at the exact same moment. I overcorrected, brushed past a big Yukon too close, and wobbled for a split second "Whoops."

"Daphne!"

"I'm fine." Racing into oncoming traffic was always easier if they didn't see you coming. Twitchy drivers caused crashes, so I'd just have to go faster. I dropped a gear, picked up speed, and voiced my premonition out loud. "I was just going to say that I have a feeling that this is going to be incredibly painful for both of us."

"Daphne..."

It made me feel sick. The idea of Romeo being hurt literally made me nauseous. I hoped I was wrong.

You're not wrong. You need to trust yourself more, my brain muttered. *Before we got lost off-world, we trusted our instincts all the time. Now, we second-guess ourselves and argue with each other.*

I rolled my eyes, speeding through a tiny gap between two yellow school buses, and kept my response internal. Can you blame me? It's not easy to trust myself. Especially when I'm so obviously batshit crazy. Case in point, I'm in the habit of talking to an impulsive, bloodthirsty version of myself.

My brain kicked me. *You are me, and I am you. We're not two entities sharing a body, you fool. We started doing this because we were lonely, remember? We had nobody else to talk to for a whole decade. And we separated Heart and Brain because we sometimes had to do things that were horrible. We broke in two to survive. I make the hard choices. I keep us alive. You keep the heart soft so we remember how to love and forgive. You're only dominant because that's always been the dominant side of our personality. We're soft and kind with twenty-percent stabby and five percent kill.*

I sighed. She was right.

We. We're the same person, you numbskull.

Okay, we were right. I'd split myself in two so I could survive and not go completely insane while I was lost in the magical wilderness, trying desperately to just keep living another day. But now, it was becoming a little obvious I'd started to think of her as separate and untrustworthy.

A chill ran up my spine. Suddenly, I realized that if I

didn't figure out how to integrate the primal, survival part of me, then my mental health would only spiral.

I know what we need to do. I'm only going to say this one more time, babes. We need to learn to trust each other again.

Look at you, talking about trust. You're so suspicious of everyone.

Not everyone. And have I ever been wrong?

I frowned. Touché.

"Daphne!"

"Oh! Sorry." I was sure Romeo hadn't been talking while I was busy dissociating. "Did you say something?" Cars and trucks barreled towards me. I zig-zagged, missing them all by inches. I was going so fast they looked like streams of light in a warp-speed tunnel. None of them saw me coming.

Most of them didn't see me at all. I probably sounded like a tiny mosquito buzzing past. "We were talking about Christopher Jupiter, weren't we?" Our exit was up ahead. I hit the brakes, skidded out, revved, spun in a half-circle, and shot off towards Fitler Square, turning immediately down a quiet street.

The traffic evaporated immediately. I heard Romeo growl in my ear. "We *were* talking about Christopher Jupiter. But you decided to break every single metropolitan traffic law *and* the laws of physics, and give me a heart attack, so I stopped focusing on the conversation."

"Oh." My cheeks warmed. I slowed down even more —mostly because the church was just up ahead. I turned off the street and onto the driveway that led to the gates. "Sorry."

He followed, his motorcycle rumbling like a thundercloud behind me. I pulled up to the gates. Romeo stopped right beside me, leaned over, and hit my kill switch, turning my bike off.

"Hey!"

"I would have done that earlier, if I had been able to catch you," he growled, flicking my kickstand down and pulling me off my bike in one smooth, powerful movement.

He manhandled me like I weighed nothing. I felt a possessive need surge from him, almost a volcanic fury, as he pulled me into his lap, facing him, holding me to his chest. His muscles were rock-hard, unyielding; his arms wrapped around me and held me in place with phenomenal strength and power. There was no resisting him at all. I didn't even try.

I was glad he was still wearing his helmet. I didn't want to see his expression right now.

He leaned down and tapped his helmet against mine. "Are you trying to kill me?"

"No." *We do, or we don't. There is no try.* "Oh, you mean the traffic. Yeah, it was probably a little risky. If you were worried about following me up Spruce, you could have gone the right way on Pine." I shrugged. "To be honest, I probably didn't buy any extra seconds; I was weaving too much, and—"

"That's not what I meant," he said darkly. "Do you understand how it feels to watch someone you love do something dangerous like that?"

My core burst into flames. "It, uh." I licked my lips. "It wasn't dangerous."

"You kissed the side of that Yukon. Doing ninety, the wrong way down the street."

"It was just a little wobble. Did you see me recover?"

He exhaled, long and slow. "You ride like you want to die, Daphne." His voice got impossibly lower. "Do you want to die?"

"No. Of course not." Not today, anyway. And not right now. Even though Romeo was mad at me, I don't think I'd ever felt safer, more loved, more cherished in my entire life.

He wasn't done telling me off, though. "The last race you won in Ueno, five years back..." His arms tightened around me. "You were the only finisher. Twelve riders crashed out. Five of them died."

I frowned. How the hell did he find out about that? It was a closed-circuit street race—no recordings, invitation-only audience, multi-million-dollar betting pool. The Yakuza set it up so that other international mobsters could gather together, rub shoulders, drink vintage champagne, eat caviar, and pit the best riders they could find against each other, knowing full well that most of us would die. It was the kind of thing the richest madmen loved to do in all the realms I'd been in, and at the time, I didn't even know I was in Japan.

That race ended up being a bloodbath. "I'm not responsible for other people's bad driving, Romeo."

Well, that wasn't strictly true. I pushed myself to the limit that day, and they tried to keep up. I would feel worse if those riders were nice people, but the men in that race were absolute monsters. One of them tried to corner me and rape me before the race even started. That guy didn't even make it to the start line.

"Five of them *died*," Romeo growled.

"Well, I think you'll find that one of them actually had an aneurysm, so it doesn't count."

Romeo paused for a second and exhaled roughly. "I get it; you love to go fast." His arms tightened around me again. "It's so hard to watch. I've never been more invested in keeping someone alive before in my entire life, and for some unfathomable reason, I've chosen to fall in love with a woman who enjoys dancing on the edge of total destruction on the regular. Please, Daphne. Do me this favor. Stop riding like a maniac."

I hesitated. "Can I just promise not to do it when you're watching?"

For a second, it felt like Romeo had stopped breathing. He let out a gruff noise. "Why is this so hard?"

I smiled, even though he couldn't see it. I still had my helmet on, too. "It's called growth. This is a good lesson for both of us. You can't control everything."

And we need to learn to let ourselves be loved.

The gate buzzed and swung open. Levi's voice echoed out of the intercom. "Are you coming in, Boss?"

We had an audience. Awkwardly, I clambered off Romeo's lap and got back on my own bike, so we could ride into the church grounds.

CHAPTER
ELEVEN

It didn't occur to me that Romeo's covenmates would be unhappy to see me. It was an unexpected —and unwelcome—surprise. We sat in the living room just inside the front doors of the church in the huge, open-plan space that used to be the nave of the church, while we exchanged information.

I sat on a love seat next to Romeo. Despite the gothic horror aesthetic of the church, it was unexpectedly warm and weirdly very cozy inside. My motorcycle leathers had gotten too hot, too quickly. Romeo noticed my red face—which clashed wildly with my lavender hair—and loaned me one of his button-downs. It came down to mid-thigh on me, like a shirtdress. I looked stupid, but I was comfortable, and that was all that mattered.

Across from me, perched on a sofa, Levi sat with his back ramrod straight, giving Romeo a quick debrief of a few coven dramas, disputes, and updates on the Delaware situation. He wore chic midnight-blue suit pants and a crisp white shirt with a navy tie, his icy-white hair scraped back into a half topknot. He didn't look like a witch at all. He looked like a sexy Lord of the Rings elf who had gotten a corporate job in mergers and acquisitions.

My ears pricked up when he mentioned Delaware, which was looking better by the day.

Maybe Chloe and Prue will be out of Delaware before we know it. We can go visit.

Then, Levi shared some bad news. A few twangs of dark energy had been detected through the main ley lines today—the telltale sign of someone performing blood magic spells—and he'd been unable to trace the source. Despite talking directly to Romeo, every now and then, Levi's eyes would flick towards me and narrow.

He's pissed at us.

Brandon glared at me while he gave us a quick debrief on what he'd learned about the People of the Claw. I could understand his antipathy. He was a dragon shifter in hiding, too.

Cole was even worse. Romeo had delegated the Jupiter business interests to him—at least a dozen multi-million-dollar companies. He glared at me the whole time, while telling Romeo bluntly that he had no idea what he was doing, he was probably ruining everything, and he might as well head downtown and set all the buildings on fire.

Micah was pissed, too, but not necessarily at me. As a former human assassin and espionage agent—now a pale, dark-haired vampire who had been sent to assassinate Romeo years ago—he was responsible for coordinating the P.I. team who had been shadowing Christopher

Jupiter. Micah's dark eyes flashed red as he explained how his P.I. had lost him. "A few hours ago, Jupiter walked straight to the counter at Athens airport and bought a ticket to Madrid. He went into the bathrooms right outside customs, but he never came out again." Micah glared at the floor for a second. "The flight left, and he wasn't on it. My P.I. managed to get a look at the computers at the check-in desk and found out Christopher Jupiter left Athens on a flight to Gatwick yesterday morning. He's been in London this whole time. I figure the guy they were tailing was one of his goons wearing a glamor. Jupiter knew he was being followed. He outsmarted us."

The atoms in the air trembled for a split-second. Romeo's hands clenched into fists—an involuntary gesture of rage. "Upgrade the order."

"We've gone through this before, Rome." Micah sighed. "We can't. Not on foreign soil. If we execute Christopher Jupiter without a trial, the Russian covens will come after us. Christopher's wife is the sister of Volkhv Orlov, and he's the High Priest of almost an entire continent. That man will tear this whole country in two to avenge his brother-in-law. It would mean war."

"I don't care."

"You're facing enough diplomatic crises here at home, boss. There's no need to go nuclear yet. We just have to bring Christopher here, and then we can take him out."

"He's coming here anyway," I said softly.

Romeo turned to gaze at me, the storm in his eyes slowly settling.

"He's coming for you." Micah looked at me, too. "There's something you have that he wants."

I nodded. It didn't help my mental state that the guys were so obviously pissed at me. My anxiety got the better of me—I hated when people were mad at me. The urge to clear the air was overwhelming.

"Look... I'm sorry about all this." I met Brandon's eyes. "I'm sorry that the drama with Myf is bringing up unpleasant memories."

"That's a bit of an understatement." Brandon raised an eyebrow. "I'm trying not to explode into a firebomb and kill everyone I love, Daphne."

Drama queen, Brain-Daphne snorted. *Myf has had one week of deprogramming and her breath isn't even slightly spicy.* She kicked me. *Say it!*

No, I needed to be nice about this. "I get it, and I'm sorry."

Brandon didn't reply.

I turned to Micah. "I'm sorry you have to deal with Christopher Jupiter. Whatever he's up to, it's ultimately my fault."

Tell him to quit whining and get better at espionage! Losing Jupiter was a serious fuckup. Tell him!

Romeo gave a rumble. "Daphne, you don't have to apologize to anyone—"

"It's okay." I gave him a soft smile. "I'm just trying to clear the air." I moved on to Levi. "I know this is tough on you, too. The High Priest and dark magic and whatnot. It's a tough job, and it's my fault you've been thrown headfirst into it."

Levi glanced at me, then at Romeo, and wisely decided to keep his mouth shut.

"And Cole—" I began. "Uh... sorry?"

Cole buried his face in his hands. "I'm not cut out for the corporate world, Daphne," he mumbled. "My last job was flipping burgers."

"I know I've come into your lives and suddenly everything is messed up and a lot harder." I shrugged. "It appears to be a pattern for me. I don't know why."

"Daphne, no." Romeo shook his head, bewildered. "None of this is your fault."

"It is." It always was. My whole life, things had exploded around me. I came into your life; your life exploded. That was just how things went. Now, the whole world might get destroyed because of me. They'd find that out soon enough, best fall on my sword now and get them used to the idea.

My brain groaned. *Christ on a bike, can you hear yourself? We just had a big pep-talk about trusting ourselves. Did you not take any of it in at all?*

Brandon spoke first, breaking the uncomfortable silence. "It's not that. We're not mad at you. We're mostly annoyed because our whole job used to be protecting this guy." He pointed his thumb towards Romeo. "Now suddenly he doesn't need us to because he's got you."

"And he missed game night last night," Levi added.

"Not me." Cole shrugged. "I'm mad at you. I'm mad because you let that asshole Lennox Arran steal your kill."

Romeo glared at him. "Cole..."

I put my hand on his arm. "It's fine." I took a deep breath. Time was running out. By now, Christopher Jupiter would be sliming his way into the drawing room of the aristocracy, looking for the Stella Ostium. "Look, let's just cut to the chase. We need your help, and things are becoming urgent." I turned to Micah. "I know Romeo asked if you could use your vamp hypnosis powers to put me under and bypass my conscious state."

Romeo reached out and took my hand. "Are you sure?"

"Yeah." I nodded. "Christopher Jupiter is on the hunt for something that could destroy this whole world, and I need to tell you what it is so we can figure out how to stop him. We need to do this now. I need—"

A delicious scent of mozzarella, fresh tomato sauce, basil and stone baked bread hit me out of nowhere, and the words dried in my throat.

I almost swooned. A millisecond later, the front door cracked open. "Hey, guys!"

A woman poked her head through the door. She was astonishingly beautiful—thick, honey blonde hair pulled back into a ponytail, a heart-shaped face with high cheekbones and a pointed chin, bright blue eyes, and a small soft pink mouth with a pronounced cupid's bow on her upper lip. A few white scars—one through her left eyebrow, another couple close to her chin—enhanced her delicate doll-like features, rather than detracting from them.

Oh no. Please don't tell me that this is—

I gaped at her when the rest of her body came into view. She was tall, probably six inches taller than me, and wore what at first glance looked like casual athletic gear—cherry red tights, a matching bra top, shiny black trainers, and a black cropped bomber jacket.

My stomach churned.

It's her. Bella, the evil foster sister.

Bella carried herself with the grace of a ballerina—long, strong limbs, perfect posture, her head tilted up. She held six pizza boxes in one hand and a six-pack of beer in the other and maneuvered around the heavy oak door with an elegance and confidence that took my breath away.

She reeked of magic. A dozen varieties—pixie, troll, fae, goblin, squonk, I couldn't even pick them all out — wrapped in various containers of brass, gold, leather, shark tooth, and the slimy jellyfish thing that grows in kombucha. Her pockets must be stuffed to the brim with magical amulets and charms. Her skin even smelled like she'd been rubbing up against a witch at some point recently—there was the faintest trace of herbs and candlewax there.

All four of Romeo's covenmates whipped around. "Bella!" They howled.

She hefted the boxes on one hand, holding them high, like a trophy. "I brought pizza!"

The boys cheered and leapt to their feet. Brandon got to her first, took the beer out of her hands and pulled her into a hug. "It's so good to see you, Bell."

"You too, Bran." She pulled back and looked at him warmly, cupping his cheek with his hand.

He ran his thumb over the scar on her chin. "Is that a new one?"

"Yeah." Her cheeks grew pink; it only made her prettier. "I got it spelunking into an underground paleolithic temple in Peru. The Incan artifacts were worth it, though. I got a lovely little bone carving with the trapped spirit of a saber tooth inside."

Brandon nodded. "Nice."

Fucking tomb raider, my brain hissed. *She's literally breaking international law, stealing shit like that. How is she getting away with it? Why don't these guys care?*

I hushed my brain gently. There was no proof Bella was stealing anything. For all I knew, she was contracted by the Peruvian government to find the artifacts and return them to the tribes they belonged to.

Where is she getting all her money from, then, huh? Onlyfans?

I shushed her harder.

Micah swooped in and kissed her on both cheeks, taking the pizza boxes from her. Cole hugged her, too, rubbing up against her in a distinctly affectionate cat-like way.

That's probably where she's getting the trace of witch scent on her skin from, my brain grumbled. *She probably dry-humped one earlier. They all love her. This is bad news. She's bad news.*

Romeo got up, too. My stomach twisted so hard it almost hurt. To give him credit, he pulled me up with him, not letting go of my hand. He led me over to the stunning woman, hugging her with his free arm.

She threw both arms around him, closed her eyes, and squeezed, while I stood awkwardly beside them. "Dear brother," she murmured.

"Bell." He kissed her cheek. "I'm glad you're here."

Evil bitch. Evil, sexy, evil, evil...

I clenched my teeth together so hard, my jaw cracked. She's his *sister*.

She's wrapped around him like spandex. Look at the adoration on her face! And he obviously loves her, too.

She's his sister.

I couldn't stop the feeling. The jealousy burned. It hurt worse than physical torture, and I had the furious impulse to tear off my own skin and scrub my bones to try and get rid of the sensation. Gods, it hurt.

We have to do something.

Frantically, I tried to think through the whirl of agony. I'd never felt like this in my entire life. How the hell did I manage it?

Stab her!

I could barely move; I felt frozen, confused, almost paralyzed. While I watched Romeo and Bella embrace, I tried to remember if this is how I felt when I met Holly LeBeaux for the first time. I must have. I'd been in love with Troy, and I'd been introduced to his beautiful, brilliant fiancé.

No, I hadn't felt this way, because Holly and Troy didn't love each other.

My fingers twitched, my hands desperate to palm my blades. My brain was blowing things out of proportion, but if he hadn't told me about Bella already, I probably would be having a total meltdown right now. Brain-Daphne was right—they clearly adored each other. The squirming in my gut—hot, twisting, churning—it was so painful I almost doubled over.

Finally, after what felt like a million years, Romeo pulled back. Bella opened her eyes, cupped his face, stared at him, and smiled. "You're looking thinner, Rome. Have you been eating properly?"

"You worry too much." His eyes were soft. Finally, he tugged on my hand. "Bella, meet Daphne."

Bella turned and fixed me with a warm, happy smile. "Daphne. It's so good to meet you." She opened her arms and pulled me into a tight hug. "Romeo's told me so much about you."

I desperately tried to relax, but my body refused to obey me. Stiffly, like a robot, I hugged her back. "Nice to meet you," I managed.

The darkness inside me lurched up.

Stab her!

I clenched my teeth and forced myself to stay calm. Why was I panicking? This was stupid. She was his sister. Bella had looked after Romeo when they were frightened little kids. They were trauma bonded. I couldn't be jealous of their love for each other. I should be happy. He was lucky to have her.

That's not it. She's got darkness inside of her. Trust me, I can feel it!

My jaw clenched harder. Yeah, she's got darkness inside. The same as he does. Trauma, remember?

"Come sit by me, Bell," Levi patted the seat beside him.

She walked over and settled herself on the sofa right opposite me, in between Levi and Brandon, with an easy, happy confidence that made me shiver.

Her eyes were focused on me, though. "I wish we had

time to get to know each other properly. But I understand that the clock is ticking, and we've got work to do. Hopefully, once this is all over, we can have some girl time."

I nodded. "Sure." I forced myself to smile back at her. "I'd love that."

Mentally, I wrestled my brain back under control. Stop it right now. We're not doing this. This is Romeo's sister. Yes, she's stunningly beautiful, ridiculously graceful and confident, and Romeo clearly adores her. The guys all love her. But she's here to help us.

She's a bad person.

She's an orphan, like him. Like us! We should feel sorry for her!

That was it; that's how I would cope. I needed to shut my brain up and focus on Bella instead. Mentally, I took hold of the sickening, burning feeling inside of me, and stuffed it down. Bella had a terrible childhood, just like I did. I should feel empathy for her, not this vicious, furious jealousy.

Empathy. Kindness, softness, gentleness.

I'm telling you, she's evil.

I ground my teeth. Empathy.

My brain hissed, bared her fangs, and snarled at me. *You'll be sorry.* Finally, she retreated, and the violent surge of emotion settled down a little.

CHAPTER
TWELVE

"You were right." Bella nodded at Romeo. "Christopher Jupiter is after a Stella Ostium."

The boys spread the pizza boxes out on the table, Brandon distributed the beer. I'd finally gotten myself under control, but I didn't trust myself to speak right now, so I stayed silent.

Bella patted Micah's knee. "From what you told me about his movements in Greece, and who he's been speaking to, it makes sense. I've met some of those old Priests before. I'm guessing he intends to use it to summon a deity."

I flinched.

Her eyes shot over to me, and she hesitated, her expression filled with worry. "I'm sorry, Daphne. Romeo told me that this is painful for you to talk about—"

"It's not painful." I forced my jaw to unclench. "It's... dangerous."

"I get that. I'm not going to pretend I understand, but I get it." Bella hesitated. "We need to find this Stella

Ostium before Christopher Jupiter does. I've heard stories from people who've handled them, and I know the damage they can do if they're used to call forth something powerful. It would be easier for me to track it down if I knew what it looked like," Bella went on, unslinging a small laptop bag from her shoulder. "I have a database where I track every single mention of any large, rare, unusual gems throughout history, because most of the time they turn out to be very powerful magical artifacts. For example, the Guinness Emerald is actually the trapped spirit of a dark elf queen. And I know for a fact that if you tap on the Chaiyo Ruby, your blood will turn to liquid gold. Not that any of this matters," she added dryly, pulling out her laptop. "Since both of those stones are worth about five-hundred-million dollars and are locked in the world's most secure safes."

Brandon chuckled. "You couldn't crack them, could you?"

She grinned at him. "I'm not suicidal. And those stones hold no interest for me, anyway. But we definitely need to find this Stella Ostium before Christopher Jupiter does." She turned to Micah. "Where is he in London?"

"We don't know. We lost him." The vampire's eyes flashed red. "My guys are trying to find him. He's had almost two whole days there."

"Well"—Bella took a deep breath—"if we've got no better ideas, I can jump on the jet and head to London now and try to find him. He's obviously on the trail."

Beside me, Romeo grew tense. I could feel his frustration boiling within him. He wanted to go there now, to go there and twist Christopher's head off himself.

Bella gnawed on her lip. "I'm sorry I'm not more help. If I knew the color or the shape of the stone, it would be easier to search for it."

I knew, but I was too scared to explain. And all Romeo knew was that he had to stay with me and guard me. Another new, awful feeling writhed in my belly. I felt useless. A burden.

It didn't have to be this way.

No, my brain whispered. *Not now. And not in front of her. I'm telling you; something isn't right.*

I stomped on her almost violently. It had to be now. I couldn't just sit here uselessly while everyone risked their lives for me.

I swallowed and turned to Romeo. "We have to try the thing you said."

He stared at me for a long moment. "Are you sure?"

I nodded. "It's the only way."

CHAPTER
THIRTEEN

We retreated to the back of the church—formerly the apse, the place where the altar would have been. The dark stone columns and enormous stained-glass windows were still there, but Romeo had cleared out the pews to turn the space into a fight gym, complete with a raised boxing ring, weight racks, and a large sparring mat.

Bella helped the boys get the space ready, as they chatted happily and teased each other. Cole tackled her onto the sparring mat, wrestling with her. She let out a Tarzan howl and effortlessly wrapped him up into a choke hold.

Good grief, the woman could fight, too. Their effortless camaraderie almost made me want to vomit. "So... They're all good buddies, huh?"

Romeo leaned against the wall beside me. "Oh, yeah. The guys all love her. Bella has been there for all of us at some point in the last eight years. And we've had a rough eight years." He gestured towards Brandon, who was running towards the wrestling couple. "When Brandon was sent to assassinate me, Bella had dropped in for a visit. She literally walked in on us fighting. She got in on the action and threw some heavy-duty combat charms to slow Brandon down. Eventually, I knocked him out. Honestly, I couldn't have done it without her. I was all alone back then."

"How old were you?"

"Twenty, and I'd only just claimed the heirdom." He frowned. "After the assassination attempt, I was okay, but Brandon kept flatlining. Bella looked after both of us. Eventually, we recovered, and I brewed him the potion to inhibit the change so he'd stop trying to kill me."

"You beat him up that badly, huh?"

"A brainwashed dragon tried to assassinate me, Daphne. I did some serious damage trying to stop him. I didn't want him to die. It wasn't his fault he'd tried to attack me." Romeo's eyes drifted away from me, finding his sister again. "Anyway, while both of us were out, a couple of the People of the Claw showed up to try and take Brandon back. Bella killed them," he said simply. "She shot them both, point blank, to stop them. I don't think Brandon will ever forget it."

Cole let out a roar and tried to wriggle out from under Bella's full mount. He wasn't using his full strength at all.

"She saved Cole's life, too. He came to join me a year or so after Brandon. And before you ask, no, he didn't try to kill me." Romeo gave a little half-smile. "He was just seeking refuge."

I hadn't heard Cole's story yet. "How did she save his life?"

"Not long after I got him sorted with an illusion charm and inducted him into my coven as a witch, I sent him on an errand up to New York. While he was there, someone abducted him, and a rogue blood witch almost tortured him to death. Bella had actually been tracking the witch because he'd stolen a destiny stone. She found Cole, realized who he was, and brought him back to me. He almost died." Romeo frowned. "Technically, he *was* dead when she brought him to me. We managed to revive him, though."

Bella was a goddamned superhero. I tamped down the surge in my gut before Brain Daphne could get into her stride.

"So, the coven has always gotten on really well with your sister."

"Oh, no, she was really wary of Levi for a long time. His family in Alaska had a huge collection of very dark artifacts, so that's understandable. It took them a long time to trust each other. He won her over eventually."

"Has she ever dated any of them?" I asked hopefully.

"No."

Well, that was definite.

"Has she ever dated..." I swallowed the lump in my throat. God, this felt awful. "You?"

"No."

I relaxed a fraction.

"Well, we *did* kiss once," Romeo admitted. "It didn't feel right, though. I figured going any further would ruin everything, so we both agreed not to mess with our relationship. Neither of us know what it's like to have a sibling, so we were just trying to figure it out as we went." He glanced down and met my eye. "Don't look so worried, Daphne. She's my sister. I love her like a sister."

I smiled and nodded, even though he just said in the same breath he didn't know what a sibling relationship was like in the first place.

He waved his hand at the playfight taking place on the sparring mat. Cole finally flipped Bella on her back and wiggled around like a monkey. "She's doing this to try and distract you, you know. I told her you needed to be relaxed, so she's trying to shift the mood."

It wouldn't work. I was anything but relaxed. In fact, I don't think I'd ever felt worse in my whole life. I watched in silence as Brandon threw himself in the air and dived on the mat, slapping his palm three times like a referee. Finally, they got up and moved the sparring mat out of the way, exposing the original stone flooring. We were going to need a hard surface for the ward.

"You're not allowed in there with me," I muttered. "That's non-negotiable."

Nothing was coming out of me, I knew that for a fact. But I wasn't sure what *I* would be like if the evils ever got too strong. Dwayne had made me watch too many horror movies with him, which didn't help my imagination at all. I didn't want Romeo to see me puking pea and ham soup or masturbating with a crucifix. Not until the third date, at the very least.

The muscle in Romeo's jaw clenched. "I have to concede to that, only because there's no way around it. I need to hear what your subconscious has to tell me, so

I'm going to be right here." He pointed to the floor. "Micah and Levi will have to be inside the circle with you. Micah will put you under, put your body and your conscious mind to sleep, and try to pull your subconscious out. Levi will be maintaining your mood and monitoring your body to make sure it's safe from whatever..." He trailed off and swallowed roughly. "And Bella's going to make sure he's fully loaded with everything he needs in case things go wrong."

"A gun?" I asked hopefully.

"No, Daphne." Romeo's jaw clenched. "Not a gun."

Levi moved in with chalk and salt, making a large ring on the stone floor. He began to sketch runes on the outside of the ward lines. "We're doing a hard ward, right, boss?"

"Yeah. It needs to be soundproof. Remember, we won't be able to hear what is going on in there with you guys, so if anything goes wrong, hit the panic button on your phone, and wake her up."

I dropped my eyes. "This is crazy. I don't even know if it's going to work."

"It has to work." His arms came up to rest on my shoulders—a solid, comforting weight. "I need to know what's going on with you."

Bella walked towards us, meeting Romeo's eyes over my head. She was only a couple of inches shorter than him. They were so much better matched than he and I were. I watched them exchange a loaded glance out of the corner of my eye. My gut churned.

Why the hell was I acting like this?

I think I know.

Her gaze dropped down to me. Her expression was so full of warmth and concern, the venom I felt for her disappeared.

You're a fool.

She smiled. "Are you ready?"

"As ready as I'll ever be."

"I brought a vessel for your racetrack illusion." She took a silver necklace out of her pocket. A big, odd-looking sphere made up of a matt-black metal dangled on the chain. She held it out to Romeo, who took it.

"Thanks." He cupped it in his hands and whispered an incantation. Ultraviolet light streamed out between his fingers, as he poured magic into the charm. It smelled identical to the magic he used when he'd created the illusion in the burger joint earlier today.

Of course. Romeo couldn't come into the circle, so he was sending Levi in with a pre-packaged calming illusion. He must have already told Bella everything.

She pulled something else out of her pocket, a very old brown pouch. It looked like leather but smelled like an off-world creature skin. "And I brought an Eye of the Nephthys, just in case."

"Good idea," Romeo said.

She handed the pouch to Levi, who came to stand beside us. "If anything goes wrong, place the pebble between Daphne's eyes. Don't handle the pebble itself—tip it on her skin from the pouch." Bella turned to me. "The Eye of the Nephthys will hold you in total stasis," she explained carefully. "Don't worry, there will be no brain activity at all. No dreams, no movement, nothing."

I opened my mouth to tell her I knew what it was.

The Egyptian gods had their own realms; they'd been close to our own mortal world thousands and thousands of years ago. Many years ago, I'd fallen into a realm ruled by the Jackals and used an Eye of Nephthys to escape.

I didn't say any of this, instead, I just nodded.

"It's not dangerous," she said hastily. "I know it sounds like it, but it will just put you to sleep..." Bella's eyebrows pinched together. She glanced at Romeo and back at me. "Sorry, I didn't mean to overstep. Rome just said that we didn't know anything, so it's best to cover all our bases—"

"It's okay." I held up my hand and forced myself to smile at her.

Evil...

I stomped Brain-Daphne down.

Levi opened the pouch and looked inside. A soft blue glow rose out. "Wow," he sighed. "Where did you get this, Bell?"

"I found a temple near the Siwa Oasis a couple of months ago. Don't tell anyone. My nemesis, Professor Ulrich Lichtenstein—he's got his whole post-grad class out there right now, digging in the sand, three miles in the wrong direction."

Tomb raider, my rosy, red ass. She's a fucking grave robber. That Eye belongs to the Siwi people. Or the Shahibat Bedouin. That bitch is stealing precious artifacts from the indigenous—

I clenched my fists. Brain-Daphne grew quiet.

"Nice." Levi nodded appreciatively. "Having this on-hand makes me feel better."

They're scared of me, I realized. They're not mad.

They're scared. And Bella was here, Little Miss Tomb Raider, with all the tools to help out. A new emotion I couldn't identify reared up within me, making my hands suddenly shake.

Bella cleared her throat, looking uncomfortable. "I'm going to head on out and give you guys some privacy."

"You don't have to leave," Romeo told her.

She smiled at him. "It's best if I do."

Guilt and shame pulsed through me. Bella could obviously feel my animosity. She was his sister, and all she'd done so far was help me. I forced myself to smile at her. "It's okay. You can stay and watch the show."

Her confident grin wobbled, and a light of concern flared in her eyes.

Goddamnit, that wasn't the right thing to say. Bella had taken it wrong. She thought I meant that this would be dangerous. As far as she knew, I was about to turn into a raging monster and try to kill everyone in this church.

"On second thought, it's probably best if you do go, Bell," Romeo muttered, his brow furrowed. He'd obviously come to the same conclusion, and he wanted to make sure his foster sister was safe. I wanted to cover my face and howl like a dog.

Why was I so confused? What the hell was wrong with me?

It's not you.

Bella fixed her easy smile back on her face and patted my shoulder gently. "It's okay. It sounds like all of you have to concentrate, and I'll just be in the way. I'll hang in my car for an hour; I've got a ton of calls to make, anyway. Good luck." She punched Romeo lightly on the arm and threw me a quick wink, before turning back to face him. "Don't fuck it up, okay? I like her." Her smile grew soft. "Try and keep this one alive."

My stomach lurched. Now, what the hell did *that* mean? Bella was so damned nice, but her words made me want to scrub my whole body with sandpaper.

"I'll come with you," Cole said, wrapping his arm around her waist.

"Me, too." Brandon loped over. "I'm not needed either, so we can keep you company."

Neither of them said goodbye to me. Or good luck. They walked out without looking back. As soon as they were out of sight, though, Romeo pulled me back into his chest and wrapped his arms around me, and I instantly felt better. "I'm going to be right here in a light trance so I'll be able to sense your spirit better. Once Micah pulls you out of your body, it's going to feel weird. You'll keep trying to snap back. Try and relax."

"Don't worry; I know about weird. I fell through countless interdimensional wormholes, remember?"

We watched for a moment as Levi made the final adjustments to the warded circle, and Micah walked in to join him.

"We're good to go," Levi called out to Romeo.

Romeo bent down and kissed my lips softly, and in that moment, all my doubt vanished completely. Pulling away, he locked eyes with me. "It's going to be okay."

"I know." I turned and walked towards the circle.

CHAPTER
FOURTEEN

I sat down, cross-legged, on the cold stone floor. The air zinged around me, packed with subtle but unmistakable power.

Decades ago, the church altar had been located right here. Before that, hundreds of years prior, there would have been a sacred stone placed on this very spot. This was a ley line intersection, a point of power. The Lenape people worshipped their gods right here for thousands of years, and the white colonizers stole it from them for the same reason. It was the closest we could get to a direct line to our creators.

The circle—three concentric rings—stretched out around me. The first, a thick line of salt. After that, a plain white chalk ring. Outside of that, Levi had marked the ground with protective runes.

Nobody was taking any chances.

Levi and Micah both busied themselves, activating personal protection charms and getting settled. If I turned my head, I could see the huge rose-shaped stained-glass window behind me. Above, the gothic church soared into a point.

Breathe in, breathe out. Breathe in....

I wish you would trust me, Brain-Daphne muttered.

I wish I *could* trust you.

I've given you no reason to not trust me.

Bitch, you wanted to use my Orion blades to flay Romeo so we could wear his skin like a suit.

You know I was joking. She shrugged. *I'm just passionate, that's all. You need to trust me. Trust me, or lose me.*

Levi held out his palm, outstretched, and whispered a spell. The illusion inside the metal charm came to life. It poured out, changing the scene completely.

Suddenly, the church disappeared. I was sitting on a camp chair on the side of a practice track just outside of Tokyo. My old Suzuki Hayabusa was parked beside me. Motorcycles zipped around the track, buzzing at high speeds, so fast. The smell of motor oil and exhaust fumes drifted around me. Another scent cut through. I looked to the right and saw a food truck selling American-style hot dogs. My mouth watered.

I smiled. All I needed to perfect the scene was Romeo. To get to him, I had to let Micah put both my body and conscious mind to sleep and send my spirit twenty feet outside of this circle to talk to him.

Piece of cake.

The boys sat on camp chairs on either side of me. Micah cleared his throat. "Okay, Daphne. I need you to look at me."

I turned and looked directly into his eyes. A flare of red sparked in his pitch-black iris, and a waft of his sand-and-coppery vampire magic enveloped me completely.

"You're feeling good," he said softly. His voice echoed around me—dramatic and melodic and ambient all at the same time, like one of those old late-eighties chocolate commercials with a pretty woman sneaking a bite of candy underneath a waterfall. "You're feeling relaxed. Your whole body is letting go."

More of the lingering tension in my body eased.

Micah smiled. "Good. You can go ahead and close your eyes."

I did as he told me.

"Right now, your vision is the red brown of your eyelids. And now, it's a soft white. A soft, floaty, cloudy white. There are clouds all around you. Your footsteps are light, like you're walking on the moon."

Yeah, it was. Floaty, like a cloud. Ooh, I felt good. Every step was feather-light, like I was almost weightless.

"Listen to my voice. Every single muscle in your body is loosening," he continued. "Your shoulders are dropping, the tightness in your chest is easing. Anything that is holding on is letting go. Let *goooooo*."

An odd noise cut through the dreamy echo of Micah's voice. What was that? It sounded like a balloon slowly deflating.

It was gone now, and the relaxed, floaty feeling remained. Someone beside me sniggered. Levi?

"Was that me?" Understanding dawned. "Did I... Did I just fart?"

There was a beat of silence.

"You're feeling *so* relaxed." Micah said again. His voice echoed all around me. "*Relaxedrelaxedrelaxed...*"

Yeah, I was. So relaxed. I'd never been more relaxed in my whole life.

"There's a ladder in front of you."

Oh, look. There was. A sturdy wooden ladder. The bottom of it disappeared into the clouds below me.

"The ladder has ten rungs." Micah said. "You're going to climb down the ladder, and when you get to the bottom, you're going to leave your body behind, float out of it, and fly into the sky."

That sounded like fun. I grinned. "Okay."

"Hold the ladder, Daphne." Micah's voice was coming from a distance now—far, far away. "I'll count your steps, backwards from ten. And when I get to one, you will leave your body behind. Move onto the first step."

I placed my foot on the rung.

"Ten. You can feel yourself moving down."

Oh, I could.

"You're taking the next step now. Nine. Your body is feeling *lighterlighterlighterlighter*...."

Hoo boy, it was. I felt like part of the cloud.

Micah's voice vibrated and echoed through me as I moved slowly down the ladder. "Move down the next step, Daphne. You're taking step eight, moving down, travelling down, down down, and now, you're taking step seven, becoming weightless, now step six, and step five, letting go, letting go of everything, now you're taking step four, relaxed, relaxed... step three, let go, let go of your body, your body is safe and happy and asleep, step two..."

I felt so good, so good, like I was made of nothing at all except for a warm, golden glow.

"And now you're taking the final step, step one, and you're deep, deep *sleepsleepsleepsleep*...."

Ahhhhhh.

For what felt like a thousand years, I drifted, floating on a cloud. Suspended, weightless, no thoughts, no feelings, in a blissful, happy nothingness.

"Out!" Suddenly, a chime hit me hard, like a thunderbolt. I lurched upright, shooting to my feet instantly, panting in shock.

CHAPTER
FIFTEEN

"What the hell?" Talk about a rude awakening. I felt like I was a giant metal gong, and someone had just smacked me. Shock and outrage made my pulse race.

The chime was still ringing in my ears. One second, I was blissfully asleep, the next, I was more awake than I'd ever been in my life. "Micah, you could have given me some warning—"

The words died in my mouth. Micah wasn't there anymore.

Neither was Levi. I looked around, confused. The white clouds were gone. All I could see was a dark-colored stone. I whirled in a circle. Dark colored stone on all sides. Where the hell was I?

Hang on...

I looked down and saw everything, everywhere, all at once, the whole scene from almost every angle. The church spread out below me, but it looked nothing like I expected it to. The angle was so strange; it was as if I was giant, looking down with enormous eyes. Something absolutely breathtaking stole all my focus, making it hard for me to comprehend anything.

A beautiful white-gold light shone on the church floor, right over near the entrance to the hallway. It was so beautiful; I could barely tear my eyes away. The light shimmered, sharpening into the shape of a man.

Of course. It was Romeo. He sat on the floor. He was waiting for me.

I'd done it. Or, rather Micah had done it. He'd pulled me out of my body. Right now, I was up near the ceiling of the church in the pointy part of the roof.

Below me, I could see a pale-white opaque dome on the church floor. I couldn't see through it. I couldn't hear anything at all.

That was the warded circle. My body was down there with Levi and Micah.

If I had a pulse, it would be thudding by now.

"Ugh." A sulky voice broke the silence. "All these witches and me without my kindling and flame. God has forsaken me."

What the hell was that?

I looked around but couldn't see anything. Nothing mattered, though. Nothing but that beautiful, angelic man, down there. I had to talk to Romeo.

But how did I get down from here? I was floating in the air. I didn't seem to have arms or legs, so I couldn't try to swim. Hands.

Did I have hands?

A hand appeared in front of me, as if manifested by willpower alone. Okay, that was a start. I reached out and touched the ceiling, hoping it would push me down. My hand passed right through the stone.

"Witches, desecrating my church," the sulky man's voice grumbled. "Devil worshippers. Heathens. The damned have overrun us."

Okay, so I couldn't use my hands to push me down. Of course. I wasn't corporeal, so I couldn't touch anything. Did I have legs?

Yes, I did. As soon as I visualized them, they appeared. Toes, feet, ankles, calves, knees, thighs...

"Put some clothes on, whore of the devil!" The sulky man turned thunderous. "This is a house of God!"

I looked down at myself. Huh. I was nude. Naked as the day I was born. I'd never been ashamed of my body, and it wasn't like I was in public or anything.

With no better ideas, I bent double and tried to tip myself upside-down, lifting my legs above me. Then, I started to kick, like I was swimming. Freestyle felt weird, so I moved to breaststroke.

"Jezebel! Whore! Slut of Satan!"

I blinked. There was a man floating in the air next to me. Slowly, he came into focus. He was a white man, maybe in his mid-fifties, bald, with bushy black brows set over small brown eyes, a snub nose, puffy lips, red-veined skin. He wore a black smock with a white dog collar.

A priest. He glared at me, his jowls wobbling in outrage.

I had sensed ghosts around the church before when I came here for the very first time. Spirits of the dead had a very faint odor of their own, very subtle, almost impossible to detect, like a slight variation in ozone. They never bothered me or anyone else for that matter. On the contrary, I felt a little sorry for them. Not being able to move on to the next life was just... sad.

I kept swimming through the air. Romeo blazed in a golden glow below me, his eyes shut, his expression serene. He was keeping his mind clear, meditating, so he could sense me. I just had to get down there.

I kicked a little harder and managed to sink a couple more inches.

The priest moved closer. I caught a whiff of burnt wool. "How dare you come here and try to seduce me, lover of Lucifer! Waggling your bountiful bosoms at me!"

I sighed. Giving a ghost attention was the same as anything else—you just made them more powerful. This guy was starting to piss me off, though. "I'm not trying to seduce you."

"You lie!" he bellowed. Damn it, he'd just gotten louder. "You lie like the serpent in the garden!"

I should have kept my mouth shut. Usually, if you ignored a ghost and you didn't give them the attention they craved, they would go away. I'd never been good at ignoring people, though. It felt mean, even if they were a grumpy, outraged dead priest. I sighed and kicked harder, trying to ignore the old ghost as he shouted insults at me.

Come on, Daphne. Get down there, go talk to your boyfriend, tell him what's up. Do I need to remind you that the fate of the entire world is at stake, here? The clock is ticking...

"Lascivious lover of Lucifer!" The smell of burned

wool grew stronger. It was coming from the ghost. My gaze flicked back over towards him.

He didn't appear to have any trouble moving in his spirit form. Maybe I should ask him for tips.

Instantly, I dismissed it. No, bad idea.

I moved back into freestyle. It didn't help. I switched to dog paddle. Who would have thought the hardest thing about this whole mission would be figuring out how to move through the air? I focused on the stone floor. Down, damnit!

The priest let out a bellow. "God will come and strike you down, harlot!"

"Oh! Would he?" Surprised, I looked at the ghost beside me.

His bushy eyebrows quivered in rage. "What?"

"It's just that... I need to go down," I explained, confused. "So, if someone was to strike me down... That... That would actually be quite helpful."

The ghost priest stared at me in silence for a second. "How dare you?" he exploded, giving an outraged shout. "You mock me, slut!"

"I wasn't mocking you." I sighed. "I just misunderstood what you were trying to say."

"You are as ignorant as you are evil, you guttersnipe!"

I straightened up, let out another weary exhale, and put my hands on my hips. "Look. You're Father Benedict, am I right?"

His eyes bulged. "Demon! The demon knows my name!"

"I'm not a demon," I said patiently. "I just did my

research. You were the priest here back in seventy-two, right?"

"I am still the priest here! There has been no other!"

I made a *yeesh* face. There had been a whole bunch of them since seventeen seventy-two. Father Benedict had burned to death in front of the whole congregation when a candle was knocked over on the altar. He wasn't the only person who had died in this church, but as far as I could tell, he was the only spirit here. He was tied to this spot and couldn't move on.

I opened my mouth to say something and thought better of it. "Never mind," I sighed.

His piggy little eyes narrowed. "That is as I thought, vile hussy. Begone!" He clapped his hands. "Depart this house of God!"

"Tell you what. I'll leave, if you can give me some tips on how to get down there."

Father Benedict blustered. "Use your will, whore! Imagine yourself down there, and it shall be so."

Huh. That made sense. I pinched my eyes closed and imagined myself standing on the stone floor, right next to Romeo Zarayan's dazzling white-gold light. My chest warmed.

When I opened my eyes again, I was there, standing right next to him. The bright light shone from his chest, right over his heart, and it was glorious to behold. I gazed at him in wonder.

"I thought you were leaving, demon?" Damnit. Father Benedict stood beside me, gnashing his teeth. "Begone, back to hell with ye!"

"Okay, okay. Yeesh. I'm just going to have a talk with my boyfriend here."

"Abomination! Hussy! Whore!"

I sighed. "Just... just give me a minute, Father. Please."

The priest grumbled under his breath.

"Please?"

He glared at me. But he didn't move away. I took a deep, wholly unnecessary breath, and turned away, trying to ignore the old ghost and give Romeo my full attention.

Right, how do I do this? On instinct, I reached out and put my hand on Romeo's chest.

He opened his eyes; they glowed silver. "Daphne?" His voice rumbled all around me like an earthquake.

His name left my lips like a prayer. "Romeo."

"I can hear you." The light in his eyes flickered. "Tell me. Tell me what Christopher Jupiter wants from you."

A chime rang in my ears. I froze for a second and checked myself. I was okay. My body lay asleep on the floor, twenty feet away.

They couldn't hear me.

"Okay." I moved closer, close enough that my spirit self was overlapping with his. It felt better. "I need to tell you the whole story. I had been bouncing around wild-magic realms for over ten years, desperately trying to find my way home," I said, moving to whisper in his ear.

Romeo stayed very still, his eyes glowing silver, and listened to my story.

CHAPTER
SIXTEEN

"I had no idea I was getting further and further away from home. Every time I found a slipway, or a portal, or even a sorcerer I could fool into opening a gateway for me... I jumped through. The worlds I found myself in became stranger. The laws were different—the normal concepts of physics and logic just didn't make sense anymore. In some, my body was able to do things I never thought possible, like turn to water and flow like a river from one place to the next. In others, I was a giant, and every creature below me was like a tiny speck. Every single day I was Alice, and I was living in a nightmare Wonderland."

Romeo's silver eyes darkened. "I understand."

"In one realm, I watched as a great warrior got exasperated with how fast the sun was going across the sky—the days were too short, and they couldn't get enough done before it was dark. So, this warrior took a rope, lassoed the sun, caught him, and hit him with his club, a magic jawbone. The sun was frightened and promised to go slower across the sky from that day on."

"Maui and Tamanuiterā," Romeo murmured. "All the myths and legends."

"They're all real. They *all* happened." I paused and took a breath. I shot a look over to the opaque dome on the floor of the church, making sure it was still silent.

It was. I was okay.

Father Benedict had drifted over and floated around the dome, glaring at it. I ignored him, turned back to Romeo, and went on, "For a few months, I found myself in a realm of monsters. Strange giant beasts with scorpion tails, hideous octopus women who reminded me of Dwayne's ex-girlfriend, Norma. And giants with only one eye."

"Cyclops." Romeo was following me.

"Yeah. I didn't have any idea where I was, and I was desperate to escape. I found a tiny crack in reality at the bottom of a cave, and I jumped straight inside." I swallowed. "And I found myself in hell."

I'd never spoken about this out loud before—I'd tried to forget it had ever happened in the first place. Of all the awful places I had been lost in... all the hell dimensions, all the shadowlands, the underworlds...

It was a second before I could go on. "The realm was pitch black. I couldn't figure out if there was no light, or if I didn't have eyes in this place. And there was no way to experiment, because I couldn't move at all. I wasn't even sure if I had a physical form, except for the fact that from the second I found myself there, I was in pain."

A rumble sounded around me; Romeo clenched his fists. This was hard for him, too. "Go on."

"After a while, I realized I did have a form, but it was different here. I was a giant. The realm was tiny, and to make it worse, I was stuffed up against the worst horrors you can imagine." I paused and took a breath. "These things rubbed up against me, pinching me, burrowing into me, wiggling into my ears. They shouted and screamed the whole time, for years and years. I tried everything, but there was no escape. To make everything infinitely worse, I could hear things outside this hell realm. I heard a woman's voice."

Romeo's expression changed; an understanding dawned in his glowing silver eyes.

"I didn't understand what she was saying. I didn't know the language she used. But she didn't scream or cry. Her tone wasn't mocking or cruel. On the contrary, her voice was beautiful. Lyrical, smooth, and melodic, like angelic bells. Sometimes, when she came close, her tone changed. She was... inquisitive. Curious." I pressed my lips together for a second. "It made everything worse. I was trapped in a hell-dimension, unable to move, nestled up against the most vicious creatures you can possibly imagine, and right outside, a woman was singing, laughing, and talking. That tiny speck of hope drove me mad."

To be fair, I was crazy already, but hearing the woman made me much worse.

I went on. "Occasionally, a man's voice echoed through to the hell dimension. I didn't understand the words he said either, but I grew to love him, because whenever he spoke, the woman would go away. Sometimes, it was as if he was telling her to leave this world alone. I imagined he was telling her not to torture me with hope anymore. Then, she'd go away. And I'd be alone again, in the darkness, with evils crawling all over me."

The air rumbled again. Romeo's jaw clenched. I waited for a second and continued with my story. "With nothing else to focus on apart from the endless horror, I became obsessed with trying to kill myself so I could end it all. You can't end it if you can't move, though, and even if I did manage to suffocate myself, my primal instinct—my wolf-nature—would come out without my permission and force me to breathe again. So, I lived with the horrors for years, but I never gave up. I tried to kill myself over and over and over again, but nothing worked. After a while I decided to switch my focus and kill my wolf nature instead, because that was the thing that appeared to be keeping me alive. So, I focused my intention and went inward. Eventually, piece by piece, I devoured her, until she was trapped in my soul with me. We were no longer twin spirits but only one, sharing a body."

Romeo opened his mouth. "You became a lyconphage."

"Yes. As you know, it didn't work. I didn't kill her; I just absorbed her. There was nowhere for her to go." My voice dropped to a whisper. "Not long after that, I started hearing the woman more. I began to pick out the most common words she used, and after what felt like forever,

I started to understand her. The creatures around me mocked her words, and they, too, started to understand her language. They caught on quicker than me, and it scared me. I began to suspect that they were demons, and a powerful god had trapped them in a tiny hell-dimension. And I—the foolish, lost broken wolf-girl—had fallen through a crack in reality and found myself trapped with them."

A pulse in the air cut me off. I looked over but couldn't see any movement in the hard ward dome.

I continued, "The woman's voice became almost constant. She was so curious, so tempted. She had no idea what was in the box. She'd been told not to open it. Her husband, the man whose voice I heard from time to time, forbade it. It was a wedding gift, given with the caveat she was never allowed to lift the lid. But she didn't know what was inside, and the mystery was driving her crazy."

Father Benedict blinked into existence beside me, making me flinch. "Are you done, whore of Satan?"

I held up my hand. "Give me five more minutes."

"No!" he thundered. "Begone, foul wench of the devil!" He waved his arms frantically, trying to push me away. They passed right through me.

I huffed out an exasperated breath. "Sir, *please*."

Romeo frowned. "Daphne? What's going on?"

"Sorry." I glared. "There's a ghost here giving me a hard time."

"It's Benedict, isn't it?" Romeo's expression grew stony. "That damned priest."

"You are the one who is damned!" Benedict drew a flask out from his robe. "Burn, witch!"

Romeo couldn't hear the shouting, but he could feel the change in ozone. His eyes narrowed. "He's splashing me with holy water, isn't he."

I pursed my lips. "Yup."

"Begone, foul demon!" Benedict howled.

"It grinds his gears that there's a bunch of witches in his church." Romeo exhaled heavily. "Tell him to just move on."

I turned to face the priest, who was furiously splashing Romeo with flecks of silver that disappeared into nothingness.

"Sir. Excuse me." Benedict whipped around and glared at me, his jowls shaking in fury. I gave him my most pleasant smile. "I get that it might go against everything you believe in having to spend eternity in the place you used to rule, with hot witches ruining all your stuff, but wouldn't it be easier if you just, y'know... moved on?

"No," he grumbled.

"No, it wouldn't be easier?"

"No, witch whore. I can't."

I raised my eyebrows. "Because..."

"I am tied to my Church."

I shrugged. "Can't you just break the tie?"

"No." He pouted. "I don't want to."

I turned back to Romeo. "He doesn't want to move on."

"Figures. Daphne, just ignore him. We always do. The

most he can do is blow up the food in the microwave from time to time, anyway."

"Okay. Where was I? Oh, right." I mentally reinforced myself and continued, "I know you've figured it all out by now, who the woman was, and where I was. But you have to understand that I had no idea what was going on. I thought that the things stuck inside this Hell with me were demons, so I knew she wouldn't let them out."

"They weren't demons."

"No. And yes." I frowned. "And no. We have no word to accurately describe what they are. But in truth, they are gods themselves."

Pausing, I checked the ward. Did I imagine that pulse of energy? Father Benedict was still floating around, gibbering in outrage.

I needed to wrap this up soon. Fear made me speak faster. "They are the Evils. The personification of everything bad in this world. Sorrow, disease, grief, madness, old age, violence, vice... They are the pure essence of that evil."

Romeo nodded.

"Soon, I realized that if this woman's curiosity got the better of her and she opened the lid, the evils would escape. I could feel how much potential they had, how they would infect the entire world. They'd fly out and feed on the realm outside and grow bigger and bigger. I knew they would; they'd said as much. They promised to change everything they touched into their likeness. They'd create a new Hell in this woman's realm, then move on to the next one, and the next one, and the next one..."

The walls rumbled. "Go on," Romeo said.

"One day, it happened. The woman talked and talked, getting the courage, backing down. Finally, a bolt of lightning split the sky. The evils laughed and laughed and poured out around me. They flew out and stung the woman."

"Keep going."

"So…I climbed out too. I was already bigger than the whole world. I gathered up the evils, and… I ate them."

Romeo frowned. "You *ate* them?"

"They had to be contained, Romeo. I'd already devoured my wolf nature; I knew how to consume abstract concepts. In that place—in a magic realm where you can stuff things like the personification of sickness and doubt into a big urn—it was easy. Like snapping my fingers. I knew I could trap things inside of me, because I'd trapped my primal nature there. So, I flew after the evils, and I devoured them.

"But they'd already tainted the small realm they were let loose in. It was a tiny place, just an island surrounded by water. I could feel the whole realm, and it was already diseased and in pain. These evil gods had infected it. The woman who opened the box was rotting on the floor, the sea was boiling, and the animals had gone mad, ripping each other to pieces."

I pinched my eyes closed, and suddenly, I was right back there. "I knew I had to do something. I was so big I could brush the sky, and I could feel every single part of this tiny realm. Above me, I felt a split in the fabric of it, a slipway into the next dimension. The evils would find it eventually and go there next. So, I shoved one hand through the crack in reality, anchored myself in the next realm, gathered up the whole world as the evils ravaged it, and I stuffed it inside me."

Did I imagine it, or had the floor rumbled?

Romeo was silent for a moment. "You devoured the world."

"Yes," I said simply. "There was no other way. The evils would have turned every single realm in the universe into Hell. As it was, the realm I devoured was bigger than the box the woman opened, and the evils had already grown larger and more powerful. Speaking of the gods gives them power, so I can't acknowledge them at all. *That's* why I couldn't tell you."

Romeo shut his glowing silver eyes, then opened them again. A thump came from inside the circle.

With growing horror, I looked down at myself. "Can they hear me?"

"They shouldn't be able to. The ward is sound-proofed."

"I'm still attached, though. To my body, I mean." I gnawed on my lip. "The silver cord..." As I said it out loud, it came into view. A ghostly-white rope; the energy cord that tied my spirit to my body. "Do you think they can hear me through the silver cord?"

Romeo grimaced. "I don't know. If something goes wrong, Levi will use the Eye anyway, and you'll shoot back to your body. Please, finish the story quickly, before you disappear."

"You know it all now," I said. "I fell into Pandora's box—a tiny pocket dimension—with all the evils. When Pandora opened the box, they flew out. I ate her whole realm to stop them from spreading across all the other realms."

I moved closer, speaking faster, trying to get it all out as quickly as possible. "They're inside me. I'm Pandora's Box now, Romeo. I am the prison for the evils that Zeus sent to torment the mortal realm. If I give the Evils attention, they'll get stronger. I don't know what will happen, but they might become impossible for me to ignore. I might go crazy and summon Pandora myself, so she can let them out of me. And she's the only one who can do it—she was created specifically for that purpose. She's a goddess herself, the embodiment of the consequences of curiosity."

Romeo nodded slowly. "I understand."

"Christopher Jupiter saw the evils when he tortured me," I said, rushing my words. "The eyes are windows to the soul, and they waved at him from behind the window. He wants them, because they are powerful, and they bring suffering."

"The worst of all blood magic," Romeo muttered. "He saw the evils inside of you, and he saw power."

"Exactly." Another pulse shot through the air; I flinched. "I don't know if it will work how he wants it to—maybe the evils will destroy him just like they will destroy everything. Maybe he has a plan to make himself into a god, like them. I don't know. But Christopher is terrifyingly intelligent, so he's already figured out that the only way to open the box is to get Pandora to do it. She's a concept herself, a goddess with no power—the embodiment of careless curiosity. That's why he wants a Stella Ostium to the Hellenic realms. He wants to call the entity Pandora, so he can get her to open the box. Me," I said, pointing a thumb at my chest. "I'm the box. And all the evils of the world are inside me."

The floor under my feet rumbled; it took me a second to register it, since my feet weren't touching the ground.

"Romeo, we have to—"

Everything went black.

CHAPTER
SEVENTEEN

The first thing I noticed was the pain. My whole body hurt like I'd been thrown into a giant washing machine and tumble dried.

Everything ached. Even breathing hurt. I tried to take a deeper inhale and winced. It wasn't the first time I'd regained consciousness after being beaten to a pulp, so I knew I had to be patient. My nervous system was overwhelmed and couldn't figure out where the pain was coming from, so it was doing the only thing it could to keep me alive. It was telling me the pain was coming from *everywhere*.

I leaned into it and waited, but the agony didn't localize anywhere in particular. There was nothing internal. I didn't think I'd been stabbed or ruptured anything. But my flesh was hot and tender from head to toe.

It took me a moment to understand that the pain *was* coming from everywhere. My whole body—the outside, at least—was bruised.

At least I could move. And—silver linings—I wasn't about to be hurt worse than I already was.

Voices drifted around me. Some loud, some soft, both female and male. Some were frantic and shouting, others calm, deep, and smooth. It took a moment for my brain to filter the noises through any concept of understanding, and they untangled slowly, finally becoming comprehensible.

A woman's voice was close by. "... might be out for days. We have to move her to a hospital now. She needs to be monitored."

"No." Romeo's voice was even closer, and my battered body relaxed when it heard him. He was here; he was safe.

Memories surfaced. I'd told him everything. He knew my deepest, darkest secret.

I was Pandora's box.

And he was kneeling next to me, holding my hand so gently, like it was made of glass. Relief flooded me, drowning out the pain.

"The Eye was supposed to be a last resort," the woman said. A twang of anxiety snapped through me as I remembered who it was.

Romeo's foster sister. She sounded worried. "You weren't supposed to leave it on her head, Levi." Bella swore—a long, loud, and imaginative string of swear words—letting him know where he could shove the Eye of Nephthys next time. "Honestly, how could you be so stupid?"

"How was I supposed to know that?" Levi's tone

went up several octaves. The poor guy was frantic. "You didn't exactly give me a booklet with instructions, Bell."

"It's a powerful magical artifact," she snapped. "Not a Nyquil tablet."

"We didn't know what else to do," Micah's tone was icy. "Her body started shaking a little at first, then it would stop for a minute. She was still breathing and still asleep, and the ward was still up, so we figured it was working. Then, all of a sudden, she had a really violent seizure. I tried to use my magic to calm her down, but—"

"By the time I tipped the Eye out of the pouch, she was throwing herself all around the hard ward," Levi said. "It was freaking terrifying, like something out of the exorcist."

Gah, I knew it.

"All I could do was hold the pouch, wait for her to flail her body towards me, and try to slap the Eye on her forehead."

So that was what the rumbling was. The monsters in the box had heard me—or, at least, they'd known they were being discussed. I was still attached to my body, after all, by the silver cord. It was a ghostly connection but still. It was a connection.

I checked my psyche carefully. They were still trapped deep within me. They were a little stronger, but unexpectedly... so was I.

Romeo knew. And I felt so much better now that I wasn't carrying this burden alone.

"I was worried that she'd seize again if I took the Eye off her," Levi went on. "Rome took the ward down only a minute later."

"A minute was already too long." A feathery light touch stroked my shin. "She's so bruised." Bella sounded worried. "She might have internal injuries. Rome, *please*. The poor girl has been slammed against a hard stone floor like a rag doll. She's black and blue from head to toe. We have to get her to a hospital."

"No," Romeo grunted. "I got her." A cool sensation soothed the pounding in my head. "She's going to be okay."

"Do I have to remind you that you're not a doctor?" Bella's tone grew firmer. "You have no idea. She's unconscious. She might even be in a coma. I'm worried that the Eye has done permanent damage. She might not *ever* wake up." Bella hesitated a second. "I'll never forgive myself if she doesn't wake up, Romeo. It's all my fault. I should have told you not to let the Eye rest on her skin for too long—"

"It's not your fault, Bell," one of the boys said. Brandon, I thought. "Besides, it was only on for a minute or two."

"It's like holding a uranium rod for only a minute or two," she ground out. Jeepers, she was really worked up.

There was a rustle and a couple of barely audible taps. "Let me call my private physician's clinic. They've got everything there to monitor her. I'll get them to send an ambulance."

"I'm not moving her."

"Rome, please," she pleaded. "She's really hurt."

"She's coming back," he said. His hand smoothed my hair back from my forehead. "I can feel her."

I tried to form words. "Yar," I managed.

"Daphne!"

"You're alive!" That was Cole, howling from a few yards away.

"Yar." I tried to blink, but my eyelids weren't working. My mouth, too, wasn't moving the way it should. I couldn't seem to figure out how to move my lips.

"Don't try to move," Romeo said softly. "Your eyes are swollen shut. Your lips, too. Here." Something cool rested against my throbbing bottom lip. "Drink."

I cracked open my mouth and felt cold honey-flavored liquid pour inside. Romeo's healing elixir to the rescue. I swallowed and felt instantly better. The little bottle disappeared and was replaced by another one, which I gulped down gratefully. Soothing magic surged through me. I could feel it, radiating out from my belly, trying to find the source of my pain. Blood vessels healed, and connections were restored. Inflammation died down. The hot, bruised feeling on my skin reduced, little by little.

My eyes cracked open and focused immediately.

Bella leaned over me, watching my face intently. When she saw me open my eyes, she closed her own and clutched her chest. "You're okay. Thank God." She let out a quivering breath. "Oh, slap my ass and call me a donkey, I've never been happier to see someone open their eyes before." She sat back on her heels and took a deep breath.

Tone it down, ya frickin'-psycho-evil-pick-me-drama-queen, Brain Daphne mumbled, still a little off her game.

Just beyond Bella, Levi crouched at my feet, arms outstretched. He muttered a healing incantation under his breath. The throb of agony dulled even further. On my other side, Brandon and Cole sat just out of my line of sight. I could hear and smell them, though.

Romeo was kneeling behind me, cradling my head in his lap. I couldn't see him without opening my eyes wider, and right now, I couldn't manage it, so I closed them again.

"I'm okay," I murmured. "It's just external bruising. Nothing is broken. No internal bleeding."

Romeo stroked my cheek. "Stay still for a minute. Guys, give her some space. Cole, go heat up the leftover pizza for her. No, actually, order her a fresh one. Call on the way, ride out and get it, and bring it back here as soon as you can. Bran, you go with him."

A croak left my lips.

"And tiramisu," he added.

My mouth still hurt too much to smile, so I didn't. I breathed out. "Thank*ssss*."

I felt better already. Brandon and Cole got up and left the room.

"So..." Bella's voice broke the silence. "What happened? Did you get the information you were after?"

"Yeah." Romeo hesitated for a second. "I know everything. I'll fill you in later, Bell."

Good. He understood. They couldn't get any more attention. No more.

He let out a gruff exhale and stroked my cheek with his thumb. "I'll fix it," he whispered. "Don't worry. I've already thought of something that might help."

I licked my swollen lips. "W— What?"

"Well, for starters, I'm going to wipe Christopher

Jupiter off the face of the planet," he growled. "He'll never get close to you; I promise you that."

"That's a good start. And...?" Bella poked him. "Please tell me you've come up with something so that she doesn't have to smash herself against the stone floor again, Rome. She's too pretty to deal with that kind of shit. It's like watching someone take a sledgehammer to a Monet."

"Yeah, I've got an idea. It's a Band-Aid solution, but it will help in the interim."

The swelling in my eyes went down enough that I could look up. The sight of him, as usual, made me feel so safe. "What? What are you thinking?"

He met my eye. "A memory spell. I can remove or suppress the memory, and we won't talk specifics."

"Oh." I swallowed. "That... that could work. That's actually how I've been coping for the last four years. Just trying to forget. It was working really well until Christopher kinda blew that plan to smithereens."

"It's not permanent," he warned. "No memory spell is. And the trauma of the event will still be ingrained."

I nodded. The pain in my muscles had receded. "Yeah, I know." If any memory spells actually permanently worked, then they'd be a useful tool for a social worker like me. They never lasted long, though. Hours, usually.

But it was a good idea—a really great Band-Aid solution for now. I understood exactly what Romeo was trying to do. He'd suppress or even take out the specific memory of... the thing I was trying to avoid giving attention to, and we'd just focus on stopping Christopher Jupiter from bringing that bitch back into this world.

I felt the barriers on my psyche. "Yeah, I think it will work."

Bella sat up straighter. "I've got a bunch of stuff in the car that might help with the spell. Some charms and amulets... maybe even a stasis box for the memory vessel... Oh! Actually, I might even have a mnemosyne in my glove compartment."

I blinked.

Bella looked at me and shrugged. "Dark magic practitioners love to hunt magical artifacts, too. Sometimes when I'm on a job, I've got competition. There's a lot of nazi occultists and black witches—"

"Blood witches," I corrected automatically.

"Yeah, of course. Blood witches. Anyways, these guys are power-hungry, and they're often loaded with arcane weapons and tools, so I make sure I shake them down once I... you know." She drew her thumb over her throat.

My eyes widened. Whoa. Bella was badass.

"I'm not the only one with a low tolerance for blood magic," Romeo said.

"Twins." Bella grinned at him. "Peas in a pod. I could have used your help in Luxor last month, Rome. That necromancer raised his whole family."

"You know I've got my own shit to deal with, Bella. Besides," Romeo added, his voice lighter than I'd heard it lately. "I'm sure you took care of it easily."

"Barely." She grimaced. "That damned djinn almost drove me insane."

My stomach twisted uncomfortably for a second.

They were so alike. I cleared my throat. "So, the memory spell...?"

"Right." Bella turned her focus to me and rose gracefully to her feet, dusting off her knees. "I get it. It's urgent. Give me a second, and I'll run out to the car and see what I've got." She skipped away, light on her feet.

Romeo and I were alone. It was nice. More of the pain melted away, and the swelling was going down. I was right, I was just bruised. Romeo ran his thumb over my lips again, and I closed my eyes and sighed.

"Are you sure you're okay?"

"No." A bubble of laughter escaped my lips. "You were there, Romeo. You heard everything. Of course I'm not okay. But taking away that memory will help a lot, for now."

"I'll do it as soon as Bella comes back. You know how it works?"

I nodded. "Not the specifics, but I know you'll use magic to weave a spell with the intention of pulling the memory of... uh, *them*, out of my mind and store it in a piece of fruit. A banana or something."

It had to be a fruit or vegetable. Memories were living things—they could only be stored in something that was alive. But if a memory was stored in something sentient—and, to various degrees, all living things were sentient—the memory would be corrupted. The workaround for that problem was to store the memory in a piece of fruit, an object which had enough life to hold the memory without corrupting it. However, this meant that even the most powerful memory spells were always only temporary. As soon as there was no life remaining in the vessel, the memory returned to where it came from.

"I prefer oranges," Romeo said. "They take longer to decompose. Bananas are mush within a few days."

"Aha. Good idea."

His eyes darkened. "There will be a gap."

"I know. For now, it's okay if we just focus on stopping Christopher from finding the thing he's looking for."

"I'll get creative and fill in the blanks. Listen..." He hesitated. "If I do this spell, and I erase the memory of what you did... I just want you to know something before we do it."

I waited. "What?"

"You're not the box."

I frowned. "What?"

"You're not the box in this story, Daphne." His eyes bored into mine. He was trying to make me understand something.

"Yeah, I am." I stared up at him, puzzled. It was the first time I hadn't automatically got what he was trying to say. "That's the whole problem here, Romeo. It's the reason why I'm lying on the floor, covered in bruises."

He sandwiched both his hands around my face and stared at me urgently, his jaw clenched. "I know I can't say this without—" He swore and looked away. "But listen to me. I know what you are, and you are *not* the box."

The passion in his eyes was so intense. Like he would tear whole worlds apart to keep me safe. Gods, he'd already done that when he tore a hole in the Hidden City to get to me. What was he trying to say? If I wasn't the box...

Then who was I?

"Got it!" Bella ran back into the gym holding a perfectly square metal box, a little like a giant bronze Rubix cube. "This should do the trick." She waved her other hand. "I grabbed a pomegranate out of your fridge on the way."

"Perfect." Carefully, he lifted my head, moved out from underneath me, and laid me back gently on the ground, resting my head on his balled-up hoodie. He didn't have to be so careful with me anymore. I was almost back to normal. But I was still so emotionally bruised, I savored his gentleness.

Bella handed the cube over to Romeo and caught my eye. "It's a mnemosyne," she explained. "An arcane tool to help keep the memory from escaping out of the pomegranate when it starts to break down. The memory will stay trapped in there until there is no life left in the fruit, so you'll have a month or so, rather than the usual two weeks. And the mnemosyne will start to beep when the pomegranate is almost completely broken down, so you'll get a warning before the memory escapes and returns to you."

I knew what a mnemosyne was. I used to help make them when I was enslaved to a mad pixie mage in Faerie. I escaped from that mage by tricking him into removing the memory of me from his own mind while we were quality-checking a new prototype, and I ran away as soon as he forgot about me.

I could have told her that. But instead, all I said was, "cool."

"I'll only take that one memory." Romeo said, putting one hand on my forehead, and the other on the box next to him. "This will be quick, because it's still fresh in your mind. Just relax." He began to chant. Magic whirled underneath his fingertips—a silver-blue mist.

I closed my eyes. Fragments of memories began to flicker in my mind's eye—the mad pixie mage, Bella handing Romeo the mnemosyne, Romeo telling me that I *wasn't* the box...

This would be quicker and easier if I surrendered and got out of the way, so I visualized my favorite practice track in Nagoya, settled myself at the start line, watched the clock, and counted down the seconds until my next race began, starting from fifty.

A cool sensation washed through me. I kept counting.

After only a few more moments, Romeo brushed my cheek with his fingers. "It's done. I took the thing that needed to be taken. Are you okay, Daphne?"

I opened my eyes and squinted at him. "Who are you?"

Romeo's eyes flew wide, and I grinned. "I'm only kidding." I wriggled on the ground, feeling much lighter, and much, much better. There was a reason I'd been so battered and bruised, but when I probed that thought, I found nothing.

Romeo watched my expression change. "I had to remove a memory that was causing you a lot of pain," he explained. "We stored it in a—"

"A mnemosyne. I remember that part." I furrowed my brow. "I remember I needed to tell you something important. Did I?"

He nodded. "We got it."

I knew we'd spoken, but I couldn't remember what it was about. It was something terrible. Catastrophic, even. Something that I couldn't cope with by myself, so Romeo removed it for now, until we could figure out a way of fixing the problem together. I'd done something... or something happened to me. All I had was a vague understanding that it was a Very Big Trauma, deserving of capital letters.

But the memory of it was gone. When I tried to probe any further, all I felt was a blank space. The only thing that remained was a face—white skin, beaky nose, and a weak chin, prominent Adam's apple, and the iciest, coldest eyes I'd ever seen in my life.

He was the problem. "Christopher Jupiter," I growled. "He tortured me."

"Yes."

Bella let out a soft, horrified gasp.

I don't need your pity right now, bitch. And why the hell didn't Romeo take the memory of the torture, too? Because that sucked donkey dick, and—

My brain suddenly realized that the memory Romeo had taken was obviously so much worse than being tortured by Christopher Jupiter and decided wisely to stop speculating. *You know what, that's all in the past. Let's just focus on the now, shall we? Let's talk about the future. When are we going to cut off Bella's head?*

I ignored her. "Christopher was the one responsible

for the Great Suffocation," I mumbled. Bringing him to justice for that crime was the most important thing right now.

Fine. We can cut off her head later.

Romeo brushed my hair back. "He knows we're after him, so he's trying to get as much power as he possibly can. You know he's magically weak but very intelligent. He's trying to find a Stella Ostium. We think he's trying to summon a Hellenic god to our realm."

I nodded. I remembered that part. "Which one, though?"

Bella reached out, put a hand on Romeo's shoulder, and gave him a loaded glance. I watched the spot where she touched him and had to force the muscles in my chest to relax.

My brain growled at me. *Heart...*

I know. It's okay.

Romeo's brow furrowed. "We don't know who he wants to summon."

I frowned. "Wait, I remember you said something on our date. Christopher was in Greece, trying to figure out how to summon a figure from Greek mythology. Wasn't it Pandora?"

There was a beat of silence. Romeo and Bella glanced at each other again. The look that passed between them did something very unpleasant to my insides.

Was it because I was jealous or because of the missing memory? "That's okay," I sighed. "We'll figure it out." Suddenly, I was sick of lying down, so I tried to sit up. Despite still being bruised, I wanted to run. I wanted to find that asshole and tear him into pieces for what he'd done to the supernatural community. Thousands and thousands of people died because of him.

Bella helped me sit up. The cacophony of odors from the various magical charms and amulets she carried wafted around her like heavy perfume, almost making me sneeze, overpowering the faintest touch of the witchy herby-candle smell on her skin. But underneath all that, the absolute absence of any personal magical scent of her own made my heart thud in my chest almost painfully. She had no magic of her own. None at all.

And Christopher Jupiter wanted it *all*.

Suddenly, a strange feeling gripped me—a rock-hard certainty, a sureness that was totally at odds with the blank space in my head. It was a feeling that I hadn't had since I was a kid. Back when things were simpler, and I understood exactly who the bad guys were. I knew who I should stab and who I should hug.

Romeo had taken a very important memory from me; I knew that. But I knew that it was imperative that I surrender it to him. I loved him, and I trusted him.

And, for the first time in a long, long time, I trusted myself.

Yassss, bitch. Let's go.

I kept my face blank, took a deep breath, and looked up, meeting Bella and Romeo's eyes "Here's what I know."

CHAPTER
EIGHTEEN

"I've spent a fair bit of time in the Hellenic realms," I told them. "The first thing you need to understand is that there's more than one. There are probably dozens. The Cyclops and their cave are one of them, and it was rubbing right up against our own mortal realm once upon a time. The Scylla lives in another small one, and she would eat any mortal sailor that slipped through to her reality. The Underworld, Tartarus, Olympus, they're all real. But they're separate worlds, and they have separate laws of time and physics and whatnot."

Bella frowned. "Yeah, I know all that. I don't see how that's important."

"The rules are the point. The Greek gods are the most powerful creatures in the most powerful realm that make up the Hellenic universe. If they want to get from one realm to another, they just can't show up in their god-like splendor. They need to change forms. When we were closer, Zeus used to do it all the time. He'd show up as a white bull to abduct Europa and bring her to Crete, or as a shower of gold to knock up— who was it? Perseus's mom, I think."

"Danae," Bella said helpfully.

"That's right. Anyways, a little-known fact is that despite the stories, the gods didn't actually change forms when they came to the mortal realm. In order to be corporeal, they had to occupy something—a body of an eagle, or a thunderbolt. Now, we're too far away, and they can't come at all. Not unless they're summoned with a butt-ton of power."

Bella stared at me but stayed quiet.

"Now, I'm never going to make the mistake of underestimating Christopher's intelligence," I said, a little pointedly. "He would already know all this. That's literally why he's doing it. He wants power; he won't want to bring a god here that he can't control. He'll be inviting one here to occupy his body."

Yes, that felt right. Christopher, the evil genius, would be using the Stella Ostium to summon a deity from Greek mythology; and with that deity firmly in residence in his shitty weak-ass body, he'd have the power he wanted to wreak havoc on the world. "I don't know why Pandora was mentioned, but it won't be her."

"Why not?" Bella asked.

"I can't imagine any reason for him to want her. Not when there's so many other better options to choose from."

"Oh." Romeo stared at the ground. "So, which god, do you think?"

I shrugged. "Any of them. Remember, Christopher is

smart, so he wouldn't try one that would be offended by being summoned by a mere mortal, so the heavy hitters —Zeus, Ares, Hades—are definitely out. And I can tell you this right now, he won't summon a female deity."

Romeo and Bella exchanged another loaded glance. A stab of pain shot through me—jealousy, scalding and painful. I gritted my teeth and ignored it. "Why not?" Romeo asked.

"Because Christopher is an asshole," I said simply. "He's sexist and racist, and he's got an insane sense of entitlement. The idea of sharing his body with a female entity who is more powerful than he is would be unthinkable. No, I bet you he'll be going for a male god."

"I think it would be foolish to rule that out, Daphne." Bella said gently.

She's calling you a fool.

I didn't care. I was sure of it.

"I've spent a lot of time in Greece," Bella said. "I've read all the ancient stories in the original Greek. There are thousands of deities for him to choose from, and some even switch genders from time to time."

Reading the Iliad in the original tongue wasn't the same as actually being there. I shrugged. "This isn't about the gods themselves, Bella. It's about what Christopher would do. There's no way in hell he'd summon a female god. Not for any reason."

Bella shot Romeo another meaningful glance and backed off. "You're probably right," she said.

Is she humoring us? Is this bitch patronizing us? Can we please cut off her head now?

You know we can't. Shush.

"Let's just focus on stopping him before he does anything," Romeo said gruffly. "Do you know how the Stella Ostium works?"

"Uh huh." I dug deep into my memory banks, carefully skirting the empty space. "The easy part is activating it, it's a simple spell, and I'd assume he already found the details in Greece. Only one person can do it, so he won't need other witches to help him. The Star Door takes three hours' worth of chanting to open wide enough, but, at the end, to finish it, the summoner needs a *lot* of magic to pull the god through. Christopher's a weak witch *and* an asshole, so for him, the only way would be to use blood magic. He'll have a human sacrifice on-hand. I'm sure of it. He will hurt someone really horribly and harness their suffering to get enough power to perform the summoning. There will be a hostage of some sort with him."

"Okay," Romeo said. "So, if we rescue that hostage, he won't have the power he needs to summon the god."

"Right." I saw what he was doing; he was tagging all the fail safes we could hit to stop Christopher.

"And, just to confirm, if he does activate the Stella Ostium, we have three hours before it's wide enough, right? We have three hours to find him and kill him or rescue his hostage."

"Preferably kill him, yes. But—" I held up my finger. "This is important. Once the Star Door is activated, a part of the terrain of the Hellenic realm will come first. The door is designed to pull something familiar in from the god's world first, so they feel comfortable when they get here. It might be an ancient temple. It might be a section of Hades underworld. We might find ourselves fighting to get up the steps of Olympus. We don't know until he opens it."

Romeo nodded. "I got it. So, after it's open, we've got three hours to advance over alien terrain and kill him before he makes a sacrifice and summons a god into his body."

"Bingo." I held up a finger. "And, as an added bonus, we've got a fair bit of time to kill him after that, too. It takes a whole moon cycle for the summoned god to get a feel for the new body they're in. Zeus did three weeks partying in Crete, chilling out as a swan before he flew off to seduce Leda and knock her up."

"So that's why he was running away from that eagle," Bella mused. "I always wondered about that."

"Exactly," I said, throwing her a bright smile. It felt forced, but I did it anyway. "Zeus wasn't powerful enough at the time. So, if worse comes to worst..." I ticked off the failsafe points with my fingers. "If Christopher *does* find the Stella Ostium first, and if he does activate it, then we've got three hours to fight our way through some ancient Greek mythological terrain to get to him before he sacrifices someone horribly and completes the summoning. And finally, worst case scenario—if Christopher Jupiter does manage to summon a Greek deity into his body, we've got a whole month before he starts growing horns and snorting and pawing at earth with his hooves."

"The minotaur?" Bella rolled her eyes. "He wouldn't."

I shrugged. "He could. Or the cyclops. All monsters

are gods. All gods are monsters. The difference is always whether they like you or not."

Oooh, that's deep. I like that.

"Okay." Romeo took a deep breath. "We find the Stella Ostium first and destroy it. Do you know what it looks like?"

"Yeah." I don't know why I didn't tell them this before. "The Hellenic one, from what I recall, is made from the blood tears of Zeus."

"Blood tears?" Bella's eyebrows shot up. "The tears of Zeus? From when he realizes his son Sarpedon is going to die?" She blew out a breath and nodded. "Oh, that makes sense. That was one of the most important moments in mythology."

I nodded. She was so damn smart. "Yes, exactly. Zeus cried tears of blood that crystallized into a gem—a stone of incredible power. When the realms of the gods drifted further away and they couldn't come to the mortal realm easily—and they weren't getting the worship they desperately wanted—the gods had their ancient Greek priests mount this Tear of Zeus and turned it into a Stella Ostium. It is blood red and tear shaped. It will look like it's cut with a billion precise facets—but the facets are natural, not cut. And it's roughly the size of a man's fist."

Bella whipped out her phone and started tapping. She was onto it. I fed her more information. The faster she found it; the sooner we'd have a lead.

"The setting will be gold, and it will surround the stone completely," I told her. "You'll be looking for something that matches the geometric period. Seven-hundred B.C."

"Got it." Her eyes darted back and forth across the screen. "I'm already narrowing down the options. Something like that would have to be in a high-tech safe somewhere. I'll have to raid the coffers to get a strike team together."

Romeo tapped her knee. "Let me know what you need."

Her eyes shot up and met his. "Are you sure?"

"Of course. Anything you want, Bell, you know that." His eyes grew warm. "Just say the word, and it's yours."

My gut twisted.

Brain-Daphne gave an uncomfortable twitch. *Why does our stomach keep doing that? I thought we were all on the same page, here.*

We were. We were fine—no, *I* was fine. My physical body was having an involuntary response, that's all. I'd get used to it.

I didn't have any hope that it would stop anytime soon, so I'd have to get used to it.

Romeo's own phone beeped. He flinched and rushed to take it out of his pocket. Anxiety pulsed through me. He always had his phone on silent—only SOS notifications came through. He tapped quickly, accepting the call. "Go."

Brandon's face appeared on the screen. He looked scared. "We have a serious problem here, Rome."

"What is it?"

"Uh." The camera moved back. "See for yourself."

There was a magic rope around his neck—scarlet-red and glowing malevolently. As the camera moved back, I saw thin white fingers clutching the end of it.

"Let me talk to him," a haughty voice demanded.

The camera tilted for a second; Cole lay on the ground, unconscious. The phone moved back, and suddenly, a woman's face took up the entire screen. White, furious face, icy blue eyes, cheekbones so sharp you could use them to slice a loaf of bread. Her jaw jutted out. She was furious.

Countess Ebadorathea Greenwood narrowed her eyes. "Let me in, Warlock," she snarled. "Now. Or I shall grind his bones to make my bread."

CHAPTER
NINETEEN

"The sorceress." Bella shot up from the stone floor like she'd been stung and moved into a low crouch. "She's here."

Jeepers, she was fast. One second, her hands were empty, the next, she had a Glock in one, and a haladie in the other—an ancient Syrian double-bladed weapon that absolutely reeked of malevolent magic. Bella froze in her crouch, her eyes flashing.

"Romeo," she whispered. "Is the hidden doorway in the apse still sealed?"

I frowned. What hidden doorway? Goddamn it, Bella knew all his secrets.

Romeo climbed to his feet and held up his hands, reaching for her. "It's okay, Bell—"

She spun the haladie in her palm, a movement almost identical to how I spun my Orion blades. She looked left, then right. "Go," she hissed at him. "She's expecting you, so go on out and hit her with everything you've got. Do whatever you have to but get the boys away from her." Moving swiftly and gracefully, she holstered the Glock at her back and grabbed my hand. "I'll cover Daphne. I'll take her through the hidden exit, and we'll meet you at my apartment. Don't worry, I'll protect her."

What a sweetheart. Big sister wants to protect us.

I fought the urge to rip my hand out of Bella's grasp and rolled my eyes at my own brain. Sarcasm, huh? Is that how low we've fallen?

"Stop." Romeo brought his hands down on her shoulders and held her in place. "Bella, just wait."

"We have to get Daphne out of here," Bella snarled softly, tugging on my hand. "She's in danger."

"We're all in danger." I pulled my hand out of hers, gently, and stretched, feeling my tendons pop and muscles strain, while at the same time trying not to look at how close Romeo was standing to Bella. They were chest-to-chest, staring each other right in the eyes. Romeo looked so damn comfortable with that proximity, almost embracing her. "I hope your liquor cabinet is locked."

"It's okay." He turned. "I don't have one. We're a beer-only household."

Bella's eyes widened. "Oh no..." She stepped back from Romeo and started rummaging around in her jacket frantically. "She's already thrown a curse or something. You guys have lost your minds. I think I've got some nullifying powder in here somewhere." She pulled a pouch out of her pocket and waved her arm. "Daphne, get behind me. I'm going to get you out of here."

"Relax, Bell," Romeo said. "The countess isn't dangerous."

"Are you kidding? It's Ebadorathea *Greenwood!* You know—The Scourge of Slovakia? The Serpent of El Salvador? Romeo, whatever she's hit you with, shake it off! Cole is unconscious, and she's got Brandon by the neck, and she's coming to kill us!"

"Okay, I misspoke. She's dangerous... but she's not here to kill us."

I walked over to the front door and unlocked it, lifting the heavy bar out of the way. Bella hissed at me. "Daphne, no! What are you—"

"Bell." Romeo's voice was sharp. "She's a friend."

Bella gaped at Romeo for a second. "She's not *your* friend. You would have told me if you had started rubbing shoulders with the most infamous, terrifying sorceresses in modern history."

"Sorry." He shrugged. "It's been a busy month."

"You called me a week ago!" She jabbed a finger at him. She was furious. "You told me all about—" Her eyes flicked over to me, and she faltered for a second. "The thing with Alexei Minoff and the new Alpha. I don't remember you saying anything about cozying up to Countess Ebadorathea Greenwood."

"Sorry. It slipped my mind."

Bella turned and stared at me. "She's your friend?"

"Yeah."

"But... she's evil!"

"No, she's—" I paused, and made a face. "Well, maybe she is a little evil. Again, it depends on your perspective." I tapped Romeo's shoulder. "Let her in."

He opened an app on his phone and keyed in a code. Outside, I heard a click and a rolling noise as the automatic gates swung open.

"Well." Bella glanced at us warily. "Forgive me if I don't seem as comfortable as you guys. The countess' exploits are splattered all over the pages of history. She's committed atrocities that would make your skin crawl, Rome."

"History is usually written by the victor, Bella." I smiled at her sweetly. "But sometimes, it's written by a vengeful, petty warlord who got hung upside-down from the ramparts of his castle for a month because he said he'd be faithful, but he lied."

Bella didn't look convinced. She patted down her jacket with all her weapons and artifacts stored safely inside and backed away from the door. "Well, I, for one, do not want to be friends with that bloodthirsty maniac. Do me a favor, guys," she muttered. "Leave me out of this. I'll just be a silent observer, here in the corner."

She backed into the alcove in the right wall of the church, sat on the steps, and took her phone, palming a tiny gold amulet at the same time. "I've got work to do, anyway. If anyone needs me, I'll be balls-deep in my suspected magical artifact database."

Surreptitiously, she clicked the amulet between two fingers. The cherry-sherbert scent of a look-away charm tickled my nose. Suddenly, I didn't want to look in her direction anymore.

She's good, Brain Daphne murmured. *This bitch is smart. No wonder she's lived as long as she has without any magic of her own. She found a way around it by using other people's magic.*

Yeah, Bella was smart. And beautiful, talented, and strong. The overwhelming protective act she'd pulled, trying to save me—that was impressive, too. The way she held that haladie, flicking her wrist expertly... She was obviously skilled at combat.

I could see exactly why Romeo loved her.

My brain squirmed in discomfort. *Gods, I wish this damned body would get with the program. Jealousy feels so icky. I don't suppose I can talk you into stabbing her when her back is turned, anyway?*

The door cracked open, and Brandon walked in, carrying Cole—still unconscious—over his shoulder. "Incoming," he called out sarcastically. "Watch out, they're right behind me."

I frowned. "They?"

The countess walked in—looking more menacing than usual in a black leather dress under a huge fluffy black fur coat. To complete the terrifying picture, she also carried a limp body over her shoulder.

I gasped. "Dwayne!"

My beautiful Alpha looked like he'd been beaten up. His feathers were ruffled, and some stuck out like they were broken. Black scorch marks marred the tips of his wings. Deep scratches scored his orange webbed feet. One of his eyes was bruised and swollen shut. His head bounced on the countess's back with every step.

Urgh, he moaned. **Handle with care, woman! Can't you see I'm dying here?**

I rushed forward. "Dwayne, are you—"

The countess held up her hand, stopping me in my tracks. "Back away, child," she snapped. "As if I didn't have enough to deal with!" She stomped inside, and, with a vigorous swing, she hefted Dwayne's body off her shoulder.

He landed with a thump on the sofa. I knelt next to him, smoothing his disheveled feathers and brushing off some of the scorch marks. Despite his injuries, I couldn't bring myself to get too close to him. He absolutely reeked of whiskey.

I glanced up at the countess. "What happened to him?"

I'm fine, baby girl. He lay prone on the couch, his eyes closed. **I jussht need some rest. And rehab, probably. And a priessht to deliver the last rites, maybe. Urghhhhhh.**

"He got into a fight with Myf, that's what happened," the countess snapped. "I came home—from a very important trip, I should add—to find both of them sozzled drunk and trading blows mid-air above the woods in the Hidden City. Really, child." She stood, ramrod straight, and put her hands on her hips, thrusting out her chest. "What the hell were you thinking? I leave you alone for a few days, and you organize a supernatural fight club?"

Dwayne let out a huff of laughter, which turned into a groan of pain. **I can't believe she bought that sshtupid story.**

I took a deep breath, counted to ten, and exhaled. This was the *worst* possible time...

"There's no supernatural fight club," I said to the

countess. "Myf has been depressed, and she's been drinking. Dwayne has been depressed too, because his new girlfriend has gone home on extended leave, and he's suffering from extreme dopamine and serotonin withdrawals."

Yeah, about that. Dwayne twitched uncomfortably in his prone position on the sofa. **There's probably something I should tell you—**

"Everyone saw her!" The countess's furious voice cut him off. "By now, the whole City will be buzzing with the news that there's a dragon hiding in one of the buildings. I managed to knock Myf out of the air, get her to change, and get her back to your apartment, but she's severely unstable, Daphne. She needs gentle treatment, not roughhousing mid-air with a god of chaos!"

I groaned. I didn't need any extra mental labor right now. "I'm sorry, Countess." I shot a glare at Dwayne. "He was supposed to be watching her, not getting stupid drunk with her, *again*, and fighting her in her dragon form. *Again*."

It was good for her, he slurred in my head. **Myf was pretty pissed when she woke up after I knocked her out the first time. She needed to let the beast out to have a little fun. She's not used to being powerful, you know. She liked it.**

"Well, she certainly beat the crap out of you, sir." I smoothed his feathers down gently.

I got a few good shots in. She's a damned big dragon. She's got breath spicier than yours after a pico binge.

I held my nose. Gods, he reeked of booze. "She's burned off your wingtips. Can't you heal yourself?"

I will, he sighed miserably. **As soon as I remember how.**

The countess sniffed. "Well, he's really messed up now. As soon as Myfanwy emerges from her drunken stupor, she's going to feel even worse than she did before. Not only that." She glared at me. "She was seen in her dragon form in the City. You know what will happen next."

I knew. She was a great beast of unfathomable power. "The People of the Claw will come for her."

"I'm not worried about the People, you dolt," the countess snapped. "I'm worried about that idiot brute, Lennox Arran."

"Oh." I shot a glance over towards Romeo. His shoulders had stiffened.

"He's the Alpha Shifter now," the countess continued. "So, technically, she is his responsibility. I'm not worried about her being enslaved, Daphne. I'm worried about her emotional state. No matter what she turns into, the truth is, she's a scared, vulnerable girl."

Guilt squirmed in my chest, hot and sloshy. I'd deal with the Lennox Arran problem later. I should be there for Myf. "I'm so sorry, your grace," I said again. "I know I've neglected her. I've got a lot going on right now."

"Yes." She lifted her chin. "I know. That's why I'm here." Her eyes roamed around my face for a second. She paused, frowned, and stepped closer.

Pinching my chin between two bony fingers, she stared into my eyes for a moment. "Huh." Abruptly, she spun in a circle, turning towards where Romeo was reviving Cole on the sofa opposite us.

"Warlock," she growled. "What did you do?"

He paused mid-incantation and met her gaze calmly. "I let her forget."

"Oh." Her eyebrows shot up. "I see. Well, I hope that doesn't backfire."

"It won't." He looked at her, the storm surging in his eyes. "And exactly how do *you* know about it?"

"Dear boy." The countess gave a haughty little chuckle, but it had no humor in it at all. On the contrary, her voice chilled me to the bone. "I was there in Castlemaine when she had her little therapy session and plunged the whole town into darkness."

"What?" My head whipped between her and Romeo. "What are you talking about?"

"That Julie woman should have lost her license," the countess grumbled. "Imagine thinking it was a good idea to magically animate a specter of someone's trauma like that?"

I spluttered, confused. I vaguely remembered that session... "Julie was a great therapist! She helped me a lot."

"Oh, she helped, alright. Once the town's mass terror alarms were reset and everyone calmed down, she realized quickly that the only way to help you was to make you forget. So I stepped in. There's a reason I go through so much fruit, you know."

"I thought it was because of all the daiquiris. You *said* it was because of all the daiquiris!"

But..." the countess heaved a weary sigh and ignored

me. "Apparently, I'm the only person that can put two and two together."

I took a deep breath. "Your grace—"

"We're going to focus on stopping Christopher," Romeo said pointedly. "We're going to find the Stella Ostium before he does."

"Your grace!" I frantically waved my hand at her to get her attention, confused, and a little frightened. "Please explain?"

She spun around elegantly to face me, and her face softened. "Darling girl, you will be unsurprised to know that I have been one step ahead of you this entire time. After that vile creature Christopher burnt you to a crisp, then ran away once the Warlock rescued you, I realized he would stop at nothing to amass more magical power. He is a sniveling weakling who relies on artifacts and pre-packaged charms purchased from far more talented witches than he."

My eyes shot over to Bella in the corner. She had her nose buried in her phone, tapping away furiously. I was sure she was listening, though.

"That's a little mean," I said out loud.

"Christopher Jupiter lusts for more innate power." The countess ignored me. "The most obvious way is to invite a god to share his body."

Wow, she was good. It was uncanny the way she'd made that wild deduction, even though it was totally accurate. "That's not *really* the most obvious way—"

"Hush, child, I'm speaking. So, I figured he would want to track down a Stella Ostium. I remembered seeing a gem that fit the description eons ago, an enormous blood-red tear-shaped ruby. It was 'liberated' from Greece by a wealthy shipping magnate," she explained. "Who presented it to my friend Edward, who showed it to me one rainy afternoon at the palace. The power radiated off that thing like a space heater."

Romeo wrapped an arm around me. "The Tear of Zeus."

"That's it." The countess pursed her lips. "It was almost worth having Dirty Bertie grope me afterwards."

"Dirty Bertie?"

"King Edward," she clarified.

I frowned, got my phone out, and tapped it into the search engine. "But King Edward died in nineteen-ten."

"So?" She arched an eyebrow. "Anyway, dear, when I realized Christopher was after the Stella Ostium, I thought I'd track it down."

My heart leapt in my chest. "Did you find it?"

"No." She grimaced. "The stone was stolen from the palace treasury back in the sixties and hasn't been seen since. The theft was unreported in the media, because, of course, the English stole it from the Greeks in the first place. At the time, there was some resentment brewing in the colonies—because of all the genocide and stolen resources—so they chose to keep the stone's theft quiet. I have some leads on who stole it, but..." Something flickered in her eyes. "Unfortunately, I was forced to give up the hunt."

I stared at her. "Why?"

"That vile witch Jupiter appeared in London and has sat on my tail over the last day or so. He trailed me from the Tower of London yesterday and showed up in the records room at Sotheby's right before me. He is travelling with a foursome of Russian mages from his wife's family. If it came to a battle, I could crush him, but I'd have my hands full with those Slavic brutes." She exhaled a weary sigh. "I am worried that if I continue the hunt, he will swoop in and steal it out from under my nose."

Romeo finally succeeded in waking up Cole and stood up, towering over all of us. "We can take it from here, your grace," he said, his voice low. "We've got an artifact expert working on pinpointing the location of the Stella Ostium right now."

He didn't say Bella's name. He didn't even draw any attention to her at all. She didn't look up; she still had her nose buried in her phone. A light sheen of sweat beaded her forehead.

He's respecting her wish to stay hidden from the sorceress, my brain snarled softly.

"Good," the countess said. "Because I am compromised, and those damned Russian mages know all my weaknesses." Her eyes dropped down to Dwayne on the couch. "I will get this beast sobered up and ready to fight and impress on him the importance of not being a menace right now. There is too much at stake."

Lighten up, you old cow, Dwayne grumbled. **It's my nature. Fish gotta fly, birds gotta swim, bees gotta fuck the birds. Something like that.**

"Can you take care of Myf, too please, your grace?" I asked her.

"Of course. But, Daphne, dear." She gave me a hard look. "If Christopher gets his hands on the Tear of Zeus, make sure you call me immediately. Do you hear me? You will need all hands on deck."

"Do you know anything else about the Tear?"

"Well, the last thing I could find was that the thief sold the stone on the black market. I did a little digging and spoke to a few old friends, and I believe a mobster"—she put two fingers in the air, doing little quote marks—"named 'Frankie Two-Coins' purchased it."

"Frankie Two-Coins?"

"An ironic name, apparently, and a very shady character. He was in London at the time, spending millions of his ill-gotten gains on antiques and artworks at the city's auction houses. My contacts believe he may have purchased the stone on the black market while he was there. It makes sense—there is no trace of the Tear of Zeus showing up in England ever again."

"So, who is this guy, and where did he take it?"

"Here, my dear. He was an American gangster." She shrugged. "That's why I returned. That vile bastard Jupiter was flailing about in London last time I saw him, still digging through the records at Sotheby's. But this Frankie Two-Coins brought it here."

CHAPTER
TWENTY

Everyone leapt into action, but quickly found that there was no particular direction to leap in. The countess, having told us everything she could, hefted Dwayne over her shoulder and took him home, making me promise that I'd call her if anything went wrong.

Bella moved from the step to the couch, traded her phone for her laptop, and sandwiched herself in next to Brandon and Levi. She'd roped them into combing her databases for any mentions of Frankie Two-Coins.

"His name won't actually be Frankie Two-Coins," she told Brandon patiently. "It will be Francis or Franklin or something. Levi, you comb the internet for any famous American gangsters in the sixties with those names."

Cole was in bed. He had decided it was a fantastic idea to attack the countess outside, and she'd smacked him down with a huge wallop of magic. Romeo and Levi had healed him the best they could, but it was going to take days before he would be back in action.

Micah paced back and forth in the far corner of the vast living room, what felt like a football field away, on a conference call with Romeo's private investigators. They were in London, trying to locate Christopher Jupiter and his Russian family mages. Micah gave them everything the countess had told us and ordered them to call us the second they'd gotten a tail on him.

Romeo sat beside me, his arm around me, silent, deep in thought. His strong, thick fingers tangled in my hair. Neither of us spoke.

For the first time in my life, I didn't find the silence awkward. With anyone else, I felt the need to fill the gaps with mindless chatter, desperate to put everyone at ease. But not with him.

On the contrary, the silence between us soothed me. It wasn't solitary. It felt almost like a meditation, clearing my mind of all the madness it had been plunged into. I could finally think straight.

So, I did. I thought about a lot of things, while the Warlock's fingers combed through my long hair, and his hand caressed the back of my neck.

I trusted him. I just had to make sure that through all this, I didn't forget that.

After a while, I finally broke the silence. "Romeo?"

"Mmm?"

"Did you keep any of Aunt Marche's old things?" As the new High Priest, he should have automatically inherited anything witch-related when he took over.

He paused. "Yeah. I kept everything."

"Any books?"

"Of course. They're in the library." He nodded

towards the west side of the living room, where a cross section of the church had been hermetically sealed behind glass doors. The room inside was floor-to-ceiling bookshelves. I hadn't gone in there yet, but I'd been planning on dancing around, Beauty and the Beast-style, as soon as I got a chance.

"Marche had a lot of great reference materials." Romeo's brow furrowed. "It was actually a fight to get hold of them. The Otherworld Council cleared out her apartment, and when I went to pick up her things, I got attacked on the way home by some sort of otherworld monster. I figured she must have some ancient, valuable books in her collection."

"Does she?"

"Not that I can tell. I've gone through everything, though, and they're mostly basic witchcraft manuals and old grimoires—a few old, dangerous spells, but nothing I didn't already know. Some old journals."

"Old journals?" My heart skipped a beat. "Any gossip in them?"

"Not really. You know she wasn't the type to say mean things about anyone. She was like you." He gave me a crooked smile. "Always optimistic and she always saw the best in people."

I made a face. "You say that like it's a good thing."

He massaged the back of my neck. "It is."

"Sometimes," I muttered, leaning back, savoring his touch. "Do you mind if I take a look in the library?"

"Of course not. My home is your home. Anything in particular you're looking for?"

I closed my eyes and exhaled. His fingers felt like

heaven. "Yeah, kind of." I squirmed a little. "That ghost I met when I was astral travelling... Father Benedict. I remember talking to him."

"Oh." Romeo let out a grunt. "He's harmless. You don't have to worry about him."

"I'm not worried about him, I know he's got no power. It's just... he's tied to this church. He's stuck here, and he can't leave. It's like a magical tie. He can never get away from here. He can't move on."

"He made the tie himself, so if he's stuck here, it's his own fault."

"Yeah, I know that. I guess what I'm wondering is if there's a way for someone else to cut the tie for him."

Romeo's eyes softened. "Father Benedict is an asshole. He was an asshole when he was alive, and he's even worse now that he's dead. And you still want to help him. You're too sweet, Daphne."

I wasn't. But now wasn't the time to argue with him. "Can I help him?"

He thought about it. "I don't think so. A magical tie is an emotional contract between two subjects, and a third party can't break it."

"So, it's will-based."

He frowned. "Not necessarily. You can remove one of the subjects, and the tie will disappear. I'm not about to destroy my home just for one nasty ghost, and that damned priest doesn't want to move on. The person who forms the tie, or the other party, has to *want* to break it."

"Well..." This was all food for thought. "Maybe with a little ghostly therapy...?"

Romeo's lips twitched. "We'll take a look at it after

we've found the Stella Ostium and destroyed it." He stroked my cheek with his thumb. "I'll help you. We'll figure it out."

Bella shouted in triumph. "I've got it!" She put her laptop on the coffee table and spun it around to face us.

Everyone jolted. "You found the Tear?" Brandon tossed his laptop aside.

"No, the mobster who bought it. Franklin Cash. He's an Irish-American mobster from Chicago, he spent a bit of time in London in the sixties. I bet you anything he's Frankie Two-Coins."

Levi leaned over on her other side. "Are you sure?"

"He's the most likely suspect, and he's come up on my radar before. Franklin Cash had a huge collection of jewelry—including some siren pearls that might turn your legs to flippers." She spun the laptop back around and scanned the screen. "Only if you eat them, though, and I doubt anyone would. There's no mention of a giant fist-sized ruby in his collection, but that doesn't mean anything. If he bought something insanely valuable like that, then he'd be a fool to display it."

Brandon leaned closer towards her. "Is he still alive?"

"No, he died in the early eighties." She tapped on the laptop, opening another database, and scanned it quickly. "His grandson, Herbert, inherited everything, including the Cash manor house in Chicago, which he still occupies. I bet it's there in the family vault. We should go now."

Romeo got up, unfolding his huge frame powerfully and efficiently, like a huge predator sensing his prey nearby.

My heart skipped a beat. "To Chicago?"

"We'll take my jet," Bella said, tapping furiously. "We need to get there as soon as possible." She shut her laptop, slid it into her bag, and got to her feet. "Let's go."

I mouthed for a second.

Romeo turned and saw me. "Daphne?" Understanding dawned on his face. "Oh."

"What's the problem?" Bella slung her bag over her shoulder.

"Daphne can't fly."

I glanced up at him, surprised. I'd never told him that, but it was true. I was scared of flying. There was a reason I'd taken the bus cross-country from California to Philadelphia in the first place. It wasn't because I was scared of heights or even being whipped through the air at high speeds—because I'd fallen through time and space often enough to get used to *that*.

No. What really got me was the thought of being sandwiched in a giant sardine can. The fear of what might happen to all the innocent passengers seated around me if I lost control...

Well, I wasn't sure exactly. But phobias aren't particularly logical, are they? "It's true," I said honestly. "I'm scared of flying." I licked my lips. "I can sit this one out."

Romeo glared down at me. "I'm not leaving you."

"Oh." Bella hesitated. "Well... you don't have to come." Her gaze flicked towards Romeo, and then back to me again. "I can try to get the Tear myself. To be honest, I'm much more at home breaking into ancient temples than I am cracking high-tech safes, but I can do it. You just gotta be sneaky." She took a deep breath and swung her bag over her shoulder. "I'll have to dig my ninja outfit out and go stealth mode," she said, her tone breezily confident. "I've got some muffle powder and a fuck-off charm somewhere around here."

"We got you, Bell," Brandon wound his arm around her. "I'll come with you."

Bella's confident expression wavered. "Thanks, Bran."

"She said stealth-mode, not beat-up-everything mode," Romeo growled. "You'll need to move through the shadows."

Levi winked. "That's your forte, boss, not ours. They didn't teach me shadow-jumping in my family's evil witch school."

Urgh, here we go, my brain moaned. *This is going to feel disgusting. Brace yourself, babes.*

I got up from the sofa, and slipped my hand into Romeo's huge, warm palm. It reassured me a little. "It's okay. You go. I'll stay here."

He glared down at me again, then his eyes flicked back to Bella for a second. Finally, he wrenched his gaze back to me. "No."

"Yes." I squeezed his hand. "Go with Bella, get the Tear of Zeus. I'll be safe here."

"I'll be honest, Rome," Bella said softly. "I could use your help on this one. But I don't want Daphne to be left all alone either; it's not safe. So, you should stay here."

I squeezed his hand. "You'll get the Tear much faster if you go with her."

Romeo's eyes flashed for a second; it was like a lightning strike. His fists clenched. I could almost feel the storm inside him, tearing him in two. It hurt me to watch it.

He loved me because I calmed the storm. I wasn't about to stop doing that now. I squeezed his hand again. "Go."

It took him a minute. "Fine." The muscle in his jaw ticked. "The coven will stay with you. All of them. We'll be back in a few hours."

"Uh..." Bella held up a finger. "I might have to take Levi as well. I need a co-pilot."

My gut lurched. So, she was piloting the jet herself? Was there nothing she couldn't do?

"Fine," Romeo's voice was low, like a snarl. "But you two—" he pointed at Brandon and Micah. "You stay here."

Micah waved his mobile. "If our London guys get in touch to tell us Jupiter is on the move, I'll call you straight away."

Bella frowned at her phone. "Let's hope we can get a signal through. There's some rough weather over Chicago. To be honest, I was kinda hoping you would come and use your vamp hypnosis to charm the Cash staff, Micah. If the safe is hidden..." She trailed off, met Romeo's gaze, and frowned. "Maybe I should stay here instead. I can look after Daphne."

My brain exploded, catching me off guard. *Fuck off,* she snarled. *We don't need looking after. We're not some fucking damsel weakling—*

Relax. I told Brain-Daphne. It's fine. We talked about this, remember?

"Actually, that might be a good idea. It will be fun."

Bella smiled at me warmly. "We could have some girl-time. I have a ton of stories to tell you about Romeo when we were growing up. I bet you want to hear all about his emo haircut when he was eleven. I even think I've got some photos somewhere." She giggled and winked at me.

You know what, I've changed my mind, girl-time sounds fun! My brain laughed like a hyena. *Let's stay here with her, and look at photos, and eat ice cream, and cut off Bella's head with a rusty butter knife!*

I laughed with her, trying to tone down the mania in my head. "Honestly, Bella, it's okay. You're the artifact hunter; you go get the Tear. I need to sleep anyway. I'm exhausted." It was late, and it had been a long, tiring, very weird day.

Bella pinched her eyebrows together. "If you're sure...?"

"I am."

"Okay." She nodded once. "We won't be long. Guys, get your stuff. My car is right outside."

Micah and Levi scrambled. She was taking them all, and leaving Brandon, a hobbled dragon shifter, and Cole, who was sleeping off the aftereffects of the countess's magical punch, to look after me. For a second, Romeo looked like he was about to explode.

"Don't." I cut him off with a shake of my head. "I can look after myself, you know. I'm in a warded church." Smiling up at him, I ran my thumb lightly over his lips. "I remember how tough it was to break in here the first time. I'll be fine."

"I know that." Some of the darkness in his eyes lifted.

"I'm not worried about you; I'm worried about me. I—" He cut himself off abruptly and shook his head. "I just don't want to leave you."

"I know," I whispered.

He leaned down and kissed me. It was hard, possessive, and desperate.

And it made me feel much better.

CHAPTER
TWENTY-ONE

I should have used the time to get some rest. It was late, and I was tired. Instead, I went straight into the library.

The hermetically sealed door gave a hiss as it shut behind me. I turned and looked at Romeo's collection of books.

The door gave a hiss as it opened again, and Brandon strolled in behind me. "Whatcha doing?"

"Nothing. Just a little research."

"Anything I can help with?"

Romeo had obviously ordered Brandon to stay close and keep an eye on me. "No." A thought occurred to me. "Actually, yeah, maybe. You were researching old mobsters. Did you find anyone else in your search that might have been called Frankie Two-Cents?"

"Surprisingly, there's a ton of gangsters throughout history called Frank." He shrugged. "But Bella got him already, so I stopped looking."

"It might be worth continuing the search, then. Just

in case she's wrong." I ran my finger along the books on the shelf nearest me. They all looked like grimoires, but it was hard to tell. They were like mismatched special editions, with no markings on the spine. I kept moving.

Brandon laughed. "She's never wrong. Bella is as certain as the breaking dawn."

"She certainly *is* confident."

"With good reason." He wandered behind me and started fiddling with the ladder, wheeling it back and forth. "If she wants something, she'll get it."

"Is that right?" I moved on, heading to a shelf that held books with modern covers, checking the spines. "Does she always get everything she wants?"

"Yeah." Suddenly, he flinched. "I mean... shoot." He glowered at the ground for a second. "Daphne, I get it. Yeah, her and Romeo are close. But there's no need to be jealous."

"I'm not," I lied.

"He's with you. He's chosen you."

"I know." I found a section with little hardcovers. They didn't have any spine markings at all. I inhaled carefully. The faintest scent hit me, and tears welled up in my eyes.

A memory swallowed me at the same time. I was sitting on the counter in the enormous kitchen in Castlemaine. Aunt Marche was baking cookies, and she'd given me the important job of weighing out the ingredients. I cracked an egg, and it spilled out on the counter. Instead of slapping me, which is what my own grandmother would have done, she wiped up the egg and tossed me another one.

Nothing is ever too ruined, she said to me. *Nothing is ever broken beyond repair.*

"Oh, shit, Daphne... don't cry." Brandon waved his hands awkwardly around me. "Rome didn't leave you and go with Bella because he wanted to, you know. He had to go. We've got to get the Tear of Zeus."

I wiped my eyes. "Goddamnit, Brandon, I *know*."

"Why are you crying, then?" He was starting to panic.

Oh, great. This was awesome. Later on, all the coven was going to hear how I cried about Romeo ditching me to run off with his beautiful, talented foster sister.

I needed some privacy. "Can you please do me a favor? I know Bella's got it all covered, but it would make me feel better if you made a list of any known mobsters called Frank. Just in case."

He looked uncertain. "I mean, if it makes you feel better... sure."

"Do a spreadsheet." I loved spreadsheets. "Real name, nickname, location, dates of known activity, and what they were best known for—like, calling cards, what kind of crime they were into, if it was racketeering, solicitation... anything you can think of."

"Yes, ma'am. It's not like I've got anything better to do," he muttered resentfully, backing away. The door gave a hiss as it closed again.

I took a deep breath, finding Aunt Marche's scent again, and savored it.

After a short search, I found Aunt Marche's stack of journals. Romeo was right—she wasn't prone to gossip. Most of them were filled with shopping lists, names and addresses of the various solitary witches without covens that she'd taken in and trained, or the occasional funny anecdote she was sure she'd forget if she didn't write it down.

Occasionally, she wrote about the witches she caught using blood magic. Unlike Romeo, Aunt Marche never killed anyone if she could help it—she always preferred to bind the rogue witch instead, smothering their ability to channel or hold magic in their bodies. Her binding spells were exceptional.

But again, with enough magic, anything is possible. Bindings could be undone. I remembered Levi's story about his evil aunt, the one who thoughtlessly performed a small blood magic spell while on holiday in the Capital. Marche caught it, traced it, and bound her magic. Levi's aunt just went straight back to the family coven in Alaska and had the whole lot of them band together to unbind her. Levi told me that some of the things she did when she was unbound made his skin crawl.

Aunt Marche was like me; we both saw the best in people. But, unlike her, I learned from my mistakes.

As I read, I piled the journals into chronological order. I cried again when I found the first mention of Romeo. The poor orphan boy. Aunt Marche's round, loopy script grew almost incomprehensible when she first wrote about her suspicions that he might be the child of Marcus Jupiter's missing daughter, Gwendolyn. Years later, when it was confirmed, she was ecstatic. I read about how she'd petitioned for the court to reopen the question of succession.

And, in horror, I read about some of the battles she

faced when the Jupiters went after her because of it. I had no idea she'd survived so many assassination attempts.

I read every journal, from cover to cover. When I was done, I flicked back through them and used some little stickers to make annotations for things I wanted to revisit.

Then, I noticed some pages were missing. Torn out. I made more notes, then started reading them again. Here, in the sealed library, with the ghost of Aunt Marche's scent keeping me company…

I fell asleep.

CHAPTER
TWENTY-TWO

Warm, strong hands cradled me, pulling me out of my deep slumber. "Daphne."

"Romeo," I mumbled and yawned. Gods, he felt so good. The blissful feeling of his warm skin against mine almost overwhelmed me, plunging me right back into unconsciousness. I'd gotten cold sleeping uncovered on the library sofa. Romeo's embrace felt heavenly.

Reality sunk in. I could feel the tension in his chest. My eyes flew open. "Oh, no. Are you okay?"

"I am better now." His voice rumbled through me. "Now that I'm home."

I was certain he still wasn't okay. "What's wrong?"

"Christopher Jupiter left London. We got the call halfway to Chicago. Our people followed him to the airport. He took a private jet this time, but you still have to go through security. He's got four mages with him, so he was easier to follow. My guy lost him, but followed the mages, which led him to a private airport gate lounge. The plane was headed back here."

"Here, to Philadelphia?"

He shook his head. "No, he's going to New York."

I leaned into him for a moment, relishing the heat of his body. "Wait. You said you got the call halfway to Chicago?"

"Yeah."

I waited. When he didn't explain, I made some logical deductions.

Romeo's pulse was racing. He had dark circles under his eyes. He held me tight, but I could feel his muscles trembling. "You shadow-jumped out of the plane, didn't you?"

"It was stupid," he mumbled, pressing his lips to my forehead. "When we got the call that he was on the way back to the States, all I could think of was that he was coming straight for you. I couldn't stop myself."

He'd lost his damn mind. "You abandoned a plane mid-flight and shadow-jumped halfway across the country?"

His lips twitched. "We were only halfway to Chicago. So, only a quarter."

I shook my head, bewildered. No wonder he was exhausted. "Romeo... You can't keep doing this. You'll kill yourself. You can't rip holes in pocket dimensions and leap out of planes to get back to me."

"I can," he said stubbornly. "And I will."

And he did, my brain said smugly. *He abandoned Old Lara Croft mid-air.*

His racing pulse evened out; the storm died down. I

might be the sunshine, chasing away the storm inside of him, but now I was worried that I might be the one creating the storm in the first place.

"There's no rush," I said. "There's no reason for Christopher to come straight here and torture me again. He's after the Tear of Zeus, not me."

Something flickered in his eyes. "I'll never forget what he did to you."

"I suppose that's fair." Seeing my mangled, burned face would have been traumatizing. Romeo's phone buzzed in his pocket; in fact, it hadn't stopped since he woke me up. "Are you going to get that?"

"In a second." He buried his face in my hair.

I melted against him. It kept buzzing. "Romeo, I don't want to rush you, but it's in your pocket, and I'm practically sitting on it." If he didn't answer it soon, I'd explode, tear his clothes off, and rub myself on him like a cat in heat.

With a low, pained grunt, he pulled it out and hit a button. Micah's face appeared on the screen. He looked panicked. He saw Romeo, and his expression dissolved into relief. "Boss," he sighed. "You're okay."

"I'm fine."

"Where did you go?"

"Back home." Romeo rubbed a hand over his shaved head and exhaled roughly. "Did you land in Chicago?"

Micah's eyes flashed. "Just now. Bella wanted to turn the plane around. She's pissed. We have to chase this lead, Rome."

Bella yelled from behind him. "Don't ever do anything like that ever again, Romeo Zarayan, you selfish bastard! I almost had a heart attack!" The phone tilted, and Bella's furious, beautiful face filled the screen. "I could kill you. What the hell were you thinking?"

"Sorry, Bell." Romeo lowered his tone. He sounded guilty. I'd never heard that tone from him before. "I didn't think."

She stared at him for a moment, then she sighed. "Look, just... just sit tight. I'll raid the Cash manor as quickly as I can and find the Tear. We'll be home soon. Wait for us, okay? I'll call the second we've got it."

"Okay."

"Promise me, Rome." Her blue eyes flashed. "Don't do anything that stupid ever again. I swear to God, I'll kill you if you get hurt."

"I promise." He hung up.

I gnawed on my lip, feeling awkward. "Big sisters, huh."

"Yeah."

"I've never had a sister. Or a brother."

"I've had dozens of foster siblings." Romeo's tone took on a dark edge. "Bella was the only one who loved me."

I wriggled out of his lap and sat up. "Christopher Jupiter is going to New York."

"Yeah."

"Why? Is it to get the Tear of Zeus?"

Romeo hesitated. "Bella is sure it's in Chicago."

"Yeah, but we don't know for sure if Franklin Cash is Frankie Two-Coins. The connection between them was tenuous at best." I got to my feet. "Is Brandon still awake?" I pressed the button on the door to unseal the library door and strode out.

Brandon was *not* still awake. He was slumped over the long heavy oak table, fast asleep. His laptop was still open in front of him. I picked up his hand and pressed his index finger on the security keypad. He didn't stir. The screen flared to life.

"What are you thinking?" Romeo murmured from behind me.

"Well, right now, I'm thinking that you need to make sure Cole is okay, and you need to drink some of your amazing healing elixirs," I said, scanning the spreadsheet Brandon had put together.

Romeo took a vial out of his pocket, slumped on the bench seat, and nudged Brandon. "Bran. Wake up."

Brandon jolted and lifted his head, lines creasing his face from the table. "Huh? Wasssgoingon?"

"Go check on Cole, would you?" Romeo tipped the contents of the vial into his mouth and swallowed. "Then go to bed and get some sleep."

Brandon wiped his face. "Oh, yeah, sure boss, no problem." He lurched to his feet, walking like a zombie. "Yeahthanksgotitboss." He stumbled out of the living room, heading down the hallway, and disappeared.

Scanning the spreadsheet, I saw that I was right—there were dozens of mobsters with Frank-and-coin adjacent names active in the United States in the sixties. Brandon had compiled quite a list. Franklin Cash, Frank Cane, Francis Molton, Francesco Moretti, Herbert Cent—

I checked the other columns, rolling my gaze over the various crimes these guys were known for. Something macabre stood out. One of these mobsters had a particularly gruesome reputation for carving out the eyes of his enemies and replacing them with—

"Dollar coins," I breathed out.

"What?"

"This one." I traced a line from the "best known for" column and found his name. "Francesco Moretti. Italian American mobster." My fingers flew across the keyboard, and within half a second, I'd brought up several historical articles. "It says here that he was a slumlord over a thirty-year period, most active in the nineteen-twenties before he went a little quiet. Francesco Moretti made a fortune running booze during prohibition and went into property, buying crappy buildings and cramming poor tenants in. From there, he could exploit them further, and he went into loan sharking, racketeering, prostitution... you name it. But, most tellingly, his calling card was leaving dollar coins in the empty eye sockets of his enemies."

Romeo grimaced. "Let me guess. He lived in New York."

"You got it—right in Brooklyn. That's him, Romeo. Frankie Two-Coins. I'm sure of it."

"Christopher must have found a lead in London." He swore. "Bella and the guys are in Chicago—" He pulled out his phone and dialed.

No answer.

"We have to get to New York," I said. "Christopher is a step ahead of us now. Do you feel up to going for a ride?" I was itching to move, and I couldn't think of anything better than flying through the night on my motorcycle.

But Romeo froze. "Daphne." He paused and swallowed. He locked eyes with me. "If the worst happens... and he does activate the Stella Ostium and summons a god..."

I stared up at him. "What?"

"Are you sure we have a month before the god gets settled in his body?"

"I'm sure. Besides, it doesn't matter. I'm not backing down from this fight, Romeo, even if he does manage to convince one of those asshole Greek deities to wreak havoc on earth with him."

Romeo exhaled slowly and finally nodded. "Okay. Let's do this." He checked his watch. "His flight left London two hours ago. We've got five hours before he lands. We can get to New York in ninety minutes." He blinked at me, then grimaced. "Probably less than an hour the way you ride."

I grinned at him, baring my teeth. A strange exhilaration pounded through me, and I felt better than I had in weeks. I hadn't realized how much constantly being on the defensive was messing with my head. I'd turned into a shell of myself.

Not anymore. Brain-Daphne bared her teeth with me. *We're back, baby.*

We were. Back together again, finally. While it was true, I was good at diplomacy and fairness and compromise...

I was also born to attack. I was *meant* to be in the

lead. It was time to go on the offensive, and boy, it felt great.

"The hunt is on," I said.

CHAPTER
TWENTY-THREE

The wonders of technology meant that we could research Frankie Two-Coins and keep up a conversation while racing at breakneck speeds through the city. We hit the highway, turned off our headlights so nobody could see us, and flew through the night like comets.

I listened as Romeo instructed his phone's AI assistant to dig up the last known address of Francesco Moretti. There was a lot of trial and error—Frankie Two-Coins had been rotten to the core, and, compared to some of his peers, he didn't enjoy the limelight. Information about him was scant, and his real name and his gangster name were never mentioned together, not even when it was reported that he was sent to prison on a life sentence in the late sixties.

The research was made a little harder by the fact that he wasn't part of a crime dynasty. There weren't any other high-profile names linked to him. It was just Francesco Moretti and his hired goons. He had kids—

dozens, actually, but he didn't involve any of them in his business. In fact, from what we could find, he had a habit of beating his kid's moms so badly that they all ended up running away to other states. The man was a monster. None of his children claimed him. But one of them must have been his heir.

I spoke my thoughts out loud. "If the Tear of Zeus hasn't been seen since Frankie Two-Coins bought it, he kept it secret. He didn't sell it. A gem that big and that valuable would have made a lot of waves in the press."

Romeo followed me. "You think he hid it somewhere."

"Those old gangsters were notorious for burying their treasure, so to speak. If his heir didn't get it, I think Frankie might have hidden it before he went to jail, thinking he would come back to it after he got out. But he died, and the secret of the Tear's location died with him. So it's either in the house," I said. "Or whoever inherited his estate took all his valuables, locked them up in their own high-tech safes, and kept it quiet, just like he did."

We needed to find out who inherited his estate, and where he lived before he was arrested.

Finally, after listening to a true crime podcast at five times the normal speed, we hit the jackpot. When he was alive, Francesco Moretti lived by himself in a whole building in Brooklyn, a fancy three-story brownstone right on the edge of Queens next to some of the most crumbling shacks in New York. Frankie Two-Coins lived like a king while the people he exploited were crammed like sardines into run-down buildings around him.

I zipped around a semi and three SUVs as if they were standing still "I'm glad he's dead," I growled. Then, I suddenly remembered that the countess once had a fling with Edward VII and thought it best to double-check. "Frankie Two-Coins *is* dead, right?"

"Yeah." Romeo had been listening to the AI robot voice with a lot more patience than me. "He died in seventy-one. He lived a long time for a mobster, though, but I guess he was only thirteen when he started running hooch during prohibition."

"Good."

"He died in jail, too."

"Even better." We roared past Trenton like we were flying. The speed blew out all the lingering doubts in my head. "Can we get an address on his building? See who owns it now?"

"I assume it will be a corporation or something," Romeo muttered. "That whole area would be prime real estate now. This would be easier if Bella were here. She's my contact for getting into these kinds of databases, but she's still not answering my calls."

Bella can fuck off.

No, I gently chided my brain. We have to do this the right way. Out loud, I said, "I'm sure we can figure it out. If you can get an address, we can find out what happened to the building after Frankie Two-Coins died." My confident tone wavered at the end. It was four in the morning. Nobody would want to talk to us at the buttcrack of dawn.

Romeo got an address for the building, but the details of who inherited it from Frankie eluded us.

"Looks like the building has been broken up into three separate apartments since the early seventies. All with different owners. So, whoever inherited the building sold it as soon as Frankie died."

"There's no mention of any family members," I chipped in. "There must be a will. There will be records."

"If there is, I bet they will be stored in filing cabinets in an attorney's attic somewhere."

We took the turnoff and hit Goethals Bridge, heading over Staten Island, and in what felt like no time at all, we were in Brooklyn.

I turned my headlights on and slowed down to a more sedate pace. "Okay, we're four hours ahead of Christopher, and I'm going to assume that he's got better access to databases than we have. He might already know where to look for Frankie's heir."

"Right." Romeo roared up beside me.

I followed him to a leafy street in Bushwick. It was hard to imagine that this was a sewer crime slum once upon a time, but, like most of New York, the place had been gentrified to death. Property prices drove everyone but the most wealthy out of these neighborhoods. We pulled over to the curb, stopped, and got off our motorcycles and stretched.

Frankie Two-Coin's brownstone was pretty. Restored and freshly painted, everything looked new, even the rail on the stairs was gleaming wrought iron. Bushy green topiaries sat on the top step on each side of the heavy oak door. "It doesn't look much like a crime-lord's lair anymore, does it?"

"No." Romeo glared up at the building. "And we've

got no luck finding who inherited his estate just yet. As soon as Bella gets back to me, I'll get her to find out. Until then, we've only got one option." He nodded up at the building. "Search the whole place."

"You want to shadow jump inside and creep around a stranger's apartment, trying to find a precious gem under the floorboards?" I groaned. "Fine." I stretched my neck. "Let's do this."

CHAPTER
TWENTY-FOUR

We found absolutely nothing. While the outside of the building had been left to its former glory and restored, all three levels of the building had been completely remodeled—floors ripped up, modern kitchens and heating systems installed, walls reinforced and soundproofed. After sliding around on my belly like a snake under the floorboards, inhaling dust, and crawling around the walls, snorting insulation material—pink fluff that looked like cotton candy but tasted like it would kill me in ten years' time—I finally gave in to the temptation to groan.

"Romeo, it's not here." My instincts had been telling me that the whole time, but we had to be sure. "We've lost our time advantage. Christopher Jupiter and his Russian goons will be landing right about now."

Romeo let out a grunt and waved his glowing light charm on his palm, lighting up a dark corner of the wall space. Like me, his mood had slipped away with each minute we searched. "Yeah."

"Dawn is breaking." I yawned. "I'm going to head on outside and get some fresh air."

"Do you need a hand?"

"Considering we're shuffling around a wall space, and there's no way out of here... yes. And I can hear the guy upstairs waking up now." The woman on the first level was already awake and doing yoga in her living room; that's why we were rummaging around in the only apartment that was empty. A young couple lived here, but the calendar on their refrigerator told me they were skiing at Hunter Mountain for the weekend. "Can you jump us out of here, please?"

He took my hand, extinguished his light charm, and pulled me into the shadows. For a split second it was so cold, snowflakes frosted on my eyelashes. Then, we were outside, emerging from the shadow of a tree across the road.

I looked up at the building. "That was a bust."

Romeo checked his phone, then grimaced.

"Any word from Bella yet?"

"None." His eyes looked back at the building. "I'm going to try something else."

"What?"

He squared his massive shoulders. "I'm going to ask the occupants if they know anything."

"Direct," I said, nodding. "I like it."

He strode up to the building and pressed the buzzer for the first-floor apartment. A breathless woman answered. "Yes?"

"Sorry to disturb you, ma'am," he said. His low, sensual voice set my skin tingling. "I was wondering if I could ask you something about the history of your building."

"Oh, you mean the old gangster stuff?" She laughed. "We get a lot of mobster enthusiasts around here. Sorry, honey, I'm no history buff. I don't know much about the guy who built this place. I just wanted a decent rent-controlled apartment. But I made sure to smudged the joint with sage, got rid of all the bad vibes, y'know?"

"Of course."

"Julien on the third floor knows a lot more about it, I think. You could ask him, if you get desperate," she added, her perky tone disappearing. She sounded like she didn't like her upstairs neighbor very much.

We'd already searched that man's apartment. He didn't seem much like a history guy. There were no books on his bookshelves, and his apartment was minimalist and very clean. The mail on his counter told me he was an investment banker, and his magazines informed me that he was a cycling enthusiast. Not the motorbike kind, though, the ones who take up entire lanes on the road and block the traffic, making other drivers either angry, nervous, twitchy, or a combination of all three.

Heart-Daphne acknowledged that cyclists had a right to the road just as much as anyone else. Brain-Daphne, however, was incredibly prejudiced.

"Okay, I'll try him." Romeo spoke into the intercom again. "Thank you very much for your time, ma'am."

"Namaste, baby, you take care now." The intercom clicked.

Romeo pressed the buzzer for the third-floor apartment. "Yes?" a man's voice said. He already sounded annoyed.

"Good morning." Romeo said. "Sir, I was wonder—"

"No." The man cut him off rudely. "I don't want to buy anything."

"No, sir, I was just wondering."

"It's Sunday morning," Julien hissed. "Sell your shit somewhere else."

Romeo's eyes narrowed. I swear I could hear the rumbling of thunder somewhere. "I wanted to talk about the building you live in." He spoke quickly, doing a bad job of masking his rage. "I will compensate you generously for your time."

Julien's tone changed and not in a good way. "Oh, you're one of those murder podcast guys, aren't you? You idiots are all the same. Well, friend, I don't need your money, and I'm not in the mood to host some nerd with a sick mobster fetish. I've got better things to do today. Get the fuck off my doorstep." He hung up.

Vindication, Brain Daphne sniggered. *He's reinforcing my anti-cyclist prejudices nicely.*

"New plan." Romeo turned towards me. "How do you feel about waterboarding?"

"Zero stars, would not recommend." I took Romeo's hand and gently tugged, trying to pull him down the steps. "Julien's a dick, but he doesn't deserve to be tortured."

Yes, he does.

"Yes, he does," Romeo echoed Brain-Daphne. He graciously submitted to my pulling, though, and we walked back across the street, taking cover under the big tree.

"Bella's finally calling me back." He had his phone to his ear already. "Bella?"

"Rome." I heard her clearly through the phone, and she sounded angry. "We just got back to the church. Where the hell are you?"

"New York," he said shortly.

"New *York?* What the hell do you mean, you're in New York? *Where* in New York?"

"In Brooklyn."

She hesitated for a split second. "Where is Daphne? Is she okay?"

"She's with me. Listen, Bell—"

"Romeo Zarayan..." Bella took a deep breath and exhaled heavily. "You better explain yourself quickly, my love."

"No time. I need your help, Bella. I need you to find the heir of the estate of Francesco Moretti, born nineteen-twelve, died nineteen seventy-one."

There was a beat of silence. "Why?"

"Did you find any trace of the Tear of Zeus at the Cash's estate?"

"No." Bella sounded so angry, it was a miracle that the phone didn't melt in Romeo's hands. "I suppose you're at Francesco Moretti's old building in Brooklyn. Stay put," she growled. "I'm on my way."

Ha ha. No chance, my brain gloated.

Romeo pocketed his phone and let out a rough exhale. "She'll take her chopper; she won't be long." His arm wrapped around me, and he pulled me to his side, closer to the tree. "If Levi co-pilots, Bella can dig into her databases at the same time, so she'll let us know if she finds something." His jaw grew tense. "We need to get out of here, in case Christopher Jupiter shows up."

That was odd. "If he shows up, we kill him." I shrugged. "I mean, that should definitely be part of our game plan. I don't know why it's not."

"He's got Russian muscle with him."

"That wouldn't have stopped you before."

"It stopped the countess."

I raised my eyebrows. "Yeah, but the countess didn't have *me*." I didn't put much sting in my words. Something was telling me that Romeo wasn't underestimating me like everyone else did.

He glanced down at me, and his eyes met mine. I could almost hear a strange tug of war taking place in his head. The muscle in his jaw ticked. "Goddamn it, this is hard."

I glanced down, checking, then looked up again. "No, it's not."

"Daphne." He almost smiled. "Not that. It's hard not being... overprotective."

"I'm not buying it." There was more than that to it. I could tell. I decided to leave it alone. "Look, we've maybe got half an hour before that Jupiter asshole rolls up with his goons." Movement caught my eye. Down the street, three middle-aged men on racing bicycles had just ridden around the corner.

A plan exploded in my mind so hard, I almost reeled back. Romeo flinched. "Daphne. Are you okay?"

"Yup. I've got an idea. Wait here." Before he could

stop me, I bounded across the street and parked my butt on the step outside Frankie Two-Coin's old building.

Three seconds later, the men slowed down and dismounted, wheeling their bikes over towards me, and I gave a little fist-pump.

Gods, we're good. Sherlock Holmes has got nothing on us.

I got out my phone and pretended to scroll. The cyclists stopped on the pavement right beside me, holding their racing bikes. None of them had kickstands.

One, a lanky guy with short thinning hair, smiled at me. "Hello."

I glanced up and gave them all a wide smile. "Oh, hi there!"

"You're up early." He nodded up at the building behind me. "Have you been visiting someone here?" His smile grew lecherous.

Another one of the cyclists—a heavyset guy seriously testing the limits of his Lycra outfit—snorted. "She won't have been at Julien's last night. Not willingly, anyway. She'll be friends with that hippie downstairs."

I blinked for a second, letting them see my confusion. "Oh, no, I'm not friends with anyone here." Behind me, inside the building, I heard footsteps. I better lay the groundwork quickly. "No, I'm a history nerd," I said, giving the men a bright smile. "Did you know that this building was built by Molly Holyhead, the most famous gangster in Queens?"

The men all laughed. "I don't think that's right, honey."

"It was," I insisted. "I learned all about it at my college. I'm a gender studies major."

"With that hair, of course you are," the heavy guy snorted scornfully.

The door behind me clicked open, and I spoke a little louder. "I just wanted to come and see it, that's all. Molly Holyhead built this place in the late twenties and ran a counterfeit money ring out of it for thirty years."

"Bullshit."

I glanced behind me. Julien stood in the doorway, holding his bicycle. I frowned at him. "Sorry?"

"You're wrong," he said pompously. "You've got the wrong place."

"No, I haven't. Molly Holyhead was a suffragette, and a famous—"

He cut me off. "I'm telling you you've got the wrong place."

"And I'm telling you that I know more about it than you do." I smiled, trying to make it as smug and insufferable as possible. "Molly Holyhead lived here until nineteen-eighty and had twelve grandchildren. Now her daughter Genevieve owns it, and—"

"You're an idiot." Julien rolled his eyes at me. "This is Francesco Moretti's old place—Frankie Two-Coins. This building and his entire estate were sold at auction after his arrest in nineteen sixty-nine."

Bingo.

Haha, Julien, you dumb fuck, you got played.

Wait—it was sold at auction *after* his arrest but *before* his death? Hmm. I needed to milk this guy for everything he got. "No way." I laughed in his face. "You've got it all wrong. This is Molly Holyhead's place, and, for what it's worth, the police can't auction off someone's estate. In the absence of a will, it would have gone to the next of kin. Those mobsters have lots of kids." Frankie Two-Coin had lots of kids, anyway—our research had found that much. The hard part had been trying to figure out which one was his heir. "One of them would have gotten it."

"You're an idiot." Julien got right in my face. "Francesco Moretti went to prison owing thousands of dollars in restitution for his crimes. His children all filed disclaimers, rejecting any current or future inheritance, so the estate was sold at a police auction to cover the restitution fees." He sneered at me. "You won't find that information in a YouTube video or on a podcast, girlie."

That couldn't be right. The brownstone might have been worth thirty thousand dollars in the late sixties, and that would have covered the restitution. But the Tear would have been worth at least a million dollars. And even if it was still hidden somewhere, according to the countess, Frankie Two-Coins bought Old Masters paintings in London. His estate would have been worth millions, even without the Tear.

"The city can't do that." I rolled my eyes. "You're being so silly."

Julien smiled nastily. "In the sixties and seventies, there wasn't much that the Brooklyn P.D. couldn't get away with. The police weren't 'woke' like they are now. They didn't care about your feelings."

I'd have to think about all this later. For now, I ran back all the important details he'd given me—restitution, Brooklyn P.D. police auction, nineteen sixty-nine. There would be records, for sure. Someone would have bought the Tear at the auction, and for whatever reason, they kept it quiet.

Julien was still sneering at me. "Believe me, girl, you're out of your league here. Go back to your gender stu—"

Something behind me stole his attention, and the words died in his throat. Julien's face turned noticeably pale. His three Lycra-clad friends turned to see what he was looking at.

Romeo strode up the steps and took my arm. "We need to go. *Now*." I saw the reason for his urgency immediately. Three giant black SUVs had just turned onto the street in an ominous-looking convoy.

Christopher Jupiter. He was here. With his Russian mage muscle. I bared my teeth and snarled softly. Time to—

Romeo pulled me into his arms and carried me bodily down the steps, heading towards our bikes.

Looks like we were running. There must be a reason why. I trusted Romeo, so I let him carry me away.

"Cycling is for losers," I shot over my shoulder before he jammed my helmet over my head.

CHAPTER
TWENTY-FIVE

We rode to East Midwood, staying within the speed limits, which grated on me. But now wasn't the time for a police chase.

"We could have fought him, you know," I said to Romeo as soon as we took off.

I was itching to punch someone. Even though I'd gotten exactly what I wanted from that asshole Julien, I wasn't satisfied at all. I had to live with the fact that he'd go about his day thinking he won an argument with a gender studies major with colorful hair. The thought alone made me want to punch someone. "We could have ended it right there."

"Jupiter might have more than four mages with him. Those SUVs looked packed."

"Still." I wasn't ready to let it go.

Romeo was silent for a second. "Not in public."

That was a good point, but it wasn't exactly the reason why he'd chosen to run. Romeo had done a risk assessment and decided fighting was too dangerous. And coming from a man who had torn a hole in the fabric of a pocket universe...

He was protecting me. It must have something to do with the memory he took from me. I decided to let it go.

We trust him, and we trust ourselves.

Yeah, we do. "Fine. So, I guess we're headed to a Brooklyn P.D. precinct?"

"Normally, I'd say no, because police auctions are done by a third party, and they're all online. But—"

"Back in nineteen sixty-nine..."

"Yeah. If they kept records of police auctions, they'd be put on microfilm or something. Let's go into the biggest precinct and ask."

We drove to the seventy-eighth, parking our bikes a little way down from the precinct but still in full view of the entrance. The city was starting to spring to life in the early morning, but it was freezing, so there wasn't much foot traffic. Romeo pulled off his helmet and stayed astride his bike. "You go in and ask." He gave me a crooked smile that melted me. "I think we've established that you're the smooth talker."

"Why do I get the feeling that you're staying here to guard the entrance?"

"I am."

I waited but got nothing more out of him. "Fine," I said, handing him my helmet. I turned, and walked up the steps, pulling off my gloves to blow on my fingers and keep them warm.

A single, middle-aged Black woman in a uniform arched her eyebrow as I approached the front desk. I smiled at her, not sure what angle to go with. "Hello, ma'am. I was wondering if I could trouble you for some information. You see, I'm doing a story—"

"I don't care." She eyeballed me. "Tell me exactly what you want, and do it fast, because we got twelve drunk sorority girls getting hauled in behind you in a minute."

"Oh." I only hesitated for a second—wasting her time would make her mad. I blurted it all out. "I need to find the records of a police auction that was held here in Brooklyn in nineteen sixty-nine—"

"New York City Municipal Archives," she deadpanned, cutting me off. "All the auction details are on digital archives, on microfilm. But—" She jabbed a finger at me. "If you're looking to find anything before the Knapp Commission, it might not be there."

"Uh—"

"Commissioner Bonner had some of the more 'controversial' records boxed up and stored in a non-government document storage facility in the Bronx." She pursed her lips. "Under the excuse that they're low-priority documents that will eventually get scanned to digital files. For now, they're still on paper and rotting in boxes. The current commissioner is probably hoping it all catches fire one day and disappears."

I gaped at her. I didn't understand anything she said. Not one word.

"That's it." She waved her hand. "Go. And you didn't hear this from me, y'hear? Lord knows I love my job, but I got both morals *and* opinions."

"Um." I needed to say something. "Me too?"

"That's right." She nodded sharply. "We don't need to cover up that shit anymore."

"Uh—"

"Now go." She gave me a glare that felt like a punch. "Get."

I dropped my eyes first and whispered to her quickly. "Thank you for your time, ma'am." I turned and scuttled away.

CHAPTER
TWENTY-SIX

I skipped down the steps, heading towards Romeo. He sat astride his motorcycle, his phone held to his ear. The darkness in his eyes noticeably lightened when he spotted me.

"Okay, thanks," he murmured. "I gotta go." He hung up. "Bella says that all the records of police auctions will be held at—"

"The New York City Municipal Archives," I finished the sentence for him.

"Okay. Let's go. She's just about to land, and she'll meet us there."

"Hold on, cowboy. Not so fast."

He hesitated. "We need to move now, Daphne. I doubt Christopher Jupiter will be as careful with his search of Frankie Two-Coin's old building. He'll know soon that it's not there. He's probably torturing Julian for the information right now."

"Ooh, I hope so." I wriggled my shoulders. "That thought makes me feel all warm and fuzzy. Just hang on." I got out my phone and spoke to it. "Hey, robot phone slave. What is the"—I squinted, trying to remember what the officer had said—"Knapp Commission?"

Romeo frowned, confused, but stayed silent as we both listened to the answer.

"Ahhh," I sighed. "That makes sense."

"No, it doesn't." Romeo shook his head. "What does a panel investigating police corruption in the seventies have anything to do with this?"

"Well, the lady at the front desk was stunningly forthcoming with information." I smiled brightly. "She barked a whole lot of information at me, and to be honest, I didn't understand any of it. But she was talking about corruption. Some of the proceeds of the police auctions back then were obviously funneled straight into the top brass's pockets. Frankie Two-Coins' estate was sold to cover his restitution fines, and that's a damned big estate, even before you factor in a giant, fist-sized ruby of exceptional clarity. If it was sold, it would be worth hundreds of millions of dollars. I'm assuming whoever bought it wanted it kept quiet, and there would have been kickbacks..."

Romeo nodded, understanding. "So we dig into the Municipal files to find what corrupt asshole got the ruby."

"That's the thing. The officer told me that a lot of the records before the Knapp Commission are kept in a non-government document storage facility in the Bronx. I'm guessing the current police commissioner doesn't want a corruption scandal erupting in the press, but he doesn't want to be a bad guy and destroy the records in case it comes back to bite him in the ass later. Covering up past police corruption is very bad for public relations."

Romeo stared at me for a second—brow furrowed, mouth slightly open. He shook his head. "Daphne." He seemed lost for words.

"Whatever moment you're having right now, Romeo, it has to wait." I tapped on my phone, searching for storage facilities in the Bronx.

"Just when I think you couldn't possibly get any more incredible than you already are..." he murmured.

I held up my finger. There were only two storage facilities in the Bronx that weren't self-storage facilities. If the commissioner had a guilty conscience, he would have put the records in a secure place, not somewhere people wandered around day and night but somewhere they could be stored for a decade or so, until he retired, and those secrets weren't his problem anymore.

And the fewer hands that went on these documents, the better. I found a specialist document storage facility, looked up, and grinned. "Got it. Let's go."

CHAPTER
TWENTY-SEVEN

Romeo gave me a charm to keep warm when we got to the storage facility. "Brace yourself," he said, pulling me into a dark doorway and giving me another crooked smile. I activated the charm, and he tugged me into the shadows.

It was lucky I'd taken a few moments to browse the business's website, or else I would have been seriously confused. The facility was one big climate-controlled warehouse lined with floor-to ceiling shelves, each one packed with boxes. The silence was intense.

I shivered. The whole place had an eerie, dead, labyrinth-like effect. And, apart from the faint red glow of motion-detectors and pest control devices, it was in almost complete darkness.

I wandered down an almost pitch-black aisle, peering at the boxes. None of them had any letters on them, just numbers. "I feel like I'm in some sort of department of government mysteries or something."

"We are." Romeo activated a glow charm on his

palm. "I bet there's far dirtier secrets in these boxes than the one we're looking for."

I tilted my head back, staring up at the illuminated boxes. They reached all the way to the ceiling. Some sections were bare and stood out like missing teeth on a giant monster. "There's millions of them."

"Yeah." Romeo let out a rough sigh.

"No identifying names. Just numbers."

"It would be deliberate, for security purposes." He poked a box with his finger. "We'd have to hack into their systems to find what numbers the Brooklyn P.D. were assigned. I think Bella would—"

I cut him off. "Let's just start looking for now." Pulling the box nearest me off the shelf, I lifted the lid and peered inside. "The boxes that were packed at the same time smell the same." I waved my hand at the row in front of me. "This whole section belongs to..." I looked at the document. "A law firm in Flushing." I scanned the paper. "Looks like Bernie is getting grandma's house in the will."

He glanced at me. "Where should I start?"

"These boxes, from the fifth one along," I said, pointing. "Then check one on the next row, one up from there, then move to the next aisle."

We began searching, row by row, aisle by aisle. Romeo carefully levitated some of the boxes on higher shelves down so we could check them, mindful of motion sensors brushing the ground to check for hungry rats gnawing on the documents rather than two preternatural busybodies like me and Romeo.

"Huh. This lot of boxes are old Department of Human

Services files," Romeo muttered, quickly scanning a document that had yellowed with age. "I suppose they're here for the same reason." His tone turned dark. "No system is perfect, but the system I grew up in left a lot to be desired."

"I know." I gave him a soft smile. "It's why I wanted to be a social worker. I wanted to make things better."

He gazed at the box, a deep sadness in his eyes. "I wish you could work in the human department. They need more good people there. The Otherworld CPS is so much smaller, and we've got supe leaders who are responsible for the kids of their species."

"Responsible, yes," I said. "Kind? *Definitely* not. That's Asherah, Zofia, Alexei and Lennox you're talking about, there."

"Hmm. Good point." He floated another box down to check. "I suppose I'm biased. My whole life changed for the better when I got shifted from the normie system to the Otherworld system."

I smiled. "You mean your life changed when you met Aunt Marche."

He glowered at the floor for a second. "I suppose that's true. I still haven't forgiven her, though. I'm still *so* angry at her." His fists clenched. "I don't know why, but it feels almost impossible to let go of."

I decided to give him the safest response. "She lied to you, Romeo. She betrayed your trust, and she left this world before she could make it up to you. I don't blame you for being angry at her."

He stared at a document moodily and slammed the lid back on.

Gently, now, my brain cautioned.

I've got this. "She told you she needed your help to do a spell to cure her cancer. And instead, she had you perform a spell that killed her. Did she have good reasons to do it? Yes, she did. She didn't want to keep living, and she wanted the transfer of power to you to be seamless and unquestionable. You don't have to forgive her right now," I said gently. "But you should try to do it soon, just for your own sake."

"I want to." His voice was gruff. "I really do. It's like a weight that I can't seem to get rid of. I still hate her so much."

I let the silence fall between us for a moment. "I understand." Time to switch topics. "And, for what it's worth, it sounds like it was more that your life changed once you all got out of that horrible group house. Bella's life changed for the better when she moved up to Vermont, didn't it?"

"Yeah. Well, not at first," he amended, rummaging around an almost-empty box. "She had a really rough time to start with. She was like a cornered stray cat, spitting and hissing. Her emails and messages broke my heart." He furrowed his brow. "But she got better. I think, like me, she finally understood that her strict foster parents had her best interests at heart. It also helped that they indulged her in her passion for relics and artifacts—not knowing they were magical, of course. They were older, both university professors, and they were into archeology." He hitched his massive shoulders in a shrug. "It was probably the bonding opportunity they needed.

They funded her education all the way through to her doctorate."

"Are they still close?"

He frowned. "I don't know. They're normies—they have no idea what her real day job is. So there's probably not much she can share with them. It's hard for her as an Orbiter."

I buried my head in between a row, trying to get my hands on a solitary box just out of reach in the middle of the shelf. "I feel so bad for her," I whispered. "Whatever happened to make her an Orbiter must have been awful. You said her mom was a sex worker. Are you sure she wasn't a witch?"

"Yeah." Romeo waved his hand, and the box shifted a few inches towards me. I grabbed it. "At first I assumed she must have been, since Bella seemed to instinctively know the basics of witchcraft from a really young age. But Bell had all her mom's details from an early age, because she was murdered. Her mom was an illegal migrant—a runaway from Yugoslavia who came here on a tourist visa and never left. I, uh, looked through Marche's records once I became High Priest, and I couldn't find any mention of Bella's mom, and the Otherworld authorities weren't called to the crime scene when she was murdered, so there were no supes involved in her death. Her mom was definitely not a witch, and the person who murdered her wasn't either." His tone softened. "I always thought Bella would have made a great witch. She's got so much potential."

"What about her dad? Bella never looked for her real dad?"

He raised his eyebrows. "Yeah, she did, and she found him, too. He was one of her mom's clients. I don't know if he was a supe or not. All she said was that he was a useless piece of shit, and not worth knowing." He grimaced. "I actually get the feeling that she killed him, but she will neither confirm nor deny that."

"Whoa. Really? She killed her own dad?" Romeo gave me a knowing look, and my cheeks warmed. "Yeah, yeah, I get it," I said, a little embarrassed. "People in glass houses shouldn't throw stones."

I'd killed my own mother. I actually might have killed my father, too. I didn't know who he was, but he was an Ironclaw wolf, and I killed a lot of Ironclaw wolves that day. "I suppose I shouldn't be judgmental," I added grudgingly.

He gave a low chuckle. "Daphne, you stabbed that goblin dad last week. You know, the one who wasn't feeding—"

"Hey," I interrupted. "*Technically*, that was Dwayne, and I was just trying to make the claw marks less ragged so they'd heal together more cleanly."

"Okay. Sure. Whatever you say."

On the next aisle, all the boxes belonged to an accountancy firm, so we moved to the next one. I got Romeo to lift down a few boxes for me so he could move to the next aisle just to speed things up. The urgency started to grate on me. We weren't getting through this place as quickly as I would have liked.

I shuffled another box off the shelf, opened the lid, peered inside, and got chills. "I think we've got something." The first file had a police badge stamp on it.

Romeo stalked back towards me. "Which boxes?"

"From that one," I said, pointing at one still on the shelf. "To the end of this row, and then the whole row below it. They all smell the same, so it's a safe assumption that they were all packed on the same day, by the same people."

He shook out his hands, then muttered under his breath. Power surged off his fingertips. Carefully, he lowered all the boxes I'd pointed out down to the floor and counted them. "Thirty-eight boxes."

I pushed one over to him. "Get to it, Lord of Shadows."

"I hate that nickname," he muttered, crouching next to me. He opened a box and flicked quickly through the files inside.

"I thought it was an honorific," I said, flicking through some papers. "Like a royal title or something."

"Hell no. Some gossip magazines came up with it. If I had my way, they'd never mention it again. It was hard enough getting the press to stop calling me Romeo Jupiter." He blew out an exasperated breath. "It's such an asshole name."

"Yeah, it is." I chuckled. "Where does Zarayan come from, anyway?"

It took him a second to answer. "My mom chose it for me. She died as a Jane Doe. The last thing she said to the person who found her dying on the sidewalk outside the Jupiter mansion was that she wanted me to be called Romeo Zarayan. The hospital followed her wishes, and I kept it."

I made sure my tone was gentle. "Do you think it was your father's last name?"

"No." He glanced at me. "I wouldn't have kept it if I thought that. I checked. There's no wizard by that name in any of the coven records."

That was because Romeo's father wasn't a witch. On some level, he knew that. Romeo's power was off the charts—he could do things that were unheard of in witch circles.

It was fae magic. Not just standard fae but high royal fae, I was sure. It was wild, unpredictable, and volatile. Trauma and magic had something in common—they made it easy to forget certain things.

We should tell him.

Agreed. But not now. He's got enough on his plate. We all do.

"I thought about changing it at one stage," he said, opening up another box. "Bella changed hers when she finally accepted her new foster parents. But my mom wanted me to be called Zarayan. She specifically didn't want me to identify as a Jupiter."

"I don't blame her." My hands suddenly tightened around a very old manilla folder. "I think I've got something." I held up the folder. "It's an evidence log from Brooklyn P.D., nineteen sixty-four. These are their old files."

But he wasn't looking. He'd gone very still, his eyes darting left and right through the gap in the aisle. "There's someone here."

CHAPTER
TWENTY-EIGHT

I blinked. "Security?"

"No, I took care of that. No human is stepping foot in here." He took out a black pouch from his pocket. "Stay quiet," he breathed out. "I'll go see." Moving backwards, Romeo let the darkness swallow him, and he disappeared.

Shit. We'd just found the boxes. Quickly, I assessed them, lifting the lids and checking the first few folders stacked inside. Out of over thirty boxes, there were five that held folders stamped with Brooklyn P.D. stamps. Could I carry five boxes out of here?

We could, but the documents we needed might not be in these five boxes. I ground my teeth, lifted a stack of folders out of the first box, and started quickly flicking through them. Incident reports, confiscated item logs, a thick folder of complaints...

A male voice shouted in the distance. I flinched. A flare of blazing red light sparked, and the voice shouted again.

Russian. He shouted in Russian.

I bounced to my feet, snuffing out the lumination charm Romeo had left me. Even with my wolfy eyesight, I couldn't see through the labyrinth of shelves. "Romeo?"

A huge body ghosted in beside me, and I melted into him immediately. "It's Christopher and his mages," he whispered. "We need to get out of here. Come on."

I pulled my hand out of his grip. "Not without the auction report. It's in here somewhere," I said, gesturing at the five boxes at my feet.

His eyes flicked over the boxes and hardened. "I can't carry all of them through the shadows. We need to leave them behind." He reached for my hand again. "Let's go."

"I'm not leaving," I said stubbornly. "Let's fight him!"

"There's more than four mages with him." The muscle in his jaw clenched. "He's found reinforcements here in New York, probably more distant family members to work as hired magical muscle. There's at least ten volkhv out there."

"Then the odds are still in our favor." I shrugged. I was only faking my confidence. I had a wild impulse for violence right now, and I knew it was a fear response. When I was scared and backed into a corner, the only thing to do was fight. "Let's go." I turned and began to walk down the aisle—

Romeo pulled me backwards. "I'm not messing around, Daphne," he growled. "We need to leave."

"If we do, Christopher will find the files, and he'll get the Tear of Zeus before us." I faced him and set my jaw stubbornly. "I'm not running away, Romeo."

He glared down at me. Just then, I noticed the fear in his eyes.

Romeo would never run from Christopher Jupiter. He wouldn't shy away from a fight with a dozen Russian wizards—volkhv. This was about me. It was something to do with the gap in my memory. He knew what I was capable of, and right now, he was scared for me.

The atoms in the air around him started to vibrate. Romeo's eyes blazed silver in the darkness, and he growled. "Daphne..."

"Ooh, scary," I said, keeping my voice light. "Tell you what, if you're that worried about me, let me stay here and find the file. You can hold them off, can't you? Or is ten volkhv too much for you?"

Manipulative, my brain sniggered. *That's not like you, Heart, but I like it. He's itching to punch someone just as much as we are.*

Romeo stared at me for another long moment, then let out a soft snarl. "Fine." He slung a thin gold chain with a protective charm around my neck, stepped back, and raised his hands, palms up, in a classic mage pose. Sparks of blazing ultraviolet magic began to swirl off his fingertips. He glared down at me, his expression thunderous. "Stay right here and find the file. I'll hold them off." He stepped back, and the shadows swallowed him.

CHAPTER
TWENTY-NINE

Shouts and screams echoed around the warehouse. Scarlet spells and blazing violet curses lit up the darkness, flashing, searing, then disappearing. Mages cursed in Russian and bellowed in the universal language of pain. The smell of burned flesh turned the air acrid.

Every now and then, Romeo ghosted into view, giving updates. "Christopher is in a hard ward at the entrance with one of his goons, trying to work a location spell," he ground out. "I can't hit him."

"Christopher and his damned wards," I muttered, flicking through a thick sheath of papers.

"I'm doing my best to distract him."

The file I held looked like an auction results report. I scanned the paper inside quickly. "Item, start bid, winning bid, name of buyer... Romeo." I glanced up at him. "I think this is it—"

A faint scent hit my nose, and my words died in my

throat. I turned, trying to confirm what my senses screamed at me.

"What is it?"

"I can smell Levi and Micah." I inhaled deeply again. "Bella, too." Her scent was a confusing cacophony because of the many magical artifacts she carried. "They're here, Romeo."

His head whipped towards the exit. "Good." The darkness pulled him away again.

I desperately shuffled through the box between my legs, pulling out each folder. The folders weren't stored in chronological order; someone had jammed them in the box carelessly. I could just pick up the box and—

No, I had to be sure. I still had three boxes left to check. I opened the folders and started to read frantically.

A scent bloomed closer. I checked it and stiffened a little, before forcing my shoulders to relax.

Bella was headed this way. I kept flicking through the documents. Auction results, October, nineteen sixty-five. Auction Results, November, nineteen sixty-eight. Come on... come on...

A flash lit up the back of the warehouse behind me, and a male voice screamed in agony. The mages were getting closer now. Christopher was at the entrance to the warehouse, but he'd sent his goons down the aisles on both sides. Eventually, they'd circle around and find me.

"Daphne!" Bella bolted towards me down the aisle, rearing out of the darkness. "There you are." She slid elegantly to a stop and held out her hand. "Come on, we've got to get you out of here."

I didn't even look up. "No chance, sorry, Bella." The next file in the box was dated nineteen sixty-nine; my fingers clutched it desperately. Was this it? I scanned the first page, looking for anything to indicate the auction was Frankie Two-Coins' seized property. Would it even mention his name?

I didn't see any names on the other auction reports. There was no point looking for any mention of Francesco Moretti.

"Daphne, come on!" Bella waved her hand in front of my face. A tiny petty part of me noticed she was wearing black leather pants and a skin-tight black ballistics shirt under a Kevlar vest shaped to look like a corset. She looked sexy as hell—a total badass. "You're in danger, honey. We gotta go!"

"I'm good," I replied shortly, running my eyes down the item columns. The police auction items were insane—cars, antiques, and classic motorcycles that made my heart thud painfully. Every time I caught a mention of jewelry, I concentrated harder. The documents were handwritten and barely legible.

Bella wasn't leaving. She reached down and took my hand impatiently; I shook her off. She let out an exasperated, frustrated noise. "I'm trying to help you, Daphne! We're surrounded by mages." Her voice grew strained. "Christopher Jupiter is here. We really need to go."

"I get that, Bella," I said, not taking my eyes off the paper. "And I don't mean to be rude, but I'm a little busy here."

"Daphne..." I could hear her inhaling loudly through her nose. I glanced up and saw her chest rise and fall rapidly. "Now."

"No."

Bella's voice took on a hard edge. "Girlfriend, I'm sorry, but I have to insist." She stared down at me. "Believe me, you don't know how serious this situation is. I don't want to scare you, but it's to do with the memory we took from you."

My confidence wobbled for a second. There was a huge blank space in my memory...

Nope. My brain flicked me in the sinuses, making me flinch. *We're not doing this again. No hesitation, no regrets, no doubts, and we trust ourselves. We trust Romeo, too. He left us to fight. He knows how important it is that we find the Tear.*

Right.

I gave Bella a reassuring smile. "It's okay. I'm almost done. I appreciate that you want to protect me, but you don't have to." *Besides, bitch, we would never need you to protect us. We could end your life twelve ways before you could even blink.* My smile wavered. I swallowed and decided to redirect her the same way I'd done with Romeo. "You can go fight with the guys, if you want. I know you're itching to get in there."

Bella hesitated for only a second, then shook her head. "No chance. You're too important, and they're all idiots. I need to get you somewhere safe." She thrust her hand down and snapped her fingers at me. "Come on."

Okay, we're going to have to be more direct to get rid of her. Do it quick before I cut off her snappy little fingers.

I dropped my eyes back to the paper in front of me, dismissing her. "I'm a werewolf, Bella," I said coldly. "I can handle myself. Go." I looked up and gave her the hardest stare I could summon. "Go. Help the others."

Her jaw clenched, and a flash of anger sparked in her eyes. Bombshell Bella clearly wasn't used to hearing the word no. "Romeo will kill us if anything happens to you."

"You better go get rid of the mages who are trying to kill us, then," I sang, scanning the next page. Was I reading this right? Did the Brooklyn P.D. auction off someone's pet cheetah?

Yep, it was a cheetah. The fool who bought it also won the auction for the gold-plated cheetah enclosure.

After hesitating for another moment, Bella let out a snarl. "Fine. I'll guard the end of this aisle." She dropped a silver charm the size of a matchbox in my lap. "Crush that in your fist if you get captured, okay?" Whirling around, she raced down the aisle.

I gave it a tentative sniff. It was a knock-out charm. It was potent—it wouldn't just knock out whoever grabbed me, it would render me unconscious, too. I carefully put the little box on the ground and poked it under the shelf beside me. I would not be activating any of Bella's artifacts anytime soon.

CHAPTER
THIRTY

The fight raged on. Every now and then, through the gaps in the boxes on the shelves, I caught a glimpse of bodies moving in the darkness, flying down the aisles on either side of me. Once, I watched Bella fight hand-to-hand with a black-cloaked, hooded volkhv, whirling her haladie in her hand, slashing at his arms and ducking as he tried to fling curses at her.

She was damned good. I had to work hard not to get sidetracked by the scalding burn of jealousy that reared up within me and just concentrate on the box of papers.

July nineteen sixty-nine was a big month for auctions—there were hundreds of items listed. Desperately, I scanned the pages.

Bella let out a piercing scream. I flinched. Immediately, Romeo's deep voice rolled through the warehouse. "Bella!"

Just keep looking, my brain wound back a kick. *Focus.*

I exhaled shakily and kept reading. A collection of high heels, twelve leisure tracksuits...

"Rome..." Bella's voice moaned. "I'm hit." She was two aisles away, but I could hear and smell them both as clear as if they were right in front of me.

"It's okay, Bell." Romeo's voice was shaky. "It's okay. I've got you. I've got you."

"Goddamnit, it hurts." Fabric ripped, and she inhaled sharply. The sudden waft of rotting flesh made me nauseous. "Don't leave me, Rome," she whimpered. "Please."

"Never. I'll never leave you." The passion in his words made my gut twist.

I clenched my jaw and kept reading. An antique Louis XIV table, a six-foot rope of pearls, an Edwardian snuffbox... A minute passed, then another.

"It was a rot-curse," he muttered. "It's okay; I've stopped it and cleared it. Drink this."

"Oh, that's better. Thanks." She sighed.

"It shouldn't scar. You'll have a big scab on your calf muscle for a week, though."

"Jesus, is that all?" She huffed out a bark of laughter. "I thought I was going to die."

His tone darkened. "You would have if we hadn't stopped the curse in time."

Bella took a deep breath in and let out a long, quivering sigh. "God, I'm so glad I've got you, Rome. I love you so much."

His voice turned gruff. "I love you too, Bell. Now." I heard him get up off the floor. "Are you ready to go kick some ass?"

"Of course."

It was a moment before I could concentrate on the file again.

CHAPTER
THIRTY-ONE

Further down the page, the script turned sloppy. It was harder to make out the words. I clenched my teeth. To make things worse, I could hear Christopher Jupiter shouting orders at his goons. He screamed in Russian, which I didn't understand, but the urgency in his tone set my teeth on edge.

He knows where we are.

Curses and spells zipped through the air, lighting up the warehouse. I held the paper almost to my nose, trying to decipher the words. The auction, held on a Saturday in April, had some expensive stuff. I struggled to make out the items. An antique silver cigarette holder. A Louis XIV armoire. A small pouch of uncut diamonds.

Suddenly, a huge man wrapped in a black cloak charged up the aisle towards me, brandishing a black flame on his palm—eyes wide, teeth bared, coming almost out of nowhere. Taken off-guard, I lurched to my feet and fumbled with my blade.

Just then, a blazing white figure flew in from above

me, crash-landing right in the volkhv's face. The volkhv went flying backwards.

My heart skipped a beat. Dwayne? Where the hell did he come from?

My beautiful goose Alpha stood on the man's chest, and, with a strange, tired, morose movement, he dropped his neck, headbutting the volkhv right between the eyes. The sound it made when the skull cracked made me shiver. Blood bubbled up and poured down the man's face, pooling on the ground beneath him.

Dwayne sighed sadly and turned to face me.

Hey, baby girl. Just thought I'd check in on you. He slumped his neck over, still depressed, and stomped up the aisle towards me, his beautiful white feathers backlit by neon curses streaking through the air behind him.

"This isn't a great time, sir," I said shakily, using my finger to follow the line of auction items. My heart was thudding out of control. The answer was here; I knew it. "Or, it is a great time, if you want to go help the guys. We're under attack, here."

Dwayne made no move to run away, instead, he squatted beside me. **Yeah, right, sure. Okay. Gotta confess something first, though. It's been eating at me.**

My fingers clutched the paper I was holding, crumpling it. "Myf? Dwayne, please tell me Myf is okay?"

No, it's not her. He pursed his lips, always an impressive feat considering it was a rock-hard beak. **That winged ginger bitch is doing just fine. The**

countess has moved her into her closet and keeps topping up her Stanley cup with long island iced tea.

I moaned again. "Am I the only adult here? For the love of all that's holy, Dwayne, she's *seventeen*."

She's a moody flying cow, that's what she is, he grumbled. **Anyway, I'm not here to talk about her. I've got a confession to make.**

I closed my eyes, hunched over the page I was holding, and groaned. "Dwayne, please. Can it wait? In case you haven't noticed, we're in a magical firefight with a bunch of evil mages. And I'm trying to find something important, or else Christopher Jupiter might summon Zeus to earth to wreak havoc and destruction on all mankind!"

Nah.

"What do you mean, nah?" My voice rose several more octaves.

That fucker won't come here. Dwayne made a face. **Not after what happened in Crete.**

"Oh, dear gods. Do I even want to know?"

Probably not. He shrugged idly. **But it involves twelve serving maidens, a vat of warm butter, and a fistfight with a donkey. My point is; this realm isn't big enough for the two of us. Zeus won't show his smug ugly mug on earth. Not while I'm here.**

That's what I figured, too. Zeus didn't like sharing the spotlight, and nowadays there were too many powerful creatures that could be considered gods here. Our realm was a lot closer to Faerie now, and the chance that the Morrigan or Oonagh might show up at any point was enough to keep Zeus away. It didn't mean that

Christopher wasn't going to summon one of the other asshole Greek gods, though.

I forced my eyes back to the paper. "This realm can't deal with two horny pansexual egomaniac gods at the same time, I suppose. Now, please, Dwayne, I'm begging you. I have to concentrate." A loud bang a few aisles over made me jump; the scream that followed it sent a jolt down my spine. "Can this wait?"

No, it can't wait. I feel... He squirmed. **Guilty. I don't like it.**

"Why do you feel guilty?" I held the page closer. A jeweled chalice. Fifty bottles of vintage champagne. A Monet painting of some water lilies.

Dwayne extended his foot and dragged a claw in a puddle of blood, making little circles. **I might have fucked up.**

I glanced up from the paper and narrowed my eyes. "Why?"

He wouldn't meet my gaze. It took him a second to answer. **Asherah wanted me to come with her. To Faerie. To meet her mom.**

Oh, crap. My pulse quickened. "Dwayne..."

Lemmie finish, little one. Anyway, I told her that — Suddenly, he lunged past me, shooting like a white arrow. I turned just in time to see him stab a big, black-bearded man with his beak, right in the heart. An acrid curse smoldered in the mages hand, burning through his own flesh.

Christopher Jupiter's goon had snuck up on me. I needed to find this damned auction report, and I needed to find it *now*.

Dwayne unstuck his beak and stabbed again, then ripped the mage's lower belly with his clawed feet. He removed his head from the man's chest cavity with a sharp pop, pulling out his still-beating heart. Tossing his head, the heart soared like a blood-splattered comet through the air. The mage collapsed behind me, falling onto a pile of boxes.

I arched my eyebrow. "You're lucky I already checked those ones."

Anyway, as I was saying... Dwayne wiped the blood off his face with his wing and spat a few times. **Asherah invited me home to meet her mom, but I respectfully declined. I told her I had other responsibilities and had to stay close to home.** Dwayne dropped his head and casually made doodles in the blood with his claws again. **She was kinda mad.**

"Mad, as in angry? Or mad, as in batshit crazy?"

Uh. He shrugged. **Both?**

She was batshit crazy in the first place. Overpowered, impulsive, insane... I swallowed roughly. "Dwayne. Did you tell her it was because of me?"

I might have.

I pinched my eyes closed. "You told her you had to stay here and watch your 'wayward ward' didn't you?"

He lowered his head. **Mayyybe.**

"Dwayne!"

I wasn't lying, little one. You're my ward, and I'm your alpha, so I should stay here and watch you.

"You're *not* watching me! The man who tortured me is at the other end of this warehouse, trying to find the document we need to track down this damn Tear of

Zeus. I'm literally surrounded by volkhv who are attempting to kill me!"

Dwayne rolled his eyes. **And I've already taken out two of them. You *could* show a little gratitude, baby girl.**

I let out a little sob. "You told Asherah that you're choosing me over her. This is great. Just *great.*"

Well, I had to tell her something. I didn't want to go. He shrugged. **Honestly, it's mostly because I hate Faerie. Too much glitter, and I'm not fond of their beer. Anyway, she was... cross.**

"Cross?" My voice moved through five octaves in the one syllable. "She was *cross?*"

I might be understating that. He cleared his throat awkwardly. **She might have burned down a building or two. She's a wild woman,** he added, shaking his head in admiration.

"And now she's mad at *me.*" This was the worst possible thing that could happen, not just now, but ever. Asherah was jealous of women Dwayne hadn't even looked at. "This is just great. Now I have an incredibly powerful and terrible fae princess gunning for me. It's *just* what I needed."

Dwayne made a show of looking around the room. **I know this might be rubbing salt in the wounds, but you're not exactly living the soft life right now, sweetheart.**

"That's not the point, Dwayne!"

He gave a little goosey shrug. **You know, Ebadorathea was right. I actually do feel better now that**

I've told you. I feel quite energized. He nodded thoughtfully. **Guilt really does weigh you down, huh?**

I'd have to deal with that crisis later. I locked my teeth and ground out my reply. "I haven't forgiven you yet, sir."

Well, you will. He took a deep breath and honked it out. **Do you want a hand with the Ruski plague out there?**

"Yes, please," I moaned.

He waddled away. There was a lot more spring in his step. For a second, I was so filled with dread, I wondered what the point of it all was. Pain and death were inevitable.

My brain stepped in, muscling out the anxiety before it drowned me. *One thing at a time, babes. Besides, we can take Asherah.*

"No, we can't!" Panic made me shout out loud. "She's the most powerful and batshit crazy creature we've met in decades!"

Relax. Focus. Read the paper.

"I barely know what half this stuff is!" I wailed. "What the hell is a Modigliani?"

Stop whining. He's an artist. We know this. You're panicking and not thinking properly.

"And a paste broach?" I peered at the paper. "What the hell is a paste broach?"

Whatever it is, it only sold for three dollars. And it's sandwiched between some expensive shit, she noted. *Look it up.*

I did as my brain directed, scrolling through the results on my phone. "A paste stone is a fake gemstone made of glass." I glanced at the paper again. "It says red. Five inches."

A chime went off in my head. *Ding ding, baby.*

I let out a soft gasp. "No. No, it can't be."

But it was. It was right there in between a painting that sold for eight thousand dollars and a "fancy" jeweled egg that had the buyer's name left blank in the winner column.

"They didn't know." My lips felt numb. "They didn't know what it was. That's why it hasn't shown up in public again. It was so big, they assumed it was fake!"

I blew out an incredulous breath and scanned the rest of the items. "The corrupt fatcats got distracted by Frankie Two-Coin's Faberge egg but left the Tear of Zeus, figuring that something that big must be fake. It's listed as a five-inch red paste broach with a gold-plated setting. They had no idea what it was!

Who bought it?

"They sold it to—" I checked the buyer column. "Someone called Veronica Sterlington-Hyde. It's not a common name. We should be able to trace it." Further down, I noticed two more similar names. Bernie Sterlington-Hyde, who bought two cases of vintage champagne, and Dorothy Sterlington-Hyde, who paid two thousand dollars for a diamond necklace. But Veronica only spent three dollars and bagged herself a Stella Ostium. "This is it. We've found it."

Girl, hold your horses. Brain-Daphne was suddenly distracted. *It's gone real quiet around here.*

I stilled. It had. The periodic flashes of light and fight sounds had stopped. Carefully, I reached out with my senses. The heavy tang of damp herbs and acrid burned wood—the smell of the Volkhv—had dissipated a little. "Have they gone?"

I think so. My brain bared her teeth. *That's suspicious.*

Whatever dark thoughts occurred to me after that were blasted away in an instant as Romeo strode out of the darkness beside me. "Romeo." I leapt to my feet. "Are you okay?"

He nodded, his expression grim but triumphant. He reached out and pulled me to his hard chest, wrapping his arms around me. "They're gone. We killed most of them; there's only two of his goons left alive." His tone turned bitter. "Jupiter got away, though. His ward turned opaque, and when I finally got through the mages to take it down, he'd disappeared."

I allowed myself to melt against him for a moment, then wiggled one arm out from where it was sandwiched between us and quickly typed the name I'd found into my search engine.

To my surprise, I got a hit right away. "Veronica Sterlington-Hyde, born June 20, nineteen sixty-one." A huff of laughter left my lips. "She was only eight years old. She was there with her parents."

He frowned down at me. "Who?"

"The girl who bought the Tear of Zeus."

CHAPTER
THIRTY-TWO

Veronica Sterlington-Hyde was certainly a woman with a strong personality. Or, as Brain-Daphne so eloquently put it, she was a stuck-up, self-absorbed nightmare of a woman with absolutely zero self-awareness.

The only good thing about her was she was easy to find. "Why, hel*lo*, darling," she cooed when she spotted Romeo on the ground floor of her three-level gallery-cum-loft building in SoHo.

Ms. Sterlington-Hyde—sculptor, artist, philanthropist, and socialite—drifted down the steel staircase in a shockingly flamboyant outfit—a neon pink and purple striped leisure suit embellished by dozens of gold and diamond-encrusted chains and even more stacked rings. She tossed back her icy-white Cleopatra bob, draped herself over the banister, and smoldered at Romeo, batting her heavily lined eyelids.

"I recognize you." Her lips curled into a pouty smirk. "You're Romeo Zarayan, the Jupiter heir, aren't you? We shared column space in Town Topics magazine a few months ago, did you know that?" She winked suggestively. "You were *right* on top of me."

Veronica Sterlington-Hyde ignored me completely. It was almost impressive how laser focused she was with her attention. She had Romeo in her sights, and nothing was going to distract her. To give her credit, she ignored Bella, too, but then again Bella wasn't holding hands with Romeo right now, and I was.

Bella drifted through the semi-public ground floor gallery, checking exits, noting potential threats, and assessing the other people in the space. A small crowd gathered in groups in between odd, twisted metal-and-ostrich feather structures, murmuring to each other, stroking their chins, and nodding thoughtfully. None of them appeared to be a threat at all. One hipster-looking couple were even huddled around the fire extinguisher mounted in the corner, making oooh noises.

There was security, though. A tall Asian man with tattoos on his neck, calluses on his knuckles, and a *try me, I dare you* expression lingered at the door. His eyes followed Bella as she stalked through the room, recognizing her predatory grace, calculating how much of a threat she might be.

He barely glanced my way. I tried not to let it bother me.

As we suspected, all the people in here were normies, so if a fight broke out, we couldn't use magic in front of them. For that reason, we left Levi and Micah in the car outside. Micah still struggled with the daylight, and Levi was recovering from a minor injury from the warehouse fight, so neither of them would be able to help us much right now, anyway.

"So, Romeo Zarayan," Veronica Sterlington-Hyde cooed. "Whatever are you doing in my humble little abode?"

I let go of Romeo's hand immediately and mumbled so only he could hear me. "I think you need to take this one, baby."

He let out a pained grunt and glared down at me for a second, before turning to face Veronica Sterlington-Hyde again. "Hello."

I stifled my grin and backed away. Veronica floated down the last few steps and struck a pose on the polished concrete floor. "A man of few words, I see." She licked her lips. "I like it."

Romeo did not like it.

"So, my darling boy," she cooed, waving her arm dramatically. "Are you in town to view some spectacular artwork? Do you like anything you see?"

"Perhaps," he managed.

A skinny man wearing nothing but black leather trousers and a top hat stalked by, holding a tray. He brandished it in front of Veronica, and she swiped the bottle off it. "Champagne, darling? It's after five in Australia, you know." She gave a little laugh. "But I can add some orange juice and make a mimosa if you haven't had breakfast yet."

"No thank you, ma'am." Romeo's expression grew even more stony.

Bella stalked behind us, having completed her security check. She'd swapped her leather pants and ballistics vest for black jeans and an expensive figure-hugging cashmere sweater, but she still radiated menace.

Veronica puffed up her lips again and narrowed her eyes until all I could see was heavy black eyeliner. "Well then, my dark prince, what is it that I can do for you today?"

My brain made some gagging noises. *Okay, I've had about as much as I can take. Go and help him.*

I stepped forward and weaved my arm through his, taking his hand again. "Romeo is looking for something extraordinary," I said, smiling at her brightly. "A statement piece for the entrance hall of his main abode."

"Aha, yes! The church!" Veronica sighed dramatically, still not even looking at me. "I did read about it in Architectural Digest. But from what I understand, you refused to grant the photographer admission so they could only speculate as to what you did with the inside. I understand, of course," she said, sidling up and sandwiching herself against him on the other side of me. "I, too, value my privacy."

The woman lived here. In her art gallery. Her whole life was public.

"I would love to take a look inside that beautiful gothic structure," she continued.

My smile wavered, but I soldiered on. "He *is* after something flamboyant, something huge, outrageous and dramatic. I'm wondering if you have anything like that available for purchase, ma'am."

"Perhaps," she simpered up at his scowling face. "Although most of my most dramatic pieces are currently in exhibitions all around the world. And the lowest price point I have for something like that is in the six-figure range."

"That is no problem," Bella murmured, stalking like a panther around a sculpture to our left.

Veronica Sterlington-Hyde finally wrenched her eyes away from Romeo and glanced at her. "Well. Perhaps if you and your girlfriend want to come into my office and take a look at some photos of my work, you can pick something out." To my horror, she took Bella's hand. "Come on, darling." She slid her other arm around Romeo's, weaving it through her own. "Let's go see what we've got for you." Tugging them both, she skipped towards a glass wall behind the stairs.

She thinks Bella's his girlfriend.

I was too pissed to keep my thoughts internal. "I'm not blind. Or deaf," I growled.

Well, to be fair, they match. Same age, same hard expression, same aura of danger and menace and power. You look like a fresh-faced milkmaid, and despite my best efforts, you exude rainbows and sunshine.

"I was literally holding his hand," I ground out.

And now that puffed up, self-absorbed socialite is holding his hand. Bella's, too. They're getting away. Go catch up to them, you fool.

I scampered after the threesome, weaving around the heavy glass door just as it was shutting behind them.

Veronica Sterlington-Hyde walked into her office and tossed herself dramatically into a hot-pink chair behind her desk. "Some of my best work was featured in Peter Minchin's last photography book." She gave a smug smile and picked up a huge coffee table book and waved it at Romeo. "He was showcasing some of the most influential artists of this century. It was very flattering to be included."

"I see." Romeo folded his huge frame into the leopard-print wing chair in front of Veronica's desk. I perched myself on the fuzzy purple ottoman next to it. Bella didn't sit; instead, she lingered by the walls, looking at framed prints of odd sculptures.

Veronica slid the book over the desk. "Take a look. Some of the copper installations will go for almost a million. If you're after a statement piece, it's worth the investment."

"Indeed."

I edged further forward in my seat. We needed to hurry this along. Not only were we still in danger of Christopher finding the Tear before us—for all I knew, he'd captured the police chief responsible for the auction and tortured the information of its whereabouts out of him already—but I was finding it harder and harder to manage my proximity to Bella. Despite me trusting myself and trusting Romeo completely...

My body was still rebelling against me. It was *screaming*. Doubt, fear, anxiety... and, by the gods, it *hurt*. "Do you have anything with huge gemstones?" I asked Veronica. The words came out louder than I meant them to. "The bigger, the better?"

Again, she didn't glance my way. "I have a few things." She turned to her computer and tapped the keyboard with two extended fingers. "I have a thing for gems, as you can see." She wiggled her fingers at Romeo, showing off her gold stacks. "Aha. Here." She swiveled the screen around to show us a misshapen copper ball-like sculpture the size of a small car, imbedded with thousands of brilliant green gemstones. "It's called *Luxe Trypophobia*."

Romeo's expression didn't change. "Lovely."

I leaned forward until I was sitting right at the very edge of the ottoman. "Do you have anything with bigger gems? Mr. Zarayan has been obsessed with oversized gems since he was a child."

Romeo shuddered ever so slightly but didn't even blink at my lie.

"Oh," Veronica sighed, batting her eyelashes at him again. "Me, too, dear boy. Brilliant cut, princess set, the bigger, the better. I was lucky to have indulgent parents, so I amassed quite the collection."

Unlucky that they turned you into a spoiled moron with absolutely zero self-awareness.

I fixed a polite smile on my face. "Really? What was the biggest?"

"The real gems were always my favorite," she sighed. "I have some huge natural citrine. And a lab-grown cubic zirconia the size of a baseball."

"And your favorite piece when you were a kid?" Come on. Come *onnnn*.

"I bought a glass ruby in a faux-gold setting once." She chuckled. "It was my favorite for a long time. It was so clear and so pretty. I swear I felt it vibrate under my fingertips. My mother used to tease me about it, because it was just a paste stone, but..." Veronica took a deep breath and sighed it all out. "I loved that thing so much. There was something magical about it, I swear."

Romeo froze next to me.

Bella stalked behind us and put her hands on the back of Romeo's chair.

Brain-Daphne shoved a vision in front of my mind of me wrapping my fingers around this woman's bloated neck, squeezing, and screaming, *And where the fuck is it?!*

"It sounds lovely," I said politely. "Do you still have it?"

"I used it in a project, actually, years and years ago. A statement piece on the loss of innocence." Veronica blew her thick blonde fringe out of her eyes. "A copper and brass-woven womb-like structure, with the paste ruby on a stalk protruding out of it. The gem represented me finally giving up childish magical things in favor of the harsh brutality of the real world. The finished artwork was visually stunning, if I do say so myself."

Holy guacamole, this spoiled idiot stuck the Tear of Zeus into one of those mangled metal monstrosities. "That actually sounds like the kind of thing we're looking for, ma'am. Where is the piece now? Can we go see it?"

"Well, it's a sentimental piece, a part of my private collection, I'm not sure I can part with it." Her gaze lingered on Romeo's chest for a moment. "But, of course, for the right price..."

"We'd like to see it in person, if we could," I interrupted. I'd had enough of her crap.

She tilted her head, thinking. "Hmm. I loaned it to a friend of mine, a curator with a gallery in a little town upstate. It's called The Ironworks."

"The town is called The Ironworks?"

She rolled her eyes. "No, his gallery is called The Ironworks. The town is called Beacon, just south of Fishkill."

I blinked. "Fishkill?"

Bella murmured softly behind me. "It's a real town. Fishkill originated from the Dutch words for fish and stream. Beacon is real, too." Her voice took a hard edge. "And the Tear of Zeus is there, at an art gallery called The Ironworks."

Thanks for the history lesson and the recap, Lara Croft.

Veronica was still talking. "His gallery is a beautiful space, set on the banks of the Hudson River. I can make a few calls and—"

Romeo was already standing. "It's been a pleasure," he said coldly, his tone totally contradicting his words.

"Wait—"

He grabbed my hand and pulled me out of the office without another word.

CHAPTER
THIRTY-THREE

"Beacon is just ninety minutes north of here," Bella said as we stalked out into the freezing air outside. "I'll drive." She gestured to the giant matt-black Yukon idling at the curb, with Micah, wearing dark glasses and gloves, behind the wheel.

"I wish I could jump us there," Romeo said. "But I might have overdone it today already."

I could tell he had; he was severely magically depleted after the battle with the mages, and less than twelve hours ago, he shadow-jumped across a quarter of the country to get home to me. He was already exhausted. All of us were running on fumes.

"That's why I'm driving." Bella jabbed her finger at the Yukon. "My mech guy is working on my helicopter right now. It was due for servicing ages ago, so we can't take that. It will take us too long to get back to the helipad, anyway, so get in and let's go."

"We'll ride," Romeo said. Levi limped out of the

Yukon and handed him a jacket. He was still injured, too. We were dropping like flies. "It will be faster."

"Yeah." Bella shook her head. "But not by much."

"Yeah, we will be." I gave her a playful grin. "We'll race you." *Let's show her what we can do.*

But Bella was not amused. "I hate to be the grownup here, but it's early afternoon on a Sunday." She turned to Romeo, shrugging on a black puffer jacket that made him look even bigger and more menacing than before. "There's no way you can get away with speeding upstate without drawing attention to yourselves. A cloaking spell will run out in half an hour, and some busybody will call it in. There will be a police chase. There are police helicopters everywhere. Besides"—she gave him a frank look—"I need you with me right now."

I raised my eyebrows.

"Not locked in a police cell," she continued.

Romeo frowned. "Bella, when have I *ever* been arrested?"

"You've almost been arrested many, many times, Romeo Zarayan. And every single time, I've been right beside you, finding a way out of the mess you're about to get yourself into, or just plain old redirecting you from the trouble you seem so hellbent on finding." Bella blew out a worried breath and shook her head. "I just think we need to stick together, that's all." She reached out and grabbed his hand in a breathtakingly casual, intimate gesture that made my stomach hurt.

After a beat, she grabbed mine, too. "All of us. We should stay together. Last time we split up, I found you surrounded by Russian witches in a warehouse, under attack."

My gut lurched. How did she *do* that? How the hell did Bella make me feel like a stupid little kid?

I knew the truth—*all* of it—and the reality was that I'd outsmarted her at every turn. I'd found the right mobster first. I'd manipulated the information on what happened to Frankie Two-Coin's estate out of that asshole Julian. I'd got the officer at the Brooklyn precinct to spill her guts about the true location of the auction result files—which, obviously, was a massive stroke of luck, but I doubted she would have told Badass Bella where they were if she'd asked. I was the one who methodically combed through boxes of files to find the right piece of paper, and I was the one who figured out the Tear of Zeus had been mislabeled as a paste broach.

I'd even found Veronica Sterlington-Hyde, but that wasn't hard. She had a whole website and lived in her gallery. But still.

I'd done *everything*. And I knew the truth. But in Bella's presence, I still felt like a stupid, silly little girl.

While I had my internal mini-tantrum, Romeo bowed his head. "Bell, I just think we should ride. Someone needs to get there as soon as possible," he said softly.

"Yes, we definitely should, which is why you need to get in the car right now." Bella's face suddenly softened. She chewed on her lip for a second, looking uncharacteristically uncertain. The sudden show of vulnerability only made her look more beautiful. "Please, Rome. I've got a bad feeling, that's all. Besides, we need to talk. We need to make contingencies just in case—" Her eyes flicked towards me, and she hesitated.

I stared at her. "What?"

Bella looked away first. "Just in case Christopher Jupiter does get the Tear of Zeus."

"He won't." My body was pushing me in the direction of a total mental breakdown—I felt like vomiting or punching something. "I'm going to make sure of it." I strode over to my Kawasaki and grabbed my helmet.

"Daphne." Romeo moved with me. "Bella's got a point. You can't ride out there too fast; you'll trigger a police chase. We really don't need that right now. I can't use magic in front of the normies, so I can't help you. And we need to find the Tear."

My irritation spiked. Despite everything, I couldn't stop my emotions from bubbling over. I took a breath; it was too shallow. My chest was too tight. I couldn't get enough air in my lungs. "Romeo."

Gods, there were so many words ready to spill out of my mouth, words that sounded crazy, insane, bitter, jealous...

I forced myself to pause, and take a deeper breath, while Brain-Daphne screamed the words for me instead. *That bitch is playing you like a fiddle, you big, sexy, clueless idiot! She's just biding her time, waiting to get her hooks into you, I know it!* Brain-Daphne howled like a dog, trying to release a bit of the pressure for me so I could move past this awful, stabbing pain in my stomach. *The whole protective big sister thing is an act. Bella doesn't like me at all. She hates me, and she's going to stab me in the back— probably literally—the second she thinks she can get away with it. Don't let her do this to us, Romeo! Choose me! Choose meeeee!*

Instead of making the biggest mistake of my life and saying that all out loud, I swallowed the lump in my throat and smiled at him. "You know me, right? You understand me?"

"Come on, Rome," Bella shouted from the curb. "Leave the Ninja. I'll get someone to take it back to my apartment garage. We need to go now! Daphne, let's go!"

I couldn't get into a car with her. Not now. I huffed out another breath, and stared into Romeo's dark gray eyes, watching the storm whirl within them. "Romeo. Do you trust me?"

A crease appeared between his brows. "Yes. Of course."

And we trust ourselves. He'll choose us. I know it.

"I'm taking my bike," I said firmly. "Go with Bella. Keep an eye on her. Make sure she doesn't text and drive, okay?" I chuckled awkwardly. "I'll meet you there. And you don't have to worry, I've been arrested for speeding exactly the same number of times as I've had tiramisu before I met you."

"You'd never had tiramisu before."

"Exactly." I winked, trying to keep the gesture casual, even though I was dying inside. "They're never gonna catch me."

CHAPTER
THIRTY-FOUR

I rode like I was escaping Hell.

In truth, I was. My stomach burned, scalding hot like lava. The speed helped blow away the dark thoughts lingering in my mind. I danced around the hole in my memory—the hole that Bella kept referring to. I had no idea what memory Romeo had taken, but I trusted that he needed to take it to keep me safe. But I knew for certain that something very bad was going to happen if Christopher Jupiter got the Tear of Zeus. And it had something to do with me.

As fast as I rode, I still couldn't escape Bella. Romeo called me the second I pulled away from the curb so he could keep in touch with me the whole way, and now I was treated to the sound of both of them discussing what might happen if Christopher Jupiter got to the Tear first.

This isn't a bad thing. We can make sure she's not talking shit to anyone. Eyes on the prize, babes. We just have to get to this gallery before that asshole Jupiter.

I weaved through the traffic in the city, abiding the traffic laws as best I could—which, to be frank, wasn't much—and listened as Romeo informed Bella I was on speaker.

Bella exhaled roughly. "Okay, game plan." I heard her switch on her blinker and the roar of the Yukon. She was pushing hard, just like I was. "If Christopher summons a god, what might his powers be?"

"Like Daphne said, it would take a month for the god to settle in his body. After that, I don't know. Daphne?"

I weaved around two yellow cabs. "He'd take on the characteristic powers of that deity. Remember, I doubt he'd have any luck summoning any of the heavy hitters, but he might be able to call a minor demigod or a magical figure from that realm. So, if it's Morpheus, he'll control sleep and dreams. If it's Charon, he'll know how to steer a ferry. If it's Aristaeus, he'll suddenly become really kickass at beekeeping."

I heard Bella take a sharp breath in. "What if it's Pandora?"

"Then he'll become nosy as hell and get really good at uncovering things that are meant to stay locked away."

Romeo let out a low growl. Idly, I wondered what was pissing him off. Bella's driving, probably.

"I mean, if it *was* Pandora," I continued, "then I'm not saying it wouldn't be bad—it totally would. Christopher would probably end up letting a diseased monkey out of a research facility and causing a zombie apocalypse, or something like that."

Romeo might feel anxious at the thought of Bella taking risks when she was driving, too. The thought made me feel even more sick, so I barreled on. "But, again, like I said, I doubt he'll summon a female deity. It just doesn't fit with Christopher's M.O."

"We can't rule anything out," Bella said.

"I'm not." I finally made it to the highway and sped up. "But I understand him. I know exactly what he wants."

Bella's tone was skeptical. "You do?"

"Yeah."

"How could you—"

"I remember looking at his face, Bella, while he was burning me over and over with blue flame. I stared at him with my only unburnt eye, while the other one melted and dribbled down my cheek. He only asked me one question, over and over, because he thought I was hiding a powerful weapon, and he wanted it. So, I know exactly what he wants, because I looked into his eyes while he tortured me, and he laughed and giggled and kicked his feet in delight."

"Jesus Christ," Bella whispered.

I grinned. It was petty, but I enjoyed unsettling her. "He's weak—magically, politically, even physically. All he wants is power. *Ultimate* power. He wants people to cower before him. He won't waste the Tear summoning a benign minor deity. It will be someone who gives him the power he seeks. Deimos, the god of panic and terror, maybe. Or Kratos, the god of strength and power."

They lapsed into silence for a second, then, Bella

chimed in with a few more suggestions of minor Greek gods that I'd forgotten about or didn't know about in the first place.

The traffic got heavy, and I needed to concentrate, so I tuned them out. Further out of the city, Bella changed the subject again and started reminiscing about some of the missions she'd dragged Romeo along on. Stories of spelunking into sunken temples in Thailand and deep-sea diving in Macedonia. Running from territorial tigers in Guangdong, ducking gravedigger bullets in Luxor.

They talked like I wasn't listening. Maybe Romeo'd forgotten I was still on the line.

God, I hate her so much.

Shush, brain, we're almost there. The sign up ahead showed the turnoff to Beacon. I followed the little robot voice in my ear as the GPS directed me towards the banks of the Hudson.

A police helicopter zoomed overhead; I slowed down a fraction. An icy coil of unease unfurled in my belly.

Something was wrong. I just didn't know what it was yet.

A hint of smoke blew up my helmet, hitting my nostrils. At the same time, I rounded a corner and saw an orange glow reflected against the fat gray clouds that gathered on the horizon.

"Oh, no." *Oh, no, no, no, no.*

"Daphne? What's wrong?"

I took a shaky breath in and pulled up to a stop at the top of the hill, overlooking the river, and pulled off my helmet.

"Daphne?" Romeo's voice in my ear was urgent.

But the roar of flames was almost deafening. The building was totally engulfed. Sirens screamed in the distance.

"The Ironworks Gallery," I whispered. "It's on fire. He's got it, Romeo. Christopher Jupiter has the Tear of Zeus."

CHAPTER
THIRTY-FIVE

Romeo found me slumped on a grassy hill, overlooking the Hudson and the burning gallery below. "Daphne!" He leapt out of the Yukon and stalked towards me.

I got up slowly. An odd mix of emotions tugged at me, and my body couldn't decide what it wanted to do first. The bone-weary exhaustion and sense of defeat made me want to fall into Romeo's arms and cry like a child. The burning frustration, blind hatred, and pure panic made me want to grab him and run as fast as we could.

I had no idea where to go next, though. If I knew, I'd already be gone. I took the most seductive option and let him pull me into his arms. "He's got it, Romeo."

"We don't know that for sure." Bella had gotten out of the Yukon, too, and was walking towards us, her gaze sweeping the riverside. "This could be a coincidence. When the fire dies down, we can—"

"Actually, I do know for sure." I cut her off, not caring

that I sounded rude or abrupt. I'd played nice for long enough. My patience was gone, and I had no desire to pretend anymore.

Bella narrowed her eyes for a split second, then blinked. Her mouth opened in a soft gasp. "Sorry, Daphne. I didn't mean to sound patronizing. It's just..." She licked her lips and swallowed. "Let's get down there and have a look around before we jump to conclusions."

Fuck off with your shit, Bella. "I've already been down there. Christopher Jupiter was here, along with two of his volkhv."

The smell of burned plastic almost overpowered everything else, but I'd never forget Christopher's scent, the herb-and-candle wax smell of the witches layered with his own personal poison tang—foxglove, nightshade, oleander, a hint of poppy, toxic and vile.

Romeo swore. His arms tightened around me, and a low rumble built in his chest. "How the fuck did Jupiter find the Tear before us?"

"We don't know that he did," Bella insisted. "You guys, come on. Let's get down there."

"If Daphne says he was here, then he was," Romeo told her. "We need to figure out what to do next."

Bella shook her head and met my gaze again. Her eyebrows pinched together. "Honey, I know you've got a good sense of smell, but there's no way you've had enough time to properly sniff around."

"I've been here for twenty minutes." I hadn't even needed that much time. I could smell Christopher's stench on the wind.

Bella flinched. "Twenty minutes? You were twenty

minutes ahead of us?" She sounded like she didn't believe me.

I didn't look away. "Yeah."

She shook her head. "That's not possible."

"I told you I ride fast." I wanted to say more, but there was no time for a dick-measuring contest with Romeo's girl best friend. Regardless of how badly I wanted her to know that she'd underestimated me, now was not the time. And the time we had was running out fast.

Quickly—but reluctantly—I pulled myself out of Romeo's arms. "Jupiter needs a ley line intersection to perform the summoning. The stronger, the better. That's where he'll be going. Any ideas?"

"The most powerful one on the East Coast is at the church, which is warded and guarded heavily, so he can't get in there," Romeo said. "There's a similar ley line in Castlemaine, California."

"No chance of him heading there," I said.

"Agreed."

"Why not?" Bella demanded. "Rome... why?"

"No time to explain." I cut her off with a wave of my hand. Dropping my nepo-baby contacts on her at this stage was beneath me. I'd save it for later. "Where else could he go?"

"Back to Russia. There are several intersections there."

"Nope." Levi limped up to join us. "He's not getting out of the country. Micah's surveillance team finally managed to bribe an airport tech guy to drop a no-fly alert on Christopher Jupiter's name. We've got people at every airport, just in case."

"He'll stay in the States," I said. "Where's the next most powerful intersection?"

Romeo shook his head abruptly. He looked pissed, like a thought had just occurred to him and he didn't like it at all. "Shit."

"What is it?"

"There's lots of powerful intersections I could name right now, but they're all occupied and well-guarded. There's only one that's not, and it's my fault."

"Where?"

"The mansion."

My eyes widened. "The *Jupiter* mansion?"

He nodded. "Marcus Jupiter built that house on that spot for a reason. It's a place of power. The mansion is empty now. I threw Mina and Wesley out, but I didn't bother updating the security to exclude any of them." He glared into space for a second. "I'll admit I liked the idea of them sneaking back in so I could throw them out again. It was stupid. I let my temper get the better of me."

"We can't change the past." I stared up at him. "But we can fix the mistakes we made in the past."

"It's not all bad news. When I found out that Christopher was the one who cursed Aunt Marche, I set an alarm on the mansion door targeting him in case he—" Romeo stopped abruptly and buried a hand in his pocket. He pulled out a chain ringed with scary-looking metal boxes and orbs and swore viciously. "He's there."

"He's there *now?*" Bella shrieked. "How the hell did

he get there so quickly? That fire down there has barely spread!"

"No idea," I said tonelessly. "And it doesn't matter now. What matters is that we get back to Philly as soon as possible so we can stop him. I'm going to assume that he's working on activating the Tear of Zeus right now and will start the incantations to summon the god to our realm."

Romeo squeezed my hand. "Will we know when he's activated the star door? Will there be a sign?"

"Well, since the first part of opening the star door brings a tiny chunk of the Hellenic realm to our world, I'm going to assume there will be a little earthquake or something. Once that happens, we've got three hours to stop him before the door is open wide enough to call the god through. We need to get to Philly *now*."

Bella glanced at her phone and cursed. "My chopper is still being serviced."

I was already pulling my motorcycle jacket back on. "Newburgh airport is six miles away; I'll meet you there. Levi, make some calls, charter a helicopter, or get Micah to compel someone to hand over their keys. If you end up with a microlite, make sure there are five parachutes."

I threw my hair back off my face so I could shove my helmet on, but Romeo grabbed me and stared down at me. His eyes, looking the darkest they'd ever been, bored into mine. Not silver, or stormy-gray, but black like a thundercloud.

I could feel the raging storm inside him, tearing him in two. He was hurting, and it made me feel like ripping my own heart out.

"It's going to be okay," I whispered.

He gave a sharp nod. "It has to be." He pressed his lips to mine and kissed me, hard and hungry. I fell into it just as desperately and wished I could stay for longer.

"Guys, come on!" Bella's voice was strained. "We have to go!"

Romeo pulled away. I clung to him for a second longer than I should have.

CHAPTER
THIRTY-SIX

The pulse hit forty-five minutes later.

We were fifteen minutes from Philadelphia when it happened—a thrum through the air, a shockwave that shifted the atoms of our reality. It was subtle but powerful. We all felt it.

Romeo opened his eyes. He'd been silent the whole trip so far, recharging his energy. Neither of us felt the urge to fill the silence.

The helicopter could only seat four, so we had to leave Levi behind. Before we took off, Levi set a regenerative circle around Romeo's seat—a ring of quartz crystals—so Romeo would rest and regain some of his strength. He hadn't slept in days, and he'd been running on empty ever since he shadow-jumped from thirty-five thousand feet in the air and three hundred eighty miles west to get home to me.

Bella piloted the helicopter with Micah beside her in a full helmet covering most of his face, the rest of his skin shining with a heavy layer of SPF 100. Neither of them spoke. Both had dark circles under their eyes, too.

"That was it, wasn't it?" Romeo's voice was like a low whisper in my headset. A faint silver glow ran over his skin.

I nodded. "Unless the Delaware hellmouth has reopened in Philly... yeah. I think that was it." I set a timer on my phone. "Three hours. We've got three hours to get to him."

Romeo cursed, reached into his pocket, and pulled out another little vial of healing potion.

"I've got some zippixie stones in my bag," Bella called out. "Do you want to take one of those, Rome?"

I stiffened. Zippixies were a species of fae creatures, who, like most pixies, excreted magical dust. The stones Bella was talking about were compressed fairy poop. And, as the name suggested, they made you very zippy for about six to ten hours. It was a magical pick-me-up at best, magical meth at worst.

Romeo rubbed his face with both hands. "Yeah, thanks, Bell. That will help." She passed her bag behind her.

I took the bag, held it in my lap, and shook my head at him firmly. Romeo furrowed his brow, confused, and reached for it.

Tread carefully...

I gave him a pointed look and shook my head again. Nope. Not happening.

Bella glanced back at the same time and saw my expression. "Oh." Her face fell. She looked hurt. "Sorry, Daphne. I didn't mean to offend you." Her beautiful lips dropped into a sad frown. "I'm an animal lover, too. If you're worried about the stones, they're ethically sourced, I promise."

There was no such thing. Zippixies didn't ever donate or sell their dust, and it would take a million years for a scavenger to wander around Faerie and gather up all the poop they could find and compress it into a stone. If Bella actually had any zippixie stones, they would be the drug equivalent of blood diamonds.

I didn't say any of that, though. With effort, I relaxed my eyebrows and rearranged my face into a sheepish expression. "It's not that. I've heard horror stories, that's all."

"They're perfectly safe—"

"Please." I pouted a little. *Urgh, this feels fucking horrible.* "Just humor me."

Romeo's eyes grew stormy, but he didn't move, and he didn't say anything. After a moment, I made the decision for him and passed the bag back to the front, making sure to toss it a little so it was out of reach.

"Aww." Bella turned for a fraction of a second and gave me a sweet, conspiratorial smile. "I love that you're looking out for my boy. You're a good woman, Daphne."

Fuckin' A, I'm a good woman. I wish I could say the same for you, you goddamn piece of—

"We're almost there." Bella banked sharply, coming in over the river towards the helipad near Philly University.

"We need to run some scenarios," Romeo said. He clenched his fists, letting the silver glow flare, then fade. "Jupiter has probably warded the mansion. I'll need some help to break through. That bastard might be low-powered, but he's good at setting wards." He sat up straighter. "Bell, do you have any—"

"I'm good at getting through wards, remember?" Ugh, my voice was all squeaky.

Romeo furrowed his brow, as if he'd forgotten that. "Oh. Oh course."

"If he's warded the mansion with basic security wards, I'll be able to get through them and disable them from the other side." An awful thought occurred to me. "Did you ever find a way to break the shrinking wards?"

Romeo shook his head, his expression grim. "As far as I can tell, there's no way to break *micșorându* wards. It's a feature of their existence that they will only stop once all sides of the ward touch. Tunnelling out from underneath is the only way."

I hissed under my breath. "Damn. Well, I guess that—"

A big white bird crashed into the windscreen.

Bella banked sharply and swore. The bird slid on the windscreen from side-to-side, balled up his wing into a fist, and banged on the plexiglass. **Bitch, let me in.**

"It's Dwayne." I unbuckled my seatbelt. "I need to open the window."

Alarms blared. Bella wrestled with the controls. "What? Hell, no, are you insane, Daphne? We can't open anything! This thing is pressurized, and the goddamn wind forces will throw us into a spin! Do you want us all to die?"

Now I felt stupid. Dwayne slid on the window, trying to hold on. He was blocking most of the view. I cupped my hands around the glass and shouted to him. "Wait until we land!"

C'mon. I'm tired. I flew all the way from Harlem.

"Why were you in Harlem?" I shouted back.

What?

Bella and Micah both winced and fiddled with their headsets. Oops. I'd been shouting directly into their ears. My cheeks warmed. I had a lot of specialties, but helicopters weren't one of them. Mortified, I took off my headset and yelled at Dwayne again. "I said, why were you in Harlem?" I'd lost Dwayne after the warehouse battle, but I knew he'd show up eventually. "Actually, forget it, I probably don't want to know."

He pressed his face to the glass. **No, you probably don't. Come on, baby girl, let me in.**

I couldn't hear Bella over the roar of the rotor blades anymore, but from her side profile, I could tell she was swearing viciously under her breath.

"Dwayne!" I called out. "We're landing now! Just hang on! No, don't let go! The rotor blades will chop you to pieces! Just hold on!"

I slid my headset back on my ears in time to hear Bella mutter. "Is that damned bird brain damaged or something?" The helicopter launched left, then right, then left again. She seemed to be struggling to get back under control.

No, she's not; she is in control. She's faking it to try and throw Dwayne off, I swear. Listen to her!

I could hear her, angrily muttering curses under her breath. Gods, I was glad that Dwayne couldn't hear her. Bella finally regained control and flew straight for a minute or two, before bringing the helicopter closer to the ground.

I spotted a shaggy head of bronze hair on the helipad—Brandon had come to meet us, his Escalade idling nearby. We landed and jumped out.

I scraped Dwayne off the windscreen, tucked him under my arm, and ran.

CHAPTER
THIRTY-SEVEN

The Jupiter mansion looked exactly the same as before. There were no ancient temples blocking the street, no golden steps leading up to Mount Olympus, no vast sea filled with weird fish-monsters, no grumpy old men steering ferries loaded with confused dead people. Whatever terrain that the Stella Ostium had pulled from the Hellenic realm, it was hidden inside the mansion.

We stood on the path across the street, carefully assessing the place, all of us in fresh clothes—combat pants, ballistics shirts, and Kevlar vests. I slid my Orion blades into the sheathes at my back but rejected Micah's offer of guns.

As a former assassin, guns were his specialty. Mundane projectile weapons were notoriously unreliable in a magical firefight, and I never wanted to get used to relying on them.

Bella, however, loaded up with Heckler & Koch USP Match pistols in her thigh holsters, knives strapped to her forearms, and a katana—which smelled suspiciously like it had the ghosts of its victims trapped in the blade—strapped to her back. She also emptied the contents of her backpack into her combat pants, filling the pockets with magical artifacts and off-world charms. The punch of the odor made my nose hurt. She literally radiated strength and power and looked unbearably sexy.

"Are we ready to go, kids?" She tossed her thick ponytail, threw her shoulders back, thrust out her chest, and took a deep breath. "Let's do this."

Dwayne eyed her with interest.

Are you fucking kidding me? I kicked him gently, waited until he was looking up at me, and snarled at him softly under my breath. "What the hell is wrong with you?"

He didn't even have the grace to look ashamed. Instead, he gave a little goosy shrug. **Don't hate the player, little one, hate the game.**

I huffed out a breath. I should have seen this coming. On the surface, Bella was exactly Dwayne's type. If Asherah found out about this, she'd—

Solve all our problems for us...?

"You know what, you've got my blessing," I muttered. "Go for it, sir, fire away." If the luck gods decided to smile on me, Asherah would float in on a bubble sometime in the next couple of hours, see Dwayne hitting on Bella, and rip Bella's head off her shoulders.

Brain-Daphne chuckled darkly. *I love the new us. On the same page, dancing to the same tune.*

Don't get used to it, I told her.

With effort, I forced myself to focus. I was going to need every ounce of concentration I possessed to get through these wards. I could smell them from here, across the street. Inhaling deeply, I cataloged the layers that Christopher Jupiter had ringed around the mansion.

The first was a hard ward—a protection dome designed to keep literally anything solid from penetrating it. It was basic but thick and very strong. I could understand why Christopher had poured all his energy into this one. If it wasn't there, we could evacuate the area, fire a rocket into the mansion, and blow the whole thing up. Bada bing, bada boom, no summoning any gods today, Mr. Jupiter.

The hard ward would be tricky, but I could manage it.

The front door was just on the inside of the hard ward, though. And only six inches from that, if my nose was to be believed, was an anti-ghost ward—a ward to hold out spirits and non-corporeal entities.

Again, I understood Christopher's thinking. He'd escaped from Romeo's wrath using a ghost charm, a hideously expensive spell that turned his body non-corporeal for a few hours. I suppose he figured if we got through the hard ward using the same kind of spell, then the anti-ghost ward would stop us in our tracks.

That was it, just the two wards. Easy. Romeo squeezed my hand, and I glanced up at him.

"What do you think?" he asked.

"Well..." I took a deep breath. "I think the only hard part is the front door."

"What do you mean?"

"There are two wards. First, a hard ward. It smells

like a honeycomb hard-ward, which means that I can't break it completely, but I should be able to chip away enough of it once I'm inside to break a section open so we can crawl in—"

"How are you going to get through it in the first place?" Bella interrupted.

I turned to look at her. My emotions must have shown on my face.

"Sorry!" She leaned back and held up her hands in surrender. "It's just professional curiosity. If it was me, I'd be using a jackhammer to dig down into the concrete of the steps, then activate a mole-ball charm and drop it down, so the construct can dig up and under the edge of the ward. Then I'd feed through a—"

"I'm just going to walk through it," I interrupted her. "I've got a knack for these things."

Genuine hurt flashed in her eyes. "Oh."

"Daphne." Romeo sighed. For the first time ever, I didn't shiver when he said my name, because he sounded so disappointed. He didn't add anything else, but I could feel the words he didn't say in his tone.

Bella's an Orbiter. She doesn't have innate access to magic like you do, and it's all she has ever wanted. You're being cruel.

"Sorry." I tried to smile at her. "I mean, I'd use a mole-ball too, but, uh, magical constructs are really expensive, and I'm... uh... really poor. Anyway..." I spun back to the door. "There's a honeycomb hard ward, which will be easy as long as I can concentrate, and a ghost ward, which will be easy, too. The problem is that the front door is sandwiched between both wards."

I waited, but Bella didn't say anything. She still looked hurt.

Not genuinely, though, my brain snorted. *She's just laying it on thick for Romeo's benefit. If this was a game of tennis, it would be fifteen-love to her.*

"I won't be able to open the door," I explained. "I can move through the hard ward as long as I convince it that I'm not solid matter. But I can't convince the door that I'm not solid. With magic, intention is everything, and the ward has been set with the intention that it will keep out solid things. The door has no such intention. It's just a door."

Bella still looked a little sulky, but she was listening.

I continued, "So, I can't trick it and move through it. At best, I have to turn the handle—again, which I can't do if I'm not solid. There just isn't enough space between the hard ward and the door for me to do that. I need to get rid of the door before I hit it, while I'm concentrating my energy on not being a solid thing, if you understand me. And whatever I do to get rid of it can't be something physical, like reach out and turn the handle. Do you understand?"

"Oh." Bella frowned. "Yeah. That's a tough one."

"If I can somehow make the door disappear without consciously deciding to pick the lock or throw a vanishing curse at it or something, then I'll be able to get through both the hard ward and the door, and I'll have to move my focus back to being physical immediately so I can get through the ghost ward." I gave her a smile. It felt forced. "Do you have any ideas on what I can do to get through it? Or do you have anything in your bag of tricks that might help?"

Bella smiled back at me tentatively. "Okay, let me think." Frowning for a second, she mumbled under her breath. "So, you need something that isn't solid to dissolve the door. A gas, maybe?"

"Any gas that dissolves the door would probably choke me to death."

"Fire?"

A lump appeared in my throat; I swallowed it. "Again, I'd have to physically set fire to it. To set a fire, my intention would be that I am solid. The hard ward would sense that, and it would throw me out at best." At worst, it would squash me between the hard ward and the burning door. I'd both suffocate *and* burn to death. It wouldn't be the best idea to say that out loud in front of Romeo, though.

Bella's eyebrows rose. "What if you didn't have to think about it? What if the solution was as simple as breathing?"

"Good, good." I nodded. "If I didn't have to think about it, I could maintain my non-solid intention."

"How about a dragonbreath petal?" She patted her pockets. "I've got one of those. All you'd have to do is exhale, and a stream of fire would incinerate the door."

Panic tightened my chest. "It will burn me once I turn solid. And I have to turn solid to move through the ghost ward."

"But it's your best— Oh, shit." Bella blinked. "I'm sorry, Daphne. I forgot about what Christopher did to you. I didn't mean... You shouldn't...."

I felt like I'd turned to ice. Luckily, my brain went on ticking. *Whoa. She's an evil bitch, and she might have suggested this on purpose just to hurt you... but she's right. That could actually work. If you hold your breath and focus on moving through the hard ward, you'll automatically exhale when you get through. The dragonbreath petal will incinerate the door, and you can walk through that, too.*

I'll burn.

You'll burn for a second, but you'll be able to run once you're clear of the hard ward.

It's going to fucking hurt.

Don't be a pussy.

That's both offensive and inaccurate. Vaginas are the toughest things in the word; they can take a beating and beg for more.

Bella cleared her throat. "Is... uh. Is she okay?"

"She's fine," Romeo said quietly. "She's just thinking."

"Her face is twitching. She looks..."

The memory of torture is always way worse than the actual torture, Brain-Daphne said cheerfully. *Remember? It's just pain. Just a little burny burn. Tell your nervous system to shut the fuck up and let's get on with it.*

That was a good point. It was the best plan we had, and we were running out of time. "Give me the petal." I held out my hand.

"No." The word erupted from Romeo's mouth like a gunshot. "It's not happening."

"It will only be for a split second."

He glared down at me, his eyes almost black. "No." His hands tightened around my shoulders. "I can't see you like that again, Daphne." He turned to Bella. "Find another way."

"Well... um. I need to think." She patted her pockets.

"There's no time. Just give me the petal, Bella." I held out my hand. "We need to move."

"There's no rush. We've got over two hours to stop him, and he's just in there." She pointed her thumb at the door. "We've got time to think about this, Daphne."

"No, we don't. He's not just 'in there,' Bella, he's brought a part of the Greek god realm into our world. It's like a pocket dimension. It could be part of the Underworld. For all we know, we might have to abseil down into Tartarus." I exhaled heavily. "Give me the petal."

"No," Romeo growled. He wasn't happy.

"I'm not going to die." I blinked up at him with my best doe-eyes. "And I heal quick, remember?"

Bella put her hand in a side pocket and drew out a little pouch. "Do you know—"

"Yeah. I put it on my tongue, it reacts with the water in my saliva, and when I exhale, boom. Dragonbreath."

The muscle in Romeo's jaw was getting a workout; he glared at me, so furious, he was almost paralyzed. "No."

He's on the brink, girlfriend. We need to reign him in.

Brain-Daphne was right. Romeo's control was legendary. It had to be. He'd had a tiny taste of blood magic as a kid, and he'd never forgotten it. It was a seductive power, it overwhelmed all common sense, and you'd lie to yourself and everyone around you trying to justify using it. It was like magical heroin, but worse, because it was everywhere. The worst thing that could happen right now was not Christopher Jupiter summoning a god into his body.

The worst thing that could happen was Romeo losing control.

So far, since he'd met me, he'd torn a hole in the fabric of a pocket dimension and shadow-jumped a quarter of the way across the country. Those were things he could do with the power already inside him. But if he lost control...If someone he loved was in mortal danger...

He might reach for blood. I couldn't let that happen.

Pushing up on my tiptoes, I put my hands on both sides of his face. God, his jaw was rock hard. Tension pulled every single muscle in his body tight.

"Romeo," I murmured. "I trust you. You know that, right?"

After what felt like forever, he nodded firmly, just once.

"Do you trust me?"

Time stretched on. He stared down at me, the storm in his eyes raging out of control.

Nod, you fucker.

"Yes."

That'll do.

I smiled. "Then let me do this. You remember who I am, right?"

He nodded quicker this time. Yeah, he remembered. I healed quickly. I could handle pain.

"No hesitation, no regrets, and we trust each other. Okay?"

He scowled. I had him back again. "I don't like this."

"For what it's worth, I don't like it either. But it's only

physical pain. It's not as bad as... well, you know." Both of us knew what the worst part of torture was. The humiliation. The helplessness. The despair. "There's none of the really bad stuff in this situation, so let me do this, okay?" I smiled. "I'll get through the hard ward, incinerate the door, move through the ghost ward, and bust a hole in the hard ward so you can get through. Then, we're going to kick Christopher Jupiter's ass. Okay?"

"Fine," he growled. He clamped his hands around my wrists, pulled me in, and kissed me.

"Here's the dragonbreath petal!" Bella shouted. "Daphne, here!"

I pulled away from Romeo. My hands shook with the effort of not punching her in the face.

CHAPTER
THIRTY-EIGHT

The dragonbreath petal tasted like a habanero pepper. I'd already tucked my hair underneath a ski mask, doused my body with water from Brandon's drink bottle, and taken the deepest breath I could possibly manage. I sandwiched my lips together, turned to face the team down on the steps below me, and very nearly opened my mouth to tell them to wish me luck. It wouldn't be ideal if I incinerated everyone before we started.

Instead, I smiled and waved like an idiot, closed my eyes, and moved towards the ward.

I hope our calculations are correct, my brain muttered. *I can smell the wards all clearly. There's gotta be six inches between the hard ward and the ghost ward. I wish there was more space. This is gonna fucking sting.*

Yeah, it was. I squeezed my eyes shut tighter and concentrated. I hadn't tried to move through a basic hard ward in ages because it required some intense focus, and most of the time, if I needed to break into one, I was usually panicking and couldn't concentrate. I needed the ward to think that I wasn't solid.

And to do that, I had to believe that I wasn't.

It was easier for me than probably anyone else on earth, because I remembered what it was like. I'd been non-corporeal a bunch of times, depending on the laws of physics in whatever realm I'd ended up in as a kid. The truth was, none of us were solid, even in this realm. We were just a bunch of atoms, vibrating at a particular level. While I centered myself, I wondered idly if I could have escaped Christopher's shrinking ward. Probably not, since it moved. I needed stillness for this to work.

I concentrated and felt the edges of the ward. Then, I emptied my mind and moved into a place where nothing existed.

I'm not real. I have no form, no substance. Daphne who?

Time didn't exist, because I didn't exist. A serene buzz floated over me. *Nothing* existed. I was nothing, and I was everything. A part of the whole, no, I was the whole, we were all whole, all ghosts, drifting through space and time...

A weird sensation kissed me, stopping Ghost Daphne from going any further into the mansion. That couldn't be right. I didn't have a body. I was formless, weightless... I opened my ghost-eyes and saw the door only inches from my face. I'd moved without thinking—it was the best way. Closing my spirit-eyes, I parted my non-existent lips and exhaled.

Flame erupted out of my mouth, bright blue, instantly incinerating a hole in the door. The shock of it sapped my concentration, and I turned solid immediately and fell into the flaming door.

Fucking OWWWW.

It took a second for the door to incinerate enough that I could fall through it, but a second was enough. I was on fire.

Stop, drop, and roll, bitch! Let's gooo!

I rolled forward, moving through the ghost-ward like it wasn't even there, and kept rolling. I stayed on the ground, rolling back and forth, until I was sure the flames were extinguished.

The smell of burned hair almost choked me. My clothes were fire-retardant and soggy, but even then, it felt like most of them had burned away. I patted myself down and opened my eyes.

They stung. It took a second for my vision to adjust. The door in front of me hadn't completely burned away yet. It was on fire, every single part glowing orange as the dragonflame ate away at it.

I exhaled with relief. I'd done it.

My relief didn't last; I had to make sure I was safe. Quickly, I rolled again to check the entrance hall and found nothing but blackness behind me—almost solid black, like the light had been sucked out of the hallway completely. I inhaled deeply through my nose, trying to concentrate past the stench of burned hair and clothes.

No terrible beasts nor villainous humans were anywhere in the immediate vicinity. Instead of comforting me, a tingle of dread coiled in my stomach. There was nothing in the darkness behind me, but that meant the darkness was *huge*. I usually could smell creatures from half a mile away, and there was nothing.

Whatever was beyond this entrance hall was immense.

Then, more dread swamped me when the cold air blowing from the street outside touched my nipples in a way that it shouldn't.

I looked down. More of my shirt had burned away than I realized. Ugh.

This was the part that nobody talked about when you were fighting the forces of evil. In any battle, your clothes were the first things that took damage. Sometimes, you lost coverage; it was inevitable. Like the time I was being chased by dark elves and had to run the full length of a windy moor in Svartálfheim with my bare butt shining in the moonlight after losing my trousers climbing out of my prison tower. Or when that flock of evil *impis borowy* ate the bottom of my robe while I was sleeping, and I had to wander around the Underhill for a week, flashing my flaps to the locals.

My brain grimaced. *We're going to have to chip away the hard wards with our titties out, aren't we.*

Yeah, we are. I climbed to my feet, wincing, and pulled out my Orion blades.

"Daphne!" Romeo's face appeared in the hole in the door. He'd had to bend double to check on me. "Are you okay?"

"I'm great. Can you pass me a shirt? Oh, wait." Embarrassment distracted me. "I'm going to have to chip a hole in the hard ward first. Hang on."

The hole in the door got bigger as more of the wood

burned away. The smoke was overpowering and made me cough and splutter. I watched as the realization dawned in Romeo's eyes. "Oh."

His face disappeared. I sighed, palmed my blades in my scorched fingers, bent down, and started chipping a hole in the ward. Soon, the whole door would be gone, and they wouldn't have to bend down to see me.

"Turn around," Romeo ordered gruffly. "Don't look."

"What?" Brandon sounded confused. "Why?"

"I'm not telling you again, Bran." His voice softened. "You too, Bell. Please."

The hole in the door got bigger. I used my blades to stab little dents in the hard ward. It was softer on the inside, easier to break through—a failsafe in case anyone who cast it had to get out in a hurry.

Stab, stab, stab. I suppose this was a little like chipping a hole in an icy lake—I just had to get a deep score in the ward, then I should be able to kick it out.

The door burned away completely. I could see the guys outside now. All of them had their backs to me. I heard Romeo growl softly. "If you even dream about twitching your head, Micah, I swear—"

"Boss, relax."

"We're not moving," Brandon confirmed.

Dwayne wasn't facing away. He was watching me chip a large circle in the ward. **Ha ha**, he chuckled. **Sorry, ma'am, we were looking for the Jupiter mansion, not Hooters.**

I mouthed at him. "Shut the hell up and get me a shirt."

I don't know why you bother. Nudity is awesome.

It wasn't the nudity that bothered me, it was having to do vigorous physical labor while nude when everyone around you was fully clothed. I ground my jaw and put all my effort into quickly chipping the circle into the ward, then, funneling all my embarrassment into my muscles, I reared back my leg and donkey-kicked the ward. It cracked.

So that's why that topless women's soccer league flopped, Dwayne sniggered. **Not enough support.**

I held my boobs with one hand so they wouldn't wobble so much and kicked again. The ward finally splintered, and a glowing amber honeycomb pattern appeared in a circle in front of me. I kicked one more time, and it fell outwards, shattering on the steps outside and disappearing completely.

"It's done," I called softly.

"Nobody move," Romeo growled. "I'm going in first."

CHAPTER
THIRTY-NINE

"Whoa." Brandon shivered as he climbed through the little hole in the ward. He straightened up and swallowed. "It's, uh. It's dark in here." A shudder rolled through him again.

"Scared of the dark, Bran?" Bella said. She was already inside, assessing the entrance hall for danger and rummaging through her pockets. She pulled out a glowstick, cracked it, held it up, and smirked.

"No." He swallowed. "Of course not."

I shot a look at Romeo next to me, but he was busy summoning his own light charm. I walked over to Brandon. "It's this place, isn't it."

He gazed into the blackness beyond us, his eyes wide. "Yeah," he whispered. "It's... it's tugging at me, trying to pull out my dragon." He swallowed heavily.

"Would that be so bad?" Bella held up her glow stick, examining the darkness a little further. "We could use a dragon in this fight."

I almost screamed. Brandon was a Stolen One, like

Myf—a dragon shifter tortured and brainwashed into being a mindless assassin. He'd been sent to kill Romeo. The only reason Romeo wasn't dead was because Brandon drank a potion to suppress his animal.

"He can't shift," I said, not looking at Bella. "It's too dangerous. His programming is too strong."

"Then hold it in, honey." Bella spun around gracefully and gave him what she probably thought was an encouraging smile. "You got this."

Oh, great, I'm going to have to be the bad guy. "The Hellenic realm is filled with magic," I told her. "This place is swamped with ancient power. It's affecting him badly."

"Oh." Her face fell. "I can't feel it." For a split second, her lip quivered. She blinked her big blue eyes—now shining with unshed tears—turned, and walked away, disappearing almost instantly as the darkness swallowed her. All I could see was her stupid glowstick, floating in the air.

"Bella, wait." Romeo went after her, charging into the black.

I watched him go. Damn.

He chose her, my brain growled.

I took a deep breath. It's going to be okay. I know it is. No hesitations, no regrets, I trust myself, and I trust him.

Let's just stab her in the heart and be done with it. Brain-Daphne's patience had run out. *Oooh, look at all this blackness. No one will ever know...*

I locked my teeth, so frustrated I could cry. At this stage, I could kill her. But it might kill him, too.

Dwayne, at least, shook his head, watching the glow

stick bob in the air next to Romeo's charm. They weren't too far away. **Wow. I didn't peg her as the mopey type.** He frowned. **Boner killer.**

To make it worse, I could still hear them, even though they were both whispering. "... hates me, Rome. She really hates me."

"She doesn't," Romeo reassured Bella softly. "Daphne is sweet. She's the kindest person I've ever met. She doesn't hate anyone."

Wrong. We do hate her.

"Well, she definitely doesn't like me," Bella whispered. "She keeps rubbing it in that I'm an Orbiter, that I don't have any magic. You heard her. She's jealous, and I understand that. It must threaten her that you and I are so close. Sometimes people don't show their true colors until they're threatened."

I ground my jaw so hard my back tooth cracked.

"I'm trying so hard. I want her to like me..." Bella's voice shook. "I just want you to be happy, that's all. It's all I ever wanted."

"I know."

"And..." her voice hitched again. "If *I* can't be the one to make you happy—"

"Stop it, Bell." Romeo's tone wasn't sharp; it was so gentle it made me want to cry. "Just stop. You'll always be my sister, and you'll always be my best friend. Nothing is ever going to change that, and you know it."

She took a quivering breath in. "I just... you know I always thought that maybe, one day—"

Okay, that's enough. My brain turned on some elevator music, trying to distract me. *You don't need to hear anymore. It's just going to make you mad. Let's focus. Brandon first.*

Right.

I took a deep breath and turned to him. He was still gazing into the darkness. "Brandon." His face had gone very pale.

"There's something—"

Oh, shit, there *was* someone coming. I pulled my Orion blades first, moved automatically into an en garde position, inhaled carefully through my nose, then relaxed.

"It's okay," I whispered, sheathing my blades. "It's a friend."

A moment later, Holly LeBeaux came trotting out of the darkness, wearing a black catsuit and carrying a wriggling body over her shoulder.

Brain-Daphne let out a wolf whistle. *Just when I thought Holly couldn't get any hotter.*

The body was Troy. I couldn't see his face, but he was trussed up like a turkey, bound and gagged, arms and legs tied with a glowing rope.

Holly smiled when she spotted me. She jogged towards us. "Hey there." Her beautiful face was pink with exertion. "You got in. Thank the goddess, I was worried we were going to die in there." She stopped in front of me and grinned. "Sorry, Daphne, but I'm out. The Jupiters called in all family reinforcements, and me and Troy are all that's left. I'd stay and fight with you..." She jerked her head towards the darkness behind her. "But whatever the hell is going on back there is out of my pay grade."

I nodded. "I understand, Holly. Uh, what *is* going on back there?"

"I have no idea. Lots of marble and plenty of olive trees." She hefted Troy higher on her shoulder, getting a better grip. "My coven hasn't cancelled our marriage contract yet, so I have to take this idiot with me. He needs to stay alive so he can sign the severance papers."

I wasn't sure what to say, so I waved my hand, gesturing at the wriggling man over her shoulder. "You could have knocked him out."

"Then he would have missed all the fun of finding out I'm a traitor."

I shrugged. "Fair enough."

She clapped her hand on my shoulder. "Go with the goddess, Daphne." Moving past me, she tossed Troy unceremoniously out the still-smoldering hole in the ward. "Oh, and let's get sushi later in the week, okay? My treat." She ducked through the hole and disappeared.

Brandon moved back up beside me. "Well. That was... interesting. Maybe I have a chance with her after all."

He was still very pale, and now, trembling a little. I put my arm on his shoulder. "Do you think you should sit this one out?"

"I can't," he whispered. "We're already down Levi and Cole. Rome needs backup."

"I know you want to help," I said gently. "But, Brandon, if we were to do a risk analysis right now..."

His head dropped to his chest and huffed out a sharp breath. "Goddamnit."

Time to soften the blow. "Sacrificing yourself and

bowing out now is the brave choice, Brandon, and you know it."

"Yeah, I—" He turned, and looked at my face, and squinted. "Did you know you don't have any eyebrows, Daphne?"

"She's right, bro." Micah joined us. "If you're feeling unstable, then you can't risk it." He glanced at me. "Woah." His eyes widened. "They're really gone, huh?"

I grimaced and ran my fingers over my forehead. My skin felt scorched, but it was healing. It would start to peel in about ten minutes. And, yep, my eyebrows were gone. "Damn."

It was hard to concentrate on more than one conversation at a time, but in the twenty seconds of silence while I examined my missing eyebrows with my fingers, I heard Romeo mutter, "Bella, we really don't have time for this right now."

"It's *never* been the right time, Rome." Her voice trembled. "That's the problem. It's never the right time for us."

I wrenched my focus back to the boys in front of me. Both of them were examining my face carefully.

"Y'know, I don't mind it." Micah nodded thoughtfully. "It's... what would you say?" He nudged Brandon.

"Fashion," Brandon supplied. "Avant garde."

"No, not that. There's a word—"

"Editorial?"

"Yeah, that's it. You look really cool, Daphne." Micah winked at me. "Even cooler now that you've got some clothes on."

"*Micah.*" Romeo's voice was like a rumble of thunder.

He walked back out of the shadows, his expression so dark, both boys edged backwards.

Bella glided out behind him. She looked pissed, too.

"Boss, I'm going to sit this one out," Brandon stammered. "There's some intense energy in here that's fucking with me. And not just yours," he muttered under his breath.

It was a throwaway comment, but it was true. The clock was ticking, and Romeo's mood was becoming more and more volatile with every second.

"I'm seriously on edge," Brandon added a little louder. "I don't want to put anyone in danger. I'll watch the perimeter, if that's okay with you."

Romeo seemed to catch himself. A little of the storm died. "That's fine." He laid his huge hand on Brandon's shoulder. "Thanks for calling it early."

Brandon gave him a wobbly smile and ducked back out the hole in the ward.

I squared my shoulders. "Okay, team." I smiled around at them. Let's—"

"I'll take point," Bella said, drawing one of her guns and checking the chamber with a sharp clack. "Let's take this fucker down." She turned around again and marched off into the darkness.

CHAPTER
FORTY

My watch beeped, and I flinched. "One and a half hours," I called softly. We'd been walking through the darkness for at least a mile now, and time was slipping away from us quickly.

I should have expected this. The stories I'd heard of the Stella Ostiums always mentioned the fact that a part of the foreign realm would be pulled through first. What I didn't realize was that it would be such a huge part. It was like walking into a giant pocket dimension, except the edges of it were ripped and torn. That was what we were walking through now—the ripped parts. The nothing.

And nothing had changed except for the ground underfoot — floorboards had quickly given way to a dirt path, littered with broken rock and marble.

"I got nothing." Bella charged ahead, a charm bracelet dangling from her hand next to the glowstick. "No sentient creatures anywhere up ahead."

We were close, though. I could feel it, but I couldn't sense anything just yet. Suddenly, my nose pulled me sharply towards the east. "This way," I called.

"I think we should keep heading straight," Bella said, not altering her course at all. "North, and we'll hit something eventually. If we start to turn now, we'll just be heading in circles."

"Bella." I waited until she'd turned towards me and gave her a soft smile. "Trust me. Please?"

Her eyes flickered with rage for a split-second. Romeo was right beside me. I grabbed his hand and turned towards the east before he was forced to choose and started walking. Thankfully, Micah followed Romeo.

But Bella wasn't moving. My heart stuttered. Oh, no. *She's going to force him—*

Move your ass, toots.

"Ouch!" Bella let out a little yelp. "That damned goose just bit me!"

Relief made me giddy. Dwayne always had my back. I had to bite my lip from giggling out loud, because that really would have made me look like an asshole.

"Ow! He bit me again! Romeo... this fucking bird is attacking me!"

"Sorry, Bella!" I called out. "I'm really sorry. Dwayne can be a bit pushy. He's a herding goose. He's just trying to get you to go in the right direction, that's all."

Imma trying to get a chunk of that hot ass, that's what I'm doing. Move, bitch.

She squealed again. "What the fuck?"

I could feel Romeo's eyes on me. "Come up here and take point, Bella," I said. "I'll fall back and deal with—"

We walked into a wall of blazing sunshine, and the words died in my throat.

CHAPTER
FORTY-ONE

It took a second for my eyes to adjust and even longer for my brain to interpret what I was seeing.

There was a small mountain in front of us. A very steep, perfectly conical shape, reaching up about a thousand feet into the sky. The mountain was covered with what looked like winding, glittering white marble walls.

The rock was crumbling in some places, especially around the bottom. Some of the walls had fallen, showing glimpses of enormous statues—a beautiful carving of a goddess, fallen over and lying on her side, another of a great lion with wings. The winding walls went up and up, as far as my sore eyes could see. Every now and then I spotted the dark green leaves of an olive tree or some huge, gnarled branches.

"It's the labyrinth," I said. The sun—a huge yellow ball in a cloudless blue sky—was so bright, it hurt my already-scorched eyes.

"That's not the labyrinth." Bella gazed up at it.

"Daedalus built it next to the Palace of Knossos. It's underground." She waved her hand. "*That* thing is not underground."

"*That* thing is not from the mortal realm." It was so hard not to be short with her. I tried to soften my tone. "Daedalus built the labyrinth in Crete for King Minos based on the Labirinto di Meride in Egypt and the Lemnian labyrinth. But the inspiration for all of them came from that." I nodded towards it. "It's the East Pillar of Hyperion."

"Bullshit." Bella shook her head. "It wouldn't look like that."

"Okay." I wasn't going to waste time arguing with her. The ancient Greeks were poets and were often overwhelmed by the splendor and glory of the god-like creatures that descended on our world when our realms rubbed up against each other. Although I'd never met him, I guessed that the Titan Hyperion was probably just a shy creature who possessed the power to manipulate the light, and he'd built a labyrinth around his pillar to keep the smalltown folk from bothering him in his house.

Beside me, Dwayne whistled a western gun-fighting tune, stretched his wings forwards, and cracked his knuckles. **Let's do this.**

The air smelled potent, heavy with salt and a weird burned-flesh odor. Surreptitiously, I sniffed my shoulder. No, not me. Someone else.

Aha. The light. I let out a gasp. "Micah!"

I stepped backwards a few steps, and the darkness

fell like a curtain. I turned my flashlight back on and found him. "Hey. There you are."

Micah's skin was bright pink and steaming. "I didn't see that coming. Usually, I can smell the sunshine a mile away."

"Don't be too hard on yourself. I didn't smell it either."

Romeo stuck his head back into the blackness with me and gave Micah a hard look. "Sorry, bro, you're going to have to sit this one out, too."

"Boss, no." Micah's eyes flashed red. "I *need* this fight."

"You're out," Romeo said gruffly. "I've got spells and charms that could shield you, but they all take time. We don't have that time." He stared at Micah for a second. "I promise you, next crisis, I'll let you throw yourself into immortal danger to save us all. But for now—" He threw Micah a rope. "Stay there and hold that. We'll need someone on the outside to help us find our way back."

Micah took the rope and folded himself down into the lotus position, his face resigned. "Yes, sir."

And then there were four. Anxiety made me chew on my lip. Romeo and I passed back into the sunlight, into the slice of Hyperion's old hood, and stared up at the mountain again.

Romeo squeezed my hand and passed me a quartz ball. "Look." He pointed. "Up there."

A binocular charm. I took it, and I squinted, trying to focus. Right at the top of the mountain, a huge slab of silver marble sat underneath a giant olive tree.

"Can you see them?"

"Them? Who are you...?" I shifted the charm down slightly and saw them. Adrenaline flooded me. It was such a bitter taste in my mouth, it made me feel sick.

Christopher Jupiter stood in front of the huge stone altar, staring down at us. His lips were moving; he was muttering the incantation to open the Star Door wider. On each side of him stood Mina and Wesley Jupiter.

His parents had joined him. Wesley glared down at us, his heavy black brows furrowed. Gray smoke floated up out of his hands and drifted down the mountain. I couldn't smell the spell he was weaving, but it looked damned evil. Behind them, the last two of Christopher's volkhv stood motionless, their dark eyes fixed on the red gem sitting on the altar behind Christopher. They were guarding the Star Door.

To my horror, Mina also had her arms outstretched, palms up. Sparks of sickly orange dripped off her fingertips. I tore my eyes away and exchanged a horrified glance with Romeo, who nodded grimly.

Mina's magic had been bound. Someone had unbound it. It took a lot of magic to undo a binding. "Levi said there was a pulse of dark energy through the ley lines last week," I whispered. "He couldn't trace it. That was it; that was Mina getting her magic unbound." *Fuckkkkk.*

"I dropped the ball," Romeo muttered.

My watch beeped. Only one hour left. I took one more look through Romeo's magnifying charm, and saw Christopher's lips curved up into a smile as he continued to chant.

"Did any of you happen to pack a rocket launcher?" I ground out through clenched teeth.

"Sorry." Bella cracked her neck. "I couldn't fit it in these pants."

"We're going to have to run the Labyrinth," I whispered. "Only the gods know what's waiting for us in there." I swallowed down my fear. "Let's get moving."

CHAPTER
FORTY-TWO

We jogged up to the entrance warily, trying to balance speed and alertness.

"The labyrinth will be tricky to solve," I said, trying not to pant too loudly. My cardio fitness had taken a beating since I'd devoured my wolf-side and taken up motorcycle racing. "We've only got an hour to get to the top; we can't afford to make many mistakes." The walls around us grew taller and taller, until we couldn't see the top of the mountain anymore. The light blazed all around us even when we were deep in the labyrinth. There were no shadows, and I realized that Christopher had done this on purpose, too. He'd pulled on Hyperion's pillar so there would be endless light. There was no way of knowing what the Jupiters were going to throw at us, and there were no shadows for Romeo to jump through.

After waddling beside me at full speed for a minute or two, his feet making a furious *pat pat pat* noise, Dwayne unfolded his wings and gave a chuckle. **Forgot I**

had these. He launched himself into the sky and disappeared.

My heart leapt.

It sank a minute later when he crash-landed beside me, the tips of his feathers scorched. **It turns out I'm not very good at breaking fire wards.** He blew on his wingtips, putting out the flames. **I'm going to need a minute here, baby girl. You guys go on ahead.**

I ground my teeth and kept running. Of course, Christopher had laid another ward around himself at the top of the mountain. He wasn't taking any chances. I should have realized that, and asked Dwayne to guide us through the labyrinth from the sky instead. Although asking Dwayne to do anything was like trying to persuade a tornado to do calculus equations.

"We need a guide," I huffed out.

Bella rummaged in her pockets as we ran—her breathing annoyingly steady. "I've got a pathfinder somewhere. Ha. Here." She brought out a little copper sphere, clicked it, then threw it into the air. The magical construct burst into life and unfolded into a tiny metal bird. It buzzed left, then right, and took off.

We jogged to follow it. The labyrinth twisted and turned upon itself, occasionally opening up to a small olive grove or a courtyard with broken statues littered about—gods, goddesses, mortal men and women with arms and legs snapped off, beasts with horse heads, ridiculously ripped men's torsos, and fish tails instead of feet. At other times, the walls opened up to reveal little rose gardens ringed in crumbling decorative columns.

The Pillar had clearly taken a beating when it was pulled here from Hyperion's realm. We kept running.

A pulse pounded through the air. I skidded to a halt and looked around warily.

"What was that?" Bella whispered.

"The Star Door." My chest was tight, and I tried to take some deep breaths to relax it. I didn't want to admit it, not even to myself, but the energy in this place was unsettling me, too. Something inside me was not just nagging at me. It was screaming, demanding attention.

I had no idea what it was. For once, my intuition was drawing a blank. "Something else has come through the Star Door," I huffed out.

"A god?"

"No." I inhaled slowly, trying to calm my breath. In through my nose, out through my mouth. My pulse was still racing. "Nothing that big. The door won't be wide enough for another hour," I explained. "And Christopher hasn't made a sacrifice. I'm guessing one of the volkhv will be the final sacrifice." I shook my head and blew out another rough breath. "I can't see Christopher sacrificing either parent for this. They made him the monster he is."

"Monsters often kill their makers," Bella commented, staring up at the sky.

"Only if they hate themselves," I told her. "Christopher is proud of what he is, and his parents are proud of him. I'm sure the volkhv are the sacrifice. Whether they know it or not is another story."

"So, what was that pulse we felt?" Romeo asked.

I thought for a second. "They'd be taking advantage

of the Star Door. It's open enough to let some smaller creatures through."

A voice hit my ears—a woman's cry. I froze and strained to hear what she was saying. "Help me! Please, Daphne! Help!"

My heart leapt into my throat, and I started to run. Romeo caught my wrist and pulled me back. "Who is that?"

"I don't know!" I tugged him. "Whoever it is, she sounds—" I shook my head desperately. "I have to save her!"

"Daphne, help!"

He swung me around and looked down on me. "Baby." His arms clamped around my shoulder. "Stop. Just think. Who is that?"

I shook my head frantically. "I don't... Oh." I blinked up at him. "I don't know that voice, but that person knows my name."

He held my gaze.

The woman's voice cried out again. "Daphne, help!"

This time, I concentrated on the tone. It sounded... mocking. Scornful. Another voice joined it. "Help, Daphne!"

It sounded like Mina Jupiter. My eyes widened.

"Crocotta," I gasped. They've summoned a pack of crocotta."

Bella swore and backed into a corner of the broken courtyard, taking shelter behind a big hunk of a broken marble column. "Of course. Crocotta are mimics." She pulled her guns and moved into a crouch.

Romeo and I followed her lead, taking cover in the other corner. Romeo began to chant, pulling power to his hands. Magenta flames appeared in his palms. I pulled my Orion blades. The ground thudded very lightly under my feet.

A hideous cat-like beast—the size of a motorcycle, with sickly orange-brown fur, a sleek, powerful body, and sickle-shaped claws flashing out of enormous paws—bounded into the courtyard. Its head was comically big, with bulging neck muscles to support the weight of it. Its enormous hyena-like jaw hung open, flashing black gums and a forest of needle-like teeth. It landed on its feet lightly, claws scraping on the stone like nails down a chalkboard. It spun in a circle.

"Daphne! Help me!" Its voice mocked me.

I heard a click, then another. Bella was trying to shoot it. Her guns weren't firing—there was too much magic. Unfortunately, the crocotta heard the click and spun on its feet again.

It saw her.

She dropped her guns, and, fast as a whip, pulled the katana from her back. The whine of the dead stabbed into my ears.

The crocotta shot towards her, kicking up dust.

"Bella! Duck!" Romeo threw a magenta flame ball as she crouched and rolled away. The ball hit the beast, and it let out a squeal that hurt my ears even more. Purple flames engulfed it completely, but it stayed on its feet, still screaming. "Daphne, help me! Daphne..."

Bella leapt to her feet, shot sideways, spun, and

brought the katana down on the crocotta's neck, slicing into its rough hide.

I wanted to scream at her. Not there! Underneath!

There was no way she'd cut through all that muscle. The easy way to cut that damn thing was to do it from the inside. Bella leapt aside like a matador and tried again, slicing a tiny gash in its neck. It screamed. "Daphne!"

The noise, it was too much. My senses were overloading. I could not handle it.

Another crocotta bounded into the courtyard, screaming. Romeo ran out to meet it, his hands pouring magenta flame. Another creature darted past that one. "Help! Daphne!" It shot straight towards me.

Fuck this. We need to shut them up, or they're gonna make us crazier than we already are.

I clenched my teeth, pushed myself up, and bolted towards the crocotta as it bounded at me, its mouth wide open, grinning.

Time slowed. I feinted left, moved right, ducked, spun on my feet, reached out with my blade...

And jammed the knife into the crocotta's mouth. The angle was perfect, pointing upwards, the serpentine metal pierced into the creature's brain. Black blood poured from its mouth, splashing me with its foulness.

Then another one screamed, and my head almost exploded.

Five crocotta packed the courtyard now, one dead. I yanked out my knife, not hesitating, and threw myself in a roll towards Bella's beast as she tried in vain to sever its head while it smoldered with purple flame. I thrust up from the ground, this time jamming my Orion blade in its ear. It froze, seized once, then its legs gave out. Yanking out the knife, I turned just in time to see another crocotta leap towards me.

I moved too slow. Its shoulder slammed into me, and I went flying, rolling painfully on the stone ground.

Before I could move, another one jumped, arms outstretched, sickle claws aiming for my throat. I did the only thing I could—lurch upwards, thrusting with both Orion blades. My serpentine metal had better luck than Bella's katana; both knives sank deep into the beast's chest, sliding in between ribs. I pushed hard and twisted, aiming for the heart.

Its teeth snapped only an inch from my face. Gods, the smell. Black blood gushed over my hands, as the creature's heart blood poured out of the holes I'd made.

My strength gave out, and I slumped back. The damned crocotta fell on top of me. Groaning, I used my blades—still stuck inside its ribs—to rock it sideways until I could shimmy out from underneath it.

The last two crocotta were still alive, both on fire. Bella was using her katana to slice one of them, a nick on the shoulder there, a cut on the back leg there.

Put it out of its misery, you bitch, my brain snarled.

Romeo watched the other crocotta, waiting for a second, then dived underneath it, scoring a deep slash on the underside of its belly with his magically sharpened KaBar knife. With a sickening wet sound, its entrails slithered out, uncoiling into the dust at our feet. It finally fell, landing with a thump, still smoldering.

I limped over to the last one, and, waiting until it

whipped towards Bella, I gritted my teeth and jammed my knife in its ear. The creature screamed, then collapsed.

CHAPTER
FORTY-THREE

My chest heaved.

"Was that it?" Bella glanced ahead. "Are there any more?"

I swallowed the bitter taste in my mouth. "Maybe. I can't tell. The smell of the dead ones here is overpowering. There could be more."

Romeo carefully patted me down. "You're okay?"

I glanced up at him. "I'm fine." I had a cracked collarbone, probably a slight concussion, and something inside me was *screaming* at me... but I was fine.

Romeo had a deep slash in his shoulder. Bella walked over, pulling a tiny med kit out of her combat pants. There was no time for that.

"We have to keep moving," I said.

She unzipped the bag anyway. "They might have arcane poison on their claws," she muttered, squeezing some bright orange cream directly onto his shoulder. "He could die from it."

Romeo froze. I wanted to scream. We had less than

forty-five minutes, and from what I could see, we'd only made it halfway up the labyrinth. He wasn't going to die from a crocotta scratch, but if I argued, it would only take longer and make me look like a heartless bitch. Bella was caring for him so tenderly...

"Stay still," she ordered, opening a bandage.

To make things even worse, another pulse pounded through the air. I glanced up. "They've summoned something else."

Bella slapped on the bandage. "What now?"

"I have no idea," I said, massaging my collarbone. "But it doesn't matter. We have to run. Let's go." I took off at a jog, panic clawing at my chest.

We caught up to the little copper pathfinder bird, following it carefully as it zipped left and right. We moved upwards frustratingly slowly, jogging through bathhouse-style pool sections, empty and filled with dust, and a little olive grove.

Suddenly, a high-pitched cry tore the air above us. I flinched as I ran.

"What was that?" Bella shouted.

"If it's what I think it is, we're really going to need to take cover." We couldn't hide now, though, there was no time. We had to keep running. "Romeo, you have a shield spell?"

"Not one that lasts for longer than eight minutes."

"Cast it," I said, slowing to a power-walk. He'd have to do it on the move. "Bella, do you have anything you could use?"

Bella tossed a little leather amulet at me. "Here." She swallowed. "I can't activate it, though."

Romeo, now with a silver glow running over the top of his head, took the amulet from me, examined it for a second, then drew a rune with his finger on the back. A glowing blue shield erupted out of it. I hefted it up and held it over my head, then handed it back to Bella. "You're going to need this. Stay underneath it."

"What about you?"

I'd already caught the scent of what I needed up ahead, and the pathfinder was headed in that direction. We turned left, and another little section opened up—a combat training yard. Like the rest of the labyrinth, it was trashed—broken spears, splintered beams, cracked floor. Darting towards the wall, I hefted a bronze shield off a rack.

It would have to do. I lifted it over my head and smiled. "Sometimes the old ways are best."

A bolt slammed into the ground next to me. Bella swore and skittered away. "What the hell was that?"

Damn it, sometimes I hated being right. "It's a feather," I said, moving back into a jog.

Romeo let out a grunt. "Stymphalian birds."

"You got it."

Bella looked up and swore. "Of all the things I hoped weren't real..."

"They're real, alright. They shoot metallic feathers like arrows, they have bronze razor-sharp beaks, and they will eat you. Whole, like a pelican, after stabbing you a billion times with the aforementioned razor-sharp beak." We raced through the training yard. Three more feather-bolts slammed into the ground, gleaming silver. One missed Bella's foot by inches.

Romeo shouted, "Bella!"

She darted around it. "I'm good!"

We ran, dodging feather-bolts and ducking as the bronze birds swooped at us, snapping their beaks. The walls of the labyrinth narrowed, giving us a little more cover. We ran with our shields up. Every now and then I caught a streak of bronze-and-silver whizzing past the bright strip of blue sky above us.

Ahead, the labyrinth opened abruptly, and we darted into a large space—a huge sunken amphitheater. I glanced up, seeing at least a dozen demon murder-birds flying overhead.

The stymphalian circled. We were stuck out in the open, and we had to get to the other side.

No hesitation, no regrets. "We have to sprint across."

Romeo pushed me forward. "Go!" The silver glow of his shield spell ran all over his body, making him look even more god-like than he already was. "Get to cover, I'll catch up." He strode forward, hands whirling in a circle, as he gathered more power. I knew I had to run. He'd be safe... but I really didn't want to leave him.

"Come on." Bella grabbed my free hand and pulled me. We raced down the bowl of the amphitheater and sprinted across the flat bottom, dodging the feather bolts as they slammed into the ground around us.

A bird screamed, then another. I turned, looked up, and saw an arrow of violet light impale one through the heart. Romeo had made a poison dart curse and fired it at the bird.

It was working, too. The stymphalian flailed in the air, spiraling down, and hit the ground with a thud. Bella and I ran up the other side of the deep bowl, my lungs and calf muscles burning. The stymphalian circling above us started to swoop, not towards us, but at Romeo.

My footsteps faltered. "We can't leave him!"

Bella pushed me forward. "He's got another six and a half minutes left in his shield charm, and we've both got nothing covering our legs. He's got this. We have to get to cover. Just move, damnit!"

She was right, and besides, Romeo would be pissed if we didn't get to safety.

We bolted towards the other side of the amphitheater. The little pathfinder bird hovered at the next archway, and we ran through it. I took a second to glance back.

Romeo strode across the amphitheater floor, skin glowing silver, his arms flexed like he was holding a bow. He walked quickly, bending his arm back and firing into the air. Another stymphalian fell to the ground with an ear-splitting scream.

Goddamn, these noises. I clutched my head for a second. The sounds in this little slice of Hellenic realm were grating on me like I'd never expected, I could barely concentrate. It made me want to...

Explode.

Desperately, I pulled myself together.

Bella tugged my wrist, drawing me further under the archway. We were entering a different section of the labyrinth now. The walls towered above us on either side, the space wider than before, like a great throne room with no ceiling. Marble plinths stood at regular intervals all the way up, ending in a glittering white wall at the end, with archways leading left and right.

Broken statues littered the floor—huge sculptures of heroes, gods, and goddesses. They'd have been over twelve feet tall if they'd been standing on their plinths. The destruction was shocking. Christopher Jupiter had stolen this slice of their realm and smashed it like a spoiled child with a fragile toy.

I inhaled carefully. A tingle of fear ran down my spine.

Bella jogged away from me, down the aisle, looking at the shattered remains of the broken sculptures carefully. "What is this place?"

I followed her, moving past her down the aisle. "The Hellenic deity version of an Instagram story. Smashed to pieces."

"This is awful. I think these were real people," she muttered. "Look at this." She gestured to the statue behind her.

Movement flashed above me. I glanced up at the strip of sky overhead and shouted, "Bella!"

She looked up, flinching. I bolted forward and tripped while I yanked my shield over my head. Stumbling sideways, I kicked a big loose stone with my toe, then, lurching backwards, my foot hit another stone, and it rolled away. Ouch, that hurt.

Regaining my balance, I crouched down, huddling under my shield, and shuddered. "I hate those damned birds."

Bella glanced up at the sky through her shield. "They've gone. Come on." She ushered me forward to join her and turned to look down the aisle. At the end, the pathfinder construct fluttered in midair, waiting for us at the left exit.

"Let's get under that archway and wait for Romeo," Bella said.

"Okay." We walked down the aisle. Suddenly, a sickly thud slammed into us. I gasped. "Bella!"

A wall flashed between us for a split-second, glowing blood red, then it disappeared completely. My mouth dropped open.

She spun on her feet. "Daphne!"

I gazed at her in horror and put my hand out, palm up. "It's a shrinking ward." My voice shook. "I'm stuck. Christopher Jupiter set a trap."

"No!" She held her hand up. "Daphne... no!"

"Don't touch it!" I screamed. Bella snatched her hand back and froze. "These things are only one-way." I explained. "If you fall in, you'll be stuck, too."

She shook her head, panicking. "Do you know how to break one? Can you break out of it, Daphne?"

"No." My mouth trembled. "You can't break a shrinking ward. It won't stop until all sides touch. It's going to compress until it kills me."

She gasped.

There. There it is. Do you see it?

I saw it. The tension in Bella's eyebrows softened, the muscle in her jaw relaxed. There was no glassy sheen of terror in her eyes. They were clear and blue.

I stared at her face and let out a soft sigh. "This is good news to you, isn't it?"

Bella's mouth dropped open. "What?" She shook her

head, confused. "No, Daphne, of course not! Don't worry, we'll get you out. There's gotta be some way."

I locked eyes with her. I was right. I knew I was right. *No hesitation, no regrets, and we trust ourselves.*

My stare morphed into a glare of hatred. "You *knew* this shrinking ward was here. You're happy I'm trapped. I can see it in your face. Don't lie to me, Bella," I said softly.

Her panicked, hurt expression melted. A smile pulled at her lips.

I knew it!

I shook my head, inhaling deeply through my nose to calm my racing pulse. "It's hard to act panicked when you're ecstatic, isn't it?"

Bella started to laugh. "Oh, sweetheart. You don't know the half of it."

CHAPTER
FORTY-FOUR

"I wasn't sure it would work," Bella said, her voice calm and measured. "Christopher said it would activate once someone stumbled into it."

"You're working with him." Desperately, I tried to control my breathing. "Let me guess. You're not making enough money stealing precious stones and valuable artifacts from poor communities and flogging them for millions, and that vile weasel Christopher is paying you billions of rubles to turn on your best friend."

She threw back her head and laughed out loud. "God, you're stupid. This isn't about money, Daphne. It's never been about money." She met my eyes again, smirking. "He's going to unbind me."

I gasped. "Oh. *Oh!* You're not an Orbiter, are you? You're a bound witch."

"Now you're finally catching up." Bella clapped, mocking me. "Well done."

I stared at her face for a long moment. "Aunt Marche bound you, didn't she?"

Her face twisted, and hatred flashed in her eyes. Suddenly, she looked so ugly. "That bitch," Bella hissed. "Yes, Marcheline bound me. She had no fucking *right*. I was only seven years old, and she fucking kicked in my bedroom door one day and did a spell to bind my magic. Do you know what it feels like?" Bella's voice rose to a shout. "Do you understand what it's like to have your power taken away?" She paused, glanced down the aisle, and took a deep breath, regaining control. "You have *no* idea. I did everything I could to get my magic back—*everything*—and nothing worked. I had a gut feeling that Romeo could help me, and we tried." She shook her head. "We tried everything. I couldn't feel the magic in him, but I just knew. For years... years! I tried to get him to work a spell that could help me, but nothing worked."

"You tried to get him to do blood magic." My voice was toneless.

Her hands shook. "He *did* do blood magic. I made sure of it. I wanted that bitch to come back and bind him, too, so I could kill her."

"Like you killed your dad?"

The flip switched again. She snorted, laughing. "That idiot? He was just a low-grade witch, a nobody. A client of my whore mother. I found him when I was sixteen. That moron didn't even have enough magic to unbind me, either, so I put him out of his misery." Her lips curved up into a smirk again. "But finally, I found someone that hated Aunt Marche as much as I did."

"Christopher," I breathed out.

"No, you idiot. His parents. Mina and Wesley attended a function at the university my foster parents taught at. I recognized them because they had money and got into a conversation with them." Her mouth twisted again. "And a year later, imagine my surprise when Romeo finally told me he'd found his magic. Imagine how I felt when he told me that a wonderful woman had shown up and taken him under her wing. Imagine what it did to my heart when he informed me that the High Priestess Marcheline gently scolded him and taught him that blood magic was bad, and that he should never do it again. He loved her, and it ruined *everything*," she snarled. "That bitch bound me, but she took him in and taught him everything she knew because he had more natural power than I did."

"No." I shook my head. "That's not why—"

"What the fuck do you know about it?' Bella spat.

I raised my chin. "Let me guess. When Romeo took the Jupiter heirdom, you made a deal with them."

"I made a deal with Christopher," she continued, like I hadn't already guessed. "I'd help him if he unbound my magic. He told me it would take a while to amass that kind of power. We worked together on a few projects. I suppose, over the years, he became like a mentor to me," she mused.

That made sense. They were so similar. Low-magic, weak, power-hungry. Entitled.

"So, I'm helping him summon this god." Her eyes met mine again, and she let out a bark of laughter. "I wish I could tell you all about that hole in your memory, but he said not to stir anything up until the time was right."

That surprised me. "What?"

She laughed scornfully. "You're a fool, Daphne, but you were right about one thing. Christopher's not going to summon Pandora."

My heart thumped uncontrollably. "Why would he...?" The *why* didn't matter. Only the *who* mattered. "W-Who? Who is he going to summon?"

Her smile stretched up to her ears, snake-like. "He's going to summon her maker. The big guy."

I shook my head once. "He can't."

"With enough power he can. And he's very confident he's going to have enough power." She shrugged carelessly. "And he's confident that once Zeus is in his body, he'll have enough power to make another Pandora."

Something inside me churned. I clutched my chest, panicking.

Bella laughed. "You don't even know why you're so scared. Don't worry, Daphne, you're not going to die. Not yet, anyway."

"I'm stuck in a fucking shrinking ward!" I snarled at her.

"Oh, relax. Christopher needs you alive, so you'll stay alive. You're right, there's no breaking these wards, but he knows how to slow them down." She giggled. "He knows how to speed them up, too. That was a fun afternoon lesson. We went through about a dozen rats, getting the timing just right."

My gut lurched. I had no words.

"So in about"—she checked her watch—"twenty-five minutes, Zeus will be in Christopher's body. He'll slow this shrinking ward down enough so there will be time to chip away the rock underneath your feet to get you out, and then I can get my magic unbound." A smile pulled at her lips. "And if Romeo stops Christopher, there won't be enough time to save you." She shrugged. "Either way, I win."

"What do you want, Bella? Money? Do you want me to try and get someone to—"

Her mouth twisted. "I want what's *mine*," she hissed. Taking a moment to compose herself, she leaned back. "Once the god is in Christopher's body, he'll give me Romeo."

CHAPTER
FORTY-FIVE

I screamed long and loud. "No!"

Romeo echoed me. "No! Daphne!"

He was coming. Bella's head whipped towards him as he appeared at the end of the grand hallway, then turned her bitter, twisted face back to me.

"If you tell him any of this, I'll make sure you die in there," she spat out through clenched teeth. "Your only chance is to keep your mouth shut."

I barely heard her. Romeo was bolting towards us, too fast, his ballistics shirt torn, a gash open in his combat pants. He'd battled the birds and won, but it had cost him. "Romeo! Stop!"

He didn't stop.

"It's a shrinking ward!" I screamed. "A trap! *Stop!*"

He slid to a halt, his face hard, eyes shining almost black with fury. His chest heaved. "Daphne—"

"You can't move," I told him. "I'm trapped inside it, and you can't be trapped, too. If you come any closer, we're both screwed." My voice dropped to a whisper and shook with emotion. "Please don't move, Romeo. Please."

His fists clenched. "No."

"Don't move!" I ordered. "You hear me? We can figure a way out of this."

"We need to stop Christopher," Bella said breathlessly. She checked her watch. "We've only got twenty minutes to get to him. We go, kill him, and come back and save her. Okay?"

Romeo's shoulders flexed. He didn't take his eyes off me. The atoms in the air began to vibrate dangerously.

Tread carefully... he's right on the edge.

I held up my hand and pointed at him. "Romeo Zarayan, listen to me, because I'm only going to say this once." I pulled one Orion blade out and held it to my wrist, never breaking eye contact with him. "If you fall to blood magic to get me out of here, I swear I will die before you rip the floor out from underneath me. Do you hear me?"

He heard me. The storm inside him surged, sending a shudder through his massive shoulders.

"No!" Bella screamed. She needed me alive, too. "Romeo, don't listen to her!"

I lifted my chin. "I'll do it. You know I will. But there's another way. There's always another way. You just need to find it." *Choose me. Please, choose me.*

The marble floor trembled again.

"Romeo!" Bella shouted at him. "We need to go. Daphne is stuck, but we'll get her out. We've got time for her, but not for Christopher. Come with me. We need to go."

"No."

"Romeo…" Bella's voice held a warning. "Come on. It's the only way."

He didn't look at her. He looked at me, and I stared back at him. His eyes bored into mine. The storm surged out of control, tearing him in two.

Choose me, I silently begged him. *Please. Choose me.*

Bella screamed. "Romeo! Look at me!"

He didn't. The ground under my feet trembled. "No," he said again. "I'm not leaving her."

"Romeo, please! Come with me!"

My heart pounded uncontrollably. *Choose me.*

Power surged around him, glowing bright and pouring off his skin. "I'll never leave her." His voice deepened, echoing around the hall. "Daphne is mine. My love."

The floor shook.

"My *only*."

Something broke, an invisible string twanged, and Romeo's massive shoulders hitched and shuddered. The scent hit me—a spell of oleander and blade mace, bound in blood. It flared, choking me, then it faded away, disappearing completely.

Silence. The world was still.

"You've done it," I whispered. "It's done. You've broken the tie."

Romeo's chest heaved like he'd run a marathon. He stumbled forward, falling onto one knee. Silver sweat glistened on his brow. He stared at me, confused and overwhelmed. Speechless.

He chose me.

I let out a sob of joy. "You've done it. It's gone."

Bella felt it, too. She gazed down at her hands, trying to understand what had just happened. "What was that?"

I turned to her. "The spell Romeo did when you were kids. He told me about it. He tried to do a spell to tie you together so you couldn't be separated. He thought it hadn't worked, but it did. The magical tie has been binding you two together emotionally for two decades. Now, it's gone. Romeo is feeling his own feelings for the first time since he was a child."

My words hung in the air. I watched the thoughts play out on Bella's face—shock, confusion, chagrin, then... rage.

Defiance. Entitlement.

The tie made no difference to her. She was still going to have him.

"We don't have time for this," she said, plastering a panicked expression on her face. "Suck it up, Romeo. We have to get moving." She held out her hand and took a step forward towards him. "We have—" She took another step, hit the ward, and stumbled back. Her eyes widened. "What the *fuck?*"

I walked over to Romeo and slid my hands over his shoulder. "Just breathe for a moment, baby," I whispered. He was going to need a minute to adjust.

Let's spend that time wisely, my brain suggested. *Now that's he's free, let's take this opportunity to stab as many holes in that bitch—*

Bella let out a frustrated snarl. "Romeo!" Her hands

patted the air in front of her, feeling the ward, then she made a fist and punched it.

"That's not going to help," I said.

Bella froze. She'd finally realized it. She wasn't touching the outside of the ward. Her eyes widened in shock.

Ah, fuck, Brain Daphne sulked. *I forgot about that part. No stabby stabby, I suppose.*

Turning, I smiled at Bella. "I'm not stuck in the ward. You are."

CHAPTER
FORTY-SIX

"I could smell the edges of it," I told her. "It's a smell I'll never forget, not even for a million years. The stones that Christopher used to mark the edges for you so you could lure me into it—they were smooth river stones, and they had no place in a hall full of broken marble pieces." I shrugged. "I just kicked a couple of the marker stones over and maneuvered you around, so you'd get stuck in it instead."

"You fucking bitch!" Spit flecked from her mouth, and she slammed her hand on the ward. "You absolute fucking—" Her expression changed whip-fast, and she wiped the fury off her face. She began to wail as if her heart was breaking. "Romeo! Romeo, help me. She did this on purpose! She tricked me!"

"Sure did." I grinned at her. "And that's not going to work anymore. You can't tug on his heart. The magic tie is gone."

Besides, Romeo was still in shock, processing the emotional snapback from the broken spell. He was beginning to stir, though. His racing pulse was evening out. The sweat was no longer beading on his skin. He took deep, even breaths.

"Romeo... I'm your sister!"

"Foster sister," I corrected. "And you've been playing him like a fiddle for years. Finally, he'll be able to see it clearly, and his judgement of you won't be clouded by the magical tie between you."

"There was no tie," Bella screamed, banging a fist on the ward again. "We're family! We look out for each other. We love each other!"

I'd have to do this quickly. Romeo could hear it now; he'd recovered enough. And he needed to hear it all, like ripping off a Band-Aid.

It was going to fucking hurt. "He might have loved you as a kid, because he thought you were protecting him. The spell he cast to tie you together made him think he loved you, and because of it, he couldn't see you objectively. You're a terrible person, Bella, and you always have been. You were the one that encouraged Romeo to do blood magic, even though you knew it was wrong, because Aunt Marche bound you for doing it."

Romeo stirred. He definitely heard that. His pulse quickened again. "What did you say?"

"It happened just before you met, when you were five, and she was seven. She's not an Orbiter; she's a bound witch." I turned back to Bella and held up my fingers, quickly listing everything I had on her—out of order, but it didn't matter. "This whole time, right from the start, you've been trying to get me alone, to drag me off to 'protect' me, but you've just been trying to haul me off and deliver me to Christopher. You misdirected the hunt for the Tear of Zeus to Chicago. I was willing to blow that off as your mistake, but you knew immediately that we were chasing Frankie Two-Coins when we told you we were in New York."

Bella's eyes widened in shock.

"Then, the background stuff. You were there when Brandon was sent to assassinate Romeo. It wasn't a coincidence. You knew it was going to happen because it was the Jupiters who'd bought him from the People of the Claw and sent him to kill Romeo when he took the heirdom. Right?"

The spark of fury in her eye told me I was right.

"And you tried to stop the assassination, because you're obsessed with Romeo. The tie wouldn't let you sit on your hands and let him be killed. You were also the one who almost killed Cole in New York, right? You thought the trauma of Cole's death might finally bring you and Romeo to the next level, and you were pissed that Romeo was gathering close friends that weren't you. Right? But Cole survived."

She ground her jaw. "You fucking—"

"Oh, I'm not done. Those were just wild guesses, but I can see I was right. I've got more concrete stuff. I checked Aunt Marche's journals. There were pages ripped out, and those pages coincided with the time just before you were moved into the new group home with Romeo at seven years old."

I swallowed, suddenly feeling overwhelmed. Gods, I'd loved that woman. "Those pages would have documented Aunt Marche binding the magic of a little girl, but you went through them, found the pages that mentioned you, and tore them out."

Romeo lifted his head. His brow furrowed. He looked at Bella in the ward, as if he'd never seen her before.

I charged on. "I knew it was you that tore out the pages. I caught a hint of your scent on the journals."

"No." Bella shook her head frantically. "Don't listen to her. Romeo..."

"And you told Christopher where we were headed every step of the way in the hunt for the Tear of Zeus," I continued. "By this stage, I was sure you were betraying us. I was hoping if I kept an ear out, you wouldn't be able to tell him we were headed to the gallery, but you had him on the phone during the interview with the awful artist woman, Veronica, didn't you? That's why you repeated the name of the town, and the name of the gallery, and specified that the Tear was there—so he could get to it first. I thought if I rode there, I'd definitely get there before him, but I lost that round."

Her mouth twisted, fury overwhelming her. She wasn't denying it anymore, at least.

"Then, you got desperate. You got sloppy. Your helicopter wasn't getting serviced in New York. You gave it to Christopher so he could get to Beacon, get the Tear of Zeus, and get back to Philly. You didn't have zippixie stones in your bag. What you had was noxie stones." I glared at her. "Noxie stones aren't poop, they're the compressed internal organs of nox pixies, which is bad enough to start with, but if Romeo had taken one of those, he would have fallen unconscious within the hour. And he'd be out of action, safe for you to come and pick up once Christopher completed the summoning."

"No!" Bella started to cry. "It's not true."

"You tried to kill Dwayne on the helicopter." I pressed my attack further. "You were controlling that spiral. I don't know anything about helicopters, but I can tell when someone's in control of a machine. You were trying to throw him into the rotors."

Bella let out a desperate wail.

"And, finally..." I pointed at her. "You smell like a witch. Witches smell like herbs and candlewax. It's so, so faint, because it's missing the punch of magic to go with it. But it's still there. I suspected you were a bound witch right from the very start, and after a while, all the puzzle pieces started to click together perfectly."

Romeo, still kneeling, finally stood. He stared at Bella in the ward, his mouth slightly open. He shook his head.

Brain-Daphne took over my mouth, wanting to rub it in. "Right from the start. I knew you were an evil twisted psycho bitch. Right from the *very* start. I just had to get Romeo to break the spell, to cut the tie with you, so he could finally see who you really are."

Bella let out a sob. "Romeo, she's gone crazy. It's me. You have to believe me."

"Oh, one last thing." I waved my phone. "I taped your little confession. Romeo can listen to it now, because he's not tied to you so he'll be able to hear it properly."

Opening my video app, I pressed play, fast-forwarded to a random spot, and held up my phone. In the silence that followed, we heard Bella's voice clearly coming out of the phone. "...that *bitch*. Yes, she bound me. She had no fucking right! I was only seven years old, and she fucking kicked in my bedroom door one day and did a spell to bind my magic. Do you know what it feels like?"

I stopped the video. My alarm buzzed; we only had fifteen minutes to stop Christopher. My brain poked me. *This has been fun, babes, but we gotta wrap it up.*

Or did we? Bella said Christopher was summoning Zeus, and that really just wasn't possible. Zeus wouldn't come here, and there was no way Christopher could amass the power to compel him. The worst he could do was blow himself up.

This is a pocket dimension, jammed into the Jupiter mansion, my brain reminded me. *He might tear a hole in it and blow us all up. Anyway, we can't risk it. This ward has about twelve hours before it squishes this bitch, let's gloat later.*

Romeo unlocked his clenched jaw, narrowing his eyes on Bella. "So, it's true," he growled softly and shook his head. "It's all true, isn't it?" Rage emanated from him, but now, it was different. He wasn't being pulled in two directions anymore. His anger was justified and untainted by Bella's influence.

The storm was over; the retribution was just beginning.

"She bound *me*, but not you!" Bella threw herself at the ward, punching it with her fist. "It's not fair!"

I felt the need to defend Marche's choices, even just to rub it in. "Romeo was just using blood. You were using the suffering; *that's* why she bound you. With magic, intention is everything, and Romeo never intended on hurting anyone. The worst thing he did was the cord spell that tied you two together, because it has let you emotionally poison him ever since. And *that's* why he glossed over the fact that you're immoral, unethical, and an all-round terrible person. You steal precious artifacts off poor people and sell them for millions, you peddle the body parts of sentient creatures, you profit off of slave labor and blood diamonds."

I wasn't watching Romeo's face, but I could feel the air trembling around him. Bella was, though. She was watching him, and for the first time, she looked scared.

Good. She deserved it. "You're a piece of shit," I added. "But Romeo excused all that because of the magical tie." Something else occurred to me. I thrust a finger. "*That's* why he still hates Aunt Marche! Because *you* do. But he's broken the tie, and now he can finally forgive her."

And boy, the tie was really broken now. All these revelations were slamming into him like bullets, and I could feel the fury rolling off him like lava down a mountain.

"Bella." He growled and took a step toward her.

"Whoa, there." I grabbed him, wrapping both of my hands around one enormous bicep and tried to pull him back. "Don't get any closer, baby." My feet slid on the dusty stone as he effortlessly dragged me with him. "Romeo? The ward? Christopher? The summoning?"

He flinched and looked at his watch. "Ten minutes. We gotta go."

I directed him around the edges of the shrinking ward, and we backed away and jogged towards the exit. *One last parting shot, please?*

Go on, then. "Oh, and Bella?" I swiveled on my feet, pirouetting before we reached the archway. "Christopher could have unbound you years ago, you know. Mina's magic was bound, but she's up there at the top of the labyrinth with her son and husband, summoning monsters."

Bella curled her hands into fists. Her face screwed up in righteous anger, and she screamed like a banshee. "Fuck you!" She bashed her fists on the ward, over and over again. "Fuck you, you stupid fucking *bitch!*"

"I told you he didn't share power," I called out. We dashed through the archway, chasing the pathfinder. "You should have listened to me."

CHAPTER
FORTY-SEVEN

Almost there. We were almost there—at the very least, we were out of the labyrinth and in what I assumed was Hyperion's palace. We were so close, I could smell the magic of the Tear of Zeus now and the sharp ozone scent of the open doorway. It made my heart hammer against my ribs so hard, it knocked the breath out of me.

I told my body to relax. The chances of Christopher being able to summon Zeus were zero. He was going to be a victim of his own hubris. We were going to be fine. Although, I should check. "Did you get all the stymphalian birds?"

"Yeah," Romeo grunted. His thigh was drenched in blood, but if it was bothering him, he didn't show it. He ran with powerful and efficient strides like an elite soldier. We bolted through an open-air banquet hall, dodging golden cups and plates that littered the floor.

The ground shook, then again, and again. I checked my watch, and we slowed to a walk. "Earthquake?"

"No." Romeo's eyes narrowed. "Footsteps."

Another thump shook the floor. We ran to the nearest archway and peeked inside the next section of the palace.

A massive open-air ballroom lay before us, lined with columns that had survived the trip. The floor was an exquisite mosaic depicting a huge monster battle in gleaming marble. I leaned further inside.

A giant man wearing nothing but a dirty loincloth stumbled around the ballroom. He was at least twenty feet tall, with nut-brown skin, massive shoulders, and a thick muscular frame. His bare feet stomped on the floor, shaking the whole room.

Dwayne was in there, too. He hovered in the air in front of the giant, flapping his blackened-tipped wings lazily. A giant ball on a red string dangled from his beak.

Wait. That wasn't a ball. It was an eyeball.

I glanced at the giant again. A cyclops. He stumbled left and right.

Dwayne smirked. **Marco!**

The giant stretched out his arms, let out an angry grunt, and lunged at Dwayne, who banked left, missing the huge grasping fingers by inches. Dwayne then twirled the eyeball around on its optic nerve, winding it up, and smacked the cyclops right in the loincloth. **Polo!**

I had to do something. "Dwayne!"

He flew in a circle around the giant's head, narrowly avoiding a swipe from the cyclops's meaty fist. **Yes, baby girl?**

I didn't know what to say. I stammered for a second. "That's not how you play Marco Polo!"

Romeo let out a bark of laughter.

I turned to him, amazed. "Did you actually just laugh? You never laugh. And I'm not sure if this is funny, Romeo," I added, pursing my lips. "This might be an animal cruelty situation."

A meaty thump distracted me; the cyclops had caught Dwayne with a backhand. **Ow. Ooh, that's going to leave a mark.**

"I'm just not sure which animal is doing the cruelty," I added.

"I'm not laughing at him." Romeo gave me his beautiful crooked smile. "It's you. I never know what is going to come out of your mouth, but whatever it is, it always makes me happy."

My heart melted as the floor trembled underneath us. The giant staggered back and forth, heavy feet thumping on the mosaic floor.

"Well, make me happy and do something," I said, waving my arm at Dwayne and the Cyclops. "We need to get through that ballroom without getting squashed or hit by a giant eyeball."

"Got it." Romeo turned and called out to Dwayne. "Sir, could you please put the giant out of his misery?"

Can't. I've been trying. This big fucker is quicker than he looks. Dwayne flapped his wings, dodging a series of swipes and grabs from the enraged cyclops. **And honestly, his aim is much better since I took his eye out. I think I've unlocked some sort of sixth sense, actually.**

"He says he's been trying, but the cyclops is quicker

than he looks." I shouted into the ballroom. "We have to get through, Dwayne!"

Okay, I'll distract him, you guys make a run for it.

I huffed out a breath. "How are you going to distract him?"

Dwayne wound up the eyeball and slugged the cyclops in the groin.

"Come on." Romeo grabbed my hand, and we bolted through the ballroom, hugging the walls as the cyclops staggered around, trading blows with a god of chaos.

CHAPTER
FORTY-EIGHT

Only four minutes to go. I caught a peek of the summit, only fifty yards away, while we ran up a winding pathway in a rose garden. Christopher was still there in front of the altar, chanting with his arms outstretched. The Star Door glowed blood red behind him, and it was getting brighter.

Christopher was alone, though. Mina and Wesley had vanished. So, too, had both the big Russian mages.

"Watch out!" Romeo reached out and pulled me aside as a smoking green ball flew through the space where my head had been only a second before. It slammed into a rose bush behind me, which shriveled and turned to ash almost instantly. "They're throwing curses." Romeo met my eye. "High alert."

"Why would he send his sacrifices down to attack us? He needs them." We crept down another path, taking cover behind a low stone wall.

I smelled the curse before I saw it and yanked Romeo backwards as another smoking ball slammed into the wall beside his head. We fell backwards together. The rock wall started to melt.

"On the wall, three o'clock," Romeo said.

"The other one is, uh, on the other wall," I replied. "At, uh, ten-thirty? Ten forty-five, maybe?"

He pressed his lips together, trying not to smile. "We're in a life-or-death situation here, baby."

"I was never in the military, Romeo. What I mean is that he's somewhere closer to eleven o'clock on the wall to my left—"

Another ball shot towards us, this one flaming orange. We rolled out of the way as it splashed vile acid. Romeo rolled to his feet, springing up, a tiny violet pebble in his hand. He threw it, reared back immediately, and threw himself on top of me, covering me.

Light flashed. A man screamed, long and loud, turning into a tortured gurgle at the end.

"One down," Romeo whispered, rolling off me.

The other volkhv was quick to respond, pelting a volley of smoke-streaked curses at us. Sickly green balls hurtled through the air. We ducked and ran, taking cover behind a low wall, then crouched behind a stout marble statue of a sea monster.

"Have you got anything I can throw?" I panted. "Anything that I don't have to use magic to activate?"

Another curse smashed into the statue. I flinched. The statue started to grow fuzzy mold where the curse hit it.

"Here." Romeo handed me a grenade.

I looked at it and shrugged. "That will do." Throwing myself to the left, away from the statue, I rolled, leapt to my feet, dashed a few yards, sighted the hooded man on the wall, pulled the pin, waited... then threw the little green bomb as hard as I could.

It exploded. The sound of tumbling rocks didn't drown out the tortured scream of a Russian mage.

"That's both of them gone," I huffed in a deep breath. "Christopher has lost both his sacrifices. He can't even summon even a powerless god, now."

Romeo let out a deep exhale. "We need to end this, though."

"Agreed."

He took my hand, and we ran.

CHAPTER
FORTY-NINE

Three minutes to go. The garden opened up to an orchard, right at the top of the mountain. We could see Christopher clearly, just up a grassy hill lined with gnarled apple trees. His arms were held up high; a triumphant smile pulled at his lips.

Why is he smiling? Brain-Daphne demanded. *Why does he look so smug?*

I glanced around the apple orchard and met Romeo's eyes.

Something was wrong. I could smell a curse being brewed. Romeo could smell it, too. His expression turned stony.

"Stay behind me," he whispered.

We moved slowly through the silky emerald blades of grass, heading uphill. The trees whispered softly, leaves brushing together overhead in a non-existent breeze.

The attack came from our left. Mina Jupiter stepped out from behind a tree and flung an armful of black smoke in the air, screaming words of power. The smoke whirled, morphing into the shape of a wyvern. I skittered backwards, giving Romeo room to counter it.

Fuck this, my brain snarled. *Let's go and hunt.*

That was a fantastic idea. I pulled out my blades. While Romeo drew on his magic to create his own smoke-demon to counter Mina's curse, I moved into a crouch, ducked behind a fat apple tree, pausing for a moment, and reached out with my senses.

There. Five trees up, three to the left. I bolted to the right, giving myself more cover, and sprinted as fast as I could, one, two, three...

After the sixth tree, I did a loop, and, light on my feet, crept up on him. Wesley Jupiter crouched low behind the fat trunk of a gnarled, ancient tree, his palms brimming with purple flames. He was waiting to ambush us. From here, he had a direct line of sight to where his wife attacked Romeo, screaming curses and waving her arms, while directing the smoke-wyvern to snap out with its jaws and consume him.

I snuck up behind Wesley. There was no time for theatrics. I slid the blade in his back, found his kidney, and twisted. He let out a sharp cry of pain and convulsed. Downhill, between the trees, we both watched as Romeo batted Mina's smoke-wyvern away almost lazily, and, spreading his fingers, made a stabbing motion towards her. Light streamed off his fingers like lasers. A beam hit Mina in the chest, striking her heart.

She gasped, her mouth wide open. Her body turned to stone—first her torso, then shoulders, followed by her arms and legs. She let out a scream as the flesh of her neck became marble, and finally, her face was frozen forever in a terrified grimace.

"This is how it ends," I whispered in Wesley's ear. There was always time for theatrics. "You finally paid for all your sins." I twisted the knife again. His cry turned into a death rattle.

My watch beeped. I flinched. "One minute!"

Romeo tossed another spell behind him as he ran—it hit the statue of Mina and exploded, vaporizing her completely.

CHAPTER
FIFTY

"Christopher's only got one minute." We dashed up the hill. "But he's got nobody to sacrifice. We just need to take down the flame ward around him," I panted. "And finally kill him."

We sprinted out of the orchard and up the grassy hill towards the altar and the huge olive tree. Christopher hadn't moved—his arms were held high as he chanted.

And he was still smiling in triumph.

His grin grew wider as we approached. Maybe he thought we were dumb enough to run into the fire ward. "There." I pointed at the line where the fire ward started. "It's there, Romeo. Please take it down quickly."

"He can't summon anything," Romeo mumbled to himself as he pressed his fingertips to the ground. A dark yellow glow appeared in front of us. Christopher locked eyes with me through the ward, smiled, and kept chanting.

"I need a minute," Romeo grunted.

My watch beeped. Thirty seconds. Not enough time. It didn't matter though, because—

An awful scream tore through the air. I whirled around and looked down. From up high, I could see the whole labyrinth spread out below us.

Bella screamed. My eyes found her.

The edges of the shrinking ward contracted. I could see it so clearly, scraping away every speck of dust on that grand hall floor, leaving a shining ring behind it. It was getting smaller and smaller and smaller...

He can speed up the shrinking ward! my brain screamed. *He's going to kill her!*

It was already too small. Bella let out a desperate cry that cracked my heart as the invisible walls of the ward closed in on her.

"She's the sacrifice! Romeo, it's Bella! The sacrifice!" My words ran together; there was not enough time. "*Hesbetrayedherandisusinghersufferingandherblood!*"

Ten seconds.

The ward splintered and cracked. "Done." Romeo turned. "Oh, fuck."

"It's too much!" I yelled desperately, pulling him backwards. "Christopher's got too much magic now. Zeus won't come, no matter how much magic Christopher uses! It's all going to backfire! We have to get out of here! This whole place is going to explode!"

Christopher shouted the last verse of the spell. The Tear of Zeus lit up like a beacon, streaming red light into the sky.

Time slowed. I watched Romeo's expression as he took in the sight of Bella, his foster sister, his former best friend, bloody and mangled, squashed like a slab of meat until she was liquid. I watched as the realization hit him —Bella's anger at being thwarted, the heartbreak of losing him, her only obsession, to me... then the anxiety of being trapped in a shrinking ward, the fear of watching it close in, the terror of suddenly watching it speed up. Her suffering, her agony, her pain, and finally, the ultimate pain of Christopher's betrayal.

I watched Romeo turn and look at Christopher Jupiter with the hatred of a thousand suns burning in his eyes. "It's too much."

That much blood magic, *that* much suffering...

Christopher raised his hands and screamed the last words into the sky. The stream of red light behind him flashed brighter.

Romeo threw himself over me, covering me.

The Tear of Zeus exploded.

CHAPTER
FIFTY-ONE

Both of us flew through the air, landing in the orchard fifty yards away. I thudded into the grass and rolled to a stop, thankfully not losing consciousness, and shook my head, trying to clear my vision.

Up ahead, the altar burned. The Tear was gone. So was Christopher. I blinked, but I couldn't find him or any of his remains anywhere. Vaporized? Definitely. An explosion that big, there was no way he was still alive, not even with a god in his body.

Scrambling to my feet, I tried to focus. A hole appeared in the altar. It was black—too black, swallowing all the light around it, and it was growing rapidly. "Romeo!"

He lay a few yards away, blood pouring from a gash in his head. My legs buckled underneath me. They weren't working properly. I crawled over to him. "Romeo?"

My senses screamed at me, everything trying to get

my attention all at once. A dangerous scent blasted through the orchard—the distinct bitter-ozone smell of suddenly unstable atoms. The atmosphere itself was shrieking in panic.

This tiny pocket dimension was imploding.

Romeo didn't move. The gash in his head wasn't deep, but he'd been hit by a flying rock and knocked unconscious. My fingers felt for a pulse, and I let out a sob when he stirred. "Come on, baby, we have to run!"

I glanced back up and saw the altar had disappeared, swallowed by the black hole. As I watched, the mighty olive tree next to it buckled, groaned, and was dragged out of the earth and sucked into the nothingness.

Desperately, I wrenched Romeo up into a sitting position and tried to haul him over my shoulder. The whole side of my body screamed in pain. Something was broken.

Torn labrum. Push through it. We'll heal later. Go. Go!

I couldn't. My body wasn't responding to my brain's commands. Nevertheless, I tried again, rolling him from the ground and trying to lift him up, but I collapsed back into the grass.

Romeo let out a groan and blinked, trying to focus. "Daph..."

"We have to go!" I begged him. "Please, Romeo, get up!'

His voice was a rough whisper. "Leave me. Go." His eyes rolled back in his head. "Get to..."

I got this, baby girl. Dwayne clumsily swooped in beside me on burned wingtips, growing bigger as he landed and waddled a few feet forward. He was now the size of a horse. Blood streaked his white feathers.

I let out a cry of relief. "Get us out of here, please, Dwayne! This place is imploding!"

Wrap yourself up in that. He tossed something at me—a brown stained sheet—and stomped over to Romeo. The atmosphere gave another mighty shiver as he flipped Romeo over, bent his neck, and used his wingtip to scoop Romeo onto his back. **There you go, hot stuff. Hold on.**

I rolled into the middle of the bloody sheet, trying not to breathe at the overwhelming stench, and held up the four corners above my head for Dwayne to pick up in his beak. We'd done this before.

Alrighty then, Dwayne muttered in my head. **Stork mode activated.**

We lifted off. Wrapped up in this stinking sheet, I couldn't see anything, and I couldn't breathe, because if I opened my mouth, I'd suffocate to death. But I could hear Dwayne's mighty wings flapping and the rumbling sound of rocks splitting, rolling, and being dragged into the widening black hole at the top of Hyperion's pillar.

Don't panic, my brain muttered. *Don't panic. We're going to make it. We've got about twenty seconds before this dimension disappears completely. We're going to make... Wait. Wait, is this the fucking cyclops's loin cloth?*

Dwayne flew straight, soaring down the mountain, then dropped abruptly and levelled out for a few seconds. His voice hollered in my head. **Tell your fanged friend to hold on, little one!**

The world suddenly turned dark—we'd reached the ragged edges of the dimension. I heard a sharp cry, and suddenly, a hard body slammed into me.

Micah. He was still holding the rope we'd left him with. "Hold on!" I screamed at him. "We're getting out of here!"

"Daphne?"

"Yeah!" I shouted. "It's me!"

"What is that *stench?*"

I was out of breath. I sandwiched my mouth together, held my nose, and counted the seconds.

Brace yourselves. This is going to be a rough landing. Dwayne's tone turned grim. **When we hit the ground, we got about three seconds to get out before this whole place collapses.**

My heart pounded in my chest. The rumble around us grew to deafening levels. I took a breath and regretted it. I braced myself, arms loose, legs primed and ready.

Three, two, one—

My feet scraped along the ground. Dwayne let go, and I rolled in a ball, getting tangled in the putrid loincloth. Ignoring the pain in my hip, I scrambled to my feet and threw off the sheet.

Right in front of us, a perfect circle displayed a tiny fragment of the park in Fitler Square. We'd made it. Micah, scraped and bloody from the rough landing, grabbed my hand and bolted towards it.

A roar deafened me. Dwayne shoved me from behind with his head. **Don't look back. Go, go, go!**

Micah tugged me through the hole in the ward, and

we dived out into the fresh air, thumping painfully down the concrete steps.

Romeo's Escalade idled at the curb. Brandon thrust his head out the window. "Get in, now!"

No, not yet. Is he there? Is he okay?

Panic clutched my chest. I looked back. The size he was now, there was no way Dwayne was getting through that hole—especially with Romeo on his back. Ignoring the pain in my side, I crawled frantically back up the steps, just in time to see Dwayne toss Romeo unceremoniously in the direction of the hole.

Romeo landed half-in-half-out. Dwayne gave him a little kick. **This is your stop, hot stuff.**

The mansion shook. Stone cracked like gunfire. The whole place was going to collapse on top of us. I reached in the hole and pulled, helping Romeo through as he staggered out on all fours, Dwayne shoving him from behind with his head at the same time. Finally, Romeo got free of the hole, and I let out a wild cry of relief.

Dwayne, shrinking rapidly, ducked out behind him, and used Romeo's body as a ramp, running down his back. **Move your ass, people.**

Suddenly, Brandon was at my side, helping me up. Micah hefted Romeo to his feet, and we staggered towards the open doors of the Escalade.

The mansion collapsed.

One second it was standing, the next, it was a broken pile of concrete and stone. Smoke and dust mushroomed into the air, choking us and pelting the Escalade with shrapnel.

What wasn't crushed burst into flames. Sirens screamed in the distance.

The Jupiter mansion—and the Jupiters themselves—were gone for good.

CHAPTER
FIFTY-TWO

I hated Mondays.

This one was especially bad. Nobody ever told you how depressing it was to have to drag yourself back to the office the day after saving the world.

I was tired, battered, bruised, heartsick, and, to top it off, I had to endure a machine-gun scolding from my boss, Monica.

"... have to be available, Daphne, that's what on-call means, you're supposed to answer your phone when it rings, and I've had to deal with four different emergency services blowing up my inbox because they couldn't get hold of the O-CPS on-call last night..."

Monica, as usual, didn't stay still, she paced back and forth behind her desk like a video game character stuck on a basement level.

To make it worse, Judy was watching. I could see her out of the corner of my eye, her puffy face scrunched up, nodding in self-righteous disapproval.

And, as if things couldn't get any worse... I deserved

this. In all the drama of chasing the Tear of Zeus, playing a deadly game of chess with Bella, and bringing down Christopher Jupiter, I'd forgotten I was supposed to be on-call this weekend. Four urgent O-CPS calls had come in, and I hadn't answered any of them. The guilt made me feel nauseous.

"... we were very, very lucky that Sergeant Hart realized you were AWOL," Monica said. "Because he called James, who diverted the on-call number to his phone and took the rest of the emergency calls yesterday, but we had four little kiddos who were forced to sit in police interview rooms for hours waiting for an O-CPS officer to come and get them!"

"I'm so sorry, Monica." I hung my head in shame. "I messed up, and I feel really awful."

"You should, Daphne, because this has ruined our stats for this month!" Monica darted back and forth. Hopefully she'd run out of caffeine soon, because I wasn't sure how much of this I could take. "Judy says I should go easy on you because you were obviously out partying and getting drunk and high, and you just forgot that you were on call but seriously, doll, you're a grown-up now, you need to take responsibility and answer your work phone when it rings..."

Tell her to shove her work phone up her ass, Brain-Daphne muttered. *We saved the whole damn world yesterday.*

I wasn't sure we had. Christopher Jupiter never had a chance. His hubris was the death of him in the end. Anyone that knew Zeus understood that he would never come to the mortal realm ever again, and being summoned by a mere witch—even one who'd amassed as much blood magic as Christopher—would offend him terribly.

I never thought Christopher would be that arrogant, my brain mused. *Not to the point of stupidity. Are we sure it was Zeus he wanted?*

Bella said it was, and she knew what he was up to better than anyone. I did remember she was being a little weird about it, talking about how Christopher wasn't going to summon Pandora—and of course he wasn't, why would he want her?—but Christopher was going to summon Zeus, the one who'd made her, so he could be super-powerful *and* make another Pandora.

She got that wrong, though. Zeus didn't make Pandora; he made the box. It was the dude with the broken feet who made her... What's his name? Hephaestus. That's it.

An icy shiver ran through me, but I chased it away. It didn't matter. Christopher was gone—nothing survived that explosion, not even the mansion that held the dimension. He'd put everything on that one chance, and the blowback killed him.

It almost killed us, too. The mansion was destroyed completely. Within seconds, the rubble was swarmed by normie emergency services, searching for survivors. All they found was Wesley's body underneath a pile of concrete.

"So that's it." Monica stomped her feet, clicking her heels on the floor in a weird tap-dancing movement that I'd come to understand meant she was almost done talking. "You're on call for the rest of the week, all night, every night, no exceptions."

"Monica..." I moaned. Romeo and I had been planning a debrief night—

Both kinds, my brain sniggered.

"No exceptions," Monica snapped, pointing her whiteboard marker at me. "You answer every callout, and you cover every overnight emergency until you're off my shit list, you hear me?"

"I hear you." I hung my head again. Romeo was still injured, and we'd only had time to chug some healing potion and fall into bed next to each other last night. I was still injured, too—my hip was killing me, and I was back in my pressure garments to help ease the pain of my burned, sliced, and gravel-rashed skin.

One day, though, we would have a proper date, from start to finish.

And I would make sure that both of us finished, at least twice. Three or four times, hopefully.

James knocked on the glass door of Monica's office. "Sorry to interrupt."

"It's okay, we're done." Monica gave me one last stern look and turned to James. "What can I help you with?"

But James was looking at me. "There's a couple of normies out in the human CPS office asking for you, Daphne."

I frowned. That was unusual, but whoever it was must have gotten security clearance to get in. I got up, wincing a little. Everything was still so damn sore. "Thanks, James."

"They're at reception."

Making my way out of our little Otherworld office, I

walked through the much busier human CPS. Two men stood just to the right of the reception desk—both in suit pants, slightly crumpled white shirts, and ties—one brown, one blue. The big one on the left with the bald head had a bullish expression and was wearing too much aftershave. The one on the right—lanky and tired looking—had salt-and-pepper hair that had grown out too much and needed cutting. Both of them watched me as I walked towards them; their eyes assessing me carefully, cataloging everything—my face, my body, clothes, shoes, hair, expression.

Aha. Detectives. Human police detectives, total normies, completely unaware of the supernatural world. Occasionally I had to liaise with the human police, but I'd only ever dealt with Otherworld detectives. I didn't recognize either of them, but from the recognition in their expressions, they knew who I was.

"Daphne Ironclaw?"

"Yes?" I looked at one, then the other. "Can I help you with something?"

The bald one flipped open a wallet, flashing his badge. "Detective Boggs." He nodded towards his lanky partner. "This is Detective Hartshorn."

I nodded and smiled tightly. "What can I do for you, gentlemen?"

I don't like this, my brain said. *I really don't like the vibe I'm getting from these two. They're looking at us like we're criminals. Like they're about to tie us to a stake and set us on fire.*

Maybe I hadn't wiped the guilty expression off my

face since my scolding from Monica. I let my features relax.

Boggs snapped his wallet shut and shoved it in his pocket. "We'd like to ask you a few questions."

"Okay. Go. What is this related to?"

"We're investigating the murder of Wesley Jupiter." Boggs stared at me, watching every little twitch, every little blink. "Can you tell us where you were yesterday, Ms. Ironclaw?"

EPILOGUE

The sky darkened overhead.

A nurse in a pristine white uniform and sensible heels rushed out to the manicured lawn overlooking the Black Sea and grimaced as she saw the coming storm. The patients had just been wheeled out to enjoy the last dying moments of the afternoon sun. They'd have to come right back in before the heavens opened.

Bustling out onto the lawn, mindful of the peace enjoyed by the very wealthy patients, she gave the order silently, with hand gestures, and quietly scolded a junior for walking too slowly as they rushed to bring their charges inside.

Her newest patient—a very thin, very pale bald man with buckled and bent legs hanging awkwardly from the seat of his wheelchair—sat at the edge of the emerald-green lawn, watching the waves roll and crash below.

How did he get that far down there? She could have

sworn she left him up on the deck with the other more critical patients.

She hurried down to the edge of the lawn, moved around to face him, knelt, and bowed her head in respect. "Sir," she said, speaking in Russian. "A storm approaches. Let me help you move inside."

After a moment's hesitation, he opened his mouth. "No." The strength of his voice belied the frailness of his body. "There is no need."

She tilted her head, confused. "But sir. The rain—"

His wheelchair made a soft clicking noise, as if shifting into gear.

The nurse frowned. That chair didn't have any gears; it was a simple wheelchair...

There was a snap and a whirr, and Christopher Jupiter drove his wheelchair up the hill and disappeared inside.

TO BE CONTINUED...

Printed in Dunstable, United Kingdom